HE'S COPYING FAMOUS SERIAL KILLERS. AND THE GAME HAS JUST BEGUN.

A woman is found murdered in the woods. It seems like a simple case but it soon escalates into a terrible nightmare. Someone is replicating the killing styles of the most infamous murderers of all time. No one knows this criminal's motives . . . or who will die next.

Two ex-Secret Service agents, Sean King and Michelle Maxwell, have been hired to defend a man's innocence in a burglary involving an aristocratic, dysfunctional family. Then a series of secrets leads the partners right into the frantic hunt that is confounding even the FBI. Now King and Maxwell are playing the Hour Game, uncovering one horrifying revelation after another and putting their lives in danger. For the closer they get to the truth, the closer they get to the most shocking surprise of all.

ACCLAIM FOR THE NOVELS OF DAVID BALDACCI

HOUR GAME

"Plenty of surprises and suspense . . . rich and deeply textured . . . fastpaced . . . one of Baldacci's strongest thrillers in years."
—Associated Press

"King and Maxwell are fictional treats, a fabulously entertaining team, and the action is hot and hard."
—*New York Daily News*

"The action is suspenseful and relentless."
—*Newark Star-Ledger*

Please turn this page for more raves for the books of David Baldacci.

"The book's pace is near-gallop." —*Buffalo News*

"Utterly absorbing . . . spins in unexpected directions . . . There are terrific action sequences throughout and plenty of suspense . . . texture and depth . . . This is Baldacci's most accomplished tale . . . and a snappy surprise ending will have Baldacci's many fans remembering why they love this author so much."
—*Publishers Weekly* (starred review)

"HOUR GAME has the elements of a classic Baldacci thriller. His characters keep getting better and richer and the plots—while always tight and well executed—are becoming more intricate and realistic . . . There is no question: David Baldacci will stay on the bestseller list for a long time to come." —*Richmond Times-Dispatch*

"A page-turner, peopled with well-drawn secondary characters, that rises above the ordinary."
—*World* magazine

"This book hits the ground running . . . Chilling and compelling . . . Will keep readers glued to the pages."
—RomanceReadersConnection.com

"A wild ride of suspense . . . You won't want to stop reading even for a moment. David Baldacci is known as a master storyteller. When you read this book you will understand why he is given that title."
—BestsellersWorld.com

SPLIT SECOND

"The action is explosive. Readers will barely have time to catch their breath." —*People*

"Excellent . . . a gripping page-turner."
—Associated Press

"Genuinely scary scenes . . . driven by tense action."
—*New York Daily News*

"Great . . . A fast-paced thriller." —*Denver Post*

"The reader will enjoy the ride." —*Houston Chronicle*

"A compelling storyteller . . . a supercharged pace."
—*Orlando Sentinel*

LAST MAN STANDING

"A killer thriller . . . A heart-racer . . . *Last Man* stands tall." —*USA Today*

"Engagingly fierce . . . Baldacci's brain-teasing plot leaves you wanting more." —*People*

"The action is nearly nonstop and expertly drawn."
—*Publishers Weekly* (starred review)

"[This book] finds the author in his familiar bestselling territory, the seamy underbelly of the nation's bureaucracy." —*Entertainment Weekly*

WISH YOU WELL

"Compelling . . . stirring . . . an old-fashioned coming-of-age story." —*People*

"Utterly captivating . . . Baldacci triumphs . . . This novel has a huge heart." —*Publishers Weekly* (starred review)

"Realistic and readable . . . entertaining."
—*Washington Post Book World*

more . . .

"Succeeds as a departure for Baldacci . . . A tender . . . inspirational story . . . Some wonderfully lyric prose."
—*Denver Post*

SAVING FAITH

"Plenty of action . . . opens with a bang . . . a joy."
—*USA Today*

"Burns and churns relentlessly forward from the first page."
—*New York Post*

"A lightning-paced thriller."
—*Chicago Tribune*

"Fast-moving . . . enjoyable . . . a twisting, turning journey."
—*Denver Post*

THE SIMPLE TRUTH

"Compelling . . . finely drawn . . . a page-turner worth losing sleep over."
—*USA Today*

"Baldacci ratchets up the suspense."
—*People*

"Baldacci excels at creating really good guys and putting them at risk."
—*Newsday*

"Fascinating . . . David Baldacci is a terrific storyteller."
—*Cleveland Plain Dealer*

THE WINNER

"Baldacci has come up with another good one."
—*New York Times*

"Aptly named . . . the devilish tale of a heroine who gambles her soul."
—*People*

ALSO BY DAVID BALDACCI

DAVID BALDACCI

HOUR GAME

WARNER BOOKS

NEW YORK   BOSTON

Copyright © 2004 by Columbus Rose, Ltd.
All rights reserved. No part of this book may be reproduced in any form or by any electronic or mechanical means, including information storage and retrieval systems, without permission in writing from the publisher, except by a reviewer who may quote brief passages in a review.

Warner Books

Time Warner Book Group
1271 Avenue of the Americas
New York, NY 10020

Visit our Web site at www.twbookmark.com

Printed in the United States of America

Originally published in hardcover by Warner Books
First International Paperback Printing: April 2005
First Paperback Printing: September 2005

10 9 8 7 6 5 4 3 2 1

This novel is dedicated to

Harry L. Carrico

Jane Giles

And to the memory of Mary Rose Tatum

Three of the finest people I have ever known

HOUR
GAME

CHAPTER

1

THE MAN IN THE RAIN slicker walked slightly bent over, his breathing labored and his body sweaty. The extra weight he was bearing, though not all that substantial, was awkwardly placed, and the terrain was uneven. It was never an easy thing to tote a dead body through the woods in the middle of the night. He shifted the corpse to his left shoulder and trudged on. The soles of his shoes bore no distinguishing marks; not that it would have mattered, since the rain quickly washed away any traces of footprints. He'd checked the forecast; the rain was why he was here. The inclement weather was the best friend he could ask for.

Aside from the dead body draped over his sturdy shoulder, the man was also remarkable for the black hood he wore, on which was stitched an esoteric symbol that ran down the length of the cloth. It was a circle with crosshairs through its middle. Probably instantly recognizable to anyone over the age of fifty, the logo once inspired a dread that had significantly eroded with time. It didn't matter that no one "alive" would see him wearing the hood; he took grim satisfaction in its lethal symbolism.

Within ten minutes he'd reached the location he'd carefully selected on an earlier visit, and laid the body down with a reverence that belied the violent manner in which the person had died. He took a deep breath and held it as he undid the telephone wire holding the bundle closed, and unwrapped the plastic. She was young with features that had been attractive two days prior; the woman was not much to look at now. The soft blond hair fell away from the greenish-tinged skin, revealing closed eyes and bloated cheeks. Had the eyes been open, they might have still held the startled gaze of the deceased as she endured her own murder, an experience replicated roughly thirty thousand times each year in America.

He slid the plastic all the way free and laid the woman on her back. Then he let out his breath, fought the urge to retch caused by the stench of the body, and sucked in another lungful of air. Using one of his gloved hands and his light, he searched for and found the small, forked branch that he'd earlier placed in the bramble nearby. He used this to support the woman's forearm, which he'd positioned such that it was pointing to the sky. The body's rigor mortis, though rapidly fading, had made the task difficult, but he was strong and had finally levered the stiffened limb to the correct angle. He took the watch out of his pocket, checked with his flashlight to make sure it was set properly, and placed it around the dead woman's wrist.

Though far from a religious man, he knelt over the body and muttered a brief prayer, cupping his hand over his mouth and nose as he did so.

"You weren't directly responsible, but you were all I had. You didn't die in vain. And I believe you're actually better off." *Did he really believe what he had just said? Maybe not. Maybe it didn't matter.*

He looked at the dead woman's face, studying her features scrupulously as though a scientist observing a particularly fascinating experiment. He had never killed another person before. He'd made it quick and, he hoped, painless. In the dull, misty night the woman seemed surrounded by a yellowish glow, as though she'd already become a spirit.

He drew farther back and examined the area all around, checking for any extraneous items that might lead to evidence against him. He discovered only a piece of cloth from his hood that had caught on a bush near where the body lay. *Careless, you can't afford that.* He placed it in his pocket. He spent several more minutes looking for other such items nearing microscopic size.

In the world of criminal investigation it was these forensic "no-see-ums" that did one in. A single drop of blood, semen or saliva, a smudge of fingerprint, a hair follicle with a bit of DNA-littered root attached, and the police could be reading you your rights while prosecutors circled hungrily nearby. Unfortunately, even full awareness of that reality offered little protection. Every criminal, no matter how careful, left potentially incriminating material at the crime scene. Thus, he'd taken great care to have no direct physical contact with the dead woman as though she were an infectious agent that could cause a fatal disease.

He rolled up the plastic and pocketed the telephone

cord, checked the watch once more and then slowly made his way back to his car.

Behind him lay the dead woman, her hand upraised to the watery heavens. Her watch was slightly luminous in the dark and made a dull beacon for her new resting place. She wouldn't remain undiscovered for long. Dead bodies aboveground rarely did, even in places as isolated as this.

As he drove off, the hooded man used his finger to trace the symbol on his hood, making the sign of the cross at the same time. The crosshairs symbol also appeared on the face of the watch he'd placed on the dead woman's wrist. *That should certainly get a rise out of them.* He took a breath full of excitement as well as dread. For years he had imagined that this day would never come. For years his courage had faltered. Now that the first step had been taken, he felt a great sense of empowerment and liberation.

He shifted into third gear and sped up, his tires grabbing the slicked roadway and holding firm as the darkness swallowed up the lights of his blue VW. He wanted to get to where he was going as fast as possible.

He had a letter to write.

CHAPTER

2

MICHELLE MAXWELL picked up her pace. She'd completed the "flat" portion of her run through the hills around Wrightsburg, Virginia, sequestered southwest of Charlottesville, Virginia; the terrain would now grow much steeper. Maxwell was a former Olympic rower who'd subsequently spent nine intense years in the Secret Service. Consequently, the five-foot-ten-inch woman was in remarkable physical shape. However, an enormous high-pressure system had parked over the entire mid-Atlantic, making this spring day unusually humid, and her muscles and lungs were beginning to strain as she headed up an incline. A quarter of the way through her run she'd put her shoulder-length black hair into a ponytail, though stubborn strands still found their way into her face.

She'd left the Secret Service to start a private investigation firm in this small Virginia town, partnering with another former Secret Service agent, Sean King. King had left the Service under a dark cloud but had become an attorney and forged a new life in Wrightsburg. The two hadn't known each other while working for Uncle Sam; rather, they'd teamed up on a case the previous year while Michelle was still in the Service and King had become embroiled in a series of local murders. After bringing that matter to a successful conclusion and gaining some notoriety in the process Michelle had suggested they start their own firm, and King, somewhat reluctantly, had agreed. With the reputation they'd gained from the previous case, and their skills as investigators, the business had quickly become a success. There had come a lull in the work, though, for which Michelle was grateful. She was an outdoors woman, and she got as much satisfaction out of camping or running a marathon as she did busting counterfeiters or putting the clamps on a corporate spy.

The woods were quiet save for the rustling branches from a moisture-laden breeze that was conjuring miniature cyclones from last winter's dead leaves. However, the sudden crack of tree branches caught Michelle's attention. She'd been told that the occasional black bear could be spotted around here, but if she did encounter an animal, it was far more likely to be a deer, squirrel or fox. She thought nothing more of it, although she took comfort in the pistol riding in the clip holster attached to her fanny pack belt. As a Secret Service agent she'd never gone anywhere without her gun, not even the toilet. One never knew where a nine-millimeter SIG and fourteen rounds might come in handy.

Moments later another sound caught her attention and kept it: running feet. In her Secret Service days Michelle had heard many types of running feet. Most had been innocuous; others signaled a darker purpose: stealth, attack or panic. She wasn't sure how to classify this one yet: good, bad or out of shape. She slowed her pace a little, using her hand to shield her eyes from the sunlight breaking through the tree canopies. For a few seconds there was dead silence, then the sounds of rushing feet returned, now much closer. Okay, what she was hearing was clearly not the measured pace of a jogger. There was a level of fear in the rushed and unsteady-sounding footfalls. Off to her left now, it seemed, but she couldn't be sure. Sound tended to whipsaw here.

"Hello," she called out, even as her hand reached down and took out her pistol. She didn't expect an answer and didn't get one. She chambered a round but kept the safety on. As with scissors, one should avoid running with a loaded gun while the safety was off. The sounds kept coming; it was human feet certainly. She glanced behind her; this might be a setup. It could be done in pairs: one to draw her attention while the other got the jump on her. Well, if so, they were going to be very sorry they chose to pick on her.

She stopped now as she finally locked on the sound's source: it was to the right, above the knoll directly in front of her. The breathing was accelerated; the rush of legs, the crashing of underbrush, seemed frenetic. In another few seconds whoever it was would have to clear the rim of dirt and rock.

Michelle slipped off her gun's safety and took up position behind a wide oak tree. Hopefully, it was only another jogger, and the person wouldn't even be aware of her armed presence. Dirt and pebbles shot out over the edge of the knoll heralding the arrival of the source of all the commotion. Michelle braced herself, both hands glued around her pistol grips, ready if necessary to put a bullet between someone's pupils.

A young boy burst out from the top of the knoll, was suspended in space for an instant and then with a scream tumbled down the slope. Before he hit bottom another boy, a little older, came into view at the knoll's crest but caught himself in time and merely slid down the slope on his butt, flopping next to his companion.

Michelle would have thought they were just horsing around, except for the look of utter terror etched on both their faces. The younger one was sobbing, his face streaked with dirt and tears. The older boy pulled him up by the scruff of his shirt, and they took off running, both their faces crimson with accelerated blood flow.

Michelle holstered her gun, stepped out from behind the tree and held up her hand. "Boys, stop!"

The pair screamed and shot around on either side of her in a blur. She spun around, grabbed for one but missed. She called after them, "What's wrong? I want to help you!"

For an instant she contemplated sprinting after them, but despite her Olympian background, it wasn't certain she could catch two young boys whose feet were apparently jet-fueled by sheer fright. She turned back around and looked toward the top of the knoll. What could have scared them that badly? She quickly altered her line of thinking. Or *who* could have? She looked once more in the direction of the fleeing boys. Then she turned back and cautiously made her way up in the direction the kids had come from. *Okay, this is getting a little dicey.* She thought about using her cell phone to call for help but decided to check things out first. She didn't want to call the cops in only to discover the boys had been spooked by a bear.

At the top of the knoll she easily found the path the two had used. She slipped through the narrow trail erratically carved by their frantic flight. It ran for about a hundred feet and then opened into a small clearing. From here the path was less certain, but then she spotted the piece of cloth dangling on the lower branch of a dogwood, and she made her way through this cleft in the forest. Fifty feet later she came to another clearing, this one larger, where a campfire had been doused.

She wondered if the boys *had* been camping here and indeed been frightened by some animal. And yet they'd had no camping gear on them, and there was none here in the clearing. And the fire didn't look all that recent. *No, something else is going on.*

In an instant the direction of the wind changed and drove the smell deep into her nostrils. She gagged, and her eyes assumed their own level of panic. She'd experienced that unmistakable smell before.

It was putrefied flesh. *Human flesh!*

Michelle pulled her tank shirt up and over her mouth and nose, trying to breathe in the stink of her own sweat rather than the rank odor of a decomposing body. She made her way around the perimeter of the clearing. At 120 degrees on her mental compass she found it. Or her. In the brush that ran along the fringe of the clearing the hand was sticking up, like the dead woman was waving hello or in this case good-bye. Even from this distance

Michelle could see that the greenish skin on the arm was slipping down off the bone. She scooted around to the up-wind side of the body and took a replenishing breath.

She ran her gaze along the corpse but kept her gun ready. Though the stench from the body, its discoloration and the skin slippage showed the woman had been dead for quite some time, it could have been recently dumped here and the killer still nearby. Michelle had no desire to join the lady's fate.

The sun was glinting off something on the woman's wrist. Michelle drew closer and saw that it was a watch. She glanced down at her own watch; it was two-thirty. She sat back on her haunches, her nose cemented into her armpit. She called 911, calmly telling the dispatcher what she'd found and her location. After that she called Sean King.

"Do you recognize her?" he asked.

"I don't think her own mother would know her, Sean."

"I'm on my way. Just stay on your guard. Whoever did it might come back to admire his handiwork. Oh, and Michelle?" said King.

"Yeah?"

"Can't you just start running on a treadmill?"

She clicked off, took up a position as far away from the body as she could while still keeping it in view, and maintained a sharp lookout. The nice day and endorphin-churning run in the beautiful foothills had suddenly taken on a grim veneer.

Funny how murder had a way of doing that.

CHAPTER

3

THE SMALL CLEARING WAS seeing quite a bit of activity, all of it man-made. A wide area had been cordoned off with yellow police tape intertwined among the trees. A two-person forensics team was foraging for clues directly around the crime scene, analyzing things that seemed far too small to be of any significance. Others hovered over the body of the dead woman, while still others were threading their way through the surrounding woods and underbrush looking for items of interest and possibly the ingress and egress of the killer. One uniformed officer had photographed and then videotaped the entire scene. All the cops wore floater masks to guard against the stench, and yet one by one they took turns hustling into the woods to empty their stomachs.

It all looked very efficient and orderly, but for a seasoned observer it was clearly bad guy one, good guys naught. They were finding zip.

Michelle stood off a ways and watched. Next to her was Sean King, her partner in the private investigation firm of King & Maxwell. King was in his forties, three inches taller than the five-foot-ten Michelle, and had short dark hair graying at the temples. He was trim and broad-shouldered but had gimpy knees and a shoulder that a bullet had ripped into years ago during an arrest that had gone awry while he was working a forgery investigation as a Secret Service agent. He'd also once been a volunteer deputy police officer for Wrightsburg but had resigned, swearing off guns and law enforcement for the rest of his days.

Sean King had suffered through several tragedies in his life: a disgraceful end to his Secret Service career after a candidate he'd been guarding was assassinated right in front of him; a failed marriage and acrimonious divorce; and most recently, a plot to frame him for a series of local murders that had dredged up the painful details of his last days as a federal agent. These events had left King a very cautious man, unwilling to trust anyone, at least until Michelle Maxwell hurtled into his life. Though their relationship had started off on very rocky ground, she was now the one person he knew he could absolutely rely on.

Michelle Maxwell had started life at a dead run, streaking through college in three years, winning an Olympic silver medal in rowing and becoming a police officer in her native Tennessee before joining the Secret Service. Like King, her exit from the federal agency hadn't been pleasant: she'd lost a protectee to an ingenious kidnapping scheme. It was the first time in her life she had failed at anything, and that debacle had nearly destroyed her. While investigating the kidnapping case she had met King. At first she'd taken an instant dislike to the man. Now, as his partner, she saw Sean King for what he was: the best pure investigative mind she had ever been associated with. And her closest friend.

Yet the two could not have been more different. While Michelle craved adrenaline highs and pushing her body to the limit with intensive, lung-and-limb-shocking physical activities, King preferred spending his leisure time hunting for appropriate wines to add to his collection, dabbling in owning the works of local artists, reading good books, as well as boating and fishing on the lake that his home backed to. He was an introspective man by nature; he liked to think things out thoroughly before taking action. Michelle tended to move at warp speed and let the pieces fall where they may. This partnership of supernova and steady glacier had somehow flourished.

"Did they find the boys?" she asked King.

He nodded. "I understand they were pretty traumatized."

"Traumatized? They'll probably need therapy all the way through college."

Michelle had already given a detailed statement to the local police, in the person of Chief Todd Williams. The chief's hair had become noticeably whiter after her and King's first adventure in Wrightsburg. Today his features held a resigned expression, as though murder and mayhem were now to be expected in his tiny hamlet.

Michelle watched as a slender and attractive red-haired woman in her late thirties carrying a black satchel and a rape kit arrived on the scene, knelt down and started examining the body.

"That's the deputy medical examiner assigned to this area," King explained. "Sylvia Diaz."

"Diaz? She looks more like Maureen O'Hara."

"George Diaz was her husband. He was a very noted surgeon in the area. He was struck by a car and killed several years ago. Sylvia used to be a professor of forensic pathology at UVA. Now she's a physician in private practice."

"And a deputy M.E. on the side. Busy woman. Any children?"

"No. I guess her work is her life," said King.

Michelle put her hand up to her nose as the direction of the wind changed yet again, flinging the stench of the body directly at them. "Some life," she said. "God, she isn't even wearing a mask, and I'm about to hurl from back here."

Twenty minutes later Diaz rose, spoke with the police, popped off her examination gloves and started snapping pictures of the body and surrounding area. Finished with that, she stowed her camera and started to walk away when she noticed King. She smiled warmly and headed toward them.

Michelle whispered, "And you forgot to tell me that you two dated?"

King looked at her surprised. "We went out a few times a while back. How'd you know that?"

"After spending close-up time with a dead body, you don't get a smile like that unless there was a prior relationship."

"Thanks for the astute observation. But be nice. Sylvia's really wonderful."

"I'm sure she was, but I don't need to hear the details, Sean."

"Rest assured, you'll never hear the details while there's breath in my body."

"I see. You're being quite the Virginia gentleman."

"No, I just don't want to be critiqued."

CHAPTER

4

SYLVIA DIAZ GAVE KING A
hug that lingered a bit past "friends" status, Michelle felt,
and then King introduced the two women.

The deputy medical examiner looked at Michelle with
what the latter perceived as an unfriendly gaze.

"I haven't seen you in a while, Sean," Sylvia said, turning back to him.

"We'd been swamped with investigative work, but
things have finally slowed down."

"So," Michelle broke in, "do you have a cause of death
on our corpse yet?"

Sylvia looked at her with a surprised expression.
"That's not really something I can discuss with you."

"I was just wondering," said Michelle innocently,
"since I happened to be one of the first on the scene. I
guess you won't know for sure until you do the post."

"You'll be doing the autopsy here, won't you?" asked
King.

Sylvia nodded. "Yes, although suspicious deaths tradi-
tionally were sent over to Roanoke."

"Why no longer?" asked Michelle.

"There used to be four official facilities certified to conduct autopsies in the state: Fairfax, Richmond, Tidewater and Roanoke. However, due to the generosity of John Poindexter, a very wealthy man who was also a past Speaker of the House in the state General Assembly, we now have a certified forensics substation right here."

"Strange donation, a morgue," said Michelle.

"Poindexter's daughter was killed here years ago. Wrightsburg falls on the jurisdictional line between the medical examiner's office in Richmond and the western district office in Roanoke. Because of that, there was a fight over which office would perform the autopsy. Roanoke finally won out, but during the transfer of the body the vehicle was involved in an accident, and vital evidence was lost or compromised. Consequently, the girl's killer was never caught, and as you can imagine, her father was not very happy. When Poindexter died, his will left the money to build a state-of-the-art facility." Sylvia glanced over her shoulder at the body. "But even with a state-of-the-art facility the cause of death on this one might be tricky."

"Any idea on how long she's been dead?" asked King.

"A lot depends on the individual, environmental factors and degree of decomposition. With a body dead this long the postmortem may give us *some* idea of a time frame, but that's all."

"I see some of the fingers have been chewed off," said King.

"Animals, clearly." Sylvia added thoughtfully, "But

still there should have been more signs of invasion. They're trying to get an ID on her now."

King said, "What do you make of the hand posed like that?"

"Afraid that's for the official detectives, not me. I just tell them how the victim died and collect any evidence during the post that might be useful. I played Sherlock Holmes when I first started doing this job, and I was quickly put in my place."

"There's nothing wrong with using your specialized knowledge to help solve a crime," commented Michelle.

"You'd think so, wouldn't you?" Sylvia paused and said, "I can tell you that the arm was braced up by the stick and that it was done deliberately. Beyond that, I'm out of ideas." She turned to King. "It was good to see you again, even if it was under these circumstances." She put out her hand to Michelle, who shook it.

As the woman walked off, Michelle said, "I thought you said you *used* to date."

"We did. It's been over a year now."

"I'm not sure she got the message."

"I really appreciate the insight. Maybe you can read my palm next. You ready to go? Or do you want to finish your run?"

"Thanks, but I've had enough stimulation for one day."

As they passed close by the body, King stopped and stared at the hand that was still pointing to the sky, his face suddenly tense.

"What is it?" Michelle asked, watching him closely.

"The watch," he said.

She glanced at it, now seeing that it was set to one o'clock and didn't appear to be running. "What about it?"

"Michelle, it's a Zodiac watch."

"Zodiac?"

"Something tells me we're going to see this person's work again," said King.

CHAPTER

5

THE ISOLATED AREA ON A bluff overlooking one of the main channels of thirty-mile-long Cardinal Lake had long been a favorite place for the teenagers in Wrightsburg to gather and perform a variety of acts their parents wouldn't approve of. The night being overcast and drizzly with a wind rattling the trees, there was only one car parked up on the bluff, but the occupants were putting on an energetic show nonetheless.

The girl was already naked, her dress and undergarments folded neatly in the backseat next to her shoes. The young man was frantically trying to pull his shirt over his head while the girl was undoing his pants; it was tough going in the cramped quarters. The shirt finally came off about the time his pants and underwear were ripped down by the hard-breathing young lady, for whom patience, at least under these circumstances, was clearly not a virtue.

He slid toward the middle of the front seat after putting on a condom, and she climbed astride him, facing him. The windows of the car were fogging up now. Over her shoulder he stared out the windshield, his own breath growing faster as he closed his eyes. It was his first time, though his partner appeared far more experienced. He'd been dreaming of this moment for at least two years, his hormones building to levels of utter agony. He smiled as she moaned and rocked on top of him.

Then he opened his eyes and stopped smiling.

The figure in the black hood stared back at him through the windshield. Through the thickening condensation on the glass he saw the shotgun muzzle come up. He started to throw the girl off him, instinctively thinking he would start the car and get out of here. He never made it. The glass exploded inward. The impact of the buckshot against her back slammed the girl into him, yet her body shielded him. Still the collision with her head broke his nose, almost knocking him out. Awash in her blood but as yet not critically wounded, he clutched the dead body against his chest, as though it were a cherished security blanket capable of warding off the bogeyman. He wanted to scream yet couldn't. He finally let the girl go as he slid toward the driver's side. His movements were clumsy, his mind clouded. *Had he been shot?* He didn't know it but he was suffering from shock, his rapidly rising and falling blood pressure dragging his body through levels of stress it wasn't designed for.

He started to turn the key in the ignition when the driver's side door opened and there was the black hood again. As he stared helplessly, the shotgun muzzle glided at him like the deadliest snake in the world. The boy started to beg and then to cry, the blood pouring from his destroyed nose. He inched back away from the gunman, until he bumped against the girl's body. *"Please!"* he wailed. *"No, God, no!"*

The nine pellets of the shotgun blast hit him in the head with the collective force of a gigantic hammer, and he fell next to the dead girl. The front of her was unmarked; however, the other side was obliterated. Looking at the girl lying there on her back, one couldn't tell what had killed the young woman. The cause of death of her boyfriend was far more obvious, considering he no longer had a face.

The killer leaned his shotgun against the car's passenger side, opened the door and reached in. He placed a watch on the young man's wrist, bracing the arm up against the dash, finally wedging it between the dash and the door. Next he fiddled with the watch that the dead girl was already wearing. Then he pulled off the cheap amethyst ring the girl had on and put it in his pocket. He lifted a St. Christopher's medal from around the young man's neck. That also went into the hooded man's pocket.

Over the boy's body he said, "I'm sorry. You're not personally guilty, but you were part of the original sin. You didn't die in vain. You righted a long-overdue wrong. Take comfort in that."

He didn't bother praying over the girl. He took an object from his pocket and laid it on the floor of the car, shut the door and lumbered off. As the rain came in through the shattered windshield, the two dead and naked young people seemed to be clinging to each other.

On the floorboard was the object the killer had placed there.

It was a dog collar.

CHAPTER

6

CHIEF WILLIAMS STOPPED by the offices of King & Maxwell located in a two-story brick townhouse in the heart of the small yet posh Wrightsburg downtown. The offices had housed King's law practice before he'd taken down his legal shingle. The chief sat with his hat in his lap, eyes puffy and features strained as he filled in King and Michelle on the grisly double homicide.

"I left the police force in Norfolk so I wouldn't have to deal with this sort of crap," Williams began. "My ex-wife got me to move here for the peace and quiet. Damn, was that woman wrong! No wonder we got divorced."

King handed him a cup of coffee and then sat down across from him, while Michelle remained perched on the edge of a leather couch. "Wait'll the papers get hold of this one. And poor Sylvia. She'd just finished the autopsy on that girl, and then she had to do two more."

"Who were they?" asked King.

"Students at Wrightsburg High School: Steve Canney and Janice Pembroke. She was shot in the back; he took it full in the face. Buckshot. When I opened that car door, it cost me my breakfast. Hell, I'll be seeing them in my sleep for months."

"No witnesses?"

"Not that we know of. It was a rainy night. Theirs were the only tire tracks up there."

Michelle perked up. "Right, it was raining. So if you didn't see any tire tracks, the killer must have walked up to the car. You didn't find any traces of that?"

"Most everything was washed away. There was an inch of bloody water on the floor of the car. Steve Canney was one of the most popular kids in school, football star and everything."

"And the girl?" asked Michelle.

Williams hesitated. "Janice Pembroke had a reputation with the boys."

"As being . . . accessible?" asked King.

"Yes."

"Was anything taken? Could it have been a robbery?"

"Not likely, although two things were missing: a cheap ring Pembroke usually wore and Canney's St. Christopher's medal. We don't know if the killer took them or not."

"You said Sylvia finished the autopsies. I'm assuming you attended them."

Williams looked embarrassed. "I had a little problem halfway through Jane Doe's post, and I got tied up while she was doing the other autopsies. I'm waiting on Sylvia's reports," he added hastily. "We don't have an official homicide detective on the force, so I figured coming here and picking your brain wouldn't be a bad thing."

"Any clues?" asked Michelle.

"Not from the first killing. And we haven't identified her yet either, though we were able to fingerprint her and we're running those. We had a computerized facial composite done too, which we're circulating."

"Any reason to believe the killings are connected?" asked Michelle.

Williams shook his head. "Pembroke and Canney will probably turn out to be some love triangle thing. Kids these days will kill you in a second and think nothing of it. All the crap on TV they watch."

King and Michelle exchanged glances and then he said, "In the first killing either the murderer lured the woman into the woods or forced her to go with him. Or he killed her elsewhere and then carried her into the woods."

Michelle nodded. "If the latter, a strong man, then. With the killing of the teenagers the person might have followed them there or been waiting on the bluff."

"Well, that area is well known as a make-out place, if they still even call it that," said Williams. "Both victims were naked. That's why I'm thinking it was maybe some boy Pembroke dumped or a kid who was jealous of Canney. The Jane Doe in the woods will be the harder one to crack. That's where I'm going to need your help."

King looked thoughtful for a moment and then said, "The watch in the first murder, did you *really* notice it, Todd?"

"Well, it seemed a little bulky for the girl."

"Sylvia said the arm the watch was on was deliberately braced up."

"She can't know that for sure."

"I saw that the watch was set to one o'clock," continued King.

"Right, but it had stopped, or the stem was pulled out."

King glanced at Michelle. "Did you notice the make of the watch?"

Williams looked at him curiously. "Make of the watch?"

"It was a Zodiac watch: circle with crosshairs."

Williams almost spilled his coffee. "Zodiac!"

King nodded. "It was also a man's watch. I think the killer put it on the woman."

"Zodiac," repeated Williams. "Are you saying . . . ?"

"The original Zodiac serial killer operated in 1968 and 1969 in the Bay Area, San Fran and Vallejo," answered King. "I think *that* Zodiac would be a little long in the tooth. But there have been at least two Zodiac copycat killers, one in New York and another in Kobe, Japan. The San Fran Zodiac wore a black executioner's hood emblazoned with white crosshairs in a circle, the same symbol that's on the Zodiac watch. He also left a watch on his last victim, a cabdriver, if I recall correctly, although it wasn't a Zodiac. However, the man suspected of being the Zodiac in San Francisco owned a Zodiac watch. They believe that's where he got the idea for the crosshairs-in-a-circle logo he wore that earned him his nickname. The case has never been solved."

Williams hunched forward in his chair. "Look, this is all really speculation on your part, and quite a stretch at that."

Michelle glanced at her partner. "Sean, do you really think it's a copycat killer?"

King shrugged. "If two people copied the original,

who's to say a third person couldn't? The San Francisco Zodiac wrote to the newspapers in code—one that was finally broken. The coded letters revealed that the killer was motivated by a short story titled 'The Most Dangerous Game.' It's a story about hunting humans."

"A game about hunting humans?" Michelle said slowly.

King asked, "Did either of the bodies in the car have a watch on?"

Williams frowned. "Wait a minute, Sean, like I said, they're totally different killings. Shotguns and, well, I still don't know how Jane Doe died, but it wasn't by buckshot, that's for damn sure."

"But what about the watches?"

"Okay, both the kids had watches on. So what? Is that a crime?"

"And you didn't notice if they were Zodiacs?"

"No, I didn't. But then I didn't notice it on the Jane Doe either." He paused and considered something. "Although Canney's arm *was* sort of leaning against the dash."

"Sort of braced up, you mean?"

"Maybe," Williams said warily. "But he got hit with a shotgun blast. No telling how that would have blown him back."

"Were both watches running?"

"No."

"What was the time on Pembroke's watch?"

"Two."

"Two exactly?"

"I think so."

"And Canney's watch?"

Williams pulled out his notebook and turned some pages until he found it. "Three," he said nervously.

"Had the watch been hit by the buckshot?"

"I'm not sure," replied Williams. "I guess Sylvia can tell us that."

"The girl's?"

"Looks like a piece of glass from the windshield hit it."

"Yet her watch read two and Canney's three," said Michelle. "If the girl's watch stopped at two when she was killed by the shotgun blast, how could the boy's have stopped at three without being struck by anything?"

Williams continued to be defensive. "Come on, except for this watch business, which isn't all that convincing, I don't see any connection at all."

Michelle shook her head stubbornly. "First killing was number one, Jennifer Pembroke's was number two and Steve Canney was victim number three. That *can't* be coincidental."

"You really need to see if the watches on Steve Canney and Jennifer Pembroke were Zodiacs," King told Williams with a sense of urgency in his voice.

Williams used his cell phone to make some calls. When he finished, the police chief looked confused.

"The watch found on Pembroke was hers, a Casio. Her mother confirmed it was the one her daughter wore. But Canney's father told me that his son didn't wear a watch. I checked with one of my deputies. The watch found on Canney was a Timex."

King's brow furrowed. "So no Zodiac watch, but Canney's was possibly planted by the killer, as it probably was in the first killing. As I recall, the San Fran Zodiac also committed a lovers' lane killing. Most or all of his killings were also near bodies of water or places named after water."

"The bluff Canney and Pembroke were killed on overlooks Cardinal Lake," said Williams grudgingly.

"And Jane Doe wasn't that far from the lake," said Michelle. "You just had to go over the crest of the hill she was on, and there's a cove right there."

"What I would do, Todd," said King, "is start working the Zodiac watch connection. The killer had to get the watch from somewhere."

Williams was looking down at his hands, his brow furrowed.

"What is it?" asked Michelle.

"We found a dog collar on the floorboard of Canney's car. We just assumed it belonged to Canney. But his father just told me that they don't own a dog."

"Could it have been Pembroke's?" asked King, but Williams shook his head.

They all sat there puzzling this over when the office phone rang. King went to answer it and returned with a pleased expression. "That was Harry Carrick, retired state supreme court justice, now country lawyer. He's got a client accused of some serious things, and he wants our help. He didn't say who or what."

Williams rose and cleared his throat. "Uh, that would be Junior Deaver."

"Junior Deaver?" said King.

"Yep. He was doing some work for the Battles. It's out of my jurisdiction. Junior's in the county lockup right now."

"What'd he do?" asked King.

"You'll have to ask Harry about that." He went to the door. "I'm calling the state police in too. They've got real homicide detectives."

"You might want to think about involving the FBI as well," said Michelle. "If this is a serial killer, VICAP can do a profile," she added, referring to the FBI's Violent Criminal Apprehension Program.

"Never thought I'd have to fill out a VICAP form in Wrightsburg."

"They've simplified the paperwork a lot," she added helpfully.

After the chief left, Michelle turned to King. "I feel sorry for him."

"We'll do what we can to help."

She sat back. "So who're Junior Deaver and the Battles?"

"Junior's a good old boy who's lived here all his life. On the wrong side of the tracks, you could say. The Battles are a different story. They're the wealthiest family by far around here. They're everything you'd expect to find in a good old southern family."

"Meaning what exactly?"

"Meaning they're, well, charming, quirky . . . you know, slightly eccentric."

"You mean crazy," said Michelle.

"Well—"

"Every family's crazy," Michelle interrupted. "Some just show it more than others."

"I think you'll find the Battles are right at the top of the list in that regard."

CHAPTER

7

HARRY LEE CARRICK LIVED on a large estate on the eastern edge of Wrightsburg. As they drove over, King filled in Michelle on the jurist-turned-practicing-attorney.

"He was a lawyer here years ago and then went on the local circuit court and then onto the state supreme court for the last two decades. In fact, he swore me into the Virginia State Bar. His family goes back about three hundred years in the commonwealth. You know, *those* Lees. He's well over seventy but sharper than ever. After he left the bench, he came back here, settled down at the family estate."

"You said Junior was from the wrong side of the tracks."

"Let's say he's occasionally strayed on the other side of the law. But from what I've heard he hasn't been in any trouble for a long time."

"Apparently until now."

They passed a set of wrought-iron gates emblazoned with the letter *C*.

Michelle looked around at the expansive grounds. "Nice place."

"Harry's done well for himself and his family certainly had money."

"Married?"

"His wife died when she was young. He never remarried and doesn't have any children. In fact, he's the last of the Carricks as far as I know."

They caught a glimpse of a large brick home with white columns nestled among all the mature trees. Yet King turned away from the direction of the main house and drove down a narrow gravel road, stopping in front of a small clapboard structure painted white.

"What's this?" asked Michelle.

"The opulent law offices of Harry Lee Carrick, Esquire."

They knocked on the door and a pleasant-sounding voice called out, "Come in."

The man rose from behind the large wooden desk, his hand outstretched. Harry Carrick was about five-nine and slender with fine silver hair and a ruddy complexion. He was dressed in gray slacks, a blue blazer, a white button-down shirt and a red-and-white-striped tie. His eyes were more the color of periwinkle than true blue, Michelle decided, and were also pleasingly impish. His eyebrows were thick and the same color as the hair. His grip was firm and his melodious southern accent as smoothly enveloping as three fingers of your favorite libation and an easy chair in which to enjoy it. His energy and manner were that of a man easily twenty years younger. In short, he was the Hollywood version of what a judge should look like.

Harry said to Michelle, "I was wondering when Sean would get around to bringing you to see me. So I felt compelled to take matters into my own hands, you see."

He led them to chairs in one corner of the small room. Stout bookcases lined most of the wall space. The furniture all looked to be antique and well used. Cigar smoke hovered in the air like miniature cumuli, and Michelle spotted an old Remington typewriter on one side table, although there was also a PC and laser printer on Harry's magnificently carved desk.

"I've altogether given in to the efficiencies of the modern age," he said, his alert eyes observing her wandering gaze. "I resisted computers until the last possible moment and then threw myself wholeheartedly into their embrace. I reserve the Remington for correspondence with certain friends of advancing years who'd consider it positively disgraceful to receive a missive on anything but monogrammed bond paper graced with the touch of the manual typewriter keys, or else my own personal scrawl, which unfortunately grows ever more indecipherable. Growing old is so darn unappealing until you consider the alternative. I'd recommend always staying young and beautiful, like you, Michelle."

Michelle smiled. Harry *was* quite the gentleman, and a charmer.

He insisted on making them tea and served it in delicately worn china cups with matching saucers. Then he settled down between them.

"Junior Deaver," prompted King.

"And the Battles," said Harry.

"Sounds like an odd couple," remarked Michelle.

"The oddest," agreed Harry. "Bobby Battle was brilliant and as tough as nails. He made his fortune through his own sweat and brains. His wife, Remmy, is as fine a lady as I know. And she's made of steel too. She'd have to be, being married to Bobby."

Michelle looked at him curiously. "You said 'was.' Is Bobby Battle deceased?"

"No, but he suffered a massive stroke recently. Not too long before the incident Junior is accused of, in fact. Not sure of his recovery prospects just yet."

"Is that the whole family, Bobby and Remmy?" asked Michelle.

"No, there's a son, Edward Lee Battle, though everybody calls him Eddie. He's about forty. Bobby's full name is Robert E. Lee Battle. We aren't related. Lee was a given name for him, quite common in these parts, as I'm sure you can understand. There was another son, Bobby Jr., Eddie's twin. He died of cancer when he was a teenager."

"Then there's Eddie's wife, Dorothea. And Eddie's younger sister, Savannah," added King. "She just finished up college, I understand."

"You said Eddie's about forty and yet Savannah just graduated from college?" asked Michelle.

Harry said, "Well, Savannah was somewhat of a surprise. Remmy was over forty when that little bundle of joy arrived. Ironically, Remmy and Bobby were separated for some time before Savannah was born, and looked headed toward divorce."

"What was the problem?" asked King.

"Remmy caught him with another woman, a prostitute. It wasn't the first time; Bobby had an appalling affinity for those types. That was all hushed up back then. I really thought that was going to be the last straw, but then they patched things up."

"A baby will do that for you," said King.

"Do they all live together?" asked Michelle.

Harry shook his head. "Bobby, Remmy and Savannah live in the big house. Eddie and Dorothea live next door in what was the estate's carriage house, but which is now a separate piece of property. I've heard rumors that Savannah may move away."

"I imagine some of her trust fund is due upon her college graduation," said King.

"And probably none too soon for her," said Harry.

"I take it she doesn't get along with her parents?" said Michelle.

"Let's put it this way: Bobby was very much an absent father, and she and Remmy are both strong, independent women, meaning they don't agree on much."

"What do Eddie and Dorothea do?" asked Michelle.

Harry answered. "Eddie's a professional artist and avid Civil War reenactor. Dorothea has her own real estate firm and does quite well." Harry gave Michelle a mischievous grin. "Folks in the Battles' social circle change domestic partners at an alarming rate and thus are often in the market for new and ever more luxurious housing. While good to Dorothea's pocketbook, it must give the woman fits remembering who's with whom on a day-to-day basis."

"Sounds a little like Peyton Place," said Michelle.

"Oh, we left Peyton Place in the dust years ago," said Harry.

"And now we come to Junior," added King.

Harry put down his teacup and reached for a file on his desk. "Junior was doing some construction work for the Battles. Specifically, work in Remmy's bedroom closet. He's good; he's even done some work for me here, and for lots of people in the area."

"And the crime he's accused of?" asked King.

"Burglary. There was a hidden cupboard in Remmy's closet where she kept jewelry, cash and other valuables. It was burglarized and the contents emptied. And there was also a secret cache in Bobby's closet that was broken into. About two hundred thousand dollars' worth, I understand, including, unfortunately, Remmy's wedding ring," said Harry. As he gazed through the file, he added, "And hell hath no fury like a woman shorn of her wedding ring."

"And they suspect Junior because he was doing work there?" asked Michelle.

"Well, a certain amount of evidence seems to pin him to the crime."

"Like what?" asked King.

Harry ticked the points off on his fingers. "The burglar accessed the house through a third-story window. The window was forced and a tool mark was left as well as a bit of metal from the tool that was matched to a crowbar owned by Junior. He also owns a ladder that would reach that window. In addition they found shards of glass in the cuffs of a pair of his pants. They can't definitively match the glass found to the window at the Battles', but it's similar. Both are tinted."

"You said he forced the window," said King. "Where'd the glass come from?"

"Part of the window broke when it was forced. I suppose the theory is, he got the shards when climbing through the opening. Next we have shoe prints found on the hardwood floor in Remmy's bedroom. They match a pair of boots found at Junior's. There was some building material found on the floor of Remmy's closet: drywall powder, cement, wood dust, the sort of thing Junior would have had on his shoes, considering the line of work he's in. There was also some soil found there that has been matched to the ground outside of Junior's home. Similar evidence was also found in Bobby's bedroom and closet."

"So they maintained separate sleeping quarters?" asked Michelle.

Harry raised a single thick eyebrow. "Knowledge that I'm sure Remmy would have preferred to keep private."

"Okay, that's all incriminating but still circumstantial," said King.

"Well, there's yet another piece of evidence. Or I suppose I should say two pieces. A glove print and a fingerprint that match Junior's."

"A glove print?" said Michelle.

"It was a leather glove," answered Harry, "and those have definitive lines and such just like a fingerprint, or so they tell me."

"But if he was wearing gloves, how did one of his prints show up?" asked King.

"Presumably, it had a hole in one of the fingers. And Junior owns such a glove."

King stared at Harry. "What's Junior's story?"

"Junior declares his innocence vigorously. He was working by himself until the early morning hours at a new house he's building for him and his family over in Albemarle County. He saw no one and no one saw him. So there goes any alibi."

"When was the burglary discovered?" asked King.

"Remmy found it around five in the morning after she got home from the hospital. She was in her bedroom around eight the night before, and there were people in the house until around eleven or so. So the crime probably took place between, say, midnight and four."

"Clearly within the hours Junior says he was working alone on the house."

"And yet with all that," said Michelle, "you think he's innocent, don't you?"

Harry met her gaze. "I've represented people who were guilty before; that comes with the territory. As a judge I've seen the culpable go free and the innocent occasionally locked up, and I've usually been powerless to do anything about it. Now, with Junior my firm belief is that he didn't commit this crime for one simple reason: the poor fellow would no more know what to do with two hundred thousand dollars' worth of cash, bearer bonds and jewels than I would trying to row my way to an Olympic silver medal in women's fours and coxswain."

Michelle looked surprised because while in college she'd done that very thing.

"Yes, my dear," said Harry apologetically, "I researched you. I hope you don't mind." He patted her hand and continued. "Junior's being an incompetent thief is clearly established. Case in point: years ago he stole some truck batteries from a local auto repair shop, only he didn't bother to take them out of the bed of his truck when he went to that very same auto repair shop to have his truck worked on. That little blunder cost him six months in jail and demonstrates his lack of skill in the felony business."

"Well, maybe he's gotten better over the years," said King.

"He's doing the best he's ever done with his contracting business. His wife makes good money. They're building a new house in Albermarle. Why attempt a burglary at the Battles'?"

"Maybe with the new house they needed some extra cash. But if he didn't do it, someone is trying hard to implicate him. Why?" said King.

Harry was ready for that query. "He was working there, so he'd be suspected. The person could have gotten his tools, shoes, pants and gloves from the trailer home Junior and his family are living in now. It's in the middle of nowhere, and there's often no one there." He added, "Although the fingerprint is the most troubling. It would take an experienced person to forge that."

"What's his family like?" asked Michelle.

"Three children, the oldest around twelve. His wife is Lulu Oxley."

"Lulu Oxley?" repeated Michelle.

"She's the manager at a gentleman's club called the Aphrodisiac. Actually, she told me she now also owns a piece of the business."

"You're kidding," said Michelle. "The Aphrodisiac?"

"I've heard it's actually quite nice inside—you know,

not just a sleazy bar with topless dancers." Harry added quickly, "Though I've never been there, of course."

"That's right," said King.

Michelle looked at him. "Please don't tell me *you've* been there."

He hesitated, looked uncomfortable and then said, "It was just one time. A bachelor's party for a friend."

"Uh-huh," said Michelle.

King sat forward. "Okay, maybe Junior didn't mastermind the thing, but what if someone else did? That person knew Junior had access to the Battles' mansion and enlists him to do it. The physical evidence *is* pretty damning, Harry."

Harry was not deterred. "There *is* evidence against him. *Too* much, in fact!"

King didn't look convinced. "Okay, what do you want us to do?"

"Talk to Junior. Get his story. Visit the Battles."

"All right, suppose we check it all out and nothing pops?"

"Then I'll talk to Junior. If he still maintains his innocence, I really have no choice but to move forward. However, if the commonwealth offers a reasonable plea deal, well, I'll have to address it with Junior. He's been in jail before; he has no desire to return."

He handed King a file with all the particulars. They shook on it, and Harry turned to Michelle and took her hand. "And I have to say that finally meeting this charming young woman was well worth any price you might charge."

"You're going to make me blush, Harry."

"I'll take that as quite a compliment."

As they left Harry and walked outside, Michelle said, "I love that man."

"Good, because meeting him may be the only positive thing that comes out of this." His cell phone rang. A minute later he clicked off. "That was Todd. Let's go," he said.

"Where to?" asked Michelle.

"A real fun place called the morgue."

CHAPTER

8

THE PALE BLUE 1969 VW puttered down one of the feeder roads leading to downtown Wrightsburg. The man driving was dressed in jeans and a white button-down shirt with loafers on his feet. He also wore a baseball cap pulled low over his forehead, and heavily tinted sunglasses covered his eyes. It was probably overkill, he knew. Most people were so self-absorbed they couldn't describe anything about anyone they'd seen in passing ten seconds before.

Coming in the opposite direction was a Lexus convertible. As Sean King and Michelle Maxwell passed by on their way to the morgue, the man didn't even glance at them. He continued on his way in the VW that had over two hundred thousand miles on its odometer. The Bug had come off the assembly line a canary yellow. It had been painted many colors since it had first been stolen years ago and had gone through at least ten sets of license plates. Along the way its VIN had been expertly altered. Like a cleansed gun, it was now virtually untraceable. He loved it.

Serial murderer Theodore "Ted" Bundy had also favored VW Bugs in killing sprees that took him from coast to coast before he was executed. He often referred to the amount of "cargo" he could carry in the Bug with the backseat removed, cargo that had once been living, female and human. Bundy also applauded the Volkswagen's incredible gas mileage. He could slaughter and flee easily on one tank of fuel.

The man made a right-hand turn and pulled into the parking lot of the upscale shopping mall frequented by many of the people who lived in tiny yet very affluent Wrightsburg. It was said that Bundy and other serial killers of his ilk spent twenty-four hours a day plotting their next murders. It must have seemed easy to men like that. Bundy reportedly had an IQ of over 120. Well, the man behind the wheel of the VW possessed one north of 160. He was a member of Mensa, he did the *New York Times* crossword puzzle every Sunday with ease; he could have made a small fortune on *Jeopardy!* answering the questions before host Alex even finished asking them.

However, the truth was, you didn't need to be a genius to hunt up suitable victims; they were everywhere. And these days it was far easier than in Bundy's time for reasons that might not seem so obvious to most people but which were abundantly clear to him.

He watched the old couple totter out of the supermarket and ease into their Mercedes station wagon. He wrote down the license plate number. He would run it later on the Internet and get their home address. They were doing their own shopping, so they probably had no live-in help or grown children nearby. The make of the car was relatively new, so they weren't surviving solely on Social Security. The man wore a cap with the logo of the local country club. That was another potential gold mine of information he might later tap.

He sat back and waited patiently. More prospects were sure to come in this busy shopping center. He could consume all he wanted without ever once taking out his wallet.

A few minutes later an attractive woman in her thirties came out of a pharmacy carrying a large bag. His gaze swung to her, his homicidal antennae twitching with interest. The woman stopped at the ATM next to the pharmacy, withdrew some cash and then committed what should have been classified as a mortal sin for the new century: she tossed the receipt into the trash before climbing into a bright red Chrysler Sebring convertible. Her vanity plate read "DEH JD."

He quickly translated that to be her initials and the fact that she was a lawyer, the "JD" standing for Juris Doctor. Her clothes told him she was fastidious about her appearance. The tan on her arms, face and legs was deep. If she was a practicing lawyer, she probably had just come back from vacation or else had visited the tanning booth over the winter. She was very fit-looking, her calves particularly well developed. She probably worked out regularly, perhaps even ran the trails in the woods hereabouts, he further deduced. His gaze had fixed on the gold anklet she wore on her left leg as she climbed in her car. That was intriguing, he thought.

She had a current-year American Bar Association bumper sticker, so the odds were she was still practicing law. And she was also single—there was no wedding ring on her finger. And right next to the ABA bumper sticker was a parking permit for a very expensive gated residential development about two miles from here. He nodded appreciatively. These stickers were very informative.

He parked, got out of the Bug, walked over to the trash can, made a show of throwing something away and in the same motion plucked out the ATM receipt. The woman really should have known better. She might as well have tossed her personal tax return in the trash. She was now naked, completely open to any probing he wanted to do.

When he got back to his car, he looked at the name on the account: D. Hinson. He'd look her up in the phone book later. And she'd also be in the business listings, so he'd know which law firm in town she worked at. That would give him two potential targets. Banks had started leaving off some of the numbers of the account because they knew their customers stupidly disposed of their receipts where they were easy pickings for people like him. Still, he didn't want her money; it was something far more personal that interested him.

He kept trolling under the warming sun. What a nice day it was shaping up to be. He reclined slightly in his seat only to perk up when off to his right a soccer mom started loading groceries in her van. He wasn't guessing there: she wore a T-shirt that announced this status. An infant rode in the car seat in the rear. A green bumper sticker announced that the woman was the mom of an honor roll student at Wrightsburg Middle School for the current school year.

Good to know, he thought: seventh or eighth grader and an infant. He pulled into the space next to the van and waited. The woman took the cart back to the front of the store, leaving the baby completely unguarded.

He got out of the Bug, leaned into the van's open driver's side window and smiled at the baby, who grinned back, chortling. The interior of the van was messy. Probably so was the woman's house. If they had an alarm system, they probably never turned it on. Probably forgot to lock all the doors and windows too. It was a wonder to him that the crime rate in the country wasn't far higher what with millions of idiots like her staggering blindly through life.

An algebra book was in the backseat; the middle school child's, no doubt. Next to it was a children's picture book, so there was at least a third child. This deduction was confirmed by the presence of a pair of grass-stained tennis shoes in the rear floorboard; they looked to be those of a five- or six-year-old boy.

He glanced in the passenger seat. There it was: a *People* magazine. He looked up. The woman had just slammed the cart back into the rack and had now paused to talk to someone coming out of the store. He reached in and drew the magazine toward him. Name and home address were on the mailing label. He already had her home phone number. She'd helpfully put it on the For Sale sign on the window of her van.

Another bingo. Her keys were in the ignition. He placed a piece of soft putty over the ones that looked like house keys, taking quick impressions. It made the breaking and entering part a lot easier when you didn't have to "break" when you "entered."

A final home run. Her cell phone was in its holder. He looked up. She was still gabbing away. Had he been so inclined, he could have killed the kid, stolen all her groceries and torched the car, and the woman would never even know it until someone started screaming at the flames shooting into the sky. He glanced around. People were far too busy with their lives to notice him.

He snatched the phone, hit the main screen button and got her cell phone number. Then he accessed her phone book, took a digital camera the size of his middle finger from his pocket and snapped pictures of screen after screen until he had all the names and phone numbers on her directory. He returned the phone, waved bye-bye to baby and slipped back into his car.

He went over his list. He had her name, home address and the fact that she had at least three kids and was married. The mailing block had been addressed to both Jean and Harold Robinson. He also had her home phone number, cell phone number and the names and numbers of a host of others important to her as well as impressions of her house keys.

She and her lovely family belong to me now.

The woman came back to her van, climbed in and drove off. He watched as she sped out of the parking lot, completely unaware that he'd become one of her intimates in the span of a few short minutes. He flicked a good-bye wave to the clueless soccer mom. *Maybe I'll be seeing you if you're extremely unlucky.*

He checked his watch: three potentials in less than twenty minutes. He breathed in the fresh air of the prosperous town of Wrightsburg, a town that had suffered a trio of brutal killings in quick succession.

Well, they hadn't seen anything yet.

CHAPTER

9

THE WRIGHTSBURG MORGUE
was located on a quiet treelined street about two miles
from the main downtown area. It was housed in part of a
small one-story building constructed of brick and glass
and had builder-grade landscaping that had flourished
with the recent wet weather. It could have housed any
type of business. People passing by would never guess it
was where dead bodies were brought to be cut open and
worked on, to determine what and/or who had killed
them. In the space right next to the morgue was a sign
proclaiming that Dr. Sylvia Diaz, M.D., also had her medical office there.

King's Lexus pulled into the parking lot, and he and
Michelle got out. A moment later a police cruiser drove in
next to them, and Todd Williams hauled out his large
body. He looked very unhappy as he tucked in his shirttail
and righted his pistol.

"Let's get this over with," he grunted before storming
ahead.

"What's with him?" whispered Michelle.

"I'll just take a flier and guess he doesn't like looking at dead bodies."

They asked for Sylvia Diaz at the front desk. The receptionist made a phone call, and a slender bespectacled man appeared. In his late twenties or early thirties the man sported a goatee and was dressed in scrubs. He introduced himself as Kyle Montgomery, Sylvia's assistant.

"She's just finishing up," he said in a monotone voice, although his eyes widened at the sight of the statuesque Michelle. "She said to bring you back to her office."

"How long have you worked here?" asked King.

Kyle squinted at him suspiciously. "Why does that matter?"

"I was just asking," he replied.

"I'm a private guy," retorted Kyle.

"I bet you went to UVA, didn't you?" asked Michelle. "What a great school," she added, smiling at him and drawing closer.

King watched with an amused expression as his partner proceeded to use her "feminine wiles" to coax information out of Kyle. She very rarely did this, but King knew it could be very effective. Kyle probably had nothing important to divulge, but it was helpful to have information on all the persons involved in the investigation.

Kyle quickly turned all his attention toward her. "Graduated pretty high up in my class," he said pompously. "I wanted to stay in the area, so I worked at UVA Hospital for a few years and then got my P.A. certification. But I got laid off from an oncology practice, and the bills started mounting up. Then this job came open. Presto, I'm a morgue tech. Thank you, God," he added sarcastically.

Michelle said, "It takes a very special person to do that sort of work."

"Yeah, it does," Kyle said cockily. "But I'm also Dr. Diaz's physician's assistant in her medical practice next door. She's there now treating a couple of patients. She actually hired me for both positions. It's a little bit of a juggling act, going back and forth, but at least the two offices are hooked together. And we don't have many deaths here that require autopsies. Hey, but that might be changing, right? Lots of action all of a sudden. Wrightsburg is really growing up. Yeah, baby." Kyle actually smiled at this.

Michelle, Williams and King exchanged disgusted glances as they followed him back.

Sylvia's office was everything Michelle imagined it would be. Very neat and orderly, tastefully decorated, at least by morgue standards, with warm feminine touches here and there to help dispel the cold, antiseptic atmosphere that dominated elsewhere in the building. On a coatrack near the door hung a woman's jacket, oversize bag and hat. On the floor next to the rack was a pair of dress shoes.

"She's very particular."

Michelle glanced over to see Kyle smiling at her. "The medical office is the same way. And Doc doesn't like to track stuff into the autopsy room, even though it's not like the most sterile place—pretty dirty, in fact. We have a locker room where we put on scrubs and shields, but sometimes I think she'd rather change out here for fear of contaminating some piece of evidence. I say get a life."

"Actually, it's nice to hear there are still dedicated people," said King stiffly.

While Kyle hung by the doorway waiting for his boss, Michelle ran her gaze around the rest of the room. On the shelf behind Sylvia's desk were several photos of a man either alone or with Sylvia. She picked one up and showed it to King with a questioning look.

"That's George Diaz, her late husband," he explained.

"She still has his pictures displayed at work?"

"I guess she really loved the guy."

"So how come you're not still seeing each other? Were there issues?" she asked in a playful tone.

"You're my business partner, not my shrink," he shot back.

A moment after Michelle put the photo back, Sylvia appeared in the doorway.

"Thank you, Kyle," she said curtly.

"Right," he said, and he and his superior smile marched off.

"Does your assistant have a slight attitude, or is it just us?" asked King.

Sylvia slipped off her lab coat and hung it on a hook on the door. Michelle took a moment to look the other woman over. A little under medium height, she was dressed in black slacks and a white linen shirt. She wore no jewelry, presumably because of her work. An earring or ring ending up in a corpse's slit-open stomach would probably not be a good thing. Her skin was smooth and lightly freckled around the jawline. Her red hair was tied back in a bun, revealing perfectly formed ears and a long, slender neck. Her brow was furrowed, and her look was one of distraction as she sat behind her desk.

"Kyle just turned thirty and doesn't really want to be here."

"I guess it's hard to pick up women in bars with the line 'Want to check out some great corpses?'" said Michelle.

"I think Kyle's dream is to be in a world-famous rock band," said Sylvia.

"Right, along with twenty million other guys," said King. "He needs to get over it. I did when I was seventeen."

Sylvia glanced at some papers on her desk, signed them, closed the file, stretched out her arms and yawned. "I'm sorry. I haven't done three autopsies so close together for quite some time, and there's been an outbreak of spring flu. That's what I was doing next door." She shook her head wearily. "It's a little schizophrenic. One minute I'm looking at the throat of a fifty-year-old woman, the next moment I'm cutting up someone to see how they were murdered. Usually, there are months when I don't even step foot inside the morgue. But not lately."

"It takes a very special person to do what you do, Sylvia," said King.

"I wasn't fishing for a compliment, just simply stating a fact, but thanks."

She turned to Williams, who was looking paler by the minute. When she spoke, her tone was not exactly one of warmth and honey. "I trust you've recovered from the first autopsy."

"I think my head has, not sure about my gut."

"I was really hoping to see you at the Canney and Pembroke posts. Having the lead investigator in attendance is usually quite helpful," she added in an admonishing tone that made her point quite clear.

Williams looked miserably at her. "I was planning to but then got called away."

"Of course." Sylvia glanced at King and Michelle with a suddenly hardened expression. "Do *you* both have strong stomachs?"

Michelle and King looked at each other. King answered for them. "Strong enough."

Sylvia turned to Williams. "Todd, do you have any objection to their seeing the bodies? Of course I also want you or at least one of your men to attend as well. It might appear strange to a jury that somebody from the police force hadn't viewed the bodies at least *post*-autopsy."

Williams looked angry but then seemed to wage an inner debate with himself. Finally, he shrugged. "Hell, let's go."

CHAPTER

10

THE AUTOPSY ROOM WAS much like Sylvia's office minus all warmth and feminine touches. Everything was stainless steel and neatly arranged. Two personal workstations with built-in desks were situated on one side of the room, and two stainless-steel examination tables with drainage holes, water tubs with hoses, a small dissection table, organ scale and trays of surgical instruments were situated on the other. The four had stopped at the locker room and donned scrubs, gloves and masks before entering. They looked like extras in a low-budget bioterrorism flick.

Michelle whispered to King as Sylvia walked ahead to speak with Kyle.

"I can see why you two dated. You both have the super mutant neatness gene. Don't worry; I hear they're working on a cure."

"Don't get your hopes up," King whispered back through his mask. "I'm never going over to the dark side."

"I'll show you Jane Doe first," said Sylvia, coming back to them.

A large stainless-steel door opened, and as Kyle emerged pushing a gurney with a sheet covering the dead woman, threads of chilly air escaped from the refrigerated room.

Michelle started shivering uncontrollably.

"You okay?" King asked.

"Of course I am," she shot back through chattering teeth. "You?"

"I was a premed student briefly before I went into law. And I worked at the morgue in Richmond over a summer. I've seen lots of bodies."

"Premed?"

"I thought it would help me pick up girls. I know, I know, but I was young and stupid."

Kyle left. Before Sylvia pulled back the sheet, she looked at Williams, and her expression was now more kindly. "Chief, just do what I told you the first time, and you'll be fine. You've already seen the worst of it. No more surprises, I promise."

He nodded, hitched up his pants and appeared to be holding his breath and praying for a natural disaster so he could get the hell out of there.

She pulled back the sheet and they all looked down.

The Y-incision running from chest to pubis made the body appear to have been unzipped. Jane Doe's organs had been removed, weighed and analyzed, and then the block of organs, muscle and tissue had been unceremoniously bagged and dumped back in the body cavity. The incision that had opened the skull was not readily apparent from their viewing angle, though the face drooped, like a doll whose supporting stitches had given way.

"The intermastoid incision is always an eye-opener," commented King dryly.

"I'm impressed, Sean," said Sylvia, staring at him.

Williams looked like he wanted to strangle King if he could only find the strength.

The smell of the body was very intense in the small room. Michelle started to cover her mouth and nose even though they were masked. Sylvia quickly stopped her.

"This room is very dirty, Michelle; germs everywhere, so don't touch your face with your hands. And trying to stop the smell that way only makes it worse. With mal-odors like this your senses will go dead in about two minutes. Just keep breathing." She glanced at Williams, who, to his credit, was taking large, rapid breaths and had one hand pushed against his belly as though trying to keep the contents in there right where they were. "At the crime scene your deputies kept running away to get fresh air and then coming back. The only thing they were doing was giving their sense of smell an opportunity to return."

"I know," said Williams between wheezes. "Puked all over their damn uniforms. We blew our whole laundry budget for the month." The police chief turned slightly green yet bravely stood his ground.

Michelle felt herself taking quick, jerky breaths. As Sylvia had said, her sense of smell was beginning to van-ish. She looked down at the body once more.

"I don't see any obvious wounds. Was it strangula-tion?" she asked.

Sylvia shook her head. "I checked that first. I used a

laser on the neck to look for ligature marks after none appeared evident under normal light. I thought there might be some hemorrhage into the muscles of the neck, but I didn't find any. And the hyoid bone and the thyroid and cricoid cartilages weren't fractured. They sometimes are in strangulation cases." She looked down at Jane Doe. "We did the sexual assault workup. It came back negative. Whoever killed her didn't rape or sexually violate her. Because of the usual order of an autopsy, I didn't discover the cause of death until near the end; up to that point it was a puzzler." She glanced sharply at Williams. "Todd, you'd already left by then."

Williams stared helplessly back at her. "Damn it, Doc, I'm trying here, okay? Cut me some slack."

"Don't keep us in suspense, Sylvia. How did she die?" exclaimed King. "And in stupid-people language if you can manage it."

Sylvia picked up a long metal rod and levered open Jane Doe's mouth.

"A twenty-two-caliber revolver was placed in her mouth and fired. The angle of the shot was about seventy-five degrees. The slug ended up lodged in her midbrain. I noticed some strange residue on her teeth. It wasn't from the discharge of the gun; that would have been a dead giveaway. The killer must've swabbed the teeth and mouth with a cleaning fluid to eliminate the evidence. The wound inside her mouth was sealed from the hot gases emitted when the gun was fired, basically cauterizing it. However, the X rays showed the bullet. We always take X rays before making any incision, but we had problems getting the film processed, so I started the post. Once I opened her up, the wound track and slug revealed themselves. When we got the X ray result, the bullet in the brain was there on the film."

"Isn't a gun in the mouth a typical method of suicide?" said Michelle.

"Not for women," replied Sylvia. "It's classic Mars versus Venus, testosterone versus estrogen. Men kill themselves with guns or by hanging. Women favor poison or drug overdoses, slitting their wrists or putting a plastic bag over their heads. Besides, there was no trace of gunpowder residue on her hands."

King mused, "The person would have to know that the cause of death would be revealed eventually even if he tried to hide it."

"Another interesting point," said Sylvia. "The woman was *not* killed in the woods. She was killed elsewhere, inside some structure, and her body was later transported to the woods. Most likely in a car, and her body was wrapped in plastic. "

"How can you be so sure?" King wanted to know.

"As you know, rigor mortis is a plain vanilla chemical process occurring upon death. It starts in the small muscles of the jaw and neck and bleeds downward to the larger muscle groups, the trunk and the extremities and is usually complete within six to twelve hours. I say usually because there are various exceptions to that rule. Body types and environmental conditions can impact the timing. An obese person may not experience rigor at death, and while cold inhibits rigor's onset, heat accelerates it. The rigidity remains anywhere from thirty hours to three days and then disappears in the same order it appeared."

"Okay, what does that tell us?" asked Michelle.

"A lot. Jane Doe was a young woman, well developed and nourished but not overweight. Rigor on her would have fallen within the normal parameters absent extraordinary environmental forces. The ambient temperatures the night before she was found had dipped into the high forties, which would have inhibited somewhat the rigor's progression. Well, rigor on Jane Doe was fully resolved and her body flaccid when I examined her at the crime scene. That means she had been dead for three days at most by that time, or at the very least thirty hours. Given the resolution of rigor despite the chilly weather, I'd lean more toward her being dead three days when she was found."

"But you said rigor's not precise. Maybe there was something else, another factor that skewed it," suggested Michelle.

"I had another check beyond the rigor. When I examined the body in the woods, it was already discolored, and swollen with gas from the bacteria engulfing the body. The skin also was blistering, and fluids were leaking from all orifices. That almost never commences until three days after death." She paused. "And if she'd lain in those woods for even thirty hours much less three days, the insect infestation would have been dramatically different than what I saw. I expected to see heavy infestation of bluebottle and greenbottle flies, both *outdoor* varieties. Flies attack a dead body almost immediately and lay their eggs. Within one to two days the eggs hatch, and the cycle keeps going. Now, when I examined the mouth, nose and eyes, I did find fly-hatched larvae, but of what turned out

to be *house*flies. The outdoor fly larvae hadn't yet
hatched. Also, burial and carrion beetles should have
been swarming the body by the time we found it. Nothing
stops insects from doing their thing. And on top of that,
after three days in those woods wild animals should have
attacked the body and removed large parts of the extremities. All that was missing were fingers."

She turned the body on its side and pointed out reddish-
purple patches on the front where the blood had settled
postmortem. "I also had yet another way to check my theory of the body's being moved. The position of the lividity really told me all I needed to know. As you can see,
lividity gives the appearance of bruising with its darkish
hues. However, here, you can also see that the discoloration is on the front of the torso and the thighs and
lower legs. The white streaks you see on the abdomen,
lower chest and parts of the legs are where the body was
lying against something hard and the resulting pressure
inhibited the process."

She shifted the body so they could see the back of it.

"You can see that there is no such discoloration on the
back or the backs of the legs. Conclusion: she was killed
and then was laid facedown, and the blood-settling
process commenced. Lividity usually first occurs around
one hour after death and is complete within three to four
hours. If the body is moved within another three to four
hours, the original discoloration may partially disappear
and new ones form as the blood shifts again. However,
fresh lividity patterns are not produced by position
changes twelve hours after death, because blood drainage
becomes fixed at that time."

She gently laid the corpse back down. "My opinion is that she was killed indoors or perhaps in a car by the shot to the head. I believe her body remained indoors for at least twenty-four to forty-eight hours and then was taken to the place where it was discovered. She couldn't have been in the woods longer than ten to twelve hours."

"And the transport by car? And the plastic?" asked King.

"What was he going to do, carry her in his arms down the road?" said Sylvia. "And neither I nor the police found any fibers on her clothing, the sorts of trace you would expect to see from the carpeting in a car or a car's trunk. And I didn't find any on the body. Plastic doesn't leave much if any residue."

Michelle said, "I found the body at around two-thirty in the afternoon. The boys would have seen it maybe minutes before that."

"Counting back," said King, "that means the body would have been dumped there, using your twelve-hour outside number, no earlier than two-thirty in the morning."

Williams had stood in the background all this time, but now he stepped forward. "Nice work, Sylvia. Wrightsburg is lucky to have you," he said.

She smiled thinly at his praise. "A postmortem doesn't tell who committed the crime unless the killer left behind things like semen, saliva or urine that we can test. The post just tells us how and what." Sylvia glanced at her notes and continued. "As I said, there was no evidence of rape, no injury to the rectum or vagina, and she'd never had a baby. I'd put her age at about mid-twenties and her health as physically sound. In life she was a well-built woman about five feet five inches tall. She'd had breast implants, and collagen injections in her lips. And she also had had her appendix removed. We'll know more when the toxicology screens come back in a couple of weeks." Sylvia pointed at Jane Doe's slit-open stomach. "Todd, she was pierced on her belly button, perhaps for a belly ring, but there was none on the body. That might help you in identifying her."

"Thanks. I'll check it out."

"The only helpful identifying mark I found was this." She picked up a magnifying glass, lifted the sheet off the lower part of the body and held up one of the legs, positioning the glass at a spot toward the inside thigh very near the woman's crotch. "It's a little difficult to make out with the extensive discoloration of the body, but it's a tattoo of a cat."

Michelle looked at the tattoo of the feline and the proximity of it to the woman's genitals and stood straight up. "I really don't want to think about that connection."

"Damn," said Williams, reddening.

"I know, not very ladylike, is it?" said Sylvia.

She looked up as Kyle entered the room.

"There's another police guy out front, wants to talk to the chief here, Doc."

"Police *guy*?" Her tone was a little strident. "Try police *officer*."

"Right, this police *officer* wants to see the chief."

"Can you ask him to come back here?"

A malicious smile passed across the young man's features. "That's the first thing I did, Doc. The police *officer* declined, without explanation. Come to think, though, he looked a little green when I suggested it."

"I'll go out front," said Williams, and he hurried off with Kyle right behind.

Five minutes later Williams returned with a nervous-looking uniformed patrolman in his wake who was introduced by Williams as Officer Dan Clancy. Williams looked stricken. "We might have an ID on the girl from the picture we circulated," he said, his voice trembling slightly as they all stared at him. "Looks like she worked briefly at the Aphrodisiac."

"The Aphrodisiac?" exclaimed King.

Williams nodded. "As an exotic dancer. Her 'stage' name was Tawny Blaze. Not real imaginative, I know. Her real name was Rhonda Tyler." He glanced at the paper in his hand. "Tyler worked there for a while but left when her contract was up."

"Will the person who recognized the picture come down and attempt to make a positive ID?" asked Sylvia. "Although with the state the body's in, I'm not sure that's possible. But if—"

Williams cut in. "That won't be necessary, Sylvia."

"Why not?" she demanded.

"We were told she has a distinguishing mark." Williams looked embarrassed.

It hit Michelle in an instant. "A tattoo of a cat next to her . . . ?"

Williams's mouth gaped even as he nodded.

"Who was the person who provided the information?" asked King.

"The manager of the Aphrodisiac. Lulu Oxley."

Now King's mouth gaped. "Lulu Oxley! Junior Deaver's Lulu Oxley?"

"How many Lulu Oxleys do you know, Sean?" asked Williams.

"I know her too," said Sylvia. "Well, we used to have the same gynecologist."

Williams said, "That's not all. We got a message from the *Wrightsburg Gazette*. They received a letter."

"What sort of letter?" asked Michelle nervously.

"A coded one," replied a very pale Todd Williams. "With the mark of the Zodiac on the envelope."

CHAPTER

11

KING ACCOMPANIED Williams to the police station to look at the note while Michelle stayed behind with Sylvia and Deputy Clancy to go over the autopsies already performed on Canney and Pembroke.

During the drive to the police station King called Bill Jenkins, an old buddy of his in San Francisco. When he made his request, his friend was understandably surprised.

"What do you need that for?" Jenkins asked.

King glanced at Williams and then said, "It's for a criminal justice class I'm teaching over at the community college."

"Oh, okay," Jenkins said. "After all the excitement you and your partner caused last year, I thought you were messed up in something like that again."

"No, Wrightsburg is back to just being a quiet, sleepy southern town."

"If you decide you ever want to rejoin the big time, give me a call."

"How soon can you have that for me?"

"You're in luck. We have a special running this week on classic serial killers. Thirty minutes. Just give me a number to fax to and a major credit card," he said, chuckling.

King got the police station fax number from Williams and gave it to his friend.

"How can you get it so fast?" King asked Jenkins.

"The timing of your call is impeccable. We conducted a long-overdue office cleaning and just last week pulled that file for archiving. Copies of the schoolteacher's notes are in there. I was just going over them the other night, in fact, for old time's sake. That's what I'll send you, the key he came up with to decipher the coded letters."

King thanked him and clicked off.

When they reached the police station, Williams strode in with King following.

Out of his professional depth or not, the chief was back on his home turf, and he was going to act like it. He bellowed for the deputy who'd called him about the coded letter and also grabbed a bottle of Advil from his secretary. King and the deputy gathered in Williams's office, where the chief plopped behind his desk and swallowed three Advil using only his saliva. Before he took the piece of paper and envelope from the deputy, he said, "Please tell me these have been checked for prints."

They had, the deputy told him. "Although Virgil Dyles, the owner of the *Gazette,* initially thought it was a joke when he got it in the mail. We wouldn't have known anything about it, but a friend of mine who's a reporter over there phoned and told me. I went right over and got it, but it's all Greek to me."

"So what did Virgil do, pass it around the damn office?" shouted Williams.

"Something like that," replied the deputy nervously. "Probably more than a few people touched it. I told my friend at the paper to keep quiet, but I think she might have told some people that she thought this was serious."

Williams's big fist came down on the top of his desk so hard both King and the deputy winced. "Damn it! This is spiraling right out of control. How the hell are we going to keep this on the q.t. if we can't even control the folks in Wrightsburg?"

"Let's look at the message," King said. "We'll worry about the media spin later."

He hovered over Williams's shoulder as the lawman examined the envelope. The postmark was local, mailed four days before, with a stamp applied very exactly. It was addressed, in block letters, to Virgil Dyles of the *Wrightsburg Gazette*. On the lower right-hand corner of the envelope was the circle with crosshairs. There was nothing written in the return address block.

"Not much there," said Williams as he unfolded the note. "Maybe there's some expert who can tell us something from how he wrote the letters, placed the stamp and such, but I sure as hell can't."

The message was written in blurred black ink, again using block letters, and the lines were in tightly structured columns arranged both horizontally and vertically.

"The blurred part is from the ninhydrin," the deputy explained. "They use that to fume the letter for prints, you know."

"Thanks. That never would have occurred to me," Williams said testily.

All the lines were in code. Some of the characters were letters; others were merely symbols. Williams sat there for some minutes going over it carefully. He finally sighed and sat back.

"You don't happen to know how to break codes, do you?" Williams asked King.

At that instant Deputy Rogers—who served with King when he'd been a part-time Wrightsburg police officer— knocked and came in, holding some pages in his hand. "This fax just came in for Sean."

King took the pages and said to Williams, "I do now."

He carried the letter and faxed pages to a small table in the corner, sat down and began to work. Ten minutes later he glanced up. This wasn't good, he thought. In fact, this was probably worse than having someone running around copying the Zodiac killer.

"Have you deciphered it?" demanded Williams.

King nodded. "I have some experience with cryptograms from my years at the Secret Service. But I recalled that a high school teacher from Salinas originally broke the code to the San Francisco Zodiac's letters. I have a friend on the force there who's very familiar with the case. I thought he might have access to the teacher's notes. That's what he faxed to me, the key to the code. That made it pretty easy."

"So what does it say?" asked Williams, swallowing nervously.

King checked his notes. "It contains misspellings and

grammatical and syntax errors, deliberate ones, I think. So did the original Zodiac."

Deputy Rogers looked at Williams. "Zodiac? What the hell's that?"

"A serial killer in California," explained Williams. "He was slaughtering people long before you were even born. He was never caught."

A look of panic appeared in Deputy Rogers's baby blues.

King began to read. *"By now, you find the girl. She's all cut up, but that ain't me. Cut her up looking for clues. Ain't none. Trust me. The watch don't lie. She was numero uno. But more numbers to come. Lots of 'em. One more thing. I ain't, repeat, ain't the Zodiac. Or his second or third or fourth coming. I am me. It ain't going to be that easy don't you know. By the time I'm done you wish it be just Zodiac."*

"So this isn't the end of it," said Williams slowly.

"Actually, I'm afraid it's just beginning," answered King.

CHAPTER

12

DEPUTY CLANCY WAS TALL and well built and trying hard not to look anxious as he stared between Sylvia and Michelle.

"Are you going to be okay?" asked Sylvia as she watched him closely. "I don't need you passing out on me."

"I'm fine, Doc," he replied gamely.

Sylvia said, "Have you seen an autopsied body before?"

"Of course," he answered curtly.

"These are shotgun wounds to the head." Sylvia looked at Michelle too as she said this.

Michelle took a deep breath. "I'm ready."

"Part of the job," said Clancy, trying to project confidence. "In fact, next month Chief Williams is sending me to the Forensic Crime Scene School."

"That's a great program, you'll learn a lot. Don't let what you're about to see dissuade you from going."

Sylvia walked over to a set of stainless-steel doors. "This is what we unofficially call the grisly room. It's for bodies that have undergone extreme trauma: burns, explosives, underwater for long periods of time. And shotgun wounds to the head," she added with emphasis. She hit a button on the wall and the doors opened. She moved inside and came back out a few moments later pushing a gurney with a body on it. She rolled the gurney to her workstation area and clicked on the overhead exam light.

Clancy coughed and put a hand up to his face mask. Sylvia quickly gave him the same lecture on sense of smell deadening. He removed his hand grudgingly but seemed to be a little unsteady on his feet. Sylvia nudged a chair over near him. Michelle noticed the movement; Clancy didn't. The two women exchanged a silent communication.

"This is Steven Canney." When she uncovered the body, Michelle's hand shot out and pushed the chair behind the deputy in time to catch him as he slumped backward, gagged and then passed out.

They rolled him in the chair to a far corner of the room, where Sylvia cracked open a tube of ammonia and stuck it under his nostrils. He came to, jerked up and shook his head, looking awful.

"If you're going to be sick, there's a restroom right there," she said, pointing.

The young man turned red. "I'm sorry, Doc. Real sorry."

"Deputy Clancy, there's nothing to be sorry about. It's a horrific sight. And the first time I saw something like that, my reaction was the same as yours."

He looked surprised. "It was?"

Yes, she assured him, it was. "I have a written report that I can give you. If you want to leave, you can. If you want to rejoin us when you feel better, that's fine too. If you just want to sit here, that's okay as well."

Deputy Clancy decided on the latter, although as soon as they turned away, he slumped down on the desk, his face in his hands.

Sylvia and Michelle went back over to Steve Canney's corpse.

"Did you really pass out your first time?" asked Michelle quietly.

"Of course not, but why make him feel even worse? The men almost always pass out. And the bigger the man, the faster."

Sylvia pointed out various areas of Canney's wounds with a long stainless-steel rod. "As you can see, the supratentorial of the brain was pretty much eviscerated, not unexpected with a shotgun wound."

She put down the rod and her face clouded over. "Canney's father came in to see his son. I advised him not to, that the wounds were very bad, but he insisted. That's the toughest part of this business. He was able to give a presumptive ID from a birthmark and a scar on his knee from an old football injury. We obtained a positive ID from dental records and fingerprints."

Sylvia took a deep breath. "My heart went out to him, although he took it pretty stoically. I've never had children, but I can imagine what it would be like, having to walk into a place like this and . . ." Her voice trailed off.

Michelle let the silence hold for a few moments and then said, "And Canney's mother?"

"She died several years ago. I guess that was a blessing of sorts."

Sylvia returned to her examination. "Determining the firing range on shotgun wounds is tricky. The most reliable way is to fire the same ammo from the exact same gun with the same choke setting. We don't have that luxury here, but you'll note that the entrance wound has no scalloping of the margin and no satellite lesions. So the distance between muzzle and victim was contact to less than two feet." She covered what was left of Canney's head with a small sheet.

"Do you know the make of the ammo?"

"Oh, yes. The wadding from the shotgun round was recovered from the wound. All the pellets also stayed in him. That's why the wound is so devastating. All the kinetic energy's used up internally." Sylvia looked at her notes. "It was a twelve-gauge loaded with nine double-ought pellets of Federal manufacture."

"And Pembroke died the same way?"

"She was shot in the back. The injuries were instantly fatal but not as devastating. There were numerous bits of the shattered windshield glass embedded in her skin as well. Conclusion: the killer fired the first shot through the windshield. Looking at the wounds alone, you'd think the range of weapon to victim was far greater. However, I think the barrel of the shotgun was near the windshield when it was discharged, or a total distance of about three feet to Pembroke. The entrance wound on her back has a characteristic scalloped margin, and there are additional satellite lesions as individual pellets separated from the main mass. Because the pellets had to break through the glass, it appears as though the shot was fired from a greater distance than was actually the case."

"Why do you think her back was to the windshield?"

"They were having sex," Sylvia said. "There was spermicidal residue from Canney's condom in her vagina. She was probably astride Canney and facing him when it happened, with her back to the windshield. That's a very natural position for intercourse in the close confines of a car. Her body acted as a shield; otherwise, Canney would have been killed from the first blast as well."

"You're sure he wasn't?"

"There were two rounds total fired. The number of pellets we found showed that. There were nine in each body. Symmetry in death," she added dryly.

"I suppose no ejected shotgun shells were found."

Sylvia shook her head. "Either the killer picked up the spent casings or the weapon was a nonpump where the fired casings have to be manually extracted."

"I guess since it was a smoothbore barrel, there's no possibility of a ballistics matching if we find a suspected weapon."

"Sometimes irregularities at the end of a shotgun's muzzle will impart scratch marks on the plastic wad. That was actually the case here. I'm not a ballistics expert, but the police may have enough to do comparisons if they ever find the shotgun. And we have the slug from Rhonda Tyler's body as well for ballistic analysis."

"There was talk that the shotgun blast that killed Steve Canney might have stopped his watch, giving the time of death."

"No. The watch was placed on him postmortem. It was stopped because the stem was pulled out. I noted that at the crime scene. I found embedded glass in his left wrist, right where the watch would have been."

"Any idea why the watch was put on him after death?"

"As a calling card perhaps? I noted that it was set to three. Pembroke's was set to around two. That also might confirm their order of death."

"And Jane Doe slash Rhonda Tyler had on a watch that didn't belong to her either and that was set to one o'clock. And it was a Zodiac."

Sylvia looked at her. "And now we have a Zodiac-style letter."

"And three people dead."

"So I guess the next one will be four o'clock, representing the fourth victim?"

"If there is a next one," said Michelle.

"There's little doubt of that. The first victim was an exotic dancer. However, the next two victims were local kids making out in a car. Once they start their murders, serial killers usually stick to one segment of the population. This guy's already showing us he's not playing by the same old rules." She paused and added quietly, "So the real question becomes, who'll be next?"

CHAPTER

13

OUTSIDE THE POLICE station, the pale blue VW Beetle drove slowly past and stopped at the intersection. The driver glanced at the one-story brick building that housed the police department. They would have gotten the letter by now. They might have also deciphered the contents. It wasn't like he'd made it very hard. The hard would come later, as in trying to stop him. *Try impossible, Mr. Policemen.*

Next they'd call in the state police's criminal investigative unit. They'd want to keep things quiet, no sense panicking people. No doubt an application for profiling assistance would be submitted to the FBI's vaunted VICAP. Important people would be contacted to see that the matter was expedited, and a profile on the killer, on him, would be quickly forthcoming.

Of course it would be totally wrong.

He'd driven past the morgue earlier, where the M.E. was probably pulling her red hair out over three bodies that represented very different things yet had common themes. The clues would be minimal. He knew what to look for and thus to remove, but no one was infallible and forensic science could dredge up much from microscopic wreckage. She'd find some things, draw some correct conclusions, but on the key points she'd come up empty. The no-see-ums wouldn't trip him up.

He drove through the intersection as several police officers ran out of the building and climbed into their patrol cars and sped off. They were probably running down irrelevant leads, wasting energy and time, which didn't surprise him considering the weak attributes of their leader, Todd Williams. However, Sylvia Diaz was first-rate in her field. And at some point, as the killings mounted, the FBI would be called in to take over the investigation. He was actually relishing the challenge.

He drove to another intersection, pulled up to the mailbox and dropped the letter in before speeding off again. When they got his next communication explaining the circumstances of Steve Canney's and Janice Pembroke's deaths, the police would know they were in for the fight of their lives.

King picked up Michelle from the morgue and filled her in on the details about the Zodiac letter. She, in turn, brought him up to speed on the autopsy results for Pembroke and Canney. Unfortunately, reciting the details didn't make the puzzle any less inexplicable.

"So it seems the killer wants to make clear that even though he's somewhat copying the Zodiac crime with Rhonda Tyler, he's *not* the Zodiac," she said. "What do you make of that?"

King shook his head. "It seems these murders are just the opening salvo."

"Do you think we'll see another letter?"

"Yes, and soon. And though Todd's not convinced of it, I'm sure it'll deal with Canney and Pembroke. He's going to talk to Lulu Oxley and obtain more info on Rhonda Tyler."

Michelle looked out the windshield. "And where are we headed?"

"To the Battles'. I called and set up an appointment." He glanced at her. "We've got a paying job, remember?" He grew silent and then added, "You've already been through a lot today. Are you sure you're up to this?"

"After what we've seen, how bad can the Battles be?"

"You might be surprised."

CHAPTER

14

THE BATTLE ESTATE WAS set on top of an imposing hill. It was a sprawling three-story structure of brick, stone and clapboard surrounded by acres of emerald grass and dotted with mature trees. It screamed old money, though the mounds of cash that had built it were only decades old. King and Michelle stopped at a pair of massive wrought-iron gates. There was a call box set on a short black post next to the asphalt drive. King rolled down his window and tapped the white button on the call box. An efficient voice answered, and a minute later the gates swung open and King drove through.

"Welcome to Casa Battle," he said.

"Is that what they call it?"

"No, just my idea of a joke."

"You said you know Remmy Battle?"

"As well as most people do, I guess. I also used to play golf occasionally with Bobby. He's gregarious and dominating, but he has balls of iron and a really nasty temper if you happen to cross him. Now, Remmy's the sort who only lets you see bits and pieces, and strictly on her terms.

And if you cross *her,* you'll need a urologist and a pack of miracles to put you back together."

"Where'd she get a name like Remmy?"

"It's short for Remington. The story I heard was that was her father's favorite brand of shotgun. Everyone who knows her thinks the woman was aptly named."

"Who knew so many interesting people lived in such a small town?" Michelle looked ahead at the imposing home. "Wow, what a fabulous place."

"On the outside yes. I'll let you be the judge of the interior."

When they knocked on the front door, it was opened almost immediately by a large, well-muscled middle-aged man dressed in a yellow cardigan sweater, white shirt, muted tie and black slacks. He introduced himself as Mason. Mrs. Battle was finishing up a few things and would meet them on the rear terrace shortly, he informed them.

As Mason led them through the house, Michelle looked around at an interior that was breathtaking. That the things she was seeing were costly there was no doubt. Yet what was also present was a sense of understatement that for some reason surprised her.

"The interior is beautiful, Sean," she whispered.

"I wasn't talking about *that* interior," he mumbled back. "I meant the ones who are breathing."

They arrived on the rear terrace to find a table laid out with both hot and cold tea and some finger foods and snacks. Mason poured the beverages of their choice and then left, closing the French doors quietly behind him. The temperature was in the seventies with a warming sun and the air a little muggy from the recent rains.

Michelle sipped her iced tea. "So is Mason a kind of butler?"

"Yes, been with them forever. He's actually more than a butler to them."

"A confidant, then? Perhaps good for our purposes."

"Probably too loyal for that option," King answered. "But then again you never really know where loyalties lie until you ask, preferably with something to give in return."

They heard a splash of water, and both went to the iron railing that partially enclosed the terrace and looked out over the exquisite rear grounds.

The sprawling outdoor entertainment area visible here included a stone pool house, a spa that could easily accommodate a dozen adults, a roofed-in dining area and a massive oval-shaped pool outlined in brick and flagstone.

"I always wondered how the really rich lived," said Michelle.

"They live just like you and me except a whole lot better."

Emerging from the clear blue and obviously heated waters of the pool was a young woman in a very revealing string bikini. She had long blond hair, was about five-seven, and her curves and bosom were solidly in the range of eye-catching. There were defined muscles in her legs, arms and shoulders and a belly ring in the navel of her flat stomach. As she bent over to pick up a towel, they could also see a large tattoo on the back of one of her partially exposed butt cheeks.

"What's that tattooed on her butt?" asked Michelle.

"Her name," answered King. "Savannah." King watched

the young woman towel off. "It's amazing what they can write on skin, and in cursive too."

"You can see that from here?" Michelle asked with raised eyebrows.

"No, I've seen it before." He quickly amended this answer. "At a pool party I attended."

"Uh-huh. Her name on her butt, what, so the guys don't forget?"

"I'm trying very hard not to think of the reason."

Savannah looked up, saw them and waved. She wrapped a short see-through robe around her, slipped on some flip-flops and headed up the brick steps toward them.

When she reached them, she gave King a hug that seemed designed to drill her large bosom right into his chest. Up close her facial features were not quite as flawless as her body; her nose, chin and jaw were a bit too sharply outlined and irregular, but that was nit-picking, Michelle decided. Savannah Battle was a very beautiful woman.

Savannah looked King up and down admiringly. "I swear, Sean King, you just get better-looking every time I see you. Now, how's that fair? We women just keep getting older." This came out in a southern drawl that Michelle thought was highly affected.

"Well, you certainly don't have to worry about that," said Michelle, extending her hand. "I'm Michelle Maxwell."

"Oh, aren't you sweet," said Savannah in a tone that wasn't sweet at all.

"Congratulations on your graduation," said King. "William and Mary, right?"

"Daddy always wanted me to go to college, and I did, though I can't say I loved it." She sat down and slowly dried off her shapely legs in what Michelle interpreted as a seductive gesture aimed at King. Then she dug into the tiny sandwiches.

"What'd you major in?" asked Michelle, thinking that the young woman must have gotten her degree in either cheerleading or throwing parties or perhaps both.

"Chemical engineering," was her surprising if mumbled reply. Apparently, no one had taught the girl not to talk with her mouth full. "Daddy made his fortune as an engineer, and I guess I took after him."

"We were sorry to hear about Bobby," said King quietly.

"He's tough; he'll pull through," she said confidently.

"I heard you might be heading out on your own," said King.

Savannah's expression darkened. "I expect people are having a good time trying to figure out what I'm going to do. Trust-fund Baby Battle," she added bitterly.

"I didn't mean it that way, Savannah," said King gently.

She waved off his apology with a dismissive karate chop through the air. "I've been dealing with that all my life, why stop now, right? I have my own way to make in the world, and it's not always easy with parents like I have. But I'll make something of myself. I'm not going through life using my credit card to buy happiness."

As she listened, Michelle felt her opinion of the young woman turning more positive.

Savannah wiped her mouth with her hand and said, "I know why you're here. It's about Junior Deaver, right? I can't figure why he would've done anything so stupid. I mean, like my mother's going to just look the other way while he walks off with her wedding ring? I don't think so."

"Maybe he didn't do it," said King.

"Sure he did," said Savannah as she toweled off her wet hair. "From what I heard he left so much evidence behind he might as well have just sat on the floor and waited for the police to show up and arrest him." She shoved another piece of sandwich into her mouth and crammed in a handful of potato chips as a chaser.

"Stop eating like some damned pig, Savannah!" the voice said sharply. "And while you're doing that, try and halfway sit like a lady, if your imagination can possibly grasp such a concept."

Savannah, who'd been slouching in her chair with her legs spread wide like a hooker on the prowl, instantly straightened up and cemented her thighs together, stretching the robe over her knees.

Remington Battle strode onto the terrace with as much presence as a Broadway legend convinced of her ability to effortlessly dominate an audience.

She was dressed impeccably in a dazzling white pleated skirt that fell several inches below the knee. On her feet were stylish if conservative low-heeled pumps. A patterned blouse of cool blue was partially covered by a white sweater that was draped around her shoulders. She was taller than her daughter by several inches—around Michelle's height—and her touched-up auburn hair and makeup were expertly done. Her features were strong, indeed almost visually overpowering. Michelle guessed that Remmy in her youth had probably been even more beautiful than her daughter. Now in her sixties she was still a very handsome woman. Yet with all that, it was the eyes that caught and held you: part eagle, part buzzard and intimidating as hell.

Remmy shook hands with King and then was introduced to Michelle. The latter felt the woman run a severe gaze over her and suspected that Remmy Battle found much to find fault with in her very casual clothes, nonexistent makeup and windswept hair. She didn't have long to ruminate on that, though, as Remmy turned her attention to her daughter once more.

"In my day we didn't greet guests without any clothes on," she said icily.

"I was swimming, Mama. I don't usually go swimming in my debutante gown," Savannah shot back, but her fingers flew to her mouth and she chewed nervously on a nail.

Remmy gave the young woman such a penetrating stare that Savannah finally grabbed another sandwich and a fistful of chips, rose, muttered something under her breath that to Michelle sounded pretty close to "old bitch" and stalked off, her wet flip-flops smacking against the brick in a series of exclamation points.

Then Remmy Battle sat down and turned her full attention to King and Michelle.

They each drew a deep breath as her gaze bored into them. To Michelle it was quite an introduction to Casa Battle. Now she understood exactly what King had meant about judging the "interior."

CHAPTER

15

"I HAVE TO APOLOGIZE for Savannah," said Remmy. "I love her, but some days I can't believe we're actually related by blood, or anything else for that matter."

"It's okay, Mrs. Battle, she's just a kid," said Michelle. "They all do crazy stuff."

Remmy snapped, "She's not a child. She's twenty-two! She's a graduate of one of the finest schools on the East Coast. Rings in her belly and tattoos on her butt! I didn't send that girl to college so she could lose her damn mind!"

Michelle looked at King for help.

"Uh, Remmy, we were sorry to hear about Bobby. How's he doing?" he asked.

"His condition is still critical," Remmy answered in the same harsh tone, and then her hand crept to her lined forehead and she said in a more restrained voice, "I'm sorry. Here I am complaining about Savannah, and I'm not exactly being Miss Hospitality myself. It's just that a lot has happened lately." She paused and said slowly,

"Bobby was in a coma for the longest time, and the damn doctors didn't know when or even if he'd come out of it. But then he did. They were even able to take him off the ventilator. Two nights ago he said his first words."

"That must be encouraging," said King.

"You'd think so, wouldn't you? Thing is, he was incoherent. Spouting off names, nothing he said made any sense. Hell, they don't know for sure if he's slipped back into the coma or not."

"I guess that's hard for the doctors to determine."

"With what they charge I expect them to walk on water and have a direct line to God," she replied bitterly.

"Is there anything *we* can do?"

"Right now a prayer or two couldn't hurt."

Mason came out carrying a tray of coffee. He poured a cup for Remmy and offered some to Michelle and King—both declined—before retreating once more.

"There's nothing like a soothing cup of coffee in the afternoon." Remmy took a long sip and then settled back in her chair. "Harry Carrick's a damn fine lawyer, and Junior's lucky to have him." She paused, took another drink of her coffee and added, "But Junior did it. I know it as though I'd seen him do it myself."

King pounced. "But that's the point, Remmy, you *didn't* see him. No one did."

She waved this comment off in a way that reminded Michelle of Savannah's earlier chopping gesture. "The evidence is overwhelming."

"Right, *too* overwhelming. He could have been framed."

Remmy looked at King as though he were speaking a

language not of this earth. "Who in their right mind would want to frame someone like Junior Deaver?"

"Whoever really broke into your home and stole all that property," replied King. "And do you really see Junior fencing bearer bonds and fine jewelry?"

"He didn't know what was in there. He got cash too. It doesn't take an Einstein to spend cash, now, does it?" she retorted.

"All we want to do is look around and talk to a few people. And even though we're working for Harry and Junior, I'm presuming you want the guilty party caught."

Remmy smiled, but there was a dangerous glint in her eyes. "You presume correctly, Mr. King, although they've already caught the guilty party." She suddenly roared, firing the words off like a .50-caliber gone haywire, "And if that big dumb son of a bitch would tell me where the *hell* my wedding ring is, I might persuade the commonwealth's attorney to drop the charges! Why don't you go back and tell Harry that! And then maybe we can put an end to this horseshit!"

Michelle noted that the woman's southern drawl was far more pronounced when she was angry and, unlike her daughter, there was absolutely nothing affected about it. Michelle set her iced tea down because she'd almost dropped it after Remmy's eruption. She silently thanked God that Remington Battle wasn't *her* mother.

Unfazed, King said in a calm voice, "Duly noted, Remmy. But can we look around now?"

Remmy stared at him for a long moment. Her lips twitched as she apparently tried to master her anger. For an instant Michelle actually thought the woman was going to hurl her cup of soothing coffee at King's head. *Maybe you should switch to decaf,* Michelle thought.

Finally, Remmy rose from her chair and motioned for them to follow. "Hell, I'll show you myself."

CHAPTER

16

REMMY BATTLE LED KING and Michelle inside and up the main staircase to the third floor. The house seemed to have been added onto over time, observed Michelle, with new wings extending out from the older central block.

Remmy apparently read her thoughts because she said, "This house has been a work in progress for decades. Many of our friends have several beautiful estates around the world, but this is the only one Bobby and I ever wanted. It's something of a mishmash at times, and some hallways just stop at a wall, but I"—she corrected herself instantly—"*we* love it."

They arrived at a door that Remmy opened and ushered them through.

It was a large and nicely furnished room, painted in comfortable colors, with a row of windows. One of those windows looked new.

Remmy pointed to it. "That's where he got in. The police said he used a crowbar. They finally gave me the okay to have everything fixed."

King stared down at a cracked picture frame that was on one of the nightstands. The glass had been pulled out. He picked it up. "What happened to this?"

Remmy scowled. "That picture was on a table over by the window. It was broken when Junior came through there. I haven't had it repaired yet."

King and Michelle looked at the drawing of a young boy inside the broken frame. The drawing was ripped right down the middle.

"Who is it?" asked King.

"It's a drawing of Bobby Jr. I'll never forgive Junior for destroying it."

King put the picture down. "I understand there was some sort of hidden drawer in your closet?"

Remmy nodded and motioned for them to follow. Her closet had elaborate mahogany built-ins throughout, and clothes, bags, shoes, hats and other accessories were arranged in precise order.

King looked at the meticulous display with unabashed admiration. He kept his own possessions in perfect order, a fact well known to Michelle. His expression of unmitigated delight clearly registered with her, for while Remmy wasn't looking, Michelle tapped King on the arm, gave an orgasmic shudder and then pantomimed having an after-sex cigarette.

"Where was the hidden drawer, if you don't mind my asking?" said King after he finished scowling at his partner.

Remmy pulled one drawer out slightly and then tapped on the front of a flat piece of wood right below it. This popped open, revealing a small space about eighteen inches across and two feet deep. "A false front," explained Remmy. "Looks like a piece of filler wood, but pulling out the drawer above primes a lever in the false front. Then tapping on the right upper corner of the false front triggers that lever, and it opens."

King examined the mechanism closely. "Pretty clever."

"Always wanted a secret drawer in my closet," said Remmy. "Ever since I was a little girl."

"But the person who robbed you didn't know how to open it?" said Michelle.

"*Junior Deaver* didn't know how to open it," she corrected. "Just about every drawer in here was clawed and busted up. Cost me a pretty penny to fix it. I'll be taking that out of Junior's hide in civil court. Be sure and tell Harry that."

"But how did anyone other than you even know there was a secret drawer in here?" Michelle wanted to know.

"Over the years I might have let that fact slip. I didn't think anything of it, because we have at least what I thought was a first-rate security system."

"And was the system on?" asked King.

"Yes, only there are no motion detectors on the third floor and the windows up here aren't wired either. The system was put in years ago after a near tragedy. I guess the philosophy back then was that second-story men don't venture to the third floor," she added in disgust.

"What near tragedy?" asked King.

Remmy turned to him. "My son Eddie was kidnapped."

"I never heard about that," he said.

"It happened over twenty years ago, while he was still in college."

"But everything turned out all right obviously," said King.

"Yes, thank God. We didn't even have to pay the five-million-dollar ransom."

"Why not?" asked Michelle.

"The FBI tracked down the kidnapper and killed him in a shoot-out. In fact, Chip Bailey, the FBI agent who rescued Eddie and killed the kidnapper, lives near here. He still works for the FBI, over in Charlottesville."

King said, "So no one was here when the burglary happened?"

Remmy sat on the edge of the large canopied bed, drumming her long, slender fingers against the carved bedpost. "Savannah was still at college. She'd graduated over the winter but decided to stay down there and have some postgraduate fun. I'm sure you could tell that my little girl truly loves her good times. Eddie and Dorothea were out of town. Mason, the household help, and Sally, the girl who handles the stables, live in the house in the far rear grounds. They wouldn't have noticed anything anyway. My bedroom windows face a pretty isolated part of the rear grounds."

"So you stay in the house by yourself?" asked Michelle.

"Bobby and me!" she said defiantly. "Our children are raised. We've done more than our share of giving friends and relatives a place to stay in our time. More often than not, this big old house was full over the years. Now it's just our home."

"But the night of the burglary the house *was* empty,"

said King. "I understand you were at the hospital with Bobby?"

"That's right, at Wrightsburg General."

"But we were told you didn't arrive back here until around five A.M.," said Michelle. "Those are pretty long visiting hours."

"I slept there in a private room down the hall from him that the hospital provided," explained Remmy.

"That was pretty accommodating of them," said Michelle.

"Our name's on the building, sweetie," Remmy said in a falsely polite tone. In a far more blunt voice she added, "Frankly, for fifteen million dollars, I thought it was the least they could do."

"Oh," said Michelle sheepishly.

"The police told me all the evidence leads to Junior, including his fingerprints."

"But he was doing work here," said King. "That could account for the print."

"They found it on the outside of one of the panes of the busted window." She added, "I hired Junior to work *in* my bedroom, not *outside* my damn window."

"And I understand that things were stolen from Bobby's closet as well."

"It was broken into."

"And what was taken?" asked Michelle.

"Come on, you can see for yourself."

She led them out of her room and down the hall, where she opened another door. They found themselves in a room that reeked of cigar and pipe smoke. It was an intensively masculine room, Michelle noted. A shotgun rack hung over the fireplace, although there was no weapon on it. A pair of antique swords hung on another wall. They were crossed one over the other, forming a large X. There were several oil paintings of splendid horses. A pipe rack stood against one corner with a number of well-chewed pipes hanging from it. In another corner was a campaign desk and chair. The bed was small, and the nightstand next to it was stacked with magazines on fishing, hunting and science. One entire wall was devoted to photos of Bobby Battle. He was a tall, thick-chested man with dark, wavy hair and features seemingly cast in iron. In most of the photos he was either fishing or hunting, but there was one of him jumping out of a plane and another where he was piloting a chopper.

Remmy waved her hand in front of her nose. "I'm sorry for the smell. We've aired it out for days, and the smell's still there. It must be in the carpet and furniture by now. Bobby loves his pipes and cigars."

As Michelle looked around at Robert E. Lee Battle's lair, images of the man seemed to flow to her apart from the photos: a bear of a man who lived life hard and took no prisoners. That such a man was lying now in a coma with bleak prospects of ever coming back made her very depressed, even though she'd never met him and was disgusted by his womanizing reputation.

Michelle pointed to several photos of Battle with large groups of people. "What are those of?"

"Some of Bobby's employees. He was an engineer-turned-businessman. Holds over a hundred patents. Looking at this room, you might think my husband was all play and no work, but Bobby is, above all else, a hard worker. The things he invented, they all made money."

"When did you two meet?" asked Michelle. She added quickly, "I know it's a personal question, but he seems such a fascinating man."

Remmy actually smiled at this. "He walked into my daddy's clothing store in Birmingham, Alabama, forty-five years ago and announced that he'd seen me at several events and I was the prettiest thing he'd ever laid eyes on and he was going to marry me. And he just wanted my daddy to know, although he said he wasn't seeking permission, which was and in many ways still is the custom down there. He said the only person he had to convince of his intentions was me. Well, he did. I was only eighteen then and hadn't seen anything of life, but I was no pushover. Yet he eventually won me."

"Quite the whirlwind," said King.

"He was ten years older than me. When we got married, he hadn't made much money, but he had the brains to and the drive. He was special. And yet he wanted *me*." This last part was said with surprising humility.

"Well, it's not like you weren't quite a catch," said King sincerely.

"I suppose I was one of the very few to stand up to him. Oh, we had our peaks and our valleys like most folks," she added quietly.

Remmy opened a door and motioned them in. "Bobby's closet."

The space was far smaller than his wife's closet but was still elaborately built out.

Remmy pushed back some pants hanging on rods and

pointed to the side of one of the cabinets where a panel of wood had been broken out.

"There's a secret cupboard there, about the same size as the one in my room. One of the drawers in this large cabinet doesn't go all the way back, you see. It's pretty clever, because from the front it's almost impossible to judge how deep the drawers are. And you can't see the little keyhole on the side unless you're looking for it. I've been in here a million times, and I never noticed it."

King shot her a glance. "So you didn't know Bobby had a secret drawer?"

Remmy looked like a woman who'd realized far too late that she'd said far too much.

"No, I didn't," she said.

"What was stolen?"

"What does it matter?" she snapped. "I know what was stolen out of mine."

"Remmy, you mean you don't know what Bobby kept in there?" asked King.

She didn't answer for a long moment. When she did, her tone was far more subdued.

"No, I don't."

CHAPTER

17

"OKAY," SAID MICHELLE once they'd left the house. "A psychiatrist could write an entire textbook on just Savannah and Remmy's relationship."

"Her not knowing what was in Bobby's secret drawer is bugging the hell out of the woman," said King as he glanced back at the mansion.

"And while her closet was all broken up, Bobby's wasn't. That's significant."

"Right. The person knew where Bobby's secret cache was but didn't have the key to open it."

Before leaving the house they'd spoken with Mason and the other household help. Their answers were incredibly consistent: they'd all been in the house in the rear grounds and had seen and heard nothing when the burglary occurred.

King and Michelle got in the car, but instead of leaving, King steered his Lexus down the asphalt road leading to the rear of the property.

"Where are we going?" she asked.

"I met Sally Wainwright, the woman who handles the stables, at a horse event last year. Let's see if she saw and heard nothing that night too."

Sally was in her mid-twenties, cute, petite but wiry with long brown hair that she kept in a ponytail. She was mucking a stall when King and Michelle drove up. She wiped the sweat from her face with a cloth and came over to the car.

"You probably don't remember me," began King. "I spent the day with you at the charity dressage event in Charlottesville last year."

Sally smiled broadly. "Of course, I remember you, Sean." She glanced at Michelle. "You and Ms. Maxwell here are pretty famous now."

"Or infamous," replied King. He looked around at the stables and horses. "So do many of the Battles still ride?" he asked.

"Dorothea never has. Eddie does quite a bit. He's into Civil War reenactments and has to saddle up sometimes in those."

"Are you into that?" asked Michelle.

Sally laughed. "I'm from Arizona. I couldn't care less about the Civil War."

"I see Savannah's home. She used to ride in competition, didn't she?" asked King.

A slight look of annoyance crossed Sally's face. "She used to." King waited expectantly to see if Sally would put a defining exclamation point on that comment.

"She's a great rider. Not so handy with mucking,

grooming and dealing with people who didn't grow up with silver spoons in their mouths." Sally suddenly looked scared as though she'd spoken out of turn.

"Not to worry, Sally," said King supportively. "I know just what you mean." He paused and added, "Does Mrs. Battle ride?"

"I've been here five years, and she hasn't saddled up once in that time." Sally leaned on her muck rake. "I saw you drive in earlier. You just visiting?"

King told her why they were there, and Sally's brow clouded as she anxiously glanced in the direction of the main house.

"I don't know anything about that," she said.

"So you were in your house with Mason and the rest the whole time, I suppose."

"Right," she said. "I go to sleep early. Have to get up at the crack of dawn."

"I'm sure. Well, if anything occurs to you, let me know." He handed her one of his business cards. She didn't even look at it.

"I don't know anything, Sean, I really don't."

"Okay. You ever see Junior Deaver around here?"

Sally hesitated and then said, "Couple times. When he was working here."

"You ever speak to him?"

"Maybe once," she said evasively.

"Well, you have a good day, Sally."

They drove off. King looked in the rearview mirror at a very nervous Sally.

"She's not telling us something," said Michelle.

"That's right," answered King.

"Where to now?"

King pointed to a large house on the other side of the board-on-board fencing. "Two more Battles to go, and then we can call it a day," he said.

CHAPTER

18

"SO THIS IS A CARRIAGE house," said Michelle as she climbed out of King's car and stared at the approximately five-thousand-square-foot red brick structure. "I always imagined them to be bigger," she added sarcastically.

"I guess it depends on the size of your carriage." King glanced at the late-model silver Volvo station wagon parked in the motor court. "That's Eddie's car."

"Let me guess, you're clairvoyant?"

"No, but I see a Confederate soldier's uniform and a painting easel in the back."

Eddie Battle answered the door and ushered them in. He was a big man, at least six-two and packing over 220 very muscular pounds. He had unruly thick dark hair and striking blue eyes, and his features were strong and weathered by the elements. The hair came from his father; his mouth and eyes came straight from his mother, Michelle observed. However, there was nothing of her sternness and cold reserve about him; indeed, his boyish manner was ingratiating. He reminded her of a handsome, albeit older, California surfer dude.

He shook their hands and sat them down in the living room. His heavily muscled and thickly veined forearms were spotted with paint, and he was wearing what appeared to be cavalry boots with his faded jeans tucked inside them. His white work shirt had several holes in it and numerous paint stains; he was also unshaven. He seemed the antithesis of a rich man's son.

He chuckled when he noted Michelle staring at his footwear. "I was killed last week during an ill-advised charge against a fortified Union position in Maryland. I wanted to die with my boots on, and I can't seem to muster the energy to take them off. Poor Dorothea is growing very annoyed with me, I'm afraid."

Michelle smiled and King said, "You're probably wondering why we're here."

"Nope. My mother called a few minutes ago. She filled me in. I'm afraid I can't tell you much. We were gone when the burglary happened. Dorothea was at a Realtor's convention in Richmond. And I fought in a fierce two-day reenactment in Appomattox and then drove straight over to Tennessee to catch the early morning light over the Smoky Mountains. I was painting a landscape," he explained.

"Sounds pretty exhausting," said Michelle.

"Not really. I get to ride around on horses and play pretend soldier and cover myself in paint. I'm a little boy who never had to grow up. I think it pains my parents to see what's become of me, but I'm a good artist, though I'll never be a great one. And on weekends I play soldier.

I'm privileged and lucky and I know that. And because of that, I try to be modest and self-deprecating. Actually, I have a lot to be modest and self-deprecating about." He smiled again and showed teeth so perfect in shape and color that Michelle concluded they were all capped.

"You're certainly frank about yourself," she said.

"Look, I'm the son of fabulously wealthy parents, and I've never really had to work for a living. I don't put on airs, and what I do I do as well as I can. However, I know that's not why you're here. So go ahead with your questions."

"Had you ever seen Junior Deaver around here?" asked King.

"Sure, he did a lot of work for my parents. Junior's also done work for me and Dorothea, and we never had a bit of trouble with him. That's why I can't understand the burglary. He was making good money off the family, but maybe not good enough. I understand there's a lot of evidence tying Junior to the crime."

"Maybe too much," answered King.

Eddie looked at him thoughtfully. "I see what you mean. I guess I haven't given the matter a lot of attention. We've been pretty preoccupied with family issues lately."

"Right. We were sorry to hear about your father."

"It's funny. I always thought he'd outlive all of us. Mind you, he still might. The man's used to getting his way."

There was a pause before King said, "This question might seem a little awkward, but I have to ask it."

"Well, I guess the whole situation is a little awkward, so fire away."

"Apparently, your father had a secret drawer in his closet that things were taken from. Your mother didn't know about the drawer and thus didn't know what might have been in it. Did you know about any of that?"

"No. As far as I knew, my parents didn't have any secrets from each other."

"Yet they kept separate bedrooms?" said Michelle abruptly.

Eddie's sunny smile faded. "That's their business. It didn't mean they didn't sleep together or didn't love each other. Dad smoked cigars and liked his room a certain way. Mom can't breathe around cigars and she likes her things a certain way. It's a big house, and they can do anything they damn well please in it."

King looked apologetic. "I told you it was awkward."

Eddie looked ready to bark at them again but then seemingly mastered this impulse. "I didn't know about any secret drawer Dad had. But I'm not his confidant."

"Does he have a confidant like that? Maybe Savannah?"

"Savannah? No, I'd cross off my little sister as a potential inside information source."

"I guess she'd been away at college," prompted Michelle.

"She's been away all right and it started long before college."

"I take it you two aren't that close," said Michelle.

Eddie shrugged. "It's no one's fault, really. I'm nearly twice her age and we have nothing in common. *I* was in college when she was born."

"Your mother mentioned to us what happened to you back then," said King.

Eddie spoke slowly. "I don't remember much about it, to tell the truth. I'd never even seen the person who kidnapped me until they showed me his body." He blew out a long breath. "I was really, really lucky. My mother and father were so happy when I got back they conceived Savannah. At least that's the official family anecdote."

"Your mother said Chip Bailey became a good friend."

"He saved my life. How do you ever repay that?"

King glanced at Michelle. "I know what you mean."

They heard a car driving up, and it screeched to a stop near the front door.

"That would be Dorothea. She doesn't like to waste time getting places," said Eddie.

Michelle glanced out the window and saw the big black Beemer. The woman who got out of the car was dressed in a tight, short black skirt with black shoes and black stockings, and her wavy hair color matched that ensemble. She took off her sunglasses, glanced sharply at King's car and then headed to the door.

Dorothea strode into the room in a pale—if jet-black—imitation of Remmy Battle, it seemed to Michelle. And then she wondered if the younger woman had consciously patterned herself after her mother-in-law in that regard. Fashionably thin with curvy hips, a round firm bottom and slender, sexy legs, the woman possessed a disproportionately large bosom that had doubtless seen professional work. Her mouth was a little too wide for her face and the lipstick a little too red for her pale complexion. The eyes were a dull green but shrewd-looking.

Greetings and introductions were made all around, and then Dorothea drew out a cigarette and lit it while Eddie explained why King and Michelle were there.

She said, "I'm afraid I can't help you, Sean." Dorothea

kept her focus on him and seemed to make a point of ignoring Michelle. "I was out of town when it happened."

"Right. Either everyone was gone or no one who was here seemed to notice anything," said Michelle, baiting the woman on purpose.

The dull green eyes shifted slowly toward her. "I'm sorry if the family and its hired help didn't work their collective schedules around Junior Deaver's felonious pursuits," she said in an icy and condescending tone. If she closed her eyes, Michelle would have sworn it was Remmy Battle speaking. Before Michelle could return fire, Dorothea looked back at King. "I think you're hunting the wrong fox here."

"Just trying to make sure an innocent man isn't sent to prison."

"Again, I think you're wasting your time," she shot back.

King rose. "Well, I certainly won't waste any more of yours," he said pleasantly.

As they left, Michelle and King heard raised voices behind them.

Michelle looked at her partner. "I bet Battle holiday get-togethers are just a hoot."

"I hope I never find out for sure."

"So now we call it a day?" asked Michelle.

"No, I lied. Next up is Lulu Oxley," replied King.

CHAPTER

19

KING AND MICHELLE
pulled up in front of a double-wide trailer set on a permanent cinder-block foundation at the end of a gravel drive.
Electrical and phone lines running to the trailer were the
only signs of a connection to the outside world. Scraggly
pines and stunted wild mountain laurel formed a weary
backdrop to the very modest home of Junior Deaver and
Lulu Oxley. An ancient, rusted Ford LTD with a cracked
vinyl top, an ashtray full of butts and an empty quart of
Beefeater on the front seat and sporting dirty West Virginia plates sat in front of the trailer like a cheap sentinel.

As they climbed out of the Lexus, however, Michelle
noted that flower boxes lined the windows of the trailer and
more pots covered with brilliant spring blooms sat on the
wooden steps leading up to the front door. The trailer itself
looked old, but the exterior was clean and in good repair.

King glanced at the sky.

"What are you looking for?"

"Tornadoes. The only time I got caught in one I was in

a trailer in Kansas. There wasn't a single blade of grass disturbed in the whole area, but that twister picked that trailer up and deposited it somewhere in Missouri. Luckily, I got out before the ride started. The guy I had gone to question about a counterfeiting ring chose to stick it out. They found him in a cornfield ten miles away."

King didn't head to the front door; instead, he went around to the side of the trailer. Directly behind the double-wide about forty feet back and enclosed on three sides by leafy trees was a large wooden shed. It had no door, and inside they could see walls lined with tools and a large air generator on the floor. As they approached the structure, an unkempt dog, ribs showing, lumbered out of the shed, saw them and commenced barking and baring its yellowed teeth. Luckily, the animal appeared to be chained to a deeply set stake.

"Okay, enough snooping around," King declared.

As he and Michelle mounted the steps to the trailer, a heavyset woman appeared behind the screened front door.

The woman's hair was big and black with silver streaks. Her dress resembled a purple sandwich board glued over her immense, square-cut frame, and her face was composed of doughy cheeks, three chins, small lips and closely set eyes. The skin was pale and virtually unwrinkled. Except for the hair color, it would have been difficult to guess her exact age.

"Ms. Oxley?" said King with his hand out in greeting. She didn't take it.

"Who the hell wants to know?"

"I'm Sean King and this is Michelle Maxwell. We've

been hired by Harry Carrick to handle an investigation on behalf of your husband."

"That'd be quite a feat considering my husband's been dead for years," was her surprising reply. "You must be wanting my daughter, Lulu. I'm Priscilla."

"I'm sorry, Priscilla," said King, glancing at Michelle.

"She's gone to get him. Get Junior, I mean." She took a sip of something in a Disney World coffee mug she was holding.

"I thought he was in jail," said Michelle.

The woman's gaze swiveled to her.

"He was. That's what *bail's* for, shug. I come up from West Virginia to help out with the kids till Junior gets himself outta this mess. If he can." She shook her large head. "Stealing from rich people. Ain't nothing dumber, but dumb is what Junior's been his whole life."

"Do you know when they'll be back?" asked King.

"They were picking up the kids from school, so ain't gonna be too long from now." Priscilla looked at them in distrust. "So exactly what are you doing here?"

"We've been retained by Junior's attorney to dig up evidence proving his innocence," explained King.

"Well, you got yourself a long road ahead."

"So you think he's guilty?" said Michelle, leaning against the banister.

Priscilla looked at her in unconcealed disgust. "He's done shit like this before."

King spoke up. "Well, maybe Junior didn't do this."

"Yeah, and maybe I'm a size six and got me my own TV show."

"If they're going to be back soon, can we come in and wait?"

Priscilla raised the pistol that she held in her other hand; it had been hidden from their view behind an outcropping of fleshy hip. "Lulu don't like me letting people in. And I don't have no way of knowing if you are who you say." She pointed the gun at King. "Now, I don't want to shoot you, 'cause you're kinda cute, but I sure as hell will, and your little skinny plaything there too, if you try anything funny."

King held up his hands in mock surrender. "No problems, Priscilla." He paused and added, "That's a fine pistol you've got there. H and K nine-millimeter, isn't it?"

"Hell if I know, belonged to my husband," said Priscilla. "But I sure know how to shoot it."

"We'll just take a stroll around outside and wait," said King, backing down the stairs and pulling Michelle with him.

"You do that. Just don't steal my Mercedes over there," said Priscilla as she shut the door.

Michelle said, "Skinny plaything? I'd like to stick that pistol right up her—"

King gripped her shoulder and led her away from the trailer. "Let's just be cool and live to play detective another day."

As they headed away from the trailer, King bent down, picked up a rock and sent it sailing into a ravine. "Why do you think Remmy Battle left the hole in the secret cupboard in Bobby's closet? She hired someone to fix the damage in her closet. Why not fix Bobby's at the same time?"

"Maybe she's pissed at him and didn't want to deal with it."

"And you think she's upset because she didn't know there was a secret drawer in his closet or what was in it?"

"While we're at it, there's something bugging me too," she said. "Why was her *wedding ring* in that drawer? She tells us what a great man her husband is, so why wasn't she wearing her ring? It couldn't be because of the secret drawer. She didn't find out about that until *after* her ring and the other things were stolen."

"She might have suspected Bobby was hiding something from her, or maybe they were having problems. Like Harry said, Bobby slept around. Or she could've been lying to us."

Michelle had a sudden thought. "Do you think Junior was hired by someone to break into the house and steal what was in Bobby's secret drawer?"

"Who would know about it other than Bobby?"

"The person who built it."

King nodded. "And that person could presume that valuables would be kept in there. In fact, it might be the same person who built Remmy's. Bobby might have hired him to do his without bothering to tell his wife."

Michelle said, "Well, I guess we can rule out Remmy's hiring Junior to break into the house and steal what was in her husband's drawer. If she knew where it was, she could've done it herself."

"*If* she knew where it was. Maybe she didn't or couldn't find it on her own, and hired Junior to find it for her and make it look like a burglary."

"But if she had hired him, she never would have called the police."

King shook his head. "Not true if Junior double-crossed her and stole her things while he was looking for Bobby's secret cache. And maybe Junior's not telling everything just yet because he wants to see how the cards fall."

"Why am I suddenly thinking this case is far more complicated than people think it is?" said Michelle wearily.

"I never thought it was simple."

They both turned in the direction of the van pulling up to the trailer.

King glanced at the occupants of the vehicle and then looked at Michelle. "Lulu must have scored the bail. That's Junior Deaver in the passenger seat. Let's see if we can get the truth out of him."

"With the way things have been going so far, don't hold your breath on that. Straight answers seem to be in short supply."

CHAPTER

20

JUNIOR DEAVER *LOOKED*
like a man who made his living with his hands. His jeans
and T-shirt were streaked with paint smears and seemed
permanently coated with drywall dust. He was over six
feet four, and his arms were thick and powerful, deeply
bronzed by the sun, and bore numerous scars, scabs and at
least five tattoos, by Michelle's count, covering a variety
of subject matter from mothers to Lulu to Harley-
Davidson. His hair was brown and thinning, and he wore
it long and pulled back in a ponytail that unfortunately
emphasized his graying and receding hairline. A small,
bristly goatee covered his chin, and his bushy sideburns
had been grown down past his Santa Claus cheeks. He
lifted his smallest child, a six-year-old girl with beautifully soft brown eyes and slender pigtails, out of the van
with a tenderness that Michelle would hardly have given
him credit for.

Lulu Oxley was thin and wore a crisp-looking black
business suit and low heels. Her brown hair was done up
professionally in a complicated braid and bun, and she

wore chic eyeglasses with slender gold frames. She held a briefcase in one hand and in the other the small hand of what looked to be an eight-year-old boy. The third child, a girl of about twelve, followed behind carrying a large school bag. All the children wore the uniform of one of the local Catholic schools.

King stepped forward and extended his hand to Junior.

"Junior, I'm Sean King. Harry Carrick hired us to work on your behalf."

Junior eyed Lulu, who nodded, and then he very grudgingly took King's hand and squeezed. Michelle saw her partner wince before the big man let go.

"This is my partner, Michelle Maxwell."

Lulu studied both of them very closely. "Harry said you'd be coming by. I just got Junior out, and I don't want him to go back in."

"I ain't going back in," growled Junior. "'Cause I ain't done nothing wrong."

As he said this, the little girl in his arms began to quietly cry.

"Oh, dang," he said, "Mary Margaret, now don't you cry no more. Daddy ain't going no place 'cept home." The little girl continued to sob.

"Mama," called out Lulu, "come and get the children, will you?"

Priscilla appeared at the door, minus the gun, and shooed the older children inside before holding out her arms for Mary Margaret and taking the sobbing girl.

She glared at Junior. "Well, I see they let anybody out of jail these days."

"Mama," exclaimed Lulu sharply, "just go inside and see to the children."

Priscilla put down Mary Margaret, and the little girl fled into the trailer. Priscilla nodded at King and Michelle. "This slick-talking feller and his chickie come 'round asking a bunch of questions. Say they're working for Junior. I say you should fire a bullet over their heads and tell them where they can go."

At the "chickie" slur King automatically grabbed Michelle's arm to hold her back from throttling the older woman. "Ms. Oxley," he said. "Like I said, we're here on Junior's behalf. We've already been to see Remmy Battle."

"Well, la-di-da," said Priscilla Oxley, who finished this statement with a snort. "And how's the queen today?"

"Do you know her?" asked King.

"I used to work at the Greenbrier Resort over in West Virginia. She and her family came there right regular."

"And she was . . . demanding?" said King.

"She was a royal pain in my fat ass," declared Priscilla. "And if Junior was dumb enough to steal from a witch like that, he deserves whatever he gets."

Lulu pointed a finger at the woman. "Mother, we have things to discuss with these people." She looked up at the front door of the trailer where Mary Margaret was listening and trembling in her distress. "Things the children don't need to hear."

"Don't you worry about that, honey." said Priscilla. "I'll fill 'em in on all their daddy's shortcomings. Only take me a couple of months."

"Now, Mother, don't be going and doing that," said Junior as he studied his large feet. He was a good foot taller than Priscilla Oxley, though he didn't outweigh her by all that much, and yet it was clear to both King and Michelle that the man was terrified of his mother-in-law.

"Don't you call me Mother. All the things Lulu and me done for you, and this is how you repay us? Getting yourself in trouble, maybe going to the electric chair!"

On this, Mary Margaret's sobs turned into earsplitting wails, and Lulu erupted into action.

"Excuse me," she said politely but firmly to King and Michelle.

She marched up the steps, grabbed a fistful of her mother's dress and pulled the larger woman into the trailer along with Mary Margaret. From behind the closed door they could hear muffled cries and angry voices, and then all became quiet. A few seconds after that, Lulu reemerged and closed the door behind her.

"Mama sometimes goes on when she's been drinking. Sorry about that," she said.

"She doesn't like me much," said Junior unnecessarily.

"Why don't we sit over here?" said Lulu, pointing to an old picnic table on the right side of the trailer.

Once settled there, King filled them both in on the visit to the Battles'.

Lulu said, "The problem is that." She pointed to the large shed behind the trailer. "I've told Junior a million times to put a door and lock on that thing."

"Old story," he said sheepishly. "Working on everybody else's house, ain't got time for my own."

"But the point," continued Lulu, "is that anybody can get in there."

"Not with old Luther back there," Junior said, nodding at the dog that had emerged once more from the shed and was barking happily at the sight of his owners.

"Luther!" said Lulu incredulously. "Sure he'll bark, but he won't bite, and he'll roll over like a baby when somebody brings him food." She turned to King and Michelle. "He has buddies coming over all the time to borrow tools. When we're not here, they leave little notes and let us know when they're gonna be bringing the things back, and sometimes they never do. And Luther sure as hell never stopped one of 'em."

"They'll leave a six-pack as a thank-you," offered Junior quickly. "They're good old boys."

"They're old boys all right, just don't know how *good* they are," said Lulu hotly. "One of them might've set you up."

"Now, baby, ain't none of them gonna do that to me."

King cut in. "But all we have to show is reasonable doubt. If the jury thinks there's an alternative out there, well, that's good for you."

"That's right, Junior," said his wife.

"But they're my friends. I ain't gonna get them in trouble. I know they ain't done nothing to hurt me. Hell, there ain't no way they coulda broke into the Battles' place. And let me tell you, they ain't gonna go up against Ms. Battle, that's for damn sure. I ain't got no college degree, but I'm smart enough not to take the woman's damn wedding ring. Shit, like I need that grief?"

"You don't have to do anything against your friends," said King emphatically. "Just give us names and addresses, and we'll check them out very discreetly. They probably all have ironclad alibis, and we can move on. But look, Junior, friends or not, unless we find other possible suspects, the evidence against you is pretty persuasive."

"Listen to him, Junior," said his wife. "You want to go back to jail?"

"Course not, baby."

"Well, then?" She looked at him expectantly.

Junior very reluctantly gave the names and addresses.

"Now, Junior," said King delicately, "I need you to be straight with me here. We're working for your attorney, so everything you say is confidential, it goes no further." He paused, choosing his words carefully. "Did you have anything to do with that break-in? Not that you did it yourself, but might you have done something to help somebody else do it, maybe even unknowingly?"

Junior stood, his hands balled into big fists. "Okay, asshole, how 'bout I mess up that face of yours!" he roared.

Michelle half rose, her hand sliding to her holstered gun, but King motioned for her to stop. He said calmly, "Junior, my partner here was an Olympic athlete, holds multiple black belts and could kick both our butts with her feet alone. On top of that she's holstering a nine-millimeter cocked and locked and could put a round between your eyes at fifty feet much less five. Now, it's been a long day and I'm tired. So sit down and start using your brain before you get yourself hurt!"

Junior glanced in surprise at Michelle, who stared back at him without a trace of concern or fear on her features. He sat, but his gaze kept skipping to her as King continued. "We don't want to be surprised down the road. So if there's anything you haven't told us or Harry, you need to correct that right now."

After a long moment Junior shook his head. "I've been straight with you. I didn't do it and I got no idea who did. And right now I'm gonna go see my kids." He rose and stomped into the trailer.

CHAPTER

21

WHEN KING AND
Michelle walked back to their car, Lulu went with them.

"Junior's a good man. Loves the kids and me," she
said. "He works hard, but he knows things don't look
good for him, and it's drilling a hole right through his
belly." She let out a long sigh. "Things were going good,
maybe too good. My job's going great, and Junior's got
more work than he can handle. We're building a new
home, and the kids are doing real good in school. Yeah,
maybe it was all going too good."

"You kept your maiden name?" said Michelle.

"I don't have any brothers," Lulu replied. "My sisters
took their husbands' names. I just wanted to keep the Oxleys around at least so long as I'm alive."

"You work at the Aphrodisiac, don't you?" asked King.

She looked a little startled. "That's right, how'd you
know?" She suddenly smiled. "Don't tell me you been
there."

King smiled back. "Once. Years ago."

"When I first went to work there, it was more a whorehouse than anything else. It was called the Love Shack back then, you know, after the B-52's song. But I saw a lot more potential than that. Over the years we've turned it into a nice club. Okay, we still have the dancers and stuff, but that's only in one section, the original part of the place. Junior did a lot of the new construction work. You should see some of the millwork in there now, wood columns, nice moldings, classy drapes and wallpaper. We got a real nice restaurant, with linen and china, a billiards room and a place to play cards, a movie theater and a first-class bar with a special ventilated place so the men can smoke cigars; and we just started a club for local businesspeople. You know, a place to come and network. We got Internet access, a business center. Revenue up eighty-six percent over last year, and last year was the best year we'd had in the last ten. And I've been pushing to change the name to something a little more . . ."

"Tasteful?" said Michelle.

"Yeah," said Lulu. "I own a piece of the place, so that's me and Junior's retirement. I want it to be as profitable as possible. I got the costs in line, manageable debt levels and strong cash flow with little direct competition, and our target demographic is golden: male high income earners who don't care how much they spend. You should see our EBITDA level compared to what it was."

"You sound like quite the businesswoman," said Michelle.

"Didn't start out that way. I didn't even finish high school. My daddy had an aneurysm when I was only sixteen. Dropped out to help nurse him. Guess I wasn't much of a nurse; he died anyway. But then I married Junior, went back and got my GED and took business courses at the community college. I started working at the Love Shack part-time. As a waitress," she added quickly. "I don't have the necessary physical equipment to be one of the dancers. Worked my way up, learned the business, and there you are."

"And one of your dancers was just killed," said King.

Lulu stiffened. "How'd you know about that?"

"We're sort of informal consultants to Chief Williams," explained King.

"She was one of our *former* dancers," corrected Lulu.

"Did you know her?" asked Michelle.

"Not really. We got lots of dancers come through. Most don't stay all that long, nature of the business. And we play it by the rules. We don't allow anything but the dancing. We're not looking to lose our license to operate because some girl wants to make some cash on the side by spreading her legs."

"Did Rhonda Tyler want to do that? Is that why she left?" asked Michelle.

"I already told the police all this. Is there some reason I got to tell you too?"

"No reason at all," said King.

"Good, 'cause I got enough on my mind without worrying why some gal got herself killed."

"I doubt she intended that to happen," said Michelle.

"Honey," said Lulu, "I been in this business long enough and seen enough that nothing—and I mean nothing—would surprise me anymore."

"I was thinking the same thing," said King.

As they drove off, Lulu watched them and then went inside the trailer.

Michelle eyed her movements in the side mirror. "She says she didn't really know the woman, and yet she was able to ID her off an artist's composite sketch, and she knew about the crotch tattoo? Come on, I'd call that a little inconsistent."

"Could be," said King.

"And while Junior may be too dumb to know what to do with bearer bonds and jewelry, I think his wife is plenty sharp enough to sell that stuff and make some decent returns."

"If that turns out to be correct, our client is guilty."

Michelle shrugged. "Those are the breaks sometimes. What next?"

"We track down who installed those secret drawers in the Battles' closets. We check out the alibis of Junior's friends, and we fill in Harry on what we've done so far."

"And we wait for the next murder to happen," added Michelle, sighing.

CHAPTER

22

DIANE HINSON LEFT HER downtown law firm as she nearly always did, at seven in the evening. She climbed into her late-model Chrysler Sebring and drove off. She picked up some carry-out dinner at a local restaurant, drove to her gated community, waved to the elderly guard inside—who carried no weapon and could have been easily overpowered by a couple of husky twelve-year-olds—and proceeded to her townhouse situated at the end of a pipestem street.

Things had been going well for Hinson this year. A newly minted partner at Goodrich, Browder and Knight, Wrightsburg's second largest law firm, she'd finally met a man she thought might be the one, a six-foot-three accountant four years her junior who liked to white-water raft and could beat her occasionally on the tennis court. She felt that any day he might pop the question, and her answer would be an immediate yes. She'd also brought a new client into the firm with billings well into the six figures that would add significantly to her personal income. She was thinking of moving into a single-family house. To do so with a ring on her finger and a husband to grow old with would be a dream come true for the thirty-three-year-old lawyer.

She parked her car in her garage and went inside. She placed her dinner in the microwave, changed into her running clothes and headed out. Three miles and a little over twenty minutes later she arrived back a little sweaty but barely short of breath. A decent middle-distance runner in college and dedicated amateur tennis player, she'd kept in excellent shape over the years.

She showered, ate her meal, caught a TV show she'd been looking forward to seeing, and received a phone call from her accountant beau, who was in Houston on a corporate audit. After some breathy promises of truly memorable sex once he returned home, she hung up, watched the late news, noted it was nearly midnight and turned off the TV. She stripped down to her panties in the bathroom, pulled on a long T-shirt she kept hanging on the door there and headed to bed.

She sensed the presence behind her, but before she could scream, the gloved hand closed around her neck, cutting off her wind and with it her voice. A very strong arm encircled her body, pinning both her limbs to her sides. Stunned, Hinson found herself being shoved facedown on the floor, unable to move or scream as a gag was placed in her mouth and her hands bound behind her with telephone cord.

As a criminal lawyer she'd defended accused rapists, getting some men off who should have gone to jail. She'd considered those professional victories. Lying facedown on the floor with a crushing weight on top of her, she steeled herself to be raped. With suffocating dread she knew that at any moment her underwear would be pulled down and the humiliating and painful violation would commence. Nauseous with fear, she told herself not to resist, let him have his way, and possibly she would survive this. She hadn't seen his face. She couldn't possibly identify him. He would have no reason to kill her. "Please," she tried to say through the gag, "don't hurt me."

Her plea went unheeded.

The knife plunged into her back, grazed the left side of her heart, was pulled free and plunged in again, tearing a two-inch gash in her left lung and slicing into her aorta on the way out. By the time it was over, a dozen wounds mottled her back. However, Diane Hinson was dead by the fourth.

The man in the black hood bent over her, careful not to step in the pool of blood forming on the carpet, and turned Hinson over on her back. He lifted her T-shirt, took a Sharpie pen from his pocket and drew a symbol on her flat belly. He made the same symbol on the wall behind her bed. He drew it large, since he didn't want anyone to miss it. The police could be such imbeciles.

He went back to the body and carefully unhooked the woman's anklet, the one he'd admired in the shopping mall parking lot, and placed it in his pocket.

He left the knife by the dead woman's side; it couldn't lead back to him. He'd pulled it from her kitchen drawer when he'd entered the house earlier. He'd been hidden behind the bushes in the darkness next to her garage door waiting for her to come home. When she opened the garage, he waited until she had gotten out of the car and gone inside. Most people closed the garage door on their way inside the house using the remote button near the door leading into the house. She'd never seen him slip inside.

He untied her hands and wedged her arm against a partially opened bureau drawer. He'd observed at the shopping mall that she wore a watch, so he hadn't bothered to bring one. He set the watch hands to where he wanted them and pulled out the stem, freezing it at that number on the dial. He said no prayer over the body. Yet he did mumble something about this being a lesson to keep one's ATM receipts.

He methodically went through the room looking for potential evidence of his presence but found none. Fingerprints and palmprints were out of the question. Not only had he worn gloves but he'd glued felt pads to each of his fingertips and palms. He slipped a small, handheld vacuum out of his coat pocket and ran it over the floor and under the bed where he'd been hiding. He did the same in the coat closet where he'd initially hidden, and continued that process on the stairs and finally the garage.

After that he took off his hood, slipped on a beard and hat and left out the back door. He made his way to his car, which he'd parked on a side road outside of the fancy gated community with its elderly, weaponless security guard. The VW started up. He drove fast but within the legal speed limit. He had another letter to write. And he knew exactly what he wanted to say.

CHAPTER

23

SEAN KING WOKE EARLY on the forty-foot houseboat that was parked at his dock. The rented houseboat *was* home, at least until he could finish building a new house to replace the one that had disappeared into a man-made crater. He donned a wet suit, drew a quick breath and then dove headfirst into the water. After a spirited swim of several hundred yards he returned to the houseboat and embarked on a two-mile trek in his Loon kayak. His partner's energetic ways were rubbing off on him, he had to grudgingly admit.

As he was paddling through the water thinking this, he looked up and saw her. He wasn't surprised, even at this hour. He often wondered if she ever slept. Could it be that his partner was really a vampire who happened to have no problem with sunlight?

Michelle was in her scull rowing with a skill, strength and intensity that King could only dream about. She was moving so fast that anyone unacquainted with the woman would have assumed her craft was under motor power.

He called out to her, his words carrying far over the calm waters.

"Time for coffee, or are you heading for the Atlantic this morning?"

She smiled, waved and headed over.

They drew their crafts up to his dock and secured them.

On the houseboat King fixed coffee while Michelle took out an energy bar from her fanny pack and started to devour it. She looked around the well-organized interior.

"You know, this boat's almost bigger than my cottage," she observed between bites.

"And it's far neater, I know," he said, pouring out juice and coffee.

It had been two days since their interview with Lulu and Junior. They'd reported back to Harry Carrick, who seemed pleased with their progress but had in turn informed them that the grand jury had, not surprisingly, indicted his client. They'd tracked down the man who had installed the secret drawers in the Battles' closets. He was elderly, retired, and seemed to have no earthly reason to break into his former clients' home. That had seemed a dead end until King asked him when Robert Battle had asked for his secret drawer to be installed.

The old man had looked a little uncomfortable at that. "Don't like keeping secrets from folks," he had said. "Mrs. Battle is a fine lady, none finer in my mind."

"So Mr. Battle didn't want her to know about it?" prompted Michelle when the old man seemed disinclined to continue.

"Sneaking in and out when she wasn't there, didn't

like it, no, sir," he said, avoiding directly answering her question.

"Any idea why Mr. Battle wanted that drawer installed?" asked King.

"Didn't ask because it wasn't my place to," he said stubbornly.

"Around what time period was that?" Michelle inquired.

The man took a minute to consider this. "Must've been about five or so years ago. Put Mrs. Battle's drawer in a few years before that."

King mused for a moment and then said, "And Mr. Battle knew about his wife's hidden drawer?"

"Don't know if he did or not. Hear he's near death's door."

"You never know with a man like that," replied King.

They'd checked out the alibis of all of Junior's friends. The men were either in a bar drinking at the time or sleeping with their wives, girlfriends or mistresses. The ladies could have been lying, of course, but it might be hard to break their testimony without a lot of digging, and in each case King had sensed they were telling the truth. Anyway, none of Junior's friends seemed remotely capable of carrying off such a burglary and setting up Junior so cleverly in the process. Their expertise seemed limited to driving nails, drinking beer and bedding women.

"Are you going to live on this houseboat the whole time while you're rebuilding?" asked Michelle.

"I don't have much choice."

"My cottage has an extra bedroom."

"Thanks, but I don't think my neatness gene could survive."

"I've gotten better."

"Better! The last time I was there you had everything from water skis to shotguns piled on a card table in your dining room, a stack of dirty laundry in the kitchen *sink* and unwashed dishes on a chair in the living room. You served dinner on paper plates on a *wakeboard* resting on two chairs—a first for me, I assure you."

"Well," she said in a hurt tone, "I thought you'd appreciate that I cooked for you. Do you know how many cans I had to open?"

"I'm sure it was a true ordeal."

He was about to say something else when his cell phone rang. It was Todd Williams. The conversation was brief, but when King clicked off, he looked badly shaken.

"Another murder?" asked Michelle as she set down her coffee and looked at him.

"Yes."

"Who was it?"

"Somebody I happened to know," he said.

CHAPTER

24

THE BRUTAL MURDER OF
Diane Hinson had not set very well in her posh, gated and
supposedly safe community. When Michelle and King arrived there, a small yet vocal crowd of angry folks had
surrounded several beleaguered men in suits representing
the management of the upscale compound. Also in the
middle of this siege was an elderly security guard who appeared so distraught he looked ready to cry.

Police cars and other emergency vehicles lined the
pipestem road to Hinson's home, and a yellow police tape
barrier stretched across the small strip of grass in front of
the home, not that many people were inclined to take a
peek. Uniformed officers came and went through the
front door and garage. King pulled to a stop and he and
Michelle got out.

Chief Williams waved to them from the front stoop.
They hurried to meet him and then all three went inside.

If possible, Todd Williams looked even more miserable than he had at the morgue. Gravity seemed to be

sucking the lawman right into the earth. "Damn," he said.
"What I did to deserve this, I don't know."

"There's been a positive ID on Hinson?" asked King.

"Yeah, it's her. Why, do you know the lady?"

"It's a small town, we're both lawyers."

"Did you know her well?"

"Not enough to be any help with the investigation.
Who found her?"

"She was supposed to be at work early this morning,
preparing for a deposition or something. When she didn't
show, people from her firm called her house and cell
phones. There was no answer. They sent someone over.
Her car was in the garage, but no one answered the door.
They got worried and called the police." Williams shook
his head. "This is the same guy who did Tyler, Pembroke
and Canney, no doubt about it."

Michelle picked up on the confident tone in his voice.
"Did you receive a letter about the high school kids?"

Williams nodded, pulled a piece of paper out of his
pocket and passed it to her. "Here's a photocopy. Damn
newspaper sat on it because it was addressed to Virgil and
he was out of town. Apparently, not one single person
over there thought to open it. And they call themselves re-
porters! My ass!"

"Was it in code like the first one?" asked King.

"Nope, that's just as we received it. And no symbol on
the envelope."

King said, "So there goes the Zodiac theory." He
looked at Michelle. "What does it say?"

Michelle scanned the letter and began reading: *"Okay,
one more down with others to follow. I told you the first time*

I wasn't the Z-man. But you're probably thinking that kid bit the dust under the Z's hand. Think again. I left the dog collar behind because the dog didn't make me do it. I don't even have a dog. I wanted to do it all by myself. And no, I'm not him either. Until next time, and it won't be long. Not SOS."

She looked up at King with a puzzled expression.

"Dog collar? And the dog made me do it?"

"You're showing your age or lack thereof, Michelle," replied King. "SOS and the dog made me do it. That's Son of Sam, David Berkowitz, the New York City killer in the 1970s. He was dubbed the lovers' lane killer because some of his victims were young dating couples killed in their cars."

"Lovers' lane, like Canney and Pembroke," said Michelle.

Williams nodded. "Berkowitz said his neighbor was some sort of demon who communicated his orders to kill through his pet dog. Crock of shit, of course."

King said, "But our guy knows exactly what he's doing. He said so."

Michelle broke in. "But I'm not getting this. Why commit murders in similar styles to past killers as a copycat would and then write letters making it clear you're *not* them. I mean, imitation is the sincerest form of flattery, right?"

"Who knows?" said Williams. "But he killed those two kids."

King stared at the chief and then looked at the letter again. "Wait a minute. He didn't say that. He says '*one more down.*'"

"Don't split grammatical hairs with a psycho," complained Williams. "He just lumped them together is all."

"Look at the letter again; he also uses the singular: 'kid,' not 'kids.'"

Williams scratched his cheek. "Well, maybe he just forgot and left off the last letter. It could be as simple as that."

"If it was intentional, which kid is he talking about?" asked Michelle.

Williams sighed deeply and then pointed up the stairs. "Well, come up and see this. I don't think it'll clear anything up, though. And I don't need a damn letter to tell me who he's *not* trying to impersonate this time."

They made their way up the stairs and entered the bedroom. Diane Hinson remained where she'd been killed. There was a blur of activity in the room as forensic techs, police officers, men in FBI windbreakers and Virginia State Police homicide investigators attended to the business of preserving the crime scene and absorbing every valuable morsel from it. If their hollow looks were any indication, however, helpful clues were apparently very hard to come by.

King observed Sylvia Diaz in one corner in deep conversation with a beefy man in an ill-fitting suit. She looked up, gave him a weary smile and then turned away. When King's gaze caught on the symbol on the wall, he jerked back.

It was a five-pointed star but drawn upside down.

"Yep, same thing I did."

He turned to see Williams staring at him. The police chief bent down and lifted Hinson's shirt. "And it's here too." They all studied the drawing on the woman's belly.

Michelle had seen the symbol on the wall as well. "It's

an upside-down pentagram," she said. She drew in a sharp breath and looked at King and Williams. "That one I know. Richard Ramirez, right?"

"The Night Stalker," said King, nodding. "Who, unless I'm mistaken, currently resides on death row almost three thousand miles from here. He drew an upside-down pentagram on some of his victims, and also on walls of at least one of his victims' bedrooms, just like here."

Williams turned Hinson to the side, and they all looked at the multiple bloody stab wounds covering her back.

"Sylvia says it looks like she was held facedown, stabbed in the back and then presumably turned over and her hand wedged against the bureau drawer."

The lawman laid her back down without any indication that he might soon forfeit his breakfast. Williams's resistance to nightmarish sights seemed to be growing stronger.

"Any clues?" asked Michelle.

"The killer used a knife from her kitchen to stab her and telephone cord from one of her phones to bind her. There are marks on her wrists that show that. But he took off the restraints to prop up her arm. There are lots of prints in here, but I'd be real surprised if the bastard wasn't wearing gloves."

"And we're sure it's a man?"

"No sign of a struggle. She was overpowered pretty quickly. And even if a woman did that maybe with a gun in hand, it'd be a little risky to tie her up. Hinson might have been able to get the upper hand. She was in great physical shape."

King looked puzzled. "And no one saw or heard anything? These are attached residential units. Somebody had to have seen or heard something."

"We're looking into that, of course, but it's too early to tell. We do know that the unit to the right of Hinson's was for sale and empty."

"When was she killed?" asked Michelle.

"You'll have to ask Sylvia that, if that FBI fellow will let her go."

King glanced over once more in Sylvia's direction. "Is he with VICAP?"

"To tell you the God's honest truth, I'm not sure. I've had so many people in here I don't know who's coming or going."

"Todd," said King, "make sure you don't say that within earshot of a defense counsel."

Williams looked confused for a moment and then said, "Oh, right, gotcha."

They went and looked at the watch.

"It's set to four o'clock," said Williams miserably.

King bent down and took a closer look. "No, it's not."

"What?" exclaimed Williams.

"It's set to one minute *past* four."

Williams knelt beside him. "Come on, Sean, I think under the circumstances that's close enough."

"This guy's been pretty precise up to now, Todd."

Williams looked skeptical. "He'd just killed a woman and wanted to get out as fast as possible. He's probably operating in the dark. Unlike with the other crime scenes, he's smack in the middle of lots of potential witnesses. In his rush he probably just didn't notice he was barely one minute off."

"Maybe," said King with equal skepticism. "But a killer who's careful enough not to leave any usable trace behind doesn't strike me as the sort to write 'kid' when he really meant 'kids' or set a watch to four-oh-one when he meant four."

"Well, if he did mean to make it one minute past, why?" asked Michelle.

King had no answer for that. He looked down at the dead woman for a long moment as Williams went off to check something else in the room.

Michelle put a hand on his shoulder. "I'm sorry, Sean, I forgot you knew her."

"She was a good person and a fine lawyer. And she sure as hell didn't deserve this—not that anyone does."

As they walked past Sylvia on their way out, she stopped them. The man in the suit had joined another group hovering over the body. He was a little shorter than King but thicker and very strongly built; his shoulders seemed to be splitting out of his suit. He had thinning brownish-gray hair, cauliflower ears and a boxer's flattened nose resting between two intense brown eyes.

Sylvia said, "Well, number four and counting. The Night Stalker. Who would have thought?" She shook her head.

"Who's the guy you were talking to?" King asked.

"FBI agent. Chip Bailey, from Charlottesville."

"Chip Bailey?" King said slowly.

"Do you know him?" asked Sylvia.

"No, but I think I'd like to."

"I can arrange something. Later, of course. People are pretty busy right now."

"That's fine." He paused and then added, "Did you note the time on the watch?"

Sylvia nodded. "One minute past four. Like Pembroke's."

"What?" King and Michelle said together.

"Pembroke's watch was set to one minute past two. Didn't I tell you that?"

"No," said Michelle, "and neither did Todd. He seems to think it was close enough to discount any significance."

"What do you think?" King asked her.

"I think it's important. I just don't know why."

"Anything else jump out at you?" asked King.

"I did a rectal temp on Hinson, after I checked for evidence of sexual assault, of course; that turned out negative. She's been dead eight to nine hours. There are *twelve* stab wounds, though."

Michelle picked up on the tone in Sylvia's voice. "That equals overkill."

"Yes. It also equals rage," said Sylvia. "There were no defensive wounds on her hands or forearms. She was obviously surprised and quickly overpowered."

She picked up her bag and nodded toward the door. "I'm heading back to the office. I've got patients to see, and then I'll do the post on Hinson."

"We'll walk out with you," said King.

They headed out into brisk air that was being quickly warmed by the sun.

"I meant to ask you, how's your investigation coming with Junior Deaver?"

King glanced at her in surprise. "How'd you know about that?"

"I ran into Harry Carrick at the grocery store. I told him you two were looking into these murders, and he told me you were doing work for him. I still can't believe Junior Deaver could have done it. He's done work at my house. I always found him very courteous and accommodating, if a little rough around the edges."

"We met with Remmy, Eddie, Dorothea and Savannah and the household staff."

"And didn't get too far, I'm sure," noted Sylvia.

"Remmy's really torn up about Bobby," said King.

"I heard he was in very bad shape."

"Well, there's hope," said Michelle. "He recently regained consciousness, even spoke, but he just rambles apparently; he's not really coherent, just spouting off names and such. But still that's a positive thing, I suppose."

"Strokes are completely unpredictable," said Sylvia. "Just when you think someone's recovering, they suddenly pass away, or vice versa."

King shook his head. "Well, for Remmy's sake, I hope he makes it." He glanced at Sylvia. "You'll let us know what you find on Hinson?"

"Todd told me to and he's the boss. At least until the FBI or the state police take over the investigation."

"Do you think that's probable?" asked Michelle.

"For purposes of finding this maniac, I think that actually would be a positive development," said Sylvia firmly.

CHAPTER

25

THE FOUR SERIAL MURD-
ders in Wrightsburg hit the national news pipeline that afternoon and continued on into the evening. Most citizens
of the small town sat in front of their TV screens as dour
anchorpersons went about dutifully explaining where the
rural Virginia municipality was, and how it had been devastated by a series of violent and apparently random murders. State and federal authorities were on the scene, the
TV people said, and hopefully, the killer would be
stopped soon. Left unsaid was the fact that no one actively involved in the investigation thought that was a
very real possibility.

Like their fellow townspeople, King and Michelle sat in
front of a television in King's office and watched and listened to the stories documenting what a slaughterhouse
their humble domicile had become. When the fact that two
letters had been sent to the *Wrightsburg Gazette* by the killer
was announced to the nation, King exclaimed, "Shit!"

Michelle nodded in understanding. "Do you think the
killer's watching?"

"Of course he is," snapped King. "The notoriety's all part of it."

"Do you really think the killings are random?"

"There's no obvious connection among any of the victims." King fell silent for a moment. "Except the reference to only one kid in the Canney and Pembroke letter. The question is, which kid?"

"I'm not following."

He looked at her. "If Pembroke was targeted specifically, for example, and Canney just happened to be there when it happened, that means there *was* a reason for Pembroke to die. Now, if there was a reason for her to die, then maybe there's a reason why the others died too. And maybe those reasons are connected somehow."

"And the watches?"

"The guy's trademark obviously, but maybe there's more to it."

"Hopefully, Sylvia will have some answers soon."

King checked his watch. "I've got a dinner I need to get to."

"Where?"

"The Sage Gentleman, with people in from out of town. You want to tag along?"

"Nope. I've got some stuff to do too."

"Date?" He smiled at her.

"Yeah, with my kickboxing instructor. Our plan is to sweat and groan a lot with our clothes on."

They headed off in opposite directions. As was typical for her, Michelle clocked an average of twenty miles over the speed limit in her white Toyota Sequoia that she'd nicknamed the Whale, in honor of Melville's fictional

creation, Moby Dick. She passed the last little-used intersection about thirty seconds before she would reach the
gravel road that wound through the woods to her cottage.
As soon as she cleared the intersection, the lights of the
pale blue VW came on and the driver put the Bug in gear,
turned right and started following her.

He slowed as she turned onto the gravel road, and
watched as her wheels kicked up dust and bits of rock and
then she was quickly out of sight in the gathering darkness.
A quarter mile up and then to the left, he knew, having
been up there already while Michelle wasn't at home.
There were no other residences within a half mile of the
place. It backed to the lake where she kept a scull, kayak
and Sea-Doo at her small floating dock. The cottage was
around fifteen hundred square feet and designed with an
open floor plan. He'd ascertained that she lived alone
with not even a dog to keep her company, and safe. However, she was a former federal agent with specialized
skills; a person not to be underestimated. He drove a little
farther down the main road, parked his car on a dirt patch
behind a screen of trees and set off on foot through the
woods toward the cottage.

When he arrived there, he saw that the Sequoia was
parked in the roundabout by the front door. The lights
were on in the house. He pulled out his binoculars and ran
them over the front of the cottage. No sign of her. Keeping well back in the trees, he made his way to the rear of
the house. A light was on in one of the rooms back there,
upper floor. Her bedroom, he surmised. There was a sheet
across the window, but he caught her silhouette twice. The
movements were straightforward: she was undressing. He

lowered his binoculars while she did so. She came out a few minutes later dressed in workout clothes, jumped in her truck and spun dirt as she headed off.

He came back around in time to see her taillights winking at him before disappearing in the darkness as she rounded the curve and then was out of sight. She certainly moved fast, he thought. He eyed the front door. It was locked, but that didn't pose much of a problem. There was no security system; he'd checked on that too. He pulled out the appropriate pick and tension tool from the set he carried.

A couple of lock-picking minutes later he was inside and looking around. The house was a mess; he marveled at the woman's ability to function amid such chaos. He placed the device behind a pile of books and CDs gathering dust in one corner of the living room. It was an FM test transmitter about the size of a quarter. He'd soldered a microphone to the transmitter, which was illegal under U.S. law because it turned the transmitter into a surveillance bug, not that he was concerned about that violation of law and privacy. He hustled upstairs to Michelle's bedroom, where he scanned her closet and found several black pantsuits, two white blouses, a trio of battered dress heels and also an abundance of jeans, sweatshirts and workout clothes and a variety of athletic shoes.

He went back downstairs. She didn't have a formal office area here; still he sorted through the stack of mail haphazardly scattered on the kitchen table. Nothing unusual there so long as one considered subscriptions to the *Shooting Magazine* and *Iron Women* normal.

He slipped outside; he had one last task to perform. Because he was hiding these bugs at different locations, he wouldn't be able to be present at all of them at the same time. Thus, he'd modified the transmitter such that it would connect wirelessly with a voice-activated digital microrecorder that he was now hiding outside of Michelle's cottage. The transmitter had an open range of a hundred meters inside a building, and the recorder had a hard drive that would allow it to store hundreds of hours of recording. He went back inside the house, spoke and then hurried back out to check the microrecorder. His snatch of conversation had been captured on it. Satisfied, he drove off. He'd already bugged King's houseboat, as well as the private investigators' office and phones. He had quickly discovered that Chief Williams was using King and Maxwell in the investigation. He realized how very helpful that could be to him. So now at least two of the people trying to find him would unwittingly provide him with advance information. As King had predicted, he *had* been listening to the news. He was well aware that an army of lawmen was being assembled to capture him. Well, he'd die first. And he'd take as many others with him as possible.

CHAPTER

26

LATER THAT NIGHT KYLE Montgomery, Sylvia's assistant and rock star wannabe, parked his Jeep in front of the morgue and got out. He was dressed in a dark hood coat with "UVA" printed across it, rumpled dungaree pants and hiking boots without socks. He noted that Sylvia's navy-blue Audi convertible was also parked in front. He checked his watch. Almost ten o'clock. Pretty late for her to be here, but there was the latest victim to dissect: the lawyer woman, he recalled. His boss had not requested his help on that one, a decision for which he was very appreciative. However, her presence here tonight made what he'd come to do a little dicey because he didn't know which facility she was in. Probably the morgue, yet if she was in the medical office, he could always make up an excuse if she discovered him. He swiped his security card in the slot by the front door, heard the lock click open and went inside Sylvia's medical office.

Only the low-level emergency lights were on. He threaded his way through the familiar surroundings, pausing only when he passed Sylvia's office. The light was on, but there was no one in there.

He slipped into the pharmacy area of the office, used his key to open one of the cabinets and withdrew a number of bottles. He took one pill from each, taking care to segregate them into Baggies which he'd earlier labeled with a black Magic Marker. He'd hack into the practice's computer system later and fudge the inventory numbers to mask his theft. Kyle only took a few pills each time, so it was easy to cover his tracks.

He was about to leave when he remembered he'd left his wallet in his locker at the morgue earlier that day. He put the pills away in his backpack and quietly unlocked the door that separated the two offices. If he ran into her, he could just tell the truth, that he'd left his wallet. He passed Sylvia's office at the morgue. It was unoccupied. He went on to the scrub area. The autopsy room was at the very back of the facility; that's where Sylvia would be attending to her silent companion. He wasn't going anywhere near there. He listened intently for a few seconds, straining to hear the sounds of the Stryker saw, water running or sterilized instruments clattering on metal, but there was only silence. That was a little unnerving, although much of what happened during an autopsy involved such quiet. The dead were not going to complain about all the poking and prodding after all.

There was a sound now, distinctly, he thought, from the rear of the place. His boss might be on the move. He quickly grabbed his wallet and withdrew into the shadows. He was suddenly fearful that if she happened upon him here, she might start asking uncomfortable questions.

She could be that way, direct and blunt. What if she asked him to open his bag? He pushed farther back into the recess of the wall, his pulse knocking in his ears. He silently cursed his lack of nerve. Minutes passed. He finally found the courage to come back into the scant light. Thirty seconds later he was out of the building and driving down the road, the stolen prescription drugs safely in his bag.

When he reached the place, the parking lot was full. He wedged his Jeep between a pair of fat SUVs and went inside.

The Aphrodisiac was full of life and activity, with virtually every table and stool at the bars taken. Kyle showed his ID to a sleepy-looking bouncer at the entrance to the room where the dancers were and spent a few minutes admiring the ladies. The shapely, barely clothed women were performing acts so lewd against the metal dancing poles that it would have caused their poor mothers to die of humiliation—after they had strangled their shameless daughters, that is. Kyle loved every minute of it.

He checked his watch and then made his way up the stairs to the second floor and down a hallway toward a thick red curtain that hung across the passageway. Beyond the red curtain was a maze of small rooms. He went to the first door, rapped out an agreed-upon signal and immediately received permission to enter.

He closed the door behind him and stood nervously, unwilling to advance far into the darkened space. This was not the first time he'd done this, but each time held its own share of risk and uncertainty.

"Do you have them?" the woman asked in a voice so low he could barely hear it.

Kyle nodded. "Right here. All the stuff you like." He dug his hand in his coat pocket and pulled out the Baggies. He held them up like a small boy proudly displaying a dead bird to his mother.

As always, the woman was clothed in a long flowing dress with a scarf wound around her head. Her eyes were hidden behind dark glasses, even though the room was poorly lit. She obviously didn't want to be recognized. Kyle had often wondered who she was but had never worked up the courage to ask. The voice seemed familiar but he couldn't definitively place it.

There'd been a note left in his Jeep one evening saying that if he'd like to make some extra money, he could call the number written on the paper. Well, who didn't want to score some extra cash? He answered affirmatively and was told that the small pharmacy Sylvia kept in her office could be a very lucrative source of income for him. Potent painkillers and other potentially mind-altering drugs were the items on the purchaser's wish list.

With no scruples impeding him Kyle had agreed to look into it, had done some homework to see the best way to access this potential gold mine and had concluded that it was doable. Terms were agreed to, the deliveries commenced and Kyle had significantly increased his income.

The long dress did not totally obscure the comely figure of the woman facing him. The private surroundings, the bed in one corner of the room and the fact that they were in a strip club always made Kyle's blood race. In a recurring fantasy he'd stride into the room, far bigger and more masculine than he actually was. He'd hold out the pills like he was doing now, but when she went to take them, he'd grab her, lift her up, laughing at her puny resistance, and throw her roughly on the bed. Then he'd fall on top of her and have his way far into the night. His sexual savagery would rise with the anguished pitch of her screams, until she finally shrieked in his ear that she wanted it; she wanted *him,* she wanted Big Kyle, so badly.

Even now he felt a rise in his pants as this wistful scenario played itself out once more in his head. He wondered if he would ever actually have the nerve to execute upon it. He doubted it. He was far too much of a chickenshit. She laid the cash down on the table and took the Baggies, then motioned with her hand for him to leave.

He immediately did so, folding the money over twice and sliding it into his pocket with a big smile.

Kyle wouldn't realize until later that something he'd seen was of great significance, chiefly because it made no sense. And it would eventually cause him to wonder. And at some point that wonder would lead to action. For now all he wondered was what to do with the money he'd just earned. Kyle Montgomery wasn't much of a saver; he was far more of a spendthrift. Instant gratification was very much a way of life for him. A new guitar, perhaps? Or a new TV and CD-DVD combo for his small apartment? By the time he'd made it back to his Jeep and driven off, the new guitar had won out. He'd order it tomorrow.

Back in the room the woman locked the door, unwound her scarf and took off her glasses. She slipped off her shoes and then removed her dress, revealing a silk camisole underneath. She examined the labels on the Baggies, took out one of the pills, crushed it and downed the powder with a glass of water followed by a chaser of straight Bombay Sapphire.

She put on some music, lay back on the bed, crossed her arms over her chest and allowed the power of the medication to send her to another place, one where she might, at least for a few brief moments, be happy. Until tomorrow, that is, when the reality of her life would come shrieking back.

She trembled, jerked, moaned and then lay still; the sweat was shooting through every pore in her body as she hit the highest high and then plunged to the lowest low. In one of the heat-charged spasms she tore off her sweat-drenched camisole and dropped to the floor in only her panties, her breath coming in huge bursts, her breasts slapping together as she rolled back and forth in a convulsion of manufactured ecstasy. Her nerves fired and mis-fired under the delicious stress of her potent concoction.

But she *was* happy. At least until tomorrow.

CHAPTER

27

KING FINISHED HIS DINNER with friends around nine-thirty and decided to call Michelle to see if she was interested in a nightcap at the Sage Gentleman to discuss the case some more. She was there in about ten minutes. When his partner arrived, King watched in amusement as many male heads in the bar turned at the sight of the tall striking brunette striding confidently through the bar wearing jeans, a turtleneck sweater, boots and a Secret Service windbreaker. The fantasies they must have been playing with, he thought. *If they only knew she was armed and dangerous and independent as hell.*

"How was the dinner?" she asked.

"Predictably boring. How about the kickboxing?"

"I need a new instructor."

"What happened to the one you have?"

"He's just not challenging enough."

As they looked around for a table in the bar area, Michelle spotted a familiar face in the far corner. "Isn't that Eddie Battle?"

At that instant, Eddie looked up, saw them and waved them over.

They sat down at his table, the remnants of a meal still there.

"Dorothea not cooking tonight?" asked King with a smile.

"That would be correct. In fact, that would be right for most of our marriage. I actually do most of the cooking," he added with a boyish grin.

"A man of many talents," said Michelle.

He was dressed in corduroy pants and a black sweater with brown elbow patches. Michelle looked down at his feet and saw loafers.

"I see you finally got the cavalry boots off."

"Not without effort. Your feet really swell up in those things."

"When's your next reenactment?" asked King.

"This weekend. At least the weather's been cooperative. Those wool uniforms are really scratchy, and if it's really hot, it's a killer. Although I'm thinking about retiring from it. My back's about gone from all the horseback riding."

"Sold any paintings lately?" asked Michelle.

"Two, both to a collector in Pennsylvania who happens to be a reenactor. Only he fights for the Union, but I won't hold that against him. Cash is cash, after all."

"I'd like to see your work sometime," said King. Michelle said the same thing.

"Well, I have it all in the studio behind the house. Give me a call whenever. I'll be glad to give you a tour." He waved to the waiter. "You two look thirsty, and as my mother would say, it's bad manners and a damn shame to drink alone."

As they waited for their cocktails, Eddie said, "So have you solved the case and gotten Junior Deaver off the hook?" He paused and added, "Although I guess you can't tell me. We're sort of on opposite sides."

"It's not an easy nut to crack," said King. "We'll see."

Their drinks came. King tasted his whiskey sour and then said, "So how's your mother doing?"

Eddie looked at his watch. "She's at the hospital, although it's around ten, so they'll be kicking her out of Dad's room soon. She'll probably sleep there though. She usually does."

"What's your dad's prognosis?"

"Actually, that's taken a turn for the better. They think he's past the worst of it."

"That's great news," said Michelle.

Eddie swallowed some of his drink. "He's got to make it. He's just got to." He looked at each of them. "I don't know if Mom could survive his dying. And while death awaits us all, I just don't see him riding off into the sunset right now." He looked down, embarrassed. "Sorry, too many gins and I start sounding pretty cliché-ish. Probably a reason why drinking alone with your problems is never a good idea."

"Speaking of drinking alone, where's Dorothea?" asked Michelle.

"At some function," said Eddie wearily. He hastily added, "A Realtor has to do all that crap. But you can't argue with her success."

"True, Dorothea has been very successful," said King quietly.

Eddie raised his glass. "To Dorothea, the world's greatest real estate agent."

Michelle and King looked at each other uncomfortably.

Eddie lowered his drink. "Look, she has her thing and I have mine. There's a certain balance to that."

"Do you have any children?" asked Michelle.

"Dorothea never wanted kids, so that pretty much settled that." Eddie shrugged. "Who knows, maybe I didn't want them either. I probably would've been a lousy dad."

Michelle said, "You could have taught your kids to paint, ride horses, maybe they would've gotten into reenactments too."

"And you still *could* have kids," added King.

"To do that, I'd have to get another wife," said Eddie with a resigned smile, "and I'm not sure I have the energy. Besides, Battles aren't supposed to divorce. It's unseemly. Hell, if Dorothea didn't kill me, my mother probably would."

"Well, it's your life," commented Michelle.

He looked at her strangely. "You'd think so, wouldn't you?" He finished his drink and said, "So I heard on the news that they've called in the big guns to help."

"Including your old friend Chip Bailey."

"I wouldn't be here if it wasn't for him."

"I'm sure your parents were really grateful to him."

"Oh, yeah. My father offered him a position as head of security in one of his companies. Big bucks."

"I didn't know that," said King. "But he obviously didn't take it."

"No. I guess he liked being a cop." Eddie tapped his spoon against his fork. "I remember when I was a kid and this area was nothing but hills and woods. It was great. We never worried about anything happening."

"And now?" asked Michelle.

"And now people are getting killed in their homes, left in the woods, shotgunned in their cars. If I ever did have a family, I don't think I'd do it here."

"Well, I guess you could live anywhere," said King.

"I'm not sure my mother would be very happy about that."

"Again, it's your life, Eddie, right?" said Michelle.

This time Eddie Battle didn't bother to answer her.

CHAPTER

28

WHILE KYLE MONT-
gomery was committing his felony and Eddie, King and
Michelle were in the bar, Bobby Battle lay in his hospital
bed under a mass of IV lines. Remmy Battle sat next to him,
her right hand clasped inside her husband's still, pale one.

Remmy's eyes were on the array of monitors that
vividly detailed the slim grasp her husband had on life.
He'd had a minor setback and gone back on the ventilator
machine, and it emitted its unnervingly high-pitched
screech whenever Bobby's breathing veered off course.
Remmy's own breathing rose and fell erratically with the
squawks of the infernal contraption.

The nurse walked in. "Hello, Mrs. Battle, everything
all right?"

"No! He doesn't know me," she snapped back. "He
doesn't know anyone."

"But he's getting stronger, the doctors said so. It'll just
take time. His vitals are much better. Even though he's back
on the ventilator, things are looking up, they really are."

Remmy's tone changed. "I thank you for telling me that. I really do, honey." She looked down at the large man in the bed.

The nurse smiled and then seemed uncomfortable. "Mrs. Battle," she began in a deferential tone undoubtedly reserved for those fortunate few who had their names on buildings.

"I know," Remmy said quietly.

"Are you going to sleep here tonight?" the nurse asked. "If so, I'll get your bed made up."

"Not tonight. I'll be back in the morning. But thank you."

Remmy rose and left. The nurse made a quick check on her patient and then exited the room a few minutes later.

Battle was the only patient on this short hallway that was otherwise largely taken up with storage rooms. The rest of the unit's ten beds emptied out onto a central area across from the nurse's station. Remmy Battle had demanded this particular room for her husband because it allowed for more privacy. There was also a rear entrance at the end of this hall that enabled her, with a special access code, to come and go without having to pass by a large number of rooms, nurses and prying glances. The room that she sometimes slept in was down this hall from her husband.

It was a few minutes after ten, and this part of the hospital, isolated from the rest, was undergoing the nightly shift change of personnel. The nurse attending Battle would spend the next forty-five minutes in the staff room with her replacement, going over the current status of the patients under her supervision as well as pertinent medication and physician instructions.

Each patient room in this unit was monitored by camera, with the live feed going to the unit's central nurse's station. The television monitors at the nurse's station were supposed to be watched constantly, although during shift change this procedure was not observed for about twenty minutes as the nurses, overworked and stretched to their limits, struggled to cram an hour's worth of work into a third of that time. However, the machinery helping keep the patients alive in each of the rooms had warning devices that would immediately alert the staff to any drastic changes in condition.

Shortly after Remmy had left, a person came in the same rear entrance that Remmy had passed through minutes earlier. Dressed in scrubs and white hospital coat with a protective mask covering the lower part of the face, and looking very much a part of the hospital world, this individual passed by the door of Bobby Battle's room, glanced inside and saw that it was empty except for the patient. A quick peek around the corner showed that the nurse's station was unattended. The intruder entered Battle's room and closed the door.

Wasting no time, the person slightly moved the camera bolted to the wall across from the bed such that the live feed wouldn't show the area to the left of the bed. Then the masked figure hurried across to the IV stand next to the bed, removed the hypodermic needle from a coat pocket and stabbed one of the medication bags above the fluid line with the needle, shooting the entire contents of the hypo into it. The person glanced once at Battle lying there, features peaceful, even with a tube down his throat. The intruder picked up his hand, placed the wristwatch on it and set it to five. Finally, the person pulled the object from another coat pocket and laid it carefully on Battle's chest.

It was a single white bird's feather.

Moments later the person had shot out the rear entrance, clambered down the stairs, slipped out into the parking lot and climbed in a car. The vehicle sped from the hospital.

The driver had a letter to write and mail.

Barely ten minutes after the car had driven off, a warning bell sounded on one of the machines in Bobby Battle's room, followed by another. Within seconds all were screaming their collective and ominous warnings.

The nurses rushed en masse to the room. A minute later a code blue was broadcast over the P.A., and a highly experienced medical crash team dashed into the room. It was all for naught. At 10:23 P.M. Robert E. Lee Battle was pronounced dead.

CHAPTER

29

AT FIRST IT WAS ASSUMED
that Battle had simply succumbed to the aftereffects of his
stroke. The white feather left on his chest by his killer had
fallen to the floor unnoticed as the medical team attempted to resuscitate him. When the feather was later
discovered by a hospital technician, he placed it on the
table next to the dead man's bed, perhaps assuming it
might have come from a pillow. The watch the killer had
placed on Battle's wrist was covered under IV lines and
also obscured by Battle's ID and medication wristbands.
An anguished and angry Remmy Battle came and went
and didn't take note of the watch or the feather. It wasn't
until a nurse called into question the feather that people
began to wonder. It hadn't come from a hospital pillow,
since they didn't contain feathers. In addition, the swift
and unanticipated change in Battle's condition was puzzling and certainly not above scrutiny.

However, it wasn't until around three in the morning,
when they were about to move Battle's body to the hospital morgue, that the watch was finally observed on the

dead man's wrist, prompting a much closer examination of the body and subsequently the IV bags. That's when the attending physician saw the puncture in the bag where the hypodermic had plunged through.

"Dear God," was all he could manage to say.

Todd Williams was roused from his bed, and on the way in he called King, who in turn called Michelle. All three arrived at the hospital at about the same time. They were surprised to see Chip Bailey there. Williams quickly introduced King and Michelle to the FBI agent.

"I was staying at a local motel, had my police scanner on," Bailey explained. "Damn, Todd, you must have your whole force here at the hospital."

"This is Bobby Battle," Williams shot back. "A leading citizen of the area."

King silently finished the man's unspoken thought. *And now you're going to receive the full wrath of the widow.*

The hospital personnel escorted them to Battle's room. The dead man was lying there with the IV lines still in him and the ventilator tube down his throat, although all the life support machines and monitors had been turned off, their squawks and digital readouts no longer needed. Michelle found herself constantly looking over at Battle, someone she'd heard much about but had never met. For some reason, and not simply the manner of his death, he seemed as fascinating dead as he had been in life.

The head nurse and attending physician gave a brief overview of what they'd discovered regarding the feather, watch and the hole in the IV bag.

"This is all highly unusual," said the doctor in the understatement of the year.

"We were pretty sure it didn't happen every night," King said.

Williams examined the watch. "Not a Zodiac," he said quietly to Michelle and King. "But it's set to *exactly* five and the stem is pulled out."

When Chip Bailey was shown the bird feather by Todd Williams, the agent's reaction was palpable, but he said nothing until the doctor and nurse had left the room.

"Mary Martin Speck," he told them when they were alone. "A nurse; she was nicknamed Florence Nightinghell. The lady killed twenty-three patients in six states over a ten-year period. Speck's currently serving a life sentence in a fed penitentiary in Georgia. Her calling card was a white bird's feather; she claimed she was doing the Lord's work."

"So we can expect another letter," said King.

"We haven't even had time to get the one on Hinson," complained Williams. "Why Bobby Battle? Why would the killer want to add him to the list? It was damn risky, coming in here like this."

However, as they quickly learned after consulting once more with the head nurse, coming in the rear door was not as difficult as they'd originally thought. The code was a simple one, 4-3-2-1, and hadn't been changed in years. There were numerous people in the hospital who knew it and quite probably had let others know.

"Do we have any idea of what was shot into the IV bag?" asked Michelle.

"The lab will analyze and run tox on the contents," said Williams. "Luckily, somebody had sharp eyes and discovered the hole in the bag before everything was taken down and discarded."

"Where's Sylvia?" asked King.

Williams shook his head. "Home sick as a dog. She finished up Hinson last night, caught a bug and is right now throwing up into the toilet. At least that's what she planned to do when I hung up. She'll be here as soon as she can."

Bailey spoke up. "The FBI too. This is the fifth connected death, at least that we know of. We're going to take a more active presence, Todd. Sorry."

"Then maybe *you* can talk to Remmy. When that woman finds out about this, she's going to have a piece of my hide."

King said, "I wouldn't do that until we receive a letter from the killer. The presence of the watch and feather makes it seem certain Bobby was another victim, but we need to be absolutely sure before we open that can of worms with Remmy."

"Good point," agreed Bailey.

"Were there any items missing from Bobby's room?" asked Michelle. "The guy we're looking for took something from all the other victims."

"We really won't know for sure until we talk to Remmy," said Williams. "Now I want to nail down the chain of events." He stepped out for a moment and returned once more with the attending physician and head nurse.

"Can you run over the timeline again for us?" Williams asked.

"Yes, sir," the nurse answered. "Mrs. Battle was here from four until right around ten. She was in the room the whole time. Mr. Battle was alive and doing fine at a few minutes after ten when his nurse last checked him. There were no other visitors during that time."

"How about before Mrs. Battle got here?" asked Michelle.

"His daughter, Savannah, came and stayed for a while early in the afternoon. I don't know the exact times. And also Dorothea Battle came in after that, say around two-thirty."

"Did they come through the rear entrance?" asked Bailey.

"Savannah did, Dorothea Battle came in the front," answered the nurse.

"We'll need exact times on those visits," Williams told them.

"Fine, we'll get them," said the doctor stiffly. "Now, can you excuse me? I have other patients to attend to." The man was surely contemplating the lawsuit that was heading right at his and the hospital's wallets, thought King.

"Hope you have better luck with them," fired back Williams, who'd obviously read the same message in the man's tone.

After he'd left, Williams continued questioning the nurse. "So at ten-fifteen Battle's condition changed."

The nurse nodded. "He went into cardiac arrest. He was flatlined when the first nurse arrived. The crash team tried to resuscitate but was unsuccessful."

King said, "So in the ten or so minutes between the nurse's checking him and his flatlining, the killer struck and the poison, if that's what we're looking at here, took effect."

"Looks that way," agreed Bailey.

"I noticed that the room has a video camera," said King.

"They all do. That way we can monitor all the patients from the nurse's station."

"But no one saw anyone else come in the room after Mrs. Battle left?"

The nurse looked nervous. "Sometimes the nurse's station isn't manned."

"Like during shift change?" said King.

"Yes. Now, if someone did come in after Mrs. Battle left, they had to come through the rear door, or else someone would have seen them."

"Understood," answered King.

"Pretty ballsy to do it with people all over the place," commented Williams.

"Well, if someone were going to try something like that," said the nurse, "they picked the right time to do it."

"Yes, they certainly did," said King.

As King and Michelle were leaving the unit, King stopped at the nurse's station.

"Mind if I take a look?" he asked the head nurse.

He went behind the large console and studied the live video feeds appearing on the monitors. "These aren't on tape, are they?" he asked.

"No. It's not for security, just for the welfare of the patients."

"Well, you might want to rethink that philosophy."

"What was that about?" Michelle asked after they'd left the hospital unit.

"It occurred to me that someone familiar with hospital procedure would also know about the cameras. You don't want to be caught on TV when you're killing someone; it really puts a crimp in your legal defense. In all the other rooms the camera was positioned such that the entire bed and all the apparatus on either side of the bed were shown. In Battle's room the feed was only of the bed and the right side."

Michelle said, "The killer moved the camera so he wouldn't be shown doing the deed in case someone was looking at the monitor."

"That's right."

On the way out of the hospital Harry Carrick met them at the exit. Though it was very early in the morning, Carrick was neatly dressed in a tweed jacket and dress shirt with an open collar.

"Harry, what are you doing here?" asked King.

"Bobby Battle and I are old friends. Well, we *were* old friends. And I'm also the general counsel for the hospital. They called me at home. I've just finished meeting with them. It's a conflict, that I readily admit. But there you are. Have you seen Remmy?"

"No, she'd already come and gone by the time we got here."

Carrick said, "I know some of what was found in Bobby's room. I'm assuming there's more to it."

"There is. We just don't know what really."

"Well, I won't keep you, but we need to reconvene shortly on Junior's case."

"How's it going?"

"What you've discovered up to this point are things I needed to know but aren't particularly helpful for our cause. I felt out the commonwealth's attorney regarding a plea deal of some sort and got stone-cold silence for my troubles. Remmy is most definitely calling the shots. She was upset before, and now with Bobby's death I don't see her aggression abating."

"Probably increasing," said Michelle.

"Probably," said Carrick glumly. "Well, I won't keep you. If you hear anything more about Bobby's death, let me know."

He turned and left them. They watched as he climbed into a perfectly restored British MG convertible and sped off into the reddish glow of the ascending sun.

Michelle turned to King. "I really feel for Harry. He's friends with the Battles, and yet he's representing Junior Deaver *and* the hospital where Bobby died."

King nodded. "I definitely see a lawsuit coming Wrightsburg General's way. Pretty ironic, suing a place that has your name on the outside of the building."

"I don't think that would deter Remmy Battle in the least."

"I wasn't thinking it would." He stretched and yawned. "I'm debating whether to go to the office or back to the boat to sleep."

"I'm going to go for a run," said Michelle. "Why don't you come with me? Endorphins are good for the brain."

"Running! You just did kickboxing!" he exclaimed.

"That was yesterday, Sean."

"God took a day off, you know."

"If he was a woman, he wouldn't have."

"Okay, you convinced me."

She looked pleased. "You're going to run with me?"

"No, I'm going back to the boat to rest. If it was good enough for God, it's good enough for me."

CHAPTER

30

THE POST OFFICE WAS under strict instructions to immediately forward any suspicious letters addressed to the *Gazette* to the police. The Hinson letter came the day after Bobby Battle had been murdered. It was simply worded.

One lawyer less, who cares? I trust you know who I'm not this time. See you soon.

Meanwhile, Sylvia Diaz had risen from her sickbed and finally performed the autopsy on Robert Battle.

At the moment she was sitting with King and Michelle in her office. Chief Williams and Chip Bailey had both attended the Battle autopsy, she told them.

"I think Todd is now thoroughly comfortable with postmortems, unfortunately simply from sheer numbers," commented Sylvia.

"So what killed Bobby?" asked King.

"I won't know for certain until the toxicology screens come back in a week or so, but it looks like someone shot a large quantity of potassium chloride into his nutrition IV bag. In less than ten minutes it would work its way through the TPN solution, into the tubing and then into his body. As soon as that happened, his heart would go into ventricular fibrillation. In his already weakened condition the end would have been quick at least and painless."

"All that suggests some medical knowledge," said King.

Sylvia considered this for a moment. "It's true that potassium chloride isn't often used to kill someone. However, if the person did have medical expertise, he was a little sloppy."

"What do you mean?"

"Battle had the standard array of IV lines: the blood thinner heparin, a saline sugar solution, a TPN or nutrition solution bag, an antibiotic to combat the pulmonary infection he caught from being on the ventilator for so long and the drug dopamine to control his blood pressure."

"Okay, so what does that tell us?" asked King.

"Well, if the person had shot the potassium chloride directly into the *tubing* instead of into the TPN bag, the same fatal result would have occurred, but it would have been undetectable. You have to understand that the TPN solution already has potassium chloride in it, and thus so did Battle's system. I was able to determine that someone had placed additional potassium chloride into the bag only by comparing the levels present there to a normal TPN bag mixture. There was over triple the standard amount, easily enough to kill him."

"So you're saying if the potassium chloride had gone into the tubing directly and not the bag, you never would have noticed it?"

"Yes. The residue in the tubing would be insufficient to

raise suspicion. In fact, it would have only been suspicious if there *hadn't* been residue of potassium chloride. And as I said, Battle already had potassium chloride in his body. It's naturally absorbed, which is why an autopsy alone wouldn't have resulted in an overdose confirmation."

"So it was like the person had some medical knowledge but wasn't an expert?" said King.

"Or else," said Michelle, "he wanted it to be discovered that Battle had been murdered. As if the watch and the feather weren't enough."

"It almost wasn't enough," King reminded her. "The feather had fallen to the floor, and the watch was covered under the IV lines and hospital tags."

"That doesn't make sense, though," said Sylvia. "I mean, isn't the first rule in murdering someone to try and make it like the perfect murder? And if so, how more perfect can you get than by making it look like no murder was even committed?"

Michelle and King both shook their heads, unable to come up with a theory that would account for the killer's behavior.

Sylvia sighed. "Not that it matters, but Battle showed evidence of arteriosclerosis. There was also some unusual wrinkling on the surface of the aorta. He also had a small tumor on his right lung, perhaps the beginnings of lung cancer. Not surprising for a smoker of his age."

"What about Diane Hinson's cause of death?" asked King. He quickly added, "Although it seemed pretty obvious."

"She died from massive internal bleeding from the multiple stab wounds. They severed her aorta and punctured her heart chamber and left lung. It would have been over in minutes for her too." She added, "Though not nearly as painless as Battle's death."

"Was she raped or sexually assaulted?" asked King.

"No evidence of that at autopsy, but lab results are still pending. I heard about the Florence Nightinghell connection, by the way. I'll guess we'll get a letter to that effect."

"The Hinson letter indicated we'd see him soon, and we did," said Michelle. "At least he's a man of his word."

King added, "First an exotic dancer, then high school kids, then a lawyer and now Bobby Battle."

"It's as though the killer is taking a greater risk with each one," commented Sylvia.

"To go from an exotic dancer he might have picked up in a bar and then shot and left in the woods to poisoning an immensely rich businessman lying in a coma in a hospital bed doesn't make a whole lot of sense," said King. "Not to sound callous, but how's the guy picking his victims: one-night stands or the social register?"

"Like I said before, this guy's operating outside the box," said Sylvia, rubbing at her bloodshot eyes.

King looked at her closely. "You look like hell," he said with a disarming smile. "You should be in bed."

"Thanks for noticing. I'll try to get to that any week now."

"Where's Kyle?" asked Michelle. "Can't he pick up the slack?"

"He's not a pathologist; he can't do the posts. And to answer your question, he called in sick. I wish that had been an option for me. I was hugging the toilet most of last night, and I have a full load of patients waiting. Thank God for antibiotics."

"What do you make of the killer's choosing to emulate Mary Martin Speck?" asked Michelle.

"Meaning a woman instead of a man?" Michelle nodded. "Well, I'm not sure what to make of it," Sylvia said. "A woman could have killed Battle. It obviously takes no physical strength to shoot a solution from a syringe into an IV bag. However, I'd stake my reputation on the murders of Rhonda Tyler and Diane Hinson being committed by a man. A woman couldn't have carried Tyler all that distance through the woods, and the knife wounds on Hinson were very deep. It was either a man or a woman so strong I'd hate to run into her in a dark alley."

"So," Michelle began slowly, "it's possible we have two killers here, a man and a woman."

"Not necessarily," argued King. "The only evidence to that effect is the reference Bailey made to Speck and the bird's feather. Until we get the letter, we won't know if the killer was mimicking Speck at all. The feather may symbolize something else, something unique to the killer."

"That's true," conceded Michelle. Sylvia nodded in agreement.

King looked at the two women. "Want to hear a really off-the-wall suggestion?"

"I'll bite," said Michelle quickly.

"Bobby Battle was a very wealthy man. I wonder who benefits under his will."

There was a long silence and then Sylvia said, "Are you suggesting a family member killed him for money and tried to make it look like one of the serial murders?"

"It couldn't have been Eddie. He was with us at the Sage Gentleman until after eleven o'clock," said Michelle.

"That's right," said King. "But Dorothea and Savannah were at the hospital earlier. They couldn't have put the poison in then, because he would have been dead long before Remmy showed up. But suppose one of them stashed the potassium chloride in the room during their earlier visit that day, then snuck back in when she saw Remmy leave, did the deed and ran like hell."

"Eddie said Dorothea was at some function," Michelle reminded him.

"We'll need to verify that."

"Well, many a murder has financial gain as the motive," said Sylvia. "You might be on to something, Sean."

"While I'm at it, here's another one to think about: Remmy was in the room with Battle for hours. Who's to say she didn't shoot that stuff into the IV bag before she left?"

"What possible motivation would Remmy have?" asked Sylvia. "She's rich."

"What if Bobby had taken up his old womanizing ways, and Remmy had simply had enough? There might not be enough money in the world to counter that."

"That's a different story, of course. Do you have evidence supporting that?"

King thought about Battle's secret drawer and Remmy's not wearing her wedding ring but decided not to mention that to Sylvia. "I'm not saying we have anything to support it. I'm just throwing out what-ifs. And maybe even more than money, a woman scorned is one of the oldest motivations for murder there is. So she exits with a built-in alibi and leaves the feather and watch as misdirection. The serial killer's M.O. has been all over the news, so she'd know those types of details."

"But the fact she was even there makes her a suspect, particularly with the delayed manner of death by poisoning," argued Sylvia. "You could make a case that if she were going to do something like that, she'd have slipped in another time, done it and left before anyone saw her. As it stands now, she really has no alibi at all."

"Well," said Michelle, "if I were the person who killed Battle and tried to pin it on our neighborhood serial killer, I'd be looking over my shoulder big-time."

"What do you mean?" said Sylvia.

"If I were the real killer, I'd be pretty upset about that."

"I'm still not following," said Sylvia.

"Look at it this way. The serial killings have been meticulously planned and executed. We have follow-up letters from the killer taunting the police. Clearly, this guy is a control freak and has some grand plan in mind. Now, if another person killed Bobby Battle and tried to pin the blame on the serial killer, our control freak may see it as tainting his masterpiece. He'll want to take out his revenge on the person who killed Battle."

"So, in effect, we may have one killer going after another," said King.

"Exactly," said Michelle.

31

"I'M DEPUTIZING YOU both," said Chief Williams as he sat eyeballing King and Michelle at their office the next day. They stared back at him, clearly stunned.

"Excuse me?" said King. "I was one of your deputies once. I have no desire to re-up, Todd."

"I'm not giving you the option. I need you!"

"They outlawed indentured servitude a long time ago," King shot back.

"What's going on, Todd?" asked Michelle.

"I'm getting squeezed out by the feds, that's what."

"But you *wanted* their help," exclaimed King.

"But I also didn't want to be shoved off the case, right here in my own town. I don't want folks to think I can't do the job. I'm willing to work with the feds, of course, even let them jointly run the investigation with me. But I'll be damned if I'm going to let them push me out of investigating my very own crime spree."

King shook his head in bewilderment. "Todd, I think you've been attending too many autopsies. Why don't you let them handle it? They've got the manpower and the experience. Let it be their headache."

"There's something to be said for pride, Sean," rejoined Williams in an offended tone. "And you two have put in a lot of time already on this thing. You've got theories and ideas. Who's to say if we work together we can't crack this thing faster than the almighty FBI? Hell, Chip Bailey's running around already like he's king of the hill. I'm just waiting for him to tell me to make him some coffee. That'll be the day. I'll shoot the son of a bitch first." He looked at them pleadingly. "Come on, you two have just as much experience as any of those guys. I know together we can get this done. And remember, we live here, they don't. We need to make Wrightsburg safe to live in again. It's our home. Everybody's counting on us."

Michelle and King exchanged glances.

Michelle spoke first. "Well, it is a challenging proposition."

"So's hang gliding; that doesn't mean you should do it," King shot back.

"Come on, Sean, this case is intriguing you, you can't deny that," she pointed out. "You'll be thinking about it whether you're working on it or not. At least if we're deputized, we can investigate with some official status. We might make more progress that way."

"And what about our investigation firm?"

"You can still do that," answered Williams quickly. "I'm not asking you to spend all your time on this. But what I'm willing to do is give you access to everything. You won't have to tag along after me everywhere. You can go and talk to people and snoop around all by yourself under my badge. I've got the power. I can deputize anybody I damn well want to."

"And Bailey won't have a problem with that?" said King skeptically. "Come on, Todd, you know better."

"So what if he gets his back up? He can't argue with your credentials. But you just leave him to me. I'll go to the mat on this one, even if I have to call the governor."

"I don't know," said King, "this could turn out to be one big turf war nightmare, and I went through enough of those with the Service."

Michelle punched him playfully in the arm. "Come on, what could it really hurt?"

"We could get killed by this psycho! I bet that would hurt."

Michelle looked at Williams and winked. "I'm in."

The police chief glanced nervously at King. "Sean?"

A long moment passed. "All right," he finally muttered.

"Good," Williams said in a relieved tone. He took a pair of silver badges out of his pocket, recited two sentences of official legalese swearing them in and handed them the badges. "Okay, you're officially deputies. Now, look at this."

He pulled out a piece of paper and handed it across to them. They read it simultaneously.

"The letter from Bobby's killer, the Mary Martin Speck wannabe, only not," said Michelle as she glanced up.

King read the letter aloud: *"Another one down. That makes five. It was a big one this time, but more to come. And no, I'm not Mary, no Florence Nightinghell here. The feather was just that, a feather for the featherweights that all of you are! See you soon. Not MMS."*

He looked up with a thoughtful expression. "Was there a Zodiac symbol on the envelope this letter came in?"

"No, it was clean. Like the Canney-Pembroke letter and the Hinson letter. We've already checked it for prints and other traces. Nothing."

"This letter says that Battle was victim number five," said King.

"Well, he *is* number five, Sean," replied Williams.

"But the Pembroke-Canney letter only mentioned the death of *one* kid. Taken literally, that would make Battle only victim number four. That's an inconsistency that's inexplicable right now."

Williams slapped his thigh with his hand. "See, that's why I want you two on board. You see things, deduce things."

"We may be entirely wrong in our deductions," countered King.

"Or you may be exactly right," rejoined Williams. "Another thing you need to know. Hinson wore an anklet, a gold one. It wasn't on the body, and it didn't turn up anywhere in her house."

King said, "Pembroke's ring, Canney's St. Christopher's medal, possibly Tyler's belly ring and now Hinson's anklet."

"Maybe he wants them as souvenirs," said Michelle, "trophies from his kills."

"Maybe. Was there anything missing from Bobby Battle?"

"Nothing that we know of." Williams studied King closely. "So what's your next move?"

King pondered this for a bit. Finally, he said, "It's time we determined once and for all if there's any connection between the killings."

"But, Sean, we know they were killed by the same person," said Williams.

"No, we *don't* know that," said King sharply. "But that's not what I meant anyway. I mean we have to find out if there's some common thread among the *victims,* if somehow *they're* connected to each other."

"But in serial killings they aren't," protested Williams.

"This one might be the exception to that rule," said King. "And while we're doing that, we're going to have to go back into the lion's den."

"Lion's den," said Michelle. "What's that mean?"

"We need to go see the Battles again," replied King.

"I think I'd rather face down Priscilla Oxley," said Michelle. "And let me tell you if that woman calls me chickie or plaything again, it won't be pretty."

After Williams had left, Michelle asked King, "So what do you really expect to find out at the Battles'?"

"With luck an answer to your question of why Remmy wasn't wearing her ring. Also the truth as to what was in Bobby's secret drawer."

"But all that's connected to the burglary, not the killings."

"Right, except Battle could have been killed because of what was in that drawer. Even if he was murdered by someone else, we need to find that someone."

"Okay, but if one of the Battles did poison him, when

we go to interview them, we're going to be talking to a murderer at some point."

"And the sooner we find out who, the better."

"So if one of them did do it, who's your money on? Eddie was with us, so is it the iron wife, the slutty daughter or the viper-tongued daughter-in-law?"

"I'll withhold judgment for now. But if Battle's death was simply a copycat murder with a separate motive, that still doesn't lead us to the person who's killed four other people and counting."

"So you think there'll be more victims?"

"Who knows?" He slapped her on the shoulder. "Just be careful out there."

"You know I can look out for myself, Sean."

"That's not what I meant. I want you around to protect *me*."

CHAPTER

32

BOBBY BATTLE'S MURDER was front-page news throughout the area. The headlines were made much more sensational by the fact that his death was attributed to the serial killer. What had been kept from the press and public were the thefts from each of the victims and the precise contents of the letters.

The citizens of Wrightsburg were locking their doors, cleaning their guns, setting their house alarms and scrutinizing their fellow citizens. The look in their eyes was clear: if someone like Bobby Battle could be killed in the middle of a busy hospital, no one was safe.

In that assumption they were actually correct.

The cave was set far back into the rolling hills east of Wrightsburg and on the way to Charlottesville. Its entrance was covered by fallen pines and sheets of thick ivy and other forest clutter, and there was no discernible trail leading to it. The hole in the rock was large enough to house several clans of black bear, which it had in the past. However, now there was only one occupant, and it walked on two legs, although it was no less a predator.

He sat brooding at a rough-hewn table in the center of the cave. It had been outfitted with enough supplies to make it livable for extended periods of time. The only illumination was from a battery-powered lantern. The man held up the hood that he'd worn when he had killed four people. He fingered the material lightly. An executioner, that's what he was, pure and simple. Yet executioners only carried out a sentence justly imposed.

He looked down at the newspaper. Staring back at him was a grainy photo of Robert Battle taken years ago. The headline read "Millionaire Businessman and Philanthropist Robert E. Lee Battle Slain in Hospital, Serial Killer Suspected."

Serial killer! Those two words beat into his brain until he balled up the paper and hurled it away. Enraged, he grabbed the lantern and slung it against the wall, plunging himself into darkness. He stood and lumbered around the room, slamming into objects, falling down, getting back up and beating his hardened fists against the rock and dirt walls until they were numb. Finally exhausted, he slumped to the cold cave floor.

He suddenly screamed so loudly that he felt his heart would burst. Eventually, the sweat broke over his skin, his breathing grew more regular and he finally calmed. He crawled back over to a trunk set against one wall, found the latch, opened it and pulled out another lantern, an oil-burning one. He fumbled for a match in his pocket, lit the wick, turned up the light, looked around and found the newspaper. He sat down at the table once more and studied the story, his gaze averted from the grainy photo of the now dead man.

This was a setback—a major one, he had to admit—but life was full of disappointment. He'd just do what he'd always done: turn an obstacle to his full advantage. The great Bobby Battle might be dead, but there was still more to do. There were more people to be killed—no, *executed*, he quickly corrected himself.

He stared at the headline, the last part of it anyway. "Serial Killer Suspected." This impersonator had stolen his thunder in the worst possible way. Stolen it and then blamed him for it. In a way he had to admire the bastard's professionalism. Admire, yes; forgive, no.

He pulled out a piece of paper upon which was written, in code, a list of his victims, ones already dead and ones he'd kill in the future. He took up a pencil and wrote a question mark on the last line of the page. He'd find this impersonator before the police did, and he'd kill him. Justice demanded it.

CHAPTER

33

"KYLE, WHAT ARE YOU doing?" asked Sylvia as she walked into the administrative office of her medical practice and saw Kyle sitting in front of the computer terminal.

He spun around in the chair. "Oh, hey, Doc, didn't expect you in this early."

"Apparently not. So what exactly are you doing?"

"Just accessing the Internet."

"I've told you before that you cannot use this computer for personal business."

"I wasn't. I was going to order some new scrubs and surgical masks that we need both for the morgue and here. I found a much cheaper deal on the Web than we're getting through our current supplier."

"Kyle, that's okay for my medical practice, but the morgue is a government entity. There are procurement procedures in place, very rigid ones. You can't just order something on your own and have a government check issued to pay for it."

"Jeez, Doc, I'm trying to save us some bucks here."

"I appreciate your initiative. I'm just telling you there are certain channels we have to go through."

"Sometimes I wonder why I even bother. Nothing but red tape."

"You think I like dealing with it? Look, just shoot me an e-mail about it, including comparison costs, and I'll put it in the system. If it's that good of a deal, we'll do it, both here and next door."

Kyle brightened. "Okay, Doc. That's cool."

She folded her arms across her chest and stared at him. "You look like you've fully recovered from being sick. Must have been a really fast bug."

"It was. How about you? Feeling better?"

"No," she said bluntly. "But I don't have a choice about showing up."

"Come on, Doc, it's not like dead people are going to know if you're a little late."

"Morgues around the country have bodies stacked up, and every minute that goes by, the victims deteriorate further and further, vital evidence is lost and the chances increase dramatically that a criminal will go free. I refuse to let that happen here."

"I hear you, Doc. You're the best."

"Uh-huh. Finish up there. We need to complete the reports on the Hinson and Battle posts, and we have a full slate of patients scheduled today."

"Right you are."

After Sylvia had left, Kyle quickly completed what he was actually doing: manipulating the pharmacy inventory records to cover up his theft. Finished, Kyle reminded himself that he'd have to find a deal on the Internet for scrubs to present to Sylvia. One thing he'd learned about the woman: she never forgot anything. If he didn't come up with it, she'd ask, and if he didn't have an answer, she'd grow suspicious. He wasn't supposed to have the pass code to get into these files, but he had scammed it from the woman who handled that part of the operation. The woman only came in three days a week, which gave him plenty of opportunity to cover his tracks each time he made a "withdrawal" from the pharmacy.

However, Kyle hadn't given Sylvia Diaz enough credit. She was already suspicious of him. And that suspicion would only deepen as time went on.

As Kyle rose to join her, he glanced at the newspaper lying on the desk next to the computer. The headline was the same one the man in the cave had ranted about: Battle murdered and the serial killer blamed. He quickly read through the accompanying story. It had happened on the same night he'd taken the woman the drugs at the Aphrodisiac. In fact, according to the newspaper account, it had occurred at the same hour Kyle had driven past the hospital on his way to the men's club. He could have passed the killer on the way, a realization that made him squirm in his seat. As his thoughts returned to that night, it suddenly struck him what he'd seen. And as Kyle had been wont to do his whole life, he immediately started to wonder how this knowledge might best serve *him*.

CHAPTER

34

JUNIOR DEAVER HEAVED a flat of asphalt shingles off his pickup truck. They landed with a thump that broke the quiet of the morning. Junior jumped off the truck and took a look at the home he was building for his family. It was all framed, the roof was on and it would soon be under shingle. It had been slow going, though. He'd done most of the work himself, calling in favors from buddies from time to time. It wasn't a large house, but it was far bigger than the double-wide trailer they were currently living in. He pulled his tool belt off the truck, put it on and headed over to fire up the gasoline generator that would power the air gun he'd use to drive the shingle nails.

It was only then that he heard the stealthy footsteps coming toward him. He spun around. He'd expected no visitors at this isolated place. No one knew he was here other than his wife. And he hadn't even heard a car pull up.

The sight of the woman drew the blood from his face.

Remmy Battle was dressed in a full-length black leather coat with the collar turned up. She had wide sunglasses on. Boots covered her feet and she was wearing gloves, though it wasn't chilly.

"Mrs. Battle? What are you doing here?"

She stopped about a foot from him. "I wanted to talk to you, Junior, just you and me."

"How'd you even know I was here?"

"I know a lot, Junior, far more than most people think. That's why I wanted to talk to you."

Junior held up his hands. "Look, I got me a lawyer. You better talk to him."

"I *have* talked to him. Now I want to talk to you."

He eyed her warily and then looked around as though he expected to see police officers swooping in to arrest him. His expression turned stubborn. "I don't see that we got anything to talk about. You already had me put in jail."

"But you're out now, aren't you?"

"Well, yeah, but we had to put up bail. Almost broke us. We ain't got that kind of money."

"Come on now, Junior, your wife makes good money over at that *club*. I know that for a fact. My husband frequented the place. She probably earned a small fortune just off him."

"I don't know nothing about that."

She ignored this. "My *dead* husband."

"I heard," Junior mumbled in reply.

"He was murdered, you know," she said in an oddly flat tone.

"Heard that too."

"You get out of jail and then he ends up dead."

He looked at her wide-eyed. "Look, you ain't gonna pin that on me, lady."

"Oh, I'm sure you have an alibi."

"You bet I do."

"Good for you, but that's not why I'm here." She drew even closer and took off her glasses. Her eyes were red and puffy.

"So why are you here?" he asked.

"I want it back, Junior. I want it back now."

"Damn it, Mrs. Battle, I didn't take your wedding ring."

She suddenly shouted, "I couldn't give a shit about the damn ring. I want the other things. You give them back to me. You give them back to me right now."

Junior slapped his thigh in frustration. "How many times do I have to say this? I don't have that stuff because I didn't break into your house."

"I'll pay you whatever you want," she persisted, ignoring his denial. She looked at the half-built house. "I'll pay for a first-rate crew to come here and finish this house for you. I'll double its size; give you a damn swimming pool, whatever you want." She drew right in front of him, one of her hands seizing his faded jean jacket in a very firm grip. "Whatever you or Lulu want I'll give you. But in return I want those things back. Just give them to me and all the charges go away, and you have yourself a really nice house. And you can keep the damn ring."

"Mrs. Battle, I—"

She slapped him across the face, stunning him into silence. He would have killed any man who did that to him. Yet he made no move to retaliate.

"But if you don't give them to me, I'll make you wish for twenty hard years in prison. You'll *beg* for that after I get through with you. I know people, Junior, don't think I don't. They'll come see you. You'll never forget their visit." She let go of his jacket. "I'll give you a little time to think about it, but not too much."

She turned to leave but then looked back at him. "One more thing, Junior. If you try to use any of it, in any way at all, or if you show it to another human being, I will come and see you myself. With a twelve-gauge shotgun that my daddy gave me right before he died. And I will blow your big, ugly head off your shoulders. Do you understand me, son?" This was all said in such a calm yet chilling tone that Junior could hear every one of his heartbeats smacking in his ears.

Remmy Battle didn't seem to think an answer to her question was necessary. She put her glasses back on, turned and left as quietly as she'd come.

Junior just stood there, his big belly heaving, and watched her go. He'd been in many a bar fight in his life against some very large men intent on doing him bodily harm; he'd even been cut up a few times. He'd been scared during those incidents. However, that was nothing compared with the terror he was feeling right now, for he had no doubt the crazy woman meant every word she'd just said.

CHAPTER

35

LATER THAT WEEK CHIP
Bailey of the FBI called an early morning meeting of all
law enforcement personnel engaged in the search for the
murderer or murderers of five people. It was held at the
Wrightsburg Police headquarters, which King—who was
in attendance along with Michelle, Todd Williams and assorted Virginia State Police and FBI folks—thought
made a cheap-shot statement as to who was now running
the show. The FBI, after all, was the eight-hundred-pound
gorilla. His resulting bad temper exhibited itself rather
quickly.

"We have a profile," said Bailey as his assistant handed
out folders to those situated around the table.

"Let me guess," said King. "Caucasian male in his
twenties to thirties, at least a high school education and
possibly even some college. I.Q. above average, but has
trouble holding a job; firstborn to working-class parents,
childhood trauma, dominant mother, possibly illegitimate, who showed interest in law enforcement and is a
loner control freak who also expressed early enthusiasm

for sadomasochistic pornography, voyeurism and torturing of small animals."

"Did you already get a copy of the report?" growled
Bailey.

"No. But most of them say that or something pretty
damn close."

"That's because serial killers share those sorts of traits.
That's been clearly established over time," Bailey fired
back. "In fact, everything in this profile has been substan-
tiated over time. Unfortunately, we've had lots of experience. Over three-quarters of the serial killers in the world
are in this country with well over one thousand murders
to their collective credit since 1977, and two-thirds of the
victims were women. The only interesting thing about
this guy is, he seems to be a mix of organized and disor-
ganized in his approach. Restraints used in one case but
not in the others. One victim transported, the others not.
One body hidden in the woods, the others left where they
fell. Weapon absent in one case, but not in the others. This
is based on hard data, Sean."

"Most of them probably do fit that profile, but not all.
Some don't fit neatly in any box."

"And you think this is one of those times?" asked
Williams.

"Think about it. None of the victims have been sexually assaulted or mutilated; in serial killings that's almost
always a component. And let's look at the targets. Most
serial killers aren't exactly brave. They grab for the low-
hanging fruit: children, runaways, prostitutes, young ho-
mosexual males and the mentally afflicted."

Bailey shot back, "One of the victims *was* an exotic

dancer and maybe a prostitute at some point. And two others *were* high school kids. And another was lying in a coma in a hospital bed. That's pretty easy pickings if you ask me."

"We don't know if Rhonda Tyler was a prostitute. And even if she was, was she killed because she was a prostitute or for some other reason? And Canney and Pembroke *weren't* runaways. And do you really think a Ted Bundy type killer is going to sneak into a hospital room and shoot stuff into an elderly stroke victim's IV bag?" He paused to let this all sink in and then added, "And Bobby Battle was a very wealthy man. There might be other people who wanted him dead."

"Meaning two killers out there?" said Bailey skeptically.

"Meaning we don't know, but we can't ignore that possibility," shot back King.

Bailey was undeterred. "I've had a little more experience doing this than you, Sean, and until something else turns up that causes me to change my mind, this is the profile we're using, and we're going under the assumption that we only have one killer at work." He eyed King closely. "I understand that you two have been deputized." He nodded at Michelle. "I want you to know that I have no problem with that. In fact, in my book, having two more seasoned professionals on the case is a good thing."

But, said King to himself.

"But," said Bailey, "we have established protocols for how we do things. We need to coordinate and keep each other informed. We all need to be on the same page."

Williams said through clenched teeth, "And of

course the Bureau will be the central clearinghouse for everything."

"That's right. If any promising leads come up, I want to know about them pronto. Then we can evaluate who's best suited to run them down."

King and Michelle exchanged brief glances. They seemed to be reading each other's mind. *That way Bailey and the Bureau can call all the shots, make the arrest and get all the credit.*

"Speaking of leads," said King, "do you have any?"

Bailey leaned back in his chair. "It's a little early to tell, but now that we've got the manpower out there, something will pop."

"Anything turn up on the Zodiac watch?" asked Michelle.

"Dead end," said Bailey. "There was no other trace of any significance at the crime scenes or on the bodies. We canvassed Diane Hinson's neighborhood. No one saw anything. We've talked to the families and schoolmates of Canney and Pembroke. There's no jealous rival out there with a guilty conscience."

"And Rhonda Tyler?" asked King. "What's her backstory?"

Bailey leafed through his notes. "Contrary to what you might think, the FBI does know how to assemble the facts, Sean," he said. "She was born in Dublin, Ohio. Dropped out of high school and hit the road to L.A. to become an actress. Right! After that dream popped, she developed a drug habit, headed east, did a little time in jail for a couple of misdemeanors and headed south. She'd been an exotic dancer for about four years in a string of clubs from Virginia to Florida. Her contract at the Aphrodisiac was up about two weeks before she was killed."

"Where was she staying when she disappeared?" asked Michelle.

"Not sure. The club has some rooms that the girls use when they're performing there. They're on the house and they come with three squares a day, so they're pretty popular with the strippers—excuse me, exotic dancers. I spoke with Lulu Oxley, the manager. She said that Tyler had stayed in one of those rooms for a while when she first came there but then found another place."

"While she was still working at the club?" asked King.

"Right. Why?"

"Well, these dancers can't make all that much money, so free room and board must be pretty hard to give up. Did she have any friends or family in the area she might have been staying with?"

"No. But we're trying to find out where she was staying during that time."

"That really needs to be followed up on, Chip," said King. "If she found herself a sugar daddy close to when she was murdered, we need to know who he is. It could very well be the guy who put a pistol in her mouth and left her for the wolves."

"Funny, we had the same thought," said Bailey, unable to hold back a sneer.

"Did you talk to the Battles yet?" asked Williams.

"I was going over there today," said the FBI man. "Care to join me?"

"Why don't you take Sean and Michelle along instead?"

"Fine," Bailey said, frowning.

After covering other points of the investigation, the meeting was adjourned. While Bailey gave additional orders to his men, Williams buttonholed King and Michelle. "Okay, I was right: the feds call the shots and take the glory."

"Maybe not, Todd," said Michelle. "I can't say they're being unreasonable. And it's more important that this psycho be caught, regardless of who does it."

"True. Still, it'd be a lot better if the people who nabbed him were *us*."

"We'll go to the Battles' and see what we can find out," said King. "But don't expect miracles, Todd. This guy knows what he's doing."

"The killer or Bailey?" he said irritably.

They drove over to the Battles' in separate cars, King and Michelle in the Whale and Bailey in his big sedan provided by the Bureau.

"The FBI always had better cars than the Secret Service," said King, eyeing Bailey's vehicle.

"Yeah, but we have better boats."

"That's because we snatched them from DEA, which confiscated them from South American drug lords."

"Hey, you do what you have to." She glanced at him. "By the way, what bee got into your bonnet at the meeting? Bailey had been pretty cooperative up until this morning. It was like you deliberately tried to piss him off."

"Sometimes that's the only way you find out what someone's really like."

As the large gates to the Battles' estate clanged shut

behind them, King said, "The one I'm worried about is Savannah."

"Savannah? Ms. Party Girl? What makes you say that?"

"Were you Daddy's little girl?"

"Well, yeah, I guess I still am."

"Well, once Daddy's little girl, always Daddy's little girl. And Savannah's daddy's gone."

CHAPTER

36

THERE WERE SEVERAL CARS parked in the motor court when they pulled up. Mason answered the door. Both King and Michelle detected it at the same time. As they followed the man in, she turned to King and whispered, "Does Mason look happier?"

"No," King whispered back. "More like he's gloating."

Remmy received them in the large library. They sat on big leather couches and watched as the lady of the house assembled herself in front of them, a queen before her court. She didn't look like a woman who had just lost her husband to murder, thought King. Yet Remmy rarely did things the way others would.

"A sad day for you, Remmy, I know," began Chip Bailey in a suitably sympathetic tone.

"I'm getting used to them," answered Remmy.

"We won't take too much of your time. I think you know Sean and Michelle."

"Yes, their last visit here was quite memorable."

King caught the edge to the woman's voice. *What exactly was memorable about it?*

Bailey cleared his throat. "You understand that Bobby's death was not from natural causes?"

"You're sure about that? It wasn't some medication foul-up?"

King briefly wondered if she'd asked because she was contemplating a lawsuit against the hospital but quickly decided she was after something else. If he could just figure out what.

"No, it was a deliberate overdose. The interaction would have been pretty quick. In fact, whoever did it probably entered your husband's room shortly after you left."

"Very shortly," added King. "Remmy, did you see anyone on your way out?"

"I left by the rear door as always. I saw some people when I got to the parking lot, but that's all. No one suspicious-looking or anything, if that's what you mean."

"How about anyone you recognized?" asked Michelle.

"No."

"And you arrived back here around what time?" asked Bailey.

Remmy looked at him pointedly. "Chip, should I take that question as meaning *I'm* under suspicion in my husband's death?"

There was an awkward silence until King broke it. "Remmy, this is an investigation. Agent Bailey here is only doing his job."

"If you don't mind, I'd like to handle this," said Bailey firmly.

Okay, thought King, *I tried to be your friend. You're on your own now, buckaroo.*

"Remmy, I have to establish where everyone was

when Bobby was killed. Just answer my question and we can move on."

At that moment Mason came in carrying a tray of coffee.

King noted that he'd already poured one for Remmy and now handed the cup to her.

Remmy said, "Thank you so much, Mason."

Mason smiled, did a half-bow to the lady and departed.

Remmy said, "I left the hospital around ten and drove home."

"Okay," said Bailey as he noted this down. "What time did you get here?"

"Around eleven or so."

"But the hospital's no more than thirty minutes from your house," King pointed out.

"I took a back road. I needed air; I drove slow, needed time to think."

"Can anyone verify when you got home?" asked Bailey.

Remmy seemed to bristle a bit but said, "Mason was still up and opened the door for me." She took a long sip of coffee. "Before I could even get my clothes off and get into bed, the phone rang and my husband was dead." She paused for a moment, seemingly studying the depths of her drink. "I called Eddie but he wasn't home."

"He was actually with us at the Sage Gentleman until a little after eleven," said King. "He was having dinner there and we joined him for a drink."

Remmy's left eyebrow hiked at this information. "Where was Dorothea?"

"At some function in Richmond, Eddie said."

Remmy snorted. "Function? She sure as hell goes to lots of those." She paused and said in a calmer tone, "I went right back to the hospital and saw my dead husband." She looked at all of them, one by one, as though daring them to challenge one word of what she was saying. "That ended the longest day of my life."

"Was there anything missing from Bobby's personal effects in the hospital?"

"No. I'm particular about that, even made the hospital put together an inventory list."

Bailey cleared his throat. "Remmy, this is going to be a difficult question to answer, but I want you to try."

Remmy seemed to stiffen. "What is it?" she said imperiously.

Bailey shot King a sideways glance before he spoke. "The other murders that seem connected to Bobby's death may not be. It's just possible that someone else killed him."

She put her cup down, sat forward and placed her hands on her knees. "What exactly is your question?"

"Just this: do you know anyone who'd want to hurt Bobby?"

She looked disappointed and sat back. "Every man has his enemies. A rich, successful man has more than most."

"Do you have anyone in particular in mind?"

"No, I don't."

"Remmy, we're just trying to get to the truth."

"So am I," she retorted.

King said, "With 'enemies' are you referring to business or personal?"

The woman's gaze swiveled to him now. "I'm sure I couldn't say. Now, if you'll excuse me, I have funeral arrangements to attend to, now that I've finally gotten back my husband's body from that *place*," she said, un-doubtedly referring to the undignified invasion of her husband's remains at the morgue.

"Remmy, we have more questions," said Bailey.

"And you know where to find me when you want to ask them," she said.

"Okay, we'll need to talk to Savannah. Is she around?"

Remmy had half risen and now stopped. "Why do you want to talk to her?"

"She was at the hospital on the day Bobby died."

"So what?"

"So that makes her someone I need to speak to," said Bailey very firmly. "You know, Remmy, I saved your son's life. I thought by that you'd realize I know what I'm doing."

King was waiting for her to erupt at this statement, but all she said was, "It might take a while. My daughter has never been an early riser." She left the room.

King couldn't help himself from asking, "So you're *not* discounting the two-killer angle, Chip?"

"In a murder investigation I don't discount anything. The fact that nothing was missing from Battle's room doesn't jibe with the other killings." He looked at King and Michelle. "So what do you two think?"

"I think the woman has her own agenda and is trying to get as much information out of us as we're trying to get out of her," answered Michelle promptly.

"And I think she won this round handily," said King with his gaze on Bailey.

CHAPTER

37

ON THE MORNING THAT the interrogation of the Battles was taking place, Kyle Montgomery sat in his apartment and fingered the new acoustical guitar he'd purchased with his drug profits. He strummed a few chords and sang a few words, his normal procedure when thinking intently. He finally put the guitar aside, slipped gloves on and pulled out a pencil and piece of paper and sat at his kitchen table. He thought about what to write and then how to write it. After several more minutes of contemplation he began to etch out large block letters. He made it halfway through, balled up the paper and threw it away. He did that twice more before settling on the final wording, chewing down a pencil in the process.

He sat back and read over it three times. It would no doubt get the person's attention; however, his dilemma was he didn't know if he actually possessed any black-mail information. Yet the beauty of it was that if the person *were* guilty, the wording of the letter would surely do its work. And his next message would carry with it a request for money, to be delivered in a very safe way that he'd think of in the meantime. He wondered how much it would be worth and then ultimately decided he couldn't determine that yet. He looked at his new guitar. One hour's work had brought that to him. One hour! When he slaved during the day for pennies! Well, maybe not too much longer.

He put the letter in an envelope, addressed it and then walked down to the corner mailbox and dropped it in. When the metal door of the postal box clanged shut, Kyle wondered for one terrifying second if he'd just made a huge blunder. However, that dread quickly left him. It was replaced by an even stronger emotion: greed.

They waited for forty-five minutes, and Bailey was just about to leave the room and find one of the household staff when Savannah Battle finally tottered into the library.

Where the mother had been all stone and ice, the daughter looked like a burning photograph a few seconds from curling up and disintegrating.

"Hello, Savannah," said King. "We're sorry we have to bother you now."

If she said something in response, none could hear it. She just stood there dressed in baggy sweatpants and a William and Mary T-shirt with no bra underneath. She was barefoot, her hair a tangled mess. Her nose and cheeks were so reddened it looked like she'd dived headfirst into a bottle of rouge. And she was chewing on her nails.

"Uh, Savannah, you want to take a seat?" asked Bailey.

The woman just stood there staring at the floor, her finger in her mouth. Michelle finally rose, guided her to the couch, poured her a cup of coffee and handed it to her. "Drink it," she said firmly.

Savannah cradled the cup in both hands and took a sip.

The ensuing interview was very frustrating. Savannah, when she did answer their questions, mumbled. When asked to repeat, she mumbled again. She'd gone to the hospital around lunchtime to see her father on the day he died. That much they managed to glean after several tedious attempts and misfires. She stayed about thirty minutes, saw no one and left. Her father was not conscious during that time. They didn't bother asking her if she had any reason to believe someone might want to kill her father. That required a level of mental acuity that the girl simply wasn't capable of right now. She'd been home the night of Bobby Battle's death but wasn't sure if anyone saw her.

As she slowly walked out of the room, Michelle touched King on the arm. "You were right. Daddy's little girl is rocked."

"But are we sure why?"

Chip Bailey received a phone call that caused him to have to make a hasty departure.

King and Michelle followed him to the front door, where King said, "We'll just hang here. You know, deputy stuff."

Bailey didn't look too pleased, but he had no grounds to argue the point.

"You're enjoying baiting him, aren't you?" said Michelle after the man had left.

"I look for the small pleasures of life wherever I can find them."

King and Michelle returned to the library, where Mason was clearing the tray.

"Here, let me help you." King reached over and pushed the coffee cups together, spilling the remains from one in the process.

"Sorry," said King. He dabbed up the spill with a napkin.

"Thanks, Sean," said Mason as he picked up the tray. They followed him into the enormous kitchen that was outfitted with professional-grade appliances and every gizmo a cook would need to transform food into art.

King whistled. "I wondered how the Battles could dish up all that wonderful cuisine at those functions I attended."

Mason smiled. "First-class. Mrs. Battle wouldn't have it any other way."

King perched on the edge of a table. "It's a good thing you were still up when Remmy came home that night. What with everything she's had to go through and all."

"It's been hard for the whole family," said Mason.

"I bet it has. So she got here around eleven?"

"Just that. I remember looking at my watch when I heard her drive up."

Michelle noted this down while King continued. "Were you still in the house when she got the phone call that Bobby had died?"

He nodded. "I was just finishing up some things and about to head out when she came running down the stairs. She was frantic, half-dressed, words coming out all jumbled. Took me a full minute to calm her down to where I could even understand her."

"She said she called Eddie to come get her."

"Only he wasn't home. I wanted to drive her to the hospital, but she told me to stay here in case anyone called. She left about ten minutes later. When she got back, she looked like a ghost, no light in her eyes at all."

Mason looked down, apparently embarrassed at his choice of words. "Anyway, then it turns out he was murdered. Now, Mrs. Battle's a strong person. She can take a shot with the best of them. But two shots and that close together, that's another story."

"She seemed very composed this morning," commented Michelle.

"She's resilient," he said, bristling. "And she has to be strong for everyone else."

"Yes, Savannah seemed a little out of it. I guess she and her father were really very close," said Michelle.

Mason offered no comment.

"Although she hasn't been home that much over the last few years."

"Hardly at all," said Mason. "Whether that's a good or bad thing I'm sure I couldn't say."

You already have, Mason, thought King. "Apparently, Savannah was home that night. I'm surprised that she didn't go to the hospital with Remmy."

"I don't know if she was home or not. If she was, I didn't see her."

"Can I speak frankly, Mason?" said King.

The man turned to him, looking a little surprised. "I guess so."

"Bobby's death might not be connected to the other killings."

"Okay," said Mason slowly.

"So if he was killed by someone else, we have to start looking at motivations."

Mason didn't say anything for a few seconds. "You mean one of the *family*?"

"Not necessarily, but that can't be discounted." He eyed the man keenly. "You've been with them a long time. It's easy to see you're far more than the hired help."

"I've been with them through the good and the bad," Mason said.

"Tell us about the bad," said King.

"Look, if you're trying to get me to say something that'll hurt Mrs. Battle—"

King interrupted. "All I'm trying to do is get to the truth, Mason."

"She would never have done anything like that!" he said sharply. "She loved Mr. Battle."

"And yet her wedding ring wasn't on her finger."

Mason started for a moment and then said, "I believe it needed repairs. She didn't want to risk further damage. I wouldn't read any more into it."

Nice comeback, thought King. "Anyone else you can think of?"

Mason thought about this but then shook his head. "I really couldn't say. I mean, I don't know anything like that," he added quickly.

Is it the former or the latter? wondered King. He produced one of his cards. "If something does occur to you, give us a call. We're far nicer than the FBI," he added.

As Mason walked them out, King stopped in front of a bookcase containing numerous photos. One in particular had caught his eye. He showed it to Mason.

"That's Bobby Jr., Eddie's twin. He was about fourteen when that picture was taken. He was born first by a few minutes; that's why he was the junior."

"You can't have been with the Battles that long," said Michelle.

"No. They'd bought this property and were building the house and they had the boys and they needed some help. I answered an ad and I've been here ever since. Other staff have come and gone, but I've always been here." His voice trailed off. He snapped back and looked at King and Michelle staring at him. "They've treated me really well. I could retire if I wanted."

"Any plans to do that?" asked Michelle.

"I can't exactly abandon Mrs. Battle now, can I?"

"I'm sure your presence here means a lot to her," said King.

Michelle looked at the young man's unnatural features in the photo. "What was wrong with Bobby Jr.?"

"He was severely mentally retarded. He was in bad shape when I started working for them. Then he got cancer and died soon after his eighteenth birthday."

"He was Eddie's twin but Eddie's fine," said King. "Isn't that unusual?"

"Well, that's what happened. They were fraternal twins."

"How did Eddie get along with his brother?"

"Did everything for him. Couldn't have been nicer. I

think Eddie knew it was only by the grace of God that it wasn't him."

"And Bobby Sr.?"

"Mr. Battle was really busy back then, traveling all over. He wasn't even here when Bobby Jr. died." He added quickly, "I have no doubt he loved the boy, though."

"It must have been pretty traumatic for Remmy when Eddie was kidnapped."

"If it hadn't been for Agent Bailey, she might have lost both her sons."

"Lucky he's on the case again," said King.

They left the house, but when Michelle started to walk over to the car, King took her arm. "It's a beautiful day. I feel like a stroll," he said, giving her a look.

"Where?"

"You'll see." He took out of his pocket the tissue he had used to clean up the coffee spill and sniffed it. He smiled at the result.

"What is it?" asked Michelle.

"Not a huge surprise, but Remmy enjoys a little bourbon with her coffee."

CHAPTER

38

KING'S CHOICE OF VENUE took them to the rear grounds. They wandered over to the spot where they could see Remmy's bedroom window. King gazed at the house where the servants lived and then back at their employer's window.

"If someone were really looking," he said vaguely.

Michelle said, "Mason definitely has a thing for Remmy. Maybe he hopes to become the new man of the estate."

King glanced over and saw the woman walking toward the stable.

"Let's go talk horses." As he was turning away, an image at one of the second-story windows caught his attention.

It was Savannah, staring at them. Yet she was gone so quickly that for an instant King wasn't even sure she'd really been there. Yet she had been. And the look on her face was clear: she was terrified.

They both greeted Sally Wainwright over by the stable. Her cheerful disposition wasn't evident today.

"God, I'm thinking about quitting," she said.

"Because Battle was murdered?" asked King.

"And four other people," said Sally as she looked over her shoulder as though for an attacker. "This was a nice, quiet town when I got here. Right now I'd probably be safer in the Middle East."

"I wouldn't do anything rash," said Michelle. "You'll probably live to regret it."

"I just want to live," Sally shot back.

King nodded. "Well, then maybe you can help us find the killer before he strikes again."

Sally looked shocked. "Me! I don't know anything."

"You may know something important, only you don't know that it is," said King. "For instance, can you think of anyone who might have intended Bobby Battle harm?"

Sally shook her head—too quickly, in King's mind.

"Come on, Sally, whatever you say goes no further."

"Sean, I really don't know anything."

He decided to try a different tack. "Why don't I throw out some possibilities, and then you can jump in if they trigger anything?"

She looked doubtful. "Well?"

"Battle was a wealthy man. People benefit from his death, right?"

"But I suppose Mrs. Battle would get most of it. And Savannah has her trust fund. I don't think she needs any more money."

"Eddie?"

Sally glanced in the direction of the carriage house. "They don't appear to be scraping dimes together. And I know for a fact that Dorothea Battle makes big bucks."

"How do you know that?" asked Michelle.

"My best friend does her nails. Dorothea likes to brag."

"Well, some people never have enough money," suggested King.

"I just don't see that being the reason," said Sally stubbornly.

"If not money, then what else?" He stared pointedly at the young woman. "I guess you probably haven't been here long enough to know about Bobby's adulterous past."

"Oh, I know more than you think," blurted out Sally. "I mean—" She stopped and looked at her dirty boots.

"It's okay, Sally," assured King, hiding his pleasure that she'd bit on his bait so quickly. "Do you know a lot about that because maybe Bobby made advances toward you?"

Sally shook her head. "No, it was nothing like that."

"So what, then?" pressed King. "It really could be important, Sally."

She remained silent a bit longer and then said, "Come on with me."

They walked past the stables and servants' house and down a paved roadway, eventually arriving at a large brick two-story building with eight old-fashioned wooden garage doors. There was an antique gas pump with a glass bubble top out front.

"This is Mr. Battle's private garage. He has, or *had*, a collection of antique cars. I guess Mrs. Battle owns them now." She pulled out a key and they entered.

The floor was covered in a black and white checkerboard pattern. The shelves held dusty trophies from antique car shows. In front of seven of the doors, sitting perfectly aligned with one another, were vintage cars ranging from a Stutz Bearcat to an imposing vehicle with cloth top and a round grille that the placard on the stand in front proclaimed to be a 1906 six-cylinder Franklin.

"I'd heard that Bobby collected old cars, but I didn't know his collection was this extensive," said King as he looked around.

"He has a bunch more on the second floor. There's a special elevator that takes them up and down," said Sally. "He used to have a full-time mechanic to take care of them." She walked down to the last space and stood. King and Michelle joined her. There was no car here. They looked at her questioningly.

She hesitated for an instant. "Look, you didn't hear this from me," she said. They both nodded in agreement. "Well, there used to be a car that sat right here. It was huge, you know, one of those big Rolls-Royces you see in the old movies?"

"What happened to it?" asked Michelle.

Sally hesitated again, as though debating whether to tell them.

Sensing this, King said, "Sally, you've gone this far."

"Okay, it was over three years ago. It was late at night, and I'd slipped down here just to look around. I wasn't supposed to have a key, but the mechanic who used to work here took a liking to me and gave me one. I was inside looking around when I heard a car coming. It was then that I noticed that one of the cars wasn't there. The door started opening and I saw the headlights. I was scared to death and sure I was going to be fired if they found me here. I ran and hid over there." She pointed to a tower of fifty-gallon oil drums that sat in one corner. "The

Rolls pulled into the garage and the motor was cut off. Mr. Battle got out and he looked bad. I mean really bad."

"How could you tell? Wasn't it dark?" asked King.

"There's an automatic trigger on the doors. At night when the doors go up, the lights come on in here."

"When you say he looked bad, how do you mean?" asked Michelle. "Sick? Drunk?"

"No, like he was really upset, worried."

"Did you ever find out what about?" asked King.

"No. Anyway, like I said, he looked bad, but then all of sudden he started smiling and then he started laughing. Laughing! Well, he did, until she showed up."

"She who, Remmy?" said King.

Sally nodded and said in a hushed tone, "If she'd had a gun, I think Mr. Battle would've been dead a long time ago."

"What happened then?" asked Michelle.

"They started arguing. Well, at first, she just was screaming at him. Not much of it made sense. But from what I could hear, there was another woman involved."

"Did it seem like Remmy knew who?" asked King sharply.

"If she did, she never mentioned her name, at least not that I heard," said Sally.

"What did Bobby do?"

"He started yelling, told her it was none of her damn business who he slept with."

"And to think I was halfway admiring the man," said Michelle in disgust.

"Well, he said something else I'll never forget," said

Sally. She paused, drew a quick breath and looked at them anxiously.

"Go ahead," said King. "I don't think anything will surprise us now."

"Mr. Battle said he wasn't the only one in the family who practiced that philosophy."

"Of sleeping around?" said King, and Sally nodded.

Michelle and King looked at each other. "And you think he was referring to Remmy?" she asked.

"I just assumed he was. But Mrs. Battle always seemed so proper and . . ."

"Supportive of her husband," suggested King.

"Yes, exactly."

"Public faces can often be deceiving," he commented.

"And the Rolls?" asked Michelle.

"It just disappeared after that night. I don't know what happened to it. In fact, Billy Edwards—he was the mechanic who used to take care of the cars—he was gone too. That's when Mr. Battle lost interest in his collection. He never came down after that, as far as I know."

"You never saw this Billy Edwards before he left?"

"No, his place was cleaned out the next day. I don't know who came and took the car. It must have been at night, or else someone would have seen it driving off."

"Thank you, Sally, you've been a big help."

They left Sally and headed back to the front of the house.

"So what do you make of that?" asked Michelle.

"It creates lots of questions. Who was Bobby seeing back then? Was the reference to sleeping around actually directed at Remmy? And why get rid of the car?" King looked pensive. "I wonder if there's any chance of tracking down this Billy Edwards and asking him about it."

"What about going directly to Remmy?"

"She'd want to know how we found out about it. And Sally's obviously not good at hiding her feelings. One look from Remmy and she'd crack. We may have to at some point, but for now we'll look for another way."

"We keep uncovering more questions and no answers," said Michelle.

"At some point the tide has to turn. We just may not like the answers we find, though."

CHAPTER

39

DOROTHEA AND EDDIE
Battle weren't home, so King and Michelle drove to the
Aphrodisiac that afternoon to speak with Lulu Oxley
about the murdered exotic dancer, Rhonda Tyler.

The parking lot was already filling up with the lunch
crowd when they arrived. As they walked past one of the
bar areas, they caught glimpses of the nearly naked ladies
dancing and the men staring and catcalling.

"I just don't get the attraction," said Michelle.

"The product isn't exactly directed at someone like
you."

"Come on, are you saying you find watching something
like that enjoyable?"

"No, but I'm afraid I'm in a minority among my gen-
der." He smiled and added, "That comes with being intel-
ligent, sophisticated and sensitive."

They were directed back to Lulu's small, cluttered office, where they found her hard at work and not looking
happy about being interrupted.

"I've told the FBI and Chief Williams everything,"

said Lulu as she snapped her lighter shut and took a drag on a fresh cigarette.

"Well, we're deputies now, so you can tell us too," said King pleasantly as he showed her his badge.

She sighed, took another puff and sat back in her chair.

"In case you hadn't heard, the surgeon general has proclaimed cigarette smoking really bad for you," said Michelle, waving the fumes away from her face.

"The surgeon general doesn't run a gentleman's club," Lulu shot back.

"We'll be happy to breathe the secondhand smoke so long as you tell us about Rhonda Tyler," said King.

"Okay, for the third time and counting, Rhonda Tyler aka whatever the hell her stage name was . . ."

"Tawny Blaze," said Michelle helpfully.

"Right, good memory," said Lulu, eyeing the woman keenly. "Anyway, she came to work here under contract. She stayed in one of the club's rooms, but shortly before her stint was up, she told us she had another place to crash. She did her contract time, and that was the last I saw of her. We'd used her before, and she'd always acted like a real professional, never any problem."

"Did she mention whether she had friends or family in the area?"

"Not to me. But with her line of work, family tends to shy away from you."

"How about a man she might have met?" prompted Michelle.

Lulu tapped ash off her cigarette into an empty paper coffee cup on her desk. "Not that I know of."

"Anyone else she might have confided in?" asked King.

"She might have talked to some of the girls."

"Can we speak with them?"

"If you can wake them up. The ones who work nights don't get out of bed until late in the afternoon. The lunch-shift girls are out onstage now."

"We'll give it our best shot," said King.

"You do that," said Lulu again, watching Michelle closely.

As they headed to the door, Michelle glanced back and saw Lulu's hand disappear inside her desk drawer. When Lulu pulled it out, there was nothing in it. Michelle looked away before the other woman could see her staring.

Lulu said, "By the way, here's a piece of information you might find interesting: the high-and-mighty Remmy Battle threatened Junior."

Both of them stared at her as she summarized the meeting between the two, including Remmy's offer to pay off Junior if he returned the stolen items.

"So she wanted something that was in the drawer, but didn't care about her wedding ring?" asked a confused King.

"Apparently, the lady has something to hide."

"Where will Junior be today?"

"Working a job in Lynchburg; you won't be able to see him. But this evening he'll be at the house he's building for us."

"Let me have the directions. And give me Junior's cell

phone number." As she did so, King asked one more question. "Did Bobby Battle ever come here?"

Lulu seemed to be trying hard not to look surprised at the question. "I think I saw him around here a few times."

"Recently?"

"What do you consider recently?"

"In the last couple of years."

"I couldn't say for sure."

I'm sure you couldn't, thought King. "Well, thanks again for all your help."

"I'll show you where the rooms are," offered Lulu.

She led them upstairs and pointed to the hallway fronted by the red curtain.

"Good luck," she said in a tone that didn't sound like she actually meant it.

As King and Michelle started off, Lulu touched Michelle on the arm. "Uh, can I ask you a question?" she said.

"We've asked *you* enough, so go ahead."

"You ever consider pole dancing?"

"Excuse me!" said Michelle, clearly stunned.

"It's just that you've got the perfect all-American, girl-next-door, come-hither thing going on. That's pretty rare in this business. You're leaner than the other gals and a little light in the chest, but I don't think the guys will mind once they see what you *do* have."

Michelle's face reddened. "You must be kidding!"

"The pay's better than you think, and you keep all the tips you get. And you can pull the night shift and still work your regular job during the day. State law doesn't allow total nudity in any strip club, so you can keep your

G-string on. But the top has to come off, that's club policy. No boobs, no bucks."

Michelle smiled tightly. "Let me put it this way: the day you see me pole dancing with only a G-string on in front of a crowd of drunken morons is the day the sky falls and kills all of us."

"I don't know," said King, who'd listened intently to this exchange. "I'd tip at least twenty bucks to see that."

CHAPTER

40

KING AND MICHELLE walked down the hallway, slipped behind the heavy red curtain and started knocking on doors. Several rooms were unlocked and unoccupied. From the others issued either a string of profanities or sleepy groans. Whenever a door was unlocked and opened—always by a scantily clad young woman with an extremely weary look—Michelle asked the same question while King averted his eyes.

"Didn't really know her," was the constant refrain. However, at the next-to-last room on the hall the voice said, "Come on in." Michelle did so. When she exited a couple of minutes later, she appeared truly shaken.

"You okay?" asked King.

"I was just propositioned by a six-foot-tall naked woman named Heidi."

"I can wait out in the car if you want."

"Shut up!"

"Must've been the come-hither look."

At the last room the door was opened by a young

woman wearing a long robe that didn't entirely hide her
heavy curves and inflated bosom. Her dyed-blond hair
was in a ponytail, and her feet were bare. She was sipping
a cup of black coffee. She introduced herself only as Pam,
and after they had told her what they wanted, she actually
invited them in.

They sat at a small table around which were placed
four chairs. The room looked comfy enough, although
King caught himself staring at the rumpled bed in the corner and the array of lingerie piled there. He turned to find
Michelle's severe gaze on him.

"So you knew Rhonda?" asked King.

"Yes, sir."

King ran his eye over her. She was so young-looking
that had he seen her half-naked rubbing against a pole, he
would have probably thrown a blanket over her and called
her father to come retrieve her. "Have the police already
talked to you?"

"Yes, sir, the FBI actually. That's what they said they
were anyway."

"Can you tell us what you told them?"

"Yes, sir."

"You don't have to call me sir, Pam. I'm Sean, this is
Michelle."

Pam looked at her stubby toes with the cracked polish
and crossed one pudgy foot over the other. "Sorry, I guess
I'm sorta nervous, Sean."

Michelle patted her hand. "There's nothing to be nervous about."

"I mean with Rhonda getting killed and all. I guess it

could've been any one of us, though Rhonda took chances I never would."

"What sort of chances?" asked King.

"We worked the same clubs together. She'd go off with men she didn't even know if they were nice to her. I only been doing this a couple of years, and I know better than that. But she always came back." Pam dabbed at some tears. "Only this time she didn't."

"Do you have any idea whom she went off with this time?" asked Michelle.

"No. Like I told them others, sometimes she tells me before she goes, other times not. This time she didn't." She took a sip of her coffee and wiped her thick lips with the back of a shaky hand. King noted that her red nail polish was chipped.

"When was the last time you saw her?"

"Couple of weeks before they found her. Our contracts were up here, but I signed on for another month. I like it here. The pay's good, and the folks here treat us nice. Not that many places give you a room and meals and all."

"And no customers back here to bother you, I take it," said King.

"No, sir, none of that," she said. "They're real particular about that."

"Did you ever see her with anyone, a man you didn't know? Did she mention anyone she was seeing?"

"No, nothing like that. Sorry."

He handed her one of his cards. "If you remember anything else, give us a call."

Both lost in thought, King and Michelle walked outside to her truck.

King was eyeing the full parking lot. "Hard to believe people find the time in the middle of the day to come here."

"It's pretty sick if you ask me," said Michelle. She was still frowning as she settled behind the wheel. "Do you know you have to be twenty-one to watch strippers, but you only have to be eighteen to *be* one? How does that make sense?"

King lowered himself into the passenger seat. "Granted it's ridiculous and degrading. Is that why you're in such a bad mood?"

"No! The *legendary* Aphrodisiac was a complete waste of time, that's why."

"How can you say that? Not only did you get a job offer as a pole dancer, which could actually come in handy when our firm's going through the inevitable lean times, but you also might have a real friend in Heidi."

A second later King was rubbing his arm where she'd slugged him. "Damn, that really hurt, Michelle," he complained.

"And it'll hurt even more if you keep it up."

CHAPTER

41

JUNIOR DEAVER STEPPED outside his half-built house and looked at the dark sky. The man was tired, having worked all day on other people's jobs before heading here to drive nails into shingles and plywood. He'd finished right before the light was gone, and then worked some on the inside. They were all looking forward to getting out of the cramped trailer.

However, the upcoming criminal trial was weighing heavily on his mind. Lulu never stopped talking about it. Could be the ruin of all our dreams, she kept saying. What if Mrs. Battle sued them? It would all be over. Then his mother-in-law would start in, and once started, Priscilla Oxley never shut up. Junior had experienced many lows in life. This one ranked right up there with the worst.

He thought about Remmy Battle's offer. If only he had something to give her. It pissed him off that no one seemed to believe him. Yet with all the evidence stacked against him he could understand how the woman thought he was guilty.

As he munched on a sandwich and sipped a beer he'd pulled from his cooler, he mulled over some things in his head. He could end this thing right now if he wanted—just tell the truth of what he'd been doing that night—but he'd rather go to jail. He just couldn't do that to Lulu. It'd been stupid, really stupid. But he couldn't take it back now.

He finished his sandwich. His cell phone was vibrating with a box full of messages. He hated the damn thing; everybody wanted something right now. He checked the list of calls. One had him puzzled: Sean King. *Wonder what he wants,* Junior thought. Well, it would have to wait.

He went back inside. It was almost eight o'clock, definitely time to call it a day. He'd been up since four in the morning. His back was killing him from climbing up and down the ladder with the shingles. He was getting too old for this kind of labor. Yet he expected to be doing it until he dropped. What else was there for a guy like him?

The blow came from directly behind him, actually cracking his skull and staggering the big man. Junior clutched his head and in the same motion wheeled around. Through the blood pouring down his face he saw the black hood coming at him, shovel upraised. He managed to block the blow with his forearm, though it shattered it. He fell back, yelling from the pain. As he lay on the cold wooden floor, he saw the shovel coming at him again. He managed to swing out his right leg and knocked the person's feet out from under him.

The man landed hard but sprang back up. Junior sat back on his butt, holding his broken arm. His big belly heaving, he kept kicking at his attacker, trying to keep him back as he scuffled away. His sandwich and beer came back up on him, covering the wooden subfloor with vomit. He managed to half raise himself, but another blow caught him across the back, and he went down again.

Junior Deaver was over six-four and weighed about 270 pounds. If he could just get in one shot on his smaller opponent, he knew things could change quickly. He'd kill the son of a bitch. Considering how badly he was already injured, Junior figured he had only one chance at this. Having been in his share of bar fights, he had some experience to draw on. He plotted to sucker his attacker in.

He knelt down, his head almost touching the floor, as though helpless. When he saw the shovel rise, he shot forward and hit his attacker directly in the gut, carrying them both across the room, where they crashed through a wall of studs.

They both hit the floor and sprawled away from each other. Junior tried to hold on to the smaller man, but the pains in his arm and shoulder were too intense. And blood was leaching through the fissure in his skull, putting pressure on his brain and causing his motor skills to rapidly deteriorate. Junior struggled to reach his feet, but the other man was quicker. He rolled away, picked up a piece of one of the broken studs and repeatedly beat Junior over the head with it, his blows becoming harder and more savage; the two-by-four splintered, popping out bent nails, and finally split in half. Junior moaned, went down, rolled over and didn't get back up. His belly heaving, blood flowing from multiple head wounds, he just lay there, his eyes closed.

The man in the hood approached cautiously, wary of another trick. He first cursed Junior and then himself for having so underestimated his target. He was sure a direct blow from a shovel to the back of the head would have felled the man. He calmed, cleared his head, told himself he had to finish the job. *So get on with it.*

His own stomach heaving, his throat cottony and a swell of lactic acid in his muscles making him dizzy, he knelt next to Junior and slipped the rounded piece of wood and length of rope out of his coat. He placed the tourniquet over Junior's head, settled it around his thick neck and slowly started to tighten until he could hear Junior gurgling for air. He kept turning it steadily, keeping constant pressure. A few minutes later the big belly heaved once more and then stopped.

The man let go of the wood and sat back on his haunches. He felt his shoulder where the impact with Junior and the studs had done him injury. He could live with that. Far more problematic was that the fight had put potential evidence in play. Using Junior's generator light, he methodically examined himself. He was covered in the man's blood, retch and mucus. Fortunately, he was wearing his hood, gloves and long sleeves because even one pulled-out hair with DNA root attached from his head or arms could prove a forensic nightmare for him.

He scoured the area and then the dead man for anything that would give him away to the likes of Sylvia Diaz. He spent much time probing under Junior's fingernails for any telltale human debris that might have ended up there. Finally comfortable that he hadn't left significant traces of himself lying around, he pulled the clown mask from his other coat pocket and placed it next to the body. It had crumpled upon Junior's impact with him, but even so, the police could hardly miss the intended meaning.

He checked Junior's pulse to ensure there was none, then sat there for five more minutes and checked it again. Subtle changes in the body upon death were well known to him, and satisfyingly, they were all taking place here. The man was gone. He reached over and gingerly raised Junior's left hand. He pulled out the watch stem and set it precisely to five o'clock—the same reading the impostor had set Bobby Battle's watch to. This would send a clear message to the police and to the impostor. He wanted them both to be informed. Instead of propping up the arm, he laid the hand back down and then pulled a black marker out from Junior's tool belt and drew an arrow on the plywood floor pointing directly to the watch. Lastly, he removed Junior's big belt buckle with a NASCAR logo and slipped it into his pocket.

The sound startled him badly until he realized what it was. Junior's cell phone was buzzing. It had fallen off in the fight. He looked at the screen. The caller ID showed that home was calling. Well, they could call all they wanted. Junior was never going home again.

He stood on shaky legs, looked down at the man with the tourniquet noose around his neck and then at the clown mask next to him, and his mouth eased into a smile. *Once more for justice,* he said to himself. He didn't intend to pray over Junior's body. With a swipe of his foot he turned off the battery-powered generator, and the area was plunged into darkness; the dead man disappeared as though by magic.

The next sound he heard shook him to his core.

It was the sound of an approaching car. He raced to the cutout of one of the front windows. Headlights were slicing through the darkness, coming right at him.

CHAPTER

42

KING AND MICHELLE climbed out of the Lexus and looked around. They'd switched vehicles at King's houseboat because one of Michelle's truck headlights was out. King pulled out a flashlight, but its thin beam did little damage against the darkness.

"His truck's here," said Michelle as she tapped the side of the battered pickup crammed with tools and construction supplies in the bed.

"Junior!" King cried out. "It's Sean King. We want to talk to you."

Michelle cupped her hands around her mouth. "Junior! Junior Deaver!"

They looked at each other.

"Maybe he's in the house."

"What, working in the pitch-dark?" said King.

"In the basement maybe and we can't see the light from here."

"Okay, so I guess we go in."

"Do you have another flashlight in your car?"

"No, but maybe Junior has one in his truck."

They looked and found one on the floorboard. Now twin beams moved through the dark.

They entered the front door and looked around.

"Junior," called out King again.

They swept the room with their lights. Over in one corner a big tarp was covering what looked to be a pile of drywall. All around were stacked wood and other building materials, tools, buckets, and bags of cement, a real mess.

"Hey, this looks just like your house," said King.

"Boy, you're in fine form today. Look, the basement steps are over here."

Michelle called down the stairs. There was no answer.

"Do you think he's hurt himself?" she said.

King looked around. "This is beginning to look a little weird," he said quietly. "Why don't you . . . ?"

Michelle already had her gun out. They went cautiously down the stairs.

In the far corner of the basement was a stack of cans. They looked behind this. Nothing. The HVAC system was in another corner of the basement. They shone their light on the mass of metal but again saw nothing.

Behind one of the large heating ducts in a space the light had missed, the man in the hood watched as they headed back upstairs. He slowly eased out of his hiding place.

Upstairs King and Michelle looked around more thoroughly. Michelle saw it first.

"Oh, no!" she hissed. She grabbed King's hand and pulled him toward her.

"Blood," she whispered in his ear, and then pointed her

light at the floor. The crimson spatters were clearly visible. Their lights followed the trail to its source: the tarp.

They crept forward, careful not to step in the spatters. King knelt, lifted up the tarp, and they saw it was Junior. King quickly felt for a pulse and found none.

"Damn it! He's dead." He shone his light around. "Oh, shit!"

"What!"

"He's got a noose tourniquet around his neck."

"Don't tell me . . ."

King pulled back the tarp some more and shone his light down the dead man's arm. "And his watch is set to five, and there's a black arrow drawn on the floor pointing right to it."

Michelle directed her light to Junior's features. "He hasn't been dead long, Sean."

"I know; he's still warm." King froze. "What was that?"

Michelle looked behind her, her light making arcs through the darkness. "What?"

"I thought I heard footsteps."

"I didn't hear anything—" Her breath caught in her throat as she saw the red laser dot appear on King's head. Its meaning was crystal clear to the firearm-savvy Maxwell. "Sean, don't move," she said hoarsely. "You're red-lighted."

"I'm wha—" But then it dawned on him what she was saying. The laser aim tracker could be followed at any moment by a bullet that would hit precisely where the dot was: in this case his brain.

As she watched, the red dot slowly moved to Michelle's gun, flitting there like some deadly wasp ready to sting. This message was also clear. She hesitated, debating whether to chance it, turn and fire. She glanced at King. He'd obviously seen the dot's location too and, reading her thoughts about trying to get off a shot, shook his head in a definite no.

She reluctantly put down her gun on the floor, pushing it away with her foot. When the red dot appeared on her flashlight, she turned it off and placed it on the floor. King slowly followed suit. The red dot then appeared on her chest and moved up and down her body, seemingly in a teasing manner, as though the person aiming the laser were fondling her.

Michelle was growing more and more irritated and beginning to gauge how far she'd have to jump to grab her weapon. While she was calculating the odds of getting off a shot before the other guy did, she failed to notice that the red dot had disappeared.

Finally realizing it, she looked at King's image in the shadowy darkness.

"Is he gone?" she said softly.

"Don't know," King whispered back. "I don't hear anything."

That changed moments later when they heard the gunshots. They both hit the floor, Michelle crawling desperately toward where she thought her gun was. One inch, one foot. *Come on! Come on!* As her fingers closed around the metal, she stopped and listened.

"Sean, are you okay?"

Seconds went by and there was nothing.

"Sean!" she whispered desperately, her hopes bottoming out when he didn't answer.

"I'm okay," he finally said.

"Damn it, you almost gave me a heart attack. Why didn't you say anything?"

"Because I fell on top of Junior, that's why!"

"Oh."

"Yeah, oh."

They waited a few more minutes. When they heard a car start up in the distance, Michelle leaped to her feet, grabbed a light and raced out, King right on her heels.

They slid into the Lexus.

"Call 911," said King. "Tell them to get the roads around here shut down as fast as possible. And then get hold of Todd."

Michelle was already on the phone.

King hit the gas and the car lumbered forward. The ride was so bumpy it knocked the phone out of Michelle's hand. He hit the brakes.

They looked at each other.

"Damn it, he shot out the tires," said King in disbelief. "That's what the gunshots were about. Let me see if I can still drive it." After a hundred feet it was very clear that if they drove over five miles an hour, they'd soon break an axle.

Michelle jumped out of the car and shone the light at the flattened front and rear tires on her side. She ran back and examined Junior's truck. There were two tires shot out there as well. Michelle called 911, gave them the information, then called Todd while King slumped against his car.

When she was finished, she came over to him and said, "Todd and his men are on their way."

"That's good to know," he said quietly.

"You never know; they might get lucky and nail the guy, Sean."

"The good guys are rarely that lucky." He crossed his arms over his chest and stared back at the half-built house.

Michelle slapped her hand against the car's hood. "God, I feel like the biggest rookie in the world for letting that guy get the drop on us. I can't believe we were probably ten feet from this maniac. Ten feet! And he got away." She grew silent, staring at the ground before glancing over at her partner. "Okay, talk to me, what are you thinking?"

He didn't answer right away. When he spoke, his voice quivered slightly. "I'm thinking that tonight three little kids lost their father and a wife her husband. And I'm just wondering when it's going to stop."

"Not until someone stops him."

King never took his eyes off the unfinished house. "Well, starting right now, that's our full-time job."

CHAPTER

43

As KING HAD PRE-
dicted, the police arrived too late to catch Junior's killer.
When news of yet another murder became public, the entire area fell into a complete frenzy. The mayor of
Wrightsburg, in a stunning show of no confidence in either Todd Williams or the FBI, demanded that the National Guard be called out and martial law declared.
Fortunately, no one granted that request. The national
news machine had descended on Wrightsburg and its en-
virons with an enormous appetite for detail, no matter
how trivial or irrelevant to the investigation. The large
media trucks and their sky antennae and news jockeys
with wireless mikes in hand became as ubiquitous as the
sprouting spring buds. The only people happy about this
situation were the local restaurateurs, innkeepers and
conspiracy buffs, who could be heard spouting endless
theories. Nearly everyone was grabbing for their fifteen
minutes of fame.

Todd Williams was inundated by the journalistic del-
uge, as was Chip Bailey. Even King and Michelle failed to

entirely escape the flood, watching in dismay as details of their previous high-profile investigative exploits were dredged up and made part of the current story.

More law enforcement resources were called in, both federal and state, and King wondered if the additional manpower was helping or hurting the investigation. The latter seemed to be the case as everyone jockeyed for position.

The letter finally came. It proclaimed that the killer of Junior Deaver was now imitating the clown prince of darkness, at least in serial killer circles: John Wayne Gacy. *And you thought he only killed young men and boys,* the message tauntingly read. *Now you know he doesn't mind knocking off big fat rednecks like Junior Deaver.*

They were all at another early morning task force meeting at the police station. The large conference room had been turned into a war room of sorts with banks of computers and telephones manned twenty-four/seven, charts, maps, stacks of files, highly specialized personnel running down all leads, tons of coffee and doughnuts and not one viable suspect anywhere in sight.

"Gacy strangled many of his victims using that ligature technique," explained Chip Bailey.

"You certainly know your serial killers," said Michelle.

"I should. I've spent years tracking them down."

"And in prison the big, jolly fellow started doing paintings of clowns," added King, "which accounts for the mask, just in case we couldn't figure it out solely from the hangman's tourniquet."

"And Junior's watch was definitely set to five o'clock,"

said Michelle. "So either our serial murderer can't count or whoever killed Bobby Battle was a copycat."

"I think we can assume there are two killers out there," conceded Bailey. "Although there's an outside possibility that there's only one killer and he's messing with the numbers for some reason."

"What, he's angling to be charged with five killings instead of six?" asked King. "I don't know about other places, but in Virginia they only execute murderers *once*."

Williams groaned and reached for the Advil. "Damn, my head's starting to hurt again."

"Have you seen Bobby Battle's will?" asked Michelle.

Williams swallowed the pills and nodded. "The vast bulk of his estate was left to Remmy."

"Did they hold the property by joint tenancy?" asked King.

"No. A lot was in Bobby's name only, including all his patents. The house went to Remmy automatically, and she had substantial property of her own."

"You said the vast bulk. Where did the remainder go?"

"Some charities. A little bit to Eddie and Dorothea. Not nearly enough to kill for, though."

"How about Savannah?" asked King.

"No, she got nothing. But she already had a big trust fund."

"But still, not to leave her anything, that was pretty callous."

"Maybe they weren't all that close," said Bailey.

King looked at him. "How well do you know the family?"

"Eddie and I see each other pretty regularly. We hunt

together, and I've gone to some of his reenactments. He's come down to Quantico and toured the FBI Academy. In fact, Remmy and Bobby came down for that, and Mason, the butler, too. I own a couple pieces of Eddie's artwork. Dorothea helped me find my house in Charlottesville. I spent an afternoon with them after his father was killed. It shook him, I can tell you that. I actually think he was more concerned about the effect it had on his mother."

King nodded. "Well, he couldn't have killed his father. He was with us."

"And he was away fighting at reenactments when Rhonda Tyler and Canney and Pembroke were killed," said Bailey.

"How about Dorothea?" asked Michelle.

"We checked. She's clean too."

"At the time Bobby Battle died too?" asked King.

"Well, she said she was driving to Richmond for a meeting the next morning."

"Alone?"

"Yes."

King said, "So she really doesn't have an alibi either. Speaking of Dorothea, do you know her well?"

"Like I said, she was my Realtor. But I don't think she's crying herself to sleep because Bobby's dead."

"Happy marriage?" asked Michelle.

"Eddie loves her, I know that. I'm not sure how much that's reciprocated. Actually, between you and me, it wouldn't surprise me if she was catching some action on the side."

"And Savannah said she was home when her father died. Was she?"

"I asked the hired help about that, but they'd all gone to their house by that time, except for Mason, and he doesn't remember seeing her. And she wasn't exactly hitting on all cylinders when we talked to her. I'm going to have to question her again."

"So she's still a suspect too. What about Bobby and Remmy?" asked King.

"What about them?"

"If I told you we had information they'd had a knock-down-drag-out three or four years ago over Bobby's sleeping around, would that surprise you?"

"No. He had that reputation. Some people thought he was over it, but old dogs rarely change their spots."

"Which might be an awfully good motive for killing her husband," said Michelle.

"Possibly," said Bailey.

"How about Remmy?" asked King.

"What, that she slept around?" King nodded. "No, never," said Bailey emphatically.

"Mason seems to really think a lot of Remmy," King said.

"I have no doubt he does, but he's not in her league and never will be, if that's what you're implying."

King stared at Bailey for a few seconds, then decided to change the subject. He looked over at Williams. "Has Sylvia finished the post on Junior?"

"Yep," answered Williams, who'd recovered enough from his misery to devour a chocolate doughnut and two cups of coffee. "He died from ligature strangulation, although he'd been beaten over the head with a shovel and a piece of wood prior to that. Damn lot of blood."

"We know," said King dryly.

"Right," said the chief. "Anyway, Sylvia thinks she might have some trace on the guy this time. And the tech team pulled up some fibers that didn't match anything Junior had on. And we also got a partial tire track nearby. Might be the car he got away in."

"Better check those fibers against my clothes," said King. "I . . . I had some contact with Junior when the shooting started."

"Speaking of shooting, you got the bullets from the tires?" asked Michelle.

"They were forty-four calibers," said Williams. "Nothing special. Hope we get a gun to match it against at some point."

"The guy had a laser aimer, that's pretty specialized," said King.

"Junior's belt buckle was also missing," noted Williams.

"Another trophy," said Michelle.

"Looks like Junior fought hard," said Bailey. "Lots of defensive wounds on his hands and forearm. And a wall of studs was taken out, probably during the struggle."

"The guy's clearly started to make some mistakes," said Williams. "You two happening along when you did really put a wrench into the works for him."

"I don't think we accomplished all that much," said Michelle, "except let him get away."

King studied the copy of the letter again. "This is the first time he's referred to a victim by name," he said.

"I noted that," said Bailey.

"Now, why would a killer do that?" wondered Williams.

"He's playing with us. He wants to jerk us around."

"For what purpose?" asked Michelle.

"Because this is all part of something a lot bigger that we're not seeing right now," replied King.

"And what might that be?" asked Bailey in a skeptical tone.

"When I figure it out, you'll be the *second* to know," said King, glancing significantly at Williams. "How did Lulu take it, Todd?" asked King in a softer tone.

Williams leaned back and shrugged his shoulders. "Didn't cry at all, but then, the kids were around. That mother of hers, though, damn lady went hysterical, screaming about how much she loved Junior, what in the world were they going to do without him. Lulu finally had to take her out of the room. Piece of work she is."

King and Michelle looked at each other and just shook their heads.

"Now we come to an interesting point," said Williams. "You told us that Remmy threatened Junior. That she wanted some things back and she didn't want Junior showing them to anyone."

King nodded. "At least that's what Lulu told us that Junior said. But it wasn't Remmy Battle who beat Junior up before strangling him to death."

"But Lulu said Remmy told Junior that she knew people."

King shook his head. "I'm not sure why Remmy would want to kill him, at least not now. According to Lulu, she was going to give Junior some time to think it over. If he's dead, he can't very well tell her where the stuff is—not that he could anyway, since I don't believe he took it in the first place."

"But if he's dead," said Bailey, "then he can't show the stuff, whatever it is, to someone else."

King remained unconvinced. "But Remmy couldn't be sure of that. He might have made arrangements in case something happened to him."

"You've got a point there," said Williams. "But it's still something we'll have to check into. Not that I'm looking forward to going down that road with Remmy."

"Well," said King, "we've got people to see and places to go."

"Where and who?" asked Bailey sharply.

"Steve Canney's father and Janice Pembroke's parents."

"We already talked to them. And to everyone connected to Diane Hinson too."

"But you don't mind another set of eyes," said Michelle.

"Go ahead," said Williams. "You have full authority."

"Just report back to me if you find anything interesting," said Bailey.

"I'll count the minutes," muttered King.

CHAPTER

44

KING AND MICHELLE drove to their office to do some work before heading out to see Pembroke's and Canney's parents. The silver Volvo station wagon and BMW Eight Series were parked in front of their office.

"Eddie and Dorothea," said Michelle as she got out of the Whale. As if on cue the doors opened on each of the vehicles and the pair got out.

"Driving separate cars," commented Michelle in a low voice.

"And maybe going in separate directions."

Eddie was dressed in gray dress slacks, white shirt and a blue blazer and carried a leather briefcase. With his deep tan and strong, weathered features, plus the nice clothes, he looked very handsome, Michelle noted appreciatively.

Dorothea was dressed all in black, which seemed appropriate under the circumstances, but King knew it had nothing to do with mourning the loss of the family patriarch: the fishnet stockings, stiletto heels and very visible cleavage were the giveaways.

King unlocked the door to the office building, and they all went inside.

When they were all settled, King said, "We're really sorry about your father, Eddie." He glanced at Dorothea but said nothing because the woman's look invited no such condolences.

"I still can't believe it," said Eddie. "Mom was there at ten, and at ten-thirty he's dead."

"Remmy told us she saw no one when she was leaving," said Michelle.

"Well, it's not like the person would've been jumping up and down in front of Remmy yelling, 'I'm going in to kill your husband now,'" said Dorothea irritably.

Eddie said, "Thanks for pointing that out, Dorothea. If you have nothing helpful to contribute, why don't you just sit there and continue sulking?"

Good for you, Eddie Battle, thought Michelle.

Dorothea looked like she was about to fire back with something suitably nasty, but she managed to restrain herself. She just sat there with her arms folded, scowling at the floor.

"What can we do for you, Eddie?" asked King.

Eddie pulled a newspaper out of the briefcase and pointed to a front-page article. King took the paper and scanned the story while Michelle read over his shoulder.

When he finished, King looked very upset. "How the hell did the account of Remmy's threatening Junior get leaked to the press?"

"Maybe Lulu," suggested Michelle. "Or her mother, Priscilla. Sounds like something she might do."

"Regardless," said Eddie, "now the whole town thinks Mom had Junior killed."

"But the *Gazette* also reported that Junior's death has been linked to the serial killings," pointed out Michelle.

Eddie slumped down in a chair. "That doesn't matter. People will think she paid someone to make it look that way."

"So how's Remmy taking it?"

"It's killing her."

"But she's not denying she threatened Junior?" asked King.

Eddie now looked wary. "I don't want to play semantics with you, Sean, but even if she threatened him, she had nothing to do with the man's death."

"I can't control what people think."

"I know that, but I just thought, well . . ."

"What do you want us to do, Eddie?" asked Michelle gently.

"Yes, it would be nice if you came to the point," said Dorothea. "I have two homes to show this morning."

Eddie ignored her and said, "Can you go and speak to Mom again? I know you came by the other day with Chip, and she sort of cut you off. But if you came by again, I know she'd see you. She needs someone to talk to right now."

"What exactly would she tell us?" asked King.

"I'm not totally sure," admitted Eddie. "But at least you can get her side of things instead of just this trash in the paper."

"I'm sure Chip and his men will do that."

"But she'd be more comfortable with you. Between

you, me and the wall, Chip and Mom don't really get along all that well."

"Even though he saved your life?"

"I don't know how to explain it. I only know it's true."

"He speaks very highly of her."

"Maybe I wasn't clear. *Mom* doesn't really care for him all that much."

"All right, we'll speak to her. But, again, that won't stop people from gossiping."

Dorothea broke in. "Since Eddie keeps beating around the bush, let me say it straight out. There's no way in the world that Remmy had anything to do with that man's death. But if you find whoever *did* kill Junior, that would stop all the talk."

"Right," said Eddie. "And then maybe you'll find who murdered Dad too."

"So you think it might be the same person?" asked King.

"It just seems very coincidental that Junior was charged with burglarizing my parents' home, and then in quick succession he and my father are killed."

"That was actually *my* idea," said Dorothea proudly. "And the reason I'm here. I got to thinking about this last night. What if somebody is using this string of murders to hide the killings of Bobby and Junior? And if so, it must be connected to what was stolen."

"That's actually something we're considering," admitted King.

"See!" exclaimed Dorothea, pointing at her husband. "I told you!"

"All right, Dorothea, all right," Eddie said. "So you think it's possible, Sean?"

"Anything's possible," said King vaguely. "Will your mother be home today?"

"Yes, but the funeral's tomorrow. A lot of people are coming in for it."

"Then we'll talk to her after that. What time's the service?"

"Two o'clock. There's a service at Christ Church and burial's at Kensington. You're welcome to come, of course."

Dorothea hunched forward. "So do you have any leads, anyone you suspect so far?"

"It's an ongoing investigation, Dorothea. We can't comment on that," replied King.

"I just thought that if we helped you, you might fill us in on things," she said bluntly.

"Sorry, it doesn't work that way. But since you're here, I have a question to ask you. You visited Bobby in the afternoon on the day he was killed?"

Dorothea stared at him blankly. "That's right. So what?"

"What was the purpose of your visit?"

"He was my father-in-law. I wanted to see how he was doing. It wasn't the first time, and I was there long before he was killed."

"And that night you went to Richmond. What time did you get there?"

"I don't remember. It was late. I went to bed."

"What hotel?"

"The Jefferson. I always stay there."

"I'm sure you do. And I'm sure they can give us the exact time you arrived."

"What the hell are you getting at? I came here this morning to try and help you, not to be interrogated."

"And I'm trying to help *you*. If you were at a hotel ninety miles away when your father-in-law was being killed, you have an ironclad alibi. I'm sure the FBI has already checked into this as well."

Dorothea stared at King for a few more moments, then rose and stalked out. Eddie thanked them both and quickly followed. King and Michelle watched through the window as they went to their cars.

Michelle said, "You don't think she was at that hotel at ten o'clock, do you?"

"I think she was somewhere she doesn't want her husband to know about. And I'm sure Bailey has already found that out but not bothered to tell us. Her answer about seeing Bobby before was total B.S. I checked at the hospital."

Michelle watched as Eddie climbed in his car. "I wonder how a nice guy like him ended up with a witch like her?"

King looked at her and smiled. "Going sweet on Eddie Battle?"

Michelle's face flushed. "Get serious, Sean."

"Do you have anything planned for tomorrow afternoon?"

"Maybe a run."

"It's canceled. We're going to a funeral."

"Why?"

"It's a little-known fact that killers very often go to their victims' funerals."

"Well, we didn't go to the other funerals."

"There haven't really been any others. Rhonda Tyler's

parents apparently didn't want to be bothered, so she was buried in a potter's field near Lynchburg. I went to the burial. The only other people there were the gravediggers."

"I'm surprised no one from the Aphrodisiac went. Like Pam maybe."

"I think they just want to forget it even happened."

"Talk about hiding your head in the sand."

"And Steve Canney was cremated without a service."

"That's a little unusual for a big football star."

"His father didn't see it that way."

"How about Pembroke?" asked Michelle.

"Her parents were so embarrassed by what she was doing with Canney when she died, they buried her at an undisclosed location out of the area."

"Hinson?"

"Her parents took her remains back to New York where she was born."

"So what do you make of Eddie and Dorothea's coming by?" she asked.

"Eddie I understand. His mother probably put him up to it. Her dutifully loyal son is a perfect tool for her. Dorothea's presence was far more interesting. She claimed it was to tell us her theory on the killer. I'm surprised she'd given it that much thought actually. I think she came principally to fish for information."

"Maybe she's just bucking for a bigger piece of the estate. Not that she needs it."

"No, I think she might," replied King.

"What do you mean? She's the queen of local real estate."

"Dorothea's become involved in some questionable real estate ventures that went south very recently."

"You did some checking?"

"I was getting tired of letting Chip Bailey have all the fun."

"And you haven't told him this?"

"He's FBI, he can find out for himself."

"So Dorothea needs money, and she's trying to get in Remmy's good graces in order to get it."

"That could be." He checked his watch. "I've arranged interviews with Roger Canney and Pembroke's parents starting in about an hour. After we finish with them, you may want to go shopping."

"Shopping? For what?"

He ran his gaze over her. "Jeans and a Secret Service windbreaker just don't cut it for proper funeral attire."

CHAPTER

45

SYLVIA DIAZ WAS COUNT-ing pills. She counted them once and then did it again. She went through her prescriptions written for the last three weeks and compared that number with the inventory counts in the pharmacy for that time period. Lastly, she went on the computer and examined the inventory numbers there. The computer records matched the levels in the pharmacy, but they didn't reconcile with the written prescriptions. Sylvia trusted her written prescriptions. There were clearly drugs unaccounted for. She called her office manager in and spoke at length with her. They went through the records together. She next spoke with her nurse-pharmacist, who filled prescriptions for patients at the office. After finishing that discussion Sylvia was convinced she knew where the problem was.

She debated what to do about it. She had no actual proof, only a fair amount of circumstantial evidence. She started to wonder when the theft or thefts might have occurred. There was one way to check. The outside door to both the morgue and her medical practice was on a keycard access system for after-hours entry and exit. An electronic log was kept that would tell her who'd entered the premises and when. She called the security company, gave the necessary information and pass code and asked her question. Aside from herself, she was told that there was only one person who'd accessed the medical office after hours in the last month: Kyle Montgomery. In fact, Sylvia discovered that he'd made his last nighttime visit around ten o'clock on the night Bobby Battle was murdered.

Janice Pembroke's mother was older than King had expected. Janice was the baby, the youngest of eight, Mrs. Pembroke explained. She'd been forty-one when Janice was born. She and her second husband, Janice's stepfather, lived in a dilapidated one-story red brick house in a run-down neighborhood. Janice had been the only child left home. Her stepfather was a short, potbellied and sour-faced man with an unlit cigarette over one ear and a Bud in his hand at nine in the morning. He apparently didn't go to work early, if at all. He smiled lasciviously at Michelle and didn't take his gaze off her after they had settled in the cluttered living room. Janice's mother was a tiny thing and exhausted-looking, understandable after raising eight children and then losing one in such a horrific manner. She also had several deep bruises on her arms and face.

"I fell down the stairs," she explained when King and Michelle had asked.

The woman spoke haltingly about her deceased daughter, frequently dabbing her eyes with a tissue. She didn't even know Janice was seeing Steve Canney, she told them.

"Different sides of the tracks," said the stepfather gruffly. "And she slept around, dirty little bitch, and it cost her. Probably thought she could get pregnant and then get herself a rich kid like Canney. I told her she was trash and all trash ever gets is more trash. Well, she got it all right." He gave King a triumphant look.

Surprisingly, Mom didn't rise to her dead daughter's defense, and King concluded that the injuries on her face and forearms were the reason.

Janice had had, to their knowledge, no enemies, and they could think of no reason why anyone would want to kill her. It was the same story they'd told the police, and the FBI after that.

"And I hope this is the last damn time we have to go through it," said the stepfather. "If she went and got herself killed, it's her own damn fault. I ain't got time to sit around and tell you people the same stuff over and over."

"Oh, are we keeping you from something important?" asked Michelle. "Like another beer perhaps?"

He lit his cigarette, took a puff and grinned at her. "I like your style, lady."

"By the way, where were *you* on the night she was killed?" asked Michelle, who was obviously working hard to keep from maiming the man.

His grin disappeared. "What the hell's that supposed to mean?"

"It means I want to know where you were when your stepdaughter was killed."

"I already told the cops that."

"Well, we're cops too. So you're just going to have to tell us again."

"I was out with some buddies."

"These buddies have names and addresses?"

They did, and Michelle wrote it all down while the man looked on nervously.

"I didn't have nothing to do with her getting killed," he said hotly as he followed them outside.

"Then you have nothing to worry about," replied Michelle.

"You're damn right I don't, baby."

Michelle spun around. "The name's Deputy Maxwell. And in case you didn't know, beating up your wife is a felony."

He snorted. "Don't know what the hell you're talking about."

"I think she might disagree," said Michelle, nodding toward Mrs. Pembroke, who cowered inside, staring through the curtains.

He laughed. "That dog won't hunt. I'm king of my castle. Why don't you come on by sometime and I'll show you, sweet-cheeks."

Michelle's entire body tensed.

"Don't do it, Michelle," warned King, who was watching her. "Just let it go."

"Screw you, Sean."

She marched over to the stepfather and spoke in a low but very clear voice. "Listen, you pathetic little moron, she doesn't have to press charges personally anymore. The state can do it for her. So when I come back here— and I will—if she even has one tiny mark on her—just one!—I'll arrest your sorry ass. After I kick the *shit* out of you first."

The cigarette fell out of the man's mouth. "You can't do that, you're a cop."

"I'll just say you fell down the stairs."

The man looked at King. "She just threatened me," he cried.

"I didn't hear any threat," said King.

"So that's the way it's gonna be, huh? Well, I ain't afraid of no skinny wench like you."

There was a five-foot-high wooden post in the front yard holding up an old-fashioned lantern. Michelle walked over to it and, with one sidekick of her powerful right leg, broke the post right in half.

After seeing that, the man's beer can joined his cigarette on the ground as he stared openmouthed at this demonstration of destruction.

"I'll be seeing *you, sweet-cheeks,*" said Michelle, and she walked to the car.

King bent down and picked up a piece of the shattered wood and said to the stricken man, "Damn, can you imagine if that were somebody's spine?" He handed him forty dollars for repairs and walked off.

As they got in the car, King said, "I think he actually wet his pants."

"I'll sleep better knowing he's not sleeping at all."

He said in a hurt tone, "Screw you, Sean?"

"I'm sorry, I was upset. But you can't always turn the other cheek either."

"Actually, I was very proud of you."

"Right. No threats on my part will make her situation

any better. A guy like that, you never know what he might do. I probably should have just kept my mouth shut."

"But you're going to go and check on her, aren't you?"

"You bet I am."

"Let me know when you're thinking of heading over."

"Why, so you can talk me out of it?"

"No, so I can hold the bastard down while you beat the crap out of him."

CHAPTER

46

HE'D FOLLOWED KING and Michelle to the Pembrokes' and was now trailing them as they headed across town to Roger Canney's home. He was not driving the blue VW today; an old pickup truck was his ride. A sweat-stained cowboy hat, shades and a stick-on beard and mustache of his own design provided satisfactory cover. The pair of investigators was starting to become a real issue, and he wasn't sure what to do about them. Pembroke could lead them nowhere; nor could the death of Diane Hinson. And by itself the murder of Rhonda Tyler was also a dead end. Canney was a different matter, though. The boy was the key that could make the entire house of cards come tumbling down.

He didn't have time to kill Roger Canney, and anyway that would raise even more suspicion about why the high school football star had to die. He had no choice but to let the interview take place, analyze what information was provided and take appropriate action. It was fortunate he'd had the foresight to bug Canney's home before he'd killed the boy. Tactics, it all comes down to tactics.

He rubbed his back where it had been bruised in the fight with Junior Deaver. He couldn't afford another encounter like that. He'd watched Michelle Maxwell snap the post in half with a seemingly effortless thrust of her leg. She was a dangerous woman. And King was even more dangerous, in his own way. In fact, Sean King was the only person he really feared could beat him. He might have to do something about that. And then he might have to kill Maxwell as well. He didn't want the woman coming after him, seeking revenge for her partner's death.

As the car ahead of him pulled into a long driveway heading up to a large brick colonial, he turned off on a side road, parked the truck and pulled down a pair of earphones that had been hidden under his hat. He tinkered with a receiver on the front seat, found the correct frequency to the transmitter he'd hidden in the Canney home, settled back and waited for the show to begin.

CHAPTER

47

"So what does Roger Canney do?" asked Michelle as she looked around the impressive home. A housekeeper had let them in and gone to get her employer.

"I don't know, but whatever it is, he does it well," answered King.

"What did his wife die of?"

"I don't know that either. I'm not friends of theirs."

Michelle kept looking around. "You know what I'm not seeing?"

King nodded. "There are no family pictures."

"What do you make of that?"

"Either they were recently pulled because of the father's overwhelming grief or they were never here."

"Overwhelming grief? Essentially, he buried his only son under cover of darkness."

"Everyone exhibits their emotions differently, Michelle. Some people, for example, kick wooden posts in half when they're upset."

Roger appeared a minute later, a tall, craggy man with

stooped shoulders and an unhappy, wan expression. He motioned them to sit on the couch in the living room, and he sat across from them. The man didn't bother to look at them when he spoke, instead resting his gaze on the beamed ceiling.

"I'm not sure why another interview is necessary," he began.

King said, "I know this is an awfully difficult time—"

Canney interrupted. "Right, right, let's just get on with it."

They went through the standard questions, to which Canney answered in extremely unhelpful monosyllables.

Frustrated, King asked, "So no enemies at school that you know of? Or that your son might have mentioned?"

"Steve was very popular. Everyone just loved him. He could do no wrong."

This was not said in the tone of a proud father, but in a mocking manner. King and Michelle exchanged puzzled glances.

"Had he ever mentioned that he was seeing Janice Pembroke?" asked Michelle.

"Steve didn't confide in me. If the kid was screwing around with some slut, that was his business. He was seventeen with raging hormones. But if he'd gotten some girl pregnant, I would have been more than upset."

"How long ago did your wife die?" asked Michelle.

Canney's gaze dropped from the ceiling to her. "Why is that relevant?"

"Just curious."

"Well, confine your curiosity to the matter at hand."

"Okay, can you think of anything at all that Steve

might have told you or that you might have overheard him say, or even one of his friends mention, that could shed some light on his murder?" she asked.

"Look, I already told you that we weren't exactly chums. We lived in the same house, but that was about it."

"Is there a reason why you and your son weren't close?" asked King.

"We both had our reasons, and they're not pertinent to his death."

"I'm afraid we need to decide that for ourselves. So if you'd answer the question . . ."

"I'm afraid I must decline," Canney said acidly.

"Well, that's up to you. Let's review what you've said. You and your son had what could reasonably be construed as an openly hostile relationship. You were perhaps upset that he was dating some slut, as you called her, and were concerned you'd have to pay for a child at some point. And then Steve and this 'slut' end up shotgunned to death. Do you own a shotgun, sir?"

Canney stood, his pale face now flushed. "What the hell are you implying? How dare you! You've twisted my words all around."

King remained impassive. "No. I'm simply making the argument any competent prosecutor would. What you've told us makes you a possible suspect in your son's death. I'm sure you were asked about your whereabouts when he was killed. I'd like you to tell us as well."

"I was home asleep."

"Alone?"

"Yes!"

"So you have no alibi," concluded King. "Well"—he

looked at Michelle—"let's go report back. At least it's another line of investigation the FBI can actively pursue." He looked back at Canney. "I'm sure the Bureau will be contacting you. Please make no plans to leave the area in the near future." He started to rise.

Canney, looking pale again, said, "Wait a minute, wait just a damned minute. I had nothing to do with Steve's murder."

"With all due respect, Mr. Canney, I never met a murderer who said otherwise," replied King.

Canney stood there, clenching and unclenching his hands while King watched him expectantly. Finally, Canney sat back down.

After a minute of silence, as though he were searching for just the right words, he said, "Steve was, quite simply, his mother's child. He adored her, worshiped her. When she died, he somehow blamed me."

"I don't recall what she died of," said King.

Canney was now rubbing his hands together nervously.

"She was in a car accident, well over three years ago now. She ran off the road and into a ravine. Died instantly."

"How could your son possibly blame you for that?" Michelle wanted to know.

"How the hell am I supposed to know!" roared Canney suddenly, and then just as quickly he calmed. "I'm sorry. As you can appreciate, this is all very difficult." They all remained silent for a bit. "There . . . there apparently was alcohol involved," Canney finally said in a very low voice.

"Your wife was intoxicated when she was killed?"

"Apparently so. It was surprising, because she'd never been a heavy drinker."

"And your marriage was a happy one?" asked Michelle.

"It was a marriage much like many others," said Canney defensively.

"Meaning?" persisted Michelle.

"Meaning it had its ups and downs."

At that moment the housekeeper entered the room and told Canney he had a phone call. He excused himself and went out of the room.

Michelle turned to her partner. "Well, that wasn't exactly what I was expecting. Do you think he had something to do with his wife's death?"

"I can't rule it out."

"He's definitely holding something back. You think he killed his son?"

"Son. That's an interesting word."

She looked at him puzzled. "What do you mean?"

"Only that Canney never referred to him as his son. Just Steve."

"That's right. Although it might just be because Steve was almost a man, and the relationship *was* strained."

"No, I think he might have given us the answer."

"Okay, Sean. What was it?"

"He was explaining why their relationship had gone wrong. He said Steve blamed him for his mother's death."

"So?"

"Well, right before that he said . . ." King pulled out his notepad and read from it. "He said, 'Steve was, quite simply, his mother's child.'"

"Right, meaning he favored his mother over his father."

"Or, more literally, that she was his mother—" King stopped and looked at Michelle.

His point finally dawned on her. "And Roger Canney was *not* his father."

Outside, the pickup truck started up. The man had heard all he needed to. It was time to act. But first he had to lay the groundwork.

CHAPTER

48

KYLE MONTGOMERY hadn't had a response to his blackmail letter yet. He had rented a post-office box a while back and had given that address for the person to respond to. He'd sent it anonymously, of course. His letter covered up the fact—very cleverly, he thought—that he actually didn't know much at all. He was counting on a guilty conscience to bring out something of importance, meaning, in his mind, something of material value. Yet he was starting to wonder if he was wrong. Well, if so, there was no harm done. Or so he thought.

He was heading to the Aphrodisiac with another delivery for his "client." He hadn't had to make another withdrawal from the pharmacy, having smartly taken extra quantities the last time. No reason to push his luck there.

He parked in the crowded lot and went inside. He didn't notice the car pull in behind him. Lost in thoughts of forthcoming cash, Kyle was completely unaware he'd been followed since leaving his apartment.

He went inside and, as was his habit, spent a few minutes watching the pole dancers. There was one in particular he favored, not that he had much of a chance with her. He had neither the looks nor, more important, the money these girls required to show him special attention.

He went upstairs and started to go behind the red curtain when a woman appeared next to him. She looked drawn and wobbly on her feet.

"Where you going?" she asked.

"To see someone," he answered nervously. "I'm expected."

"Is that right?" the obviously intoxicated woman slurred. "You got some ID?"

"ID? For what? I'm not drinking and I'm not watching the girls. And do I look like I'm underage? Or did you miss the gray hair in my goatee?"

"Don't get smart with me or your ass is out of here."

"Look, ma'am, is there a problem?" asked Kyle in a more polite tone. "I've gone back there before," he added.

"I know you have, I've seen you," said the woman.

"You come here a lot?" asked Kyle nervously. It suddenly dawned on him that earning a reputation as a regular visitor wasn't a good thing.

"I come every day," answered Lulu Oxley. She flicked her hand toward the red curtain. "Knock yourself out, slick."

Lulu staggered down the stairs while Kyle hurried through the red curtain.

He knocked on the same door and received the usual reply. He went in. The woman was lying on the bed, a blanket over her. The room was so dark he could barely make this out.

He held up his Baggie. "Here you go."

She pitched something to him. He put out his hand but missed, and the object fell to the floor. He picked it up. Ten rolled hundreds secured by a rubber band. He put the Baggie on the table and stood there, nervously looking at her. After a few seconds passed and she said nothing, he turned to leave. He stopped when he heard the bedsprings rattle and saw the lights brighten. Squinting, he looked back and saw her coming toward him. She wore the scarf and the dark glasses and had the blanket wrapped around her. When she drew closer, he could see that her shoulders were bare and she was in her stocking feet.

When she drew within a foot of him, she let the blanket drop. She had on a black lace thong and matching thigh-high stockings and bra, and that was it. He started breathing hard and felt every muscle tense. Her body was absolutely stunning, her belly flat, her hips soft, her breasts straining against the slender black material holding them in. He just wanted to rip off what little she had on.

As if sensing his thoughts, transparent as they were, she reached behind her, undid the clasp, and the bra fell to the floor and her breasts sprang free.

Kyle moaned and almost dropped to his knees. This was, without doubt, the greatest night of his life.

She reached out as if to touch him but then merely took the Baggie, picked up the blanket and covered herself again.

Kyle moved forward. "No need to do that, baby," he said in as cool a fashion as he could muster. "It'll just get in the way." He'd never come close to having a woman like this. A thousand bucks and he gets laid for free too. What could be better? He went to put his arms around her, but she shoved him back with a strength that surprised him.

His face flushed when she started to laugh.

She returned to the bed, let the blanket slip to the floor again, lay back on the bed and stretched like a cat. Then she turned over on all fours, reached over and put the Baggie on the nightstand. She did it with a slow deliberateness that gave him a long and unobstructed view of her from behind. He was so aroused now it was actually painful.

She rolled over on her back, put her feet up in the air and took her time sliding each stocking down her leg and then balled them up and tossed them at him. After that she pointed at him and laughed again. Kyle felt his blood pressure shoot upward even as other parts of him deflated.

"You little bitch!" His fantasy would finally be realized, and he was going to teach her a lesson at the same time. He rushed forward and then stopped just as quickly when the pistol swiveled in his direction. It must have been hidden under the bedcovers.

"Get out." This was the first time she'd spoken in a normal tone to him. He didn't recognize the voice. However, he wasn't focused on that. His gaze was on the gun that moved up and down, aimed first at his head and then at his crotch.

Kyle started to back up, his hands up in front of him as though to deflect a bullet. "Hey, just stay cool, lady. I'm going."

"Now," she said in a louder voice. She wrapped the

blanket around her and stood in front of him, holding the gun with both hands like she knew exactly how to use it.

He raised his hands even higher. "I'm going. I'm going! Damn!"

He turned to leave.

"Put the money on the table," she said.

He turned slowly back around. "Excuse me?"

"On the table, the money." She motioned with her gun.

"I brought you what you wanted. That costs *money.*"

In response she let the blanket drop once more and ran one hand along her curvy, nearly naked body. "So does this," she said very firmly. "Take a good look, little boy, it'll be the last time you see it."

He bristled at this insult. "A thousand dollars! For what? A frigging peep show? I wouldn't pay a thousand bucks even if I got to screw you."

"No amount of money would be enough to let you even touch me," she said bluntly.

"Oh, yeah? Boy, you're quite the catch. A druggie exhibitionist living in a room in a strip club? And hiding behind a scarf and those big dark glasses. Waving your naked ass in front of me and then not giving it up. Who the hell do you think you are? Huh?"

"You're boring me. Get out."

"You know what? I don't think you're going to fire that gun, not with lots of people around." He looked at her in triumph. The look was short-lived.

She tapped a cylindrical object attached to the gun's muzzle and said, "This is a suppressor. Really makes for a silent shot." She pointed it once more at his crotch. "Would you like a quick demonstration?"

"No," he yelled, backing away. "No." He dropped the money on the table, turned and ran out of the room, slamming the door closed behind him.

The woman locked the door, went back to her bed and swallowed several pills. A few minutes later she was moaning on the floor, happy again.

Outside the woman's door, Sylvia ducked out of the way right before Kyle came running past. She had heard everything. Rushing back outside, Sylvia was just in time to see Kyle spit gravel out of his Jeep's tires as he raced out of the parking lot. Sylvia slipped the hat off her head and let her hair down. Her suspicions had been confirmed. Kyle was stealing drugs and then selling them to the woman in the room. Sylvia decided to wait out in the parking lot to see if she came out.

Hours passed. It was very early in the morning, and Sylvia had watched well over a hundred people, mostly men, leave the building. She was just about to give up when someone emerged. It was a woman, her head was wrapped in a scarf and she wore sunglasses even though it was very dark outside. She seemed a little wobbly on her feet but got into a car parked near the rear of the building and drove away. Sylvia did not follow, because she would have been too easily spotted. However, she did see the car the woman got in. She drove off. While some questions had been answered tonight, troubling new ones had taken their place.

CHAPTER

49

THE DAY OF ROBERT E. Lee Battle's funeral started out under a blue sky that soon turned cloudy. By the time the procession reached the cemetery, a warm, gentle rain was falling. The army of black sat around the freshly dug hole under an enormous white tent.

King looked at many faces he knew and many he didn't. It was said that the regional airports in Charlottesville and Lynchburg were lined wingtip-to-wingtip with private jets belonging to friends of the Battles who'd come to pay their last respects. Morbid curiosity had probably enticed more than a few attendees.

Michelle sat next to King. She was actually wearing a dress! King knew better than to make any comment. His arm was still aching from his last wisecrack.

The Battles were in the front row, Eddie and Savannah on either side of their mother. Chip Bailey was next to Eddie. Dorothea sat at the end of the row, arms crossed. Mason stood off to one side, his gaze on the heavily veiled Remmy. *Ever the dutiful servant,* thought King.

On the other side of King sat Harry Carrick. The man was dressed as dapper as ever, his white hair even more striking against the backdrop of his dark suit. He'd given Michelle a peck on the cheek and King a firm handshake before sitting down.

"Quite a crowd," King whispered to him. Michelle leaned over to listen.

"Bobby and Remmy had lots of friends and business associates. Throw in the curious and the ones who came merely to gloat, and you have a staggering turnout."

"So I guess the Junior Deaver case is over," said King.

"Technically yes. You can't prosecute a dead man for burglary; what would be the point?"

"Technically, but . . . ," said King, watching his friend closely.

"But if my assumption is correct and Junior was innocent, I'd still like to catch the thief."

"You want us to keep investigating?"

"Yes, I do, Sean. I have his wife and children to consider. Why should his little ones grow up thinking their father was a thief if he wasn't?"

"In fact, we have our own motivation to follow that up."

"I can see that, considering how Junior was killed."

"Exactly. What are you doing after the funeral?"

"I've been invited to the Battles'," answered Harry.

"So have we. Maybe we can find a quiet corner and discuss tactics."

"I look forward to it." They all sat back and listened as the preacher commenced his talk about the dead man, the resurrection and life eternal. The rain continued to fall, making a somber afternoon even more depressing.

As the lengthy homily finally ended, the preacher went forward to comfort the family. King's gaze moved beyond the group assembled by the grave, and out in grids to the surrounding area. It was the same technique he'd used when in protection detail at the Secret Service. Then he'd been looking for potential assassins; now he was looking for someone who'd already killed.

King spotted her as she came over the slight rise of ground to the right.

Lulu Oxley was dressed all in black but, unlike Remmy Battle, wore no veil. And then it suddenly occurred to King: Junior's funeral had been today as well. And there was only one cemetery in the area. Appearing behind Lulu as she marched toward them were Priscilla Oxley and the three Deaver children.

"Oh, shit," whispered King to Harry and Michelle. Michelle had already seen them coming. Harry hadn't until King pointed her out.

Harry jerked back and said, "Oh, good Lord."

Lulu turned and motioned for her mother and children to stay where they were. They instantly obeyed, and then Lulu kept right on coming. King, Michelle and Harry rose as one to head her off. Others in the crowd had seen her too, because the murmuring was growing louder.

When they reached her, about fifty feet from the Battles, King said, "Lulu, you definitely don't want to do this."

"Get the hell out of my way!" said Lulu in a voice that told King she'd been drinking.

Harry took her by the arm. "Lulu, listen to me. You listen to me now!"

"Why the hell should I? I listened to you before and Junior's dead!" To King she looked like she might collapse any moment or else pull a gun and start shooting anything with clothes on.

"No good can come out of your being here," continued Harry. "No good. Mrs. Battle is grieving too."

"She should be rotting in hell for what she did!" She tried to jerk her arm away from Harry's grip, but the old man somehow held on.

His voice was steady and calm. "There isn't a shred of evidence that she had anything to do with Junior's death. In fact, everything points to his being killed by the same person who killed all the others, including Bobby Battle. The same person killed *both* your husbands."

"Then maybe she had her husband killed, I don't know. But she threatened Junior and now he's dead."

King looked back and saw that Remmy Battle had raised her veil and was now staring at them. And then King's worst fears were realized. Remmy went over to Mason, said something to him as she pointed at them, and then she started walking over holding an umbrella against the rain.

"Oh, this just gets better and better," muttered King under his breath. All others in the crowd sat watching, waiting for a catastrophic collision of widows.

With long, methodical strides Remmy reached them quickly. King immediately blocked her path to Lulu.

"Get the hell out of my way, Sean. This is *not* your business." Her southern drawl had never been more prominent, at least in his experience. Her look and tone brooked no opposition, and King reluctantly did as he was told.

Harry was the next barrier, but it only took a fierce expression from Remmy to move him aside as well. Probably sensing the futility of it, Michelle didn't even try.

Remmy was now face-to-face with Lulu, who stared back at her on tottering legs, the tears running down her face, which was twisted into an expression of hatred.

Without looking back at them Remmy said, "I want to talk privately with Ms. Oxley. We have some things to discuss that are just between us."

Lulu began, "I got nothing to say to—"

Remmy held up her hand, but King, who couldn't see her features, concluded it was probably the look on the older woman's face that had halted the usually indomitable Lulu from launching into her tirade.

"Please let us talk," said Remmy in a calmer tone.

The three of them slowly moved away. King remained nearby, tensed to leap if the women started throttling each other.

Remmy immediately took Lulu's arm in a firm grip. At first the other woman resisted, but Remmy leaned toward her and began to talk quickly, though none trying to eavesdrop could hear what was said. Long moments passed, and King looked on in amazement as Lulu's features calmed. Even more miraculously, after a few minutes of conversation Lulu reached out and gripped Remmy's arm for support. The two women finished their conversation and started to walk toward King.

Remmy said, "The Oxleys will be joining us at the house. But first I'm going to pay my respects to Junior."

As they walked off, King saw that Mason had col-

lected Priscilla and the children and was leading them
down to the Battles' limousine.

"In my seventy-plus years I've never seen anything as
strange and inexplicable as that," said Harry, stunned.

As the two women disappeared over the slight rise in
the ground, King said to his two companions, "Stay
here." He started off at a jog, following the two women.

Junior's grave site had no tent and was far humbler
than Bobby Battle's funeral in every other respect. It was
Saks versus Kmart, which overlooked the indisputable
fact that both men were *equally* dead.

The only people around were the two men whose task
it was to lower the simple wooden casket into the ground
and cover it with six feet of fill. King watched from behind a large ornate sculpture of a mother and child that
marked a nearby grave as Remmy spoke to the workers,
who nodded respectfully and stepped away. The two
women knelt on the fake green grass carpet in front of the
casket and clasped their hands together in prayer. They remained there for several minutes. When they rose,
Remmy went over to the coffin and placed a single red
rose on it. Lulu nodded at the men, who came forward
once more as the women walked off arm in arm.

King drew farther back as they passed by his hiding
place, and watched as they disappeared over the rise.
King turned back to Junior's grave. The cemetery workers had headed back to their nearby truck probably to get
their shovels. King thought about going over to pay Junior his own last respects. King hadn't known the man
very well, but his wife and children obviously loved him
very much; every man should leave behind such a legacy.

King hadn't seen too many tears at Bobby Battle's inter-
ment, costly though it had been.

As he was about to head back, he stopped and ducked
farther behind the statue. Someone had flitted out of a
nearby patch of trees. This person walked quickly toward
the grave, looking nervously all around. There seemed an
abundance of guilt in the figure's furtive movements.
King couldn't make out who it was or whether it was a
man or a woman, since the person's outfit consisted of
pants, a coat and a cowboy hat pulled low.

As the person knelt in front of the grave, King crept
forward for a better look. And then the hat came off as the
person's head bowed in prayer. It looked to be a woman,
given the length of the piled-up hair. However, from this
angle King couldn't make out the face. Should he walk up
and confront the person? But that would give him away as
well. He thought some more and then ducked behind the
large statue of mother and child once more, picked up a
pebble, aimed and sent it sailing toward another large
marker about twenty feet to his right and close to Junior's
grave. The result was as he'd hoped.

The woman looked up quickly at the sound of the rock
hitting the marker, giving King a clear look at her face.
She put her hat back on and ran for the cover of the trees.

King had no reason to give chase. He knew who it was.

Yet why would Sally Wainwright, the Battles' horseper-
son, be praying in front of Junior Deaver's grave?

CHAPTER

50

CASA BATTLE, THOUGH very large, was very full. Long linen-covered tables had been set up on the main floor with food and drink. After filling their plates and glasses Harry had led King and Michelle to the second-floor study to talk things over.

He explained, "I don't think we'll be interrupted here. It's far enough away from the food and, more important, the liquor. Death makes people especially thirsty, I've found."

King looked at the antique writing desk against one wall. There were fancy writing instruments, heavy bond paper with the initials *REB* on them, a leather ink blotter and several old-fashioned inkwells.

"Even more than me, Remmy is a letter writer from the old school," said Harry, who was watching King. "The lady doesn't believe in e-mails or even typewriters. And she expects missives in kind."

"I'm glad she has the time to communicate that way. I guess that comes with being really rich. I saw Remmy and Lulu go off together when we got here," said King.

"Remmy has a private chamber near her bedroom on the

third floor," answered Harry. "I'd love to be a fly on the wall there."

"I can't imagine what Remmy said to Lulu to make an instant peace," said Michelle. "Talk about miracles. I feel like I almost saw the Virgin Mary."

King took a swallow of his wine and smiled appreciatively. "Valandraud of St-Emilion; Remmy didn't hold back on the good stuff." He looked at the older man. "I can fathom a guess about Remmy and Lulu. How about you, Harry?"

Harry adjusted his bow tie and smoothed down his hair before sampling the wine and a crab cake on a plate resting on his knees. "I believe we can take what Michelle said quite literally; in other words, she did make peace, across the board."

"Meaning what exactly?" asked Michelle.

"That she told Lulu she doesn't believe Junior committed the burglary and therefore isn't going to sue for the return of the items. With the criminal prosecution dropped due to Junior's death, the matter is officially closed."

"I'm sure she added that she had nothing to do with Junior's death and is deeply sorry Lulu has lost her husband as well," commented King.

"And there was probably talk of Remmy's setting up college funds for the Oxley children," added Harry.

"And perhaps financial help for Lulu, to finish the house and all," said King. "She'd already offered that to Junior when she thought he was behind the burglary. She probably felt guilty for all the trouble she'd caused them."

Michelle stared at the two, bewildered. "You think she covered all that in a few minutes at the cemetery?"

Harry raised his wineglass in a salute of sorts. "Remmy isn't the sort to let the grass grow under her feet. She might not always make the right decision, but when the woman acts, people know it! Not unlike a certain female investigator of my acquaintance."

Michelle smiled at his remark and then quickly grew serious. "And Remmy's change of heart is due to what?"

"As we said, she knows or at least believes Junior was innocent of the burglary," said King. "In addition, there's no way Junior could have killed Bobby. Even if he had the necessary medical knowledge, which he didn't, he would have been hard to miss at the hospital. And I checked: he had an alibi for the time Bobby was killed."

"So Remmy must be thinking that the murder of her husband and the theft of the things from the house are related," said Michelle. "If Junior didn't do one, he couldn't have done the other."

"Exactly," said Harry. "Which proves he was framed."

King looked around at the walls of books and then glanced out the window at the afternoon gloom. It had started to rain harder. He watched the drops splatter on top of the cars parked in the front motor court.

"When I followed Remmy and Lulu to Junior's grave site, I saw another mourner there," said King. "A very unexpected one."

"Who?" they both exclaimed together.

"Sally Wainwright."

"The stable hand?" Harry looked puzzled.

Michelle snapped her fingers. "Sean, that day we first spoke to Sally. You asked her if she knew Junior. She said she'd seen him around, but you noted how nervous and eva-sive she seemed."

"That's right," said King.

"Paying last respects to a man you'd merely *seen around*?" mused Harry.

"I'm going to have another talk with Miss Sally," said King.

Harry motioned them to sit down on the couch across from the fire while he stood in front of them. "Now, it seems very clear that Junior's setup was done by someone with knowledge of criminal investigations."

"So our next course of action?" asked Michelle.

Deferring answering her question, Harry consulted an old-fashioned pocket watch hanging on a gold chain strung across his vest.

"That's a beautiful piece, Harry," said Michelle.

"It belonged to my great-grandfather. Having no son of my own, I'm keeping it safe for my eldest nephew." He fingered the heavy piece lovingly. "In this hurly-burly world it's comforting to know one can still ascertain the time of day in the same manner as over a hundred years ago." He snapped shut the watch's cover and looked sharply at them. "All right," he said, returning to Michelle's query. "By this time everyone downstairs will have imbibed at least one and possibly two drinks. Thus, I suggest we join the tipsy masses below and observe and listen. It's not beyond the realm of possibility that our killer is in this house right now. At the very least we might gain some information that could stop any future murders."

They adjourned their meeting and moved to the main level.

CHAPTER

51

THERE WERE SEVERAL odd pairings awaiting them downstairs. They could see Savannah out on the glass-enclosed rear porch with the two youngest Oxley children. She appeared to be playing a game with them that involved tugging on one's ear and pantomiming. The older Oxley girl stood in the corner, watching without smiling.

"Charades," concluded Michelle. "I didn't think Savannah had it in her to entertain young children."

"I think she's a lot younger in some ways than people think," said King.

Chip Bailey and Dorothea were conversing in low tones in a far corner of the living room. Eddie stood nearby apparently in deep conversation with Todd Williams, who hadn't been at the funeral but wasn't going to miss the post-burial vittles.

As they watched, Remmy and Lulu came down the staircase arm in arm. All heads turned to watch.

"Why am I reminded of Lee and Grant at Appomattox?" whispered Harry.

Chip Bailey immediately abandoned Dorothea and headed to the stairs to meet Remmy. Mason, who had been serving food, wasn't far behind.

"The hounds are circling, and the former man of the house is barely in the ground," commented Harry.

"Chip Bailey too?" said Michelle. "I wouldn't have figured that. Eddie said his mother didn't like the man."

"Being the kept husband of an enormously wealthy woman is enough of a prize to at least make an effort at changing her opinion," commented King dryly.

However, Remmy apparently had other ideas. She swept past both men and headed toward King and his group.

Remmy nodded at Harry as she walked up. "I know that you and Lulu have met, Harry, so I won't bother with introductions."

King thought he detected a twinkle in Remmy's eye as she said this.

"I'm glad *you've* made her acquaintance, Remmy," rejoined Harry. "And in what seems to be a very positive way."

"Let's just say we've come to a meeting of the minds." Remmy looked at Lulu and squeezed the other woman's hand. "I was stupid and blind and unfair, and I have communicated that to Lulu." She looked directly at the woman. "Neither of us can bring our husbands back, but I promise that you and your beautiful children will not want so long as I'm around."

"I appreciate that, Mrs. Battle, I really do." Lulu both looked and sounded lucid now.

"I know you do and please call me Remmy." She now

turned to King and Michelle. "I hope you're making progress on the case," she said.

"Every day," King replied.

She looked at him curiously but said nothing.

"We wanted to come by and talk to you at some point," said King.

"Yes, Eddie mentioned that. Well, I'm not going anywhere."

"Don't let the newspapers get you down, Remmy," said King.

"Papers? If I want to know what's happening with me, I don't consult strangers, I just ask myself."

Priscilla Oxley suddenly swooped in, juggling a large plate crammed with food and a glass of wine. "Honey," she said to Remmy, "thank you so much for everything. Why, I've always told Lulu you're a saint. Right, baby, just the other day I was saying if the world had more Remmy Battles, what a world it would be."

"Mother, please," began Lulu, but Priscilla rushed on.

"And here you and Lulu have become friends, and you brought us to your beautiful home and said you'd take care of the children. Why, when we lost *our* poor Junior, I didn't know what my daughter was going to do." Her big chest heaved, and her gravelly voice broke in her throat. It was a magnificent job, King thought.

"Mother, I have a job, a good one. It's not like the children were going to starve."

However, Priscilla was too worked up to be denied. "And now that I'll be staying on to help Lulu and everything, having that new house finished and your continued support, why, I know everything's going to be just fine." Twin tears dribbled down her flabby cheeks. "As one mother to another I can't tell you what a relief that is." She finished this off by swallowing the entire contents of her wineglass.

To King the connoisseur it was an appalling moment. Yet after her emotional performance, he thought, the woman deserved her own TV show.

"I'm just glad I could help, Priscilla," said Remmy politely.

Priscilla looked shyly at her. "You probably don't remember, but I waited on you when you used to visit the Greenbrier in West Virginia."

"Oh, I remember you *very* well, Priscilla."

Priscilla froze. "Oh, you do? Well, thanks again." And then Priscilla was gone as fast as she'd arrived.

Eddie and Bailey next joined them.

"It was a beautiful service, Remmy," said Bailey.

"Reverend Kelly does a good job," she replied. "And he had a lot of good material. Bobby led quite an extraordinary life."

"I'm going to see one of Eddie's reenactments Saturday," said Bailey.

"Which one are you doing?" asked Michelle.

"The Battle of Cedar Creek near Middleton," answered Eddie. "Phil Sheridan's Army of the Shenandoah against Jubal Early's Army of the Valley. It's usually held in October, but they moved it up this year." He looked down and then glanced at Michelle. He seemed to be about to say something but remained silent.

Harry said, "Wasn't old Jubal the only Confederate general who never formally surrendered?"

"That's right," said Eddie. "He ended up practicing law over in Rocky Mount, Virginia."

"Well, at least he took up an honorable profession after the war," said Harry.

"I think Eddie and I are going to be spending a lot more time together," said Bailey. King thought the man could not have been more obvious.

"I'm looking forward to that," said Eddie with what seemed genuine enthusiasm.

You're a good liar, Eddie, King thought.

Remmy reached out and took her son's hand. "How you doing?"

"Just hoping for happier days, Mom."

"Maybe you and Dorothea should go away somewhere, just get away."

"Yeah, maybe we'll do that," answered Eddie with not a trace of interest.

King noted that the Oxley children had come inside when they saw their mother. As Lulu joined them, King excused himself, went to the bar, got two glasses of wine and headed to the rear porch to see Savannah while she was still alone.

The young woman was sitting on the couch staring into the fire that blazed in the fireplace at one end of the room.

"Long day for you, Savannah," he said quietly.

She started and looked up, smiling when she saw who it was. He handed her one of the glasses and sat next to her. "A glass of Château Palmer can work miracles for the spirits. It's a fine French wine."

" 'Palmer' doesn't sound French," she said, staring at her glass as though she could see images in it.

"He was an English general under Wellington who came to Bordeaux with his army around 1814 and stayed. He purchased a property that eventually became known as Château Palmer, and started producing wine, which goes to show that the grape, like the pen, is mightier than the sword."

"I don't know much about wine," she said. "I'm more a Jack and Coke girl."

"One can never go wrong with Jack and Coke, but if you're interested in wine, I'd be glad to help you, although you could start learning right in this house. Your parents have a ten-thousand-bottle cellar. I nearly fainted with envy when I first saw it." He took a sip of wine and watched her watching the fire. "I saw you with the Oxley children."

"They're nice kids," she said quietly as she played with her string of pearls. "The little one, Mary Margaret, was bawling when she got here, poor thing. She really misses her daddy. I brought them out here. Mom and Ms. Oxley wanted to talk."

"They seemed to have worked everything out."

"I really thought Junior had done it." Her eyes suddenly glimmered with a layer of tears.

"So did I, at first."

"I know I wasn't much help the other day."

"You were still in shock. Whenever you're ready to talk, I'm here."

She nodded absently, and her nervous fingers played

over her pearls. He waited for her to speak, but she didn't. She simply stared into the fire.

He finally rose. "If you need anything, anything at all, just give me a call."

She glanced up and clutched at his hand. "How come you're not married?"

At first he thought she was flirting with him but then realized she was serious.

He said, "I was, a long time ago, and it just didn't work out."

"I think some people are supposed to be alone."

"You don't think you're one of those people, do you?"

She shook her head. "No. But I think my father was."

Puzzled, King sat back down. "What makes you say that?"

Before she could answer, they heard Remmy say, "I'm sure there are people who'd like to see you, Savannah."

They both looked over to see her standing in the doorway scrutinizing them.

Savannah rose obediently. "I'll see you, Sean."

He watched mother and daughter walk off before rejoining Michelle in the family room. Harry had caught Remmy and Savannah as they were coming back in and was speaking with them in a far corner.

Get as much as you can, Harry, thought King, *because I pretty much struck out.*

"Anything interesting?" asked Michelle.

"Savannah is one troubled woman. She knows something but can't get it out."

"Use your charm, Sean. She has the hots for you."

"Oh, you think so?"

"*Please*. Men are so blind when it comes to that."

"So anything happen on your end?"

"I've been invited to Eddie's next reenactment. I'm going with Chip."

King crossed his arms and stared at her. "Really?"

She stared back at him defensively. "Yeah, really. Why?"

"*Women* are so blind when it comes to that."

"Come on, he's married, Sean!"

"Yes, he is."

CHAPTER

52

MICHELLE DROVE WITH Chip Bailey to the outskirts of Middleton, Virginia. It was a crisp morning with nothing but blue skies overhead and a nice breeze to relieve the growing heat.

"Good day to fight," said Bailey.

Is there really ever a good day to slaughter each other? thought Michelle.

The big man sipped on his coffee and munched on an egg sandwich from McDonald's. Michelle chewed on an energy bar and cradled her bottle of orange juice. She wore jeans, hiking boots and her Secret Service windbreaker. Bailey had donned khakis, a sweater and wraparound shades.

"You ever been to one of these?" asked Bailey.

"No."

"They're actually pretty cool. They have all these events, infantry drilling, hospital demonstrations, bands, dances, even fancy balls, afternoon teas, candlelight tours. The cavalry charges are really something. These guys are serious about this stuff. You'll see hundreds of them out there today, although during the actual war the armies had tens of thousands of soldiers. But they put on a good show anyway."

"How did Eddie get into that? Doesn't seem like something a sensitive artist would be drawn to."

"I think it was his father who was interested in it at first. He was very much into history, even helped finance some of the battle reenactments."

"Was Eddie very close to his father?"

"I think he wanted to be. That's one reason he got into reenactments—at least that's my educated guess. But Bobby Battle was an inscrutable fellow. And he wasn't around all that much. I think he preferred sailing around the world in a hot-air balloon or building a factory in Asia to raising his kids."

"I understand he offered you a job after you rescued Eddie."

Bailey looked surprised that she knew this.

"He did but I wasn't interested."

"Mind my asking why not?"

"No big secret. I just liked being an FBI agent. I hadn't been with the agency all that long, and I wanted to make a career out of it."

"How'd you bust the case?"

"Got a tip that I ran to its source. Eddie was in college back then, and I did some digging around. Found out this guy living at the same apartment complex was a convicted felon."

"Why didn't Eddie live at home? Didn't he go to UVA?"

"No, he went to Virginia Tech over in Blacksburg, a few hours from here. Anyway, turns out this guy had found out who Eddie was, or more to the point who

Eddie's parents were. Eddie came home late one night, and next thing he knew he was tied up in a shack in the middle of nowhere."

"How'd you learn about the shack?"

"The guy had used it before for hunting. I'm not saying he was the sharpest tool in the shed, but he was dangerous. The Battles paid the money; but we were watching when the pickup was made."

"Wait a minute; I thought the Battles didn't pay the ransom."

"No, they did but they got it back—well, at least most of it."

"I'm not following."

"With kidnappings the dicey piece for the criminal is getting the payoff. Today you can do it with wire transfers and computer gimmicks and such, but it's still tricky. Twenty years ago it was far harder. But this guy thought he had it figured out. He had the drop arranged so it was at a shopping mall on a Saturday, people everywhere. He must have scoped out the place, because he knew where this back exit was. As soon as he took the bag, he disappeared into a sea of people."

"How'd you pick him up, then?"

We had two transmitters hidden on the bag. But we figured he'd think of that and toss the bag, so we had transmitters in some of the cash wrappers binding the money. We didn't think he'd throw out the money. He did, in fact, toss out the bag. But we were still able to follow him right to the shack."

"Wasn't that a risk, not arresting him on the spot?"

"The bigger risk was never finding Eddie. This guy's

past history showed him to be a loner. If Eddie was alive, and that was a big if, this guy was probably going back to either set him free or more likely kill him."

"And that's when the shoot-out happened?"

"He must have spotted us and opened fire, and we returned it. We had a sniper with us, and the kidnapper took one in the head."

"You said you recovered most of the money?"

Bailey laughed. "After he spotted us and opened fire, this idiot burned about five hundred thou of the five million total in the potbellied stove that was in the shack. I guess he was thinking we weren't going to get him *and* the money."

"Lucky you didn't hit Eddie," said Michelle.

He looked at her sternly. "It's easy to play Monday-morning quarterback."

"I'm not trying to second-guess what you did. I've been in situations like that too. It's never easy. The important thing is, Eddie lived."

"That's the way I've always seen it." Bailey pointed up ahead. "And there he is in the flesh."

They'd turned off the main highway and into a parking area filled with trucks, horse trailers, campers and RVs. Along one side numerous tents were set up. Michelle waved at Eddie, who was busy getting his gear together. They got out of the car and joined him.

"So what are you this time?" asked Bailey.

Eddie grinned. "I'm a man of many talents, so I've got multiple roles. First, I'm a major in the 52nd Virginia in an all-Virginia brigade under General John Pegram's Division. After that I saddle up as part of the 36th Virginia Cavalry Battalion, Johnson's Brigade under General

Lomax's Division. I belong to lots of different units actually; they're always looking for bodies. Hell, I've mustered up in Confederate armies in Tennessee, Kentucky, Alabama and even Texas. Done artillery, cavalry, infantry, even went up in an observation balloon once. Now, don't tell my mother, but I've suited up in Union blue on occasion too. "

"Sounds pretty involved," said Michelle.

"Oh, it's quite a show. There are primers for how to put one of these events together, complete with sample budgets, marketing plans, logistics, finding sponsors, that sort of thing."

Michelle pointed to the line of tents. "What are those?"

"They call them sutlers," replied Eddie. "During the actual Civil War merchants would follow the armies and sell them things. Sutlers nowadays sell period-style items and goods to reenactors and the public. As for the reenactors there are definitely different levels. They have the ones called thread-counters who make sure their uniforms are authentic down to fabric having the same thread count as during the real war, hence the nickname." Eddie deadpanned, "They're also referred to as the stitch Nazis." Bailey and Michelle laughed. "Then you have the other side of the spectrum, the Farbys; those are the ones who dare to have polyester in their uniforms or use plastic dinnerware during a reenactment, when those things weren't even invented at the time of the real war. I call them *Julie* instead of *Johnny* Rebs."

"So which are you, Nazi or Julie?" asked Michelle.

He grinned. "I'm a tweener. Most of my stuff is authentic, but I occasionally bend to the comforts of life at times as well." He lowered his voice, "Don't tell anyone, but my uniform has some rayon in it and, God forbid, Lycra. And if you press me on the point, I won't deny that there might be some plastic thingies on my person."

"Your secret is safe with me."

"I'm actually going to buy some stuff from the sutlers today. Everybody's gearing up for the reenactment of the Battle of Gettysburg in Pennsylvania in July. Then we got the Spotsylvania, Virginia, campaign coming up; the Road to Atlanta and the Battle of Franklin are in the fall. But this battle today is a pretty big deal. The Union outnumbered the rebels by about a third on both the infantry and cavalry side and had over twice the number of artillery pieces, but the Yanks suffered double the number of killed and wounded."

As Michelle helped him with his gun, canteen and bedroll, she looked around at all the activity. "This is like a big movie production."

"Yeah, but without the big payday."

"Little boys who never grow up," replied Bailey, shaking his head and grinning. "The toys just get bigger and more elaborate."

"Is Dorothea here?" Michelle asked.

Eddie shrugged. "My good wife would rather have all her hair pulled out one strand at a time than come and see me play soldier." A bugle sounded. "Okay, the camps are open. They'll start with a little lecture about the battle and such, some infantry field drilling, music and then a cavalry demonstration."

"You said you're riding. Where's your mount?"

Eddie pointed to a thirteen-hands-high nimble-looking

Tennessee walker tethered to a trailer parked next to Eddie's truck. "There's my ride, Jonas. Sally's taken good care of him, but that horse is ready for some real action."

They headed to the army camps. Michelle watched with great admiration as Eddie drilled on foot, then took Jonas through some very intricate paces during the cavalry demonstration. The spectators were required to leave the camps before the artillery barrage began. At the first salvo Michelle covered her ears.

Then the first day of the battle was announced.

Eddie pointed them to a spot where they could "watch me die gloriously." He also pointed out the hospitality tents. "Hot dogs and cold Buds. That's a perk no Civil War soldier ever saw," he said.

"I hear they're filming this," said Bailey.

"That's right. They shoot lots of them. For posterity," he added sarcastically.

"I'm assuming all the guns and cannon are loaded with blanks," said Michelle.

"Mine is. I sure as hell hope everyone else followed that same rule." Eddie smiled. "Don't worry, we're all pros here. There won't be any musket balls flying around." He stood and balanced all his equipment. "Sometimes I don't know how those guys walked, much less fought, with all this stuff. I'll see you later. Wish me luck."

"Good luck," said Michelle as he hustled off.

CHAPTER

53

THE MESSAGE WAS SIT-
ting on Kyle's Jeep when he came down from his apartment. He opened the envelope and read the contents, a
broad smile covering his face. It was from his prescription pill client, the crazy exhibitionist with a love for si-
lenced weapons. She wanted to meet, at a local motel,
very late that night. She had even included the room number. She apologized for what she'd done and wanted to
make amends. She promised him five thousand dollars
and, more intriguingly, consummation of what he'd expected to receive the last time. She wanted him, the letter
said. She wanted him badly. He would never forget the
experience. And she'd included another inducement: ten
one-hundred-dollar bills. It was probably the very same
cash she'd made him leave behind.

He put the money in his pocket, climbed into his Jeep
and set off. His blackmail scheme hadn't paid off; he'd
obviously been wrong about what he'd seen. But now this
new opportunity had presented itself, and with the grand
already in his pocket, how could he really lose? Okay, she

probably wasn't playing with a full deck, but he didn't
figure her for any more gun wielding. Why would she
give him this much money if she didn't mean what she
said? He would be very careful, but Kyle took this as perhaps the luckiest day of his life. And he told himself he'd
be rough with her, as a little payback for scaring him so
badly. He bet she liked it rough. Well, he'd give the bitch
more than she bargained for. Big Kyle was on the
warpath.

Michelle and Bailey watched through binoculars as the
battle, or rather the series of skirmishes, took place all
over the area: charges and countercharges and hand-to-
hand fighting that looked incredibly realistic. Every time
the cannon boomed Michelle jumped and Bailey laughed.

"Rookie," he said jokingly.

Columns of men in gray and butternut brown would
pour out to be met by walls of their counterparts in blue.
Even with all the smoke, shots, cannon fire, screams, confusion and rush of feet and smack of saber against saber
everywhere, Michelle could easily see how the real thing
would be far worse. At least no blood was pooling on the
ground, no limbs were scattered around; there were no
real sobs that heralded the dying gasps of the mortally
wounded. The worst injury they'd observed was a
sprained ankle.

Michelle became very alert when she saw Eddie and
his ragtag company explode out of the woods shrieking
the famous rebel yell. They were met by a volley of fire
by their Union opponents, and half the men fell to the dirt,

dead or dying. Eddie wasn't hit in the initial fire, and he and about a dozen of his men raced on. Eddie jumped the wooden breastworks and engaged in furious hand-to-hand combat with three Union soldiers, dropping two of them as Michelle looked on enthralled. He actually lifted one of the men up and threw him into a bush. As his soldiers were dropping all around him, Eddie pulled his saber and did some intricate swordplay with a Union captain, finally running him through.

So realistic was it all that when Eddie turned to seek out another foe and took a rifle round right in his gut, Michelle felt all her breath rush out. As Eddie dropped to the ground, she felt an almost overpowering urge to pull her own weapon, rush forward and shoot the man who'd just killed Eddie.

She turned and found Bailey's gaze on her. "I know. I felt the same way the first time I saw him get killed."

For a few minutes none of the men moved at all, and Michelle felt herself growing nervous. Then Eddie sat up, leaned over and spoke to the fallen man next to him, stood and walked over to join a relieved Michelle and Bailey.

He took off his hat, wiped his sweaty brow.

"That was absolutely amazing, Eddie," said Michelle.

"Aw, shucks, ma'am, you should've seen me at Gettysburg or Antietam. Now, there I was in fine form."

You looked pretty fine today, thought Michelle, and then she caught herself, King's remonstrations coming back to her: he was married. Even if his wife apparently didn't care for him, he was still married.

"How do you know who dies or not?" she asked.

"It's all pretty much planned out before. Most reenactments are held Friday to Sunday. On Friday people start gathering and the generals go around to everybody, tell them what they need, who's going to be where, who dies, who doesn't. A lot depends on who shows up and with what—horses, cannon, stuff like that. Most everybody here is experienced, so there's not much of a learning curve. And the fighting is choreographed, at least for the most part; but there's always some room for improvisation. The guy I picked up and dumped in the bush? That was a little payback on my part. The last battle the little shit smacked me in the head with his sword handle. Said it was an accident. I had a knot on my head for a week. So I *accidentally* picked him up and threw him into that thornbush."

She looked over where the "dead" men were still on the ground. "Are there rules about how long you have to stay there?"

"Yes, but it's flexible. Sometimes the general tells you beforehand you have to stay down until the battle's over. Or if we have ambulance carriers that show up; we may be taken off the field that way. They're filming today, so it's all a little trickier, but the cameras switched to another skirmish after I got killed, so I cheated a little and jumped ship." He added with a shy grin, "The scenery's a lot better over here."

"Compared to dead bodies? I don't think I'll take that as a compliment," said Michelle, returning his smile.

They later watched Eddie on horseback where he led his men on tactical probes of the Union line. The horsemen flashed by, racing up and down knolls and jumping obstacles in their way.

Michelle turned to Bailey. "Where'd he learn to ride like that?"

"You'd be surprised at what the man can do. Have you seen any of his paintings?"

"No, but I really want to."

Eddie rode by later and tossed his plumed cavalry hat to Michelle.

"What's that for?" she said, catching it.

"I wasn't killed. You must be my good-luck charm," he called out before dashing off again.

A ladies' tea and fashion show followed. After that was instruction on dances of the Civil War era. Eddie partnered with Michelle and helped teach her the intricate steps of several. A formal ball followed that was supposed to be for reenactors only, but Eddie had a Civil War–era dress he said he'd bought from one of the sutlers that he gave to Michelle.

She looked at it in surprise. "What am I supposed to do with this?"

"Why, milady, if we're crashing the ball, you have to have the proper accoutrements. Come on, you can change in the truck. I'll stand guard so your reputation will remain intact."

Eddie had gotten an outfit for Chip Bailey too, but the FBI agent announced he had to leave.

"I'll drive her home, then," said Eddie. "I can't stay for the second day of the battle anyway. I'm leaving tonight."

Michelle looked a little uncomfortable with this, but Eddie said, "I promise I'll be the perfect gentleman. And remember we have Jonas in the trailer as a chaperone."

They spent the next two hours dancing and eating and drinking.

Eddie finally sat down, his big chest heaving while Michelle looked barely out of breath.

"Okay, girl, you've got some wind, I'll say that."

"Well, I didn't fight in a war today."

"I'm beat and my back is killing me. I've been riding horses and doing this fighting stuff way too long. You ready to call it a day?"

"I am."

Before they left, he took a Polaroid of her in her ball gown. "I'll probably never see you dressed like that again," he explained, "so I might as well have proof of it."

She changed back into her regular clothes before the drive home. On the way they talked, first about the battle and reenactments in general and then about Michelle's background and family.

"Lots of brothers, huh?" said Eddie.

"Too many, sometimes. I was the youngest, and though he'd never admit it, my dad dotes on me. He and my brothers are all cops. When I decided to join the ranks, he was none too pleased. He still hasn't quite gotten over it."

"I had a brother," he said quietly. "His name was Bobby. We were twins."

"I know, I heard. I'm sorry."

"He was a great kid. He really was. Sweet, do anything for you, he was just not all there. I loved him. I really did and I miss him like hell."

"I'm sure it really devastated your whole family."

"Yeah, I suppose it did," he said.

"And I guess you and Savannah don't have much in common."

"She's a good kid too, really bright, but she's sort of lost. Hell, I can't blame her, look at me."

"I think you've done all right for yourself."

He glanced over at her. "That's quite a compliment coming from you, an Olympian-turned-Secret-Service-agent and now a hotshot detective. How do you like working with Sean?"

"He's great. I couldn't ask for a better partner and mentor."

"He is one smart man. But let's face it: he's lucky to have *you.*" Michelle looked out the window, obviously uncomfortable.

"I'm not being fresh, Michelle. You two work well together. It's nice to be part of something like that. I guess I'm just envious."

She looked over at him. "If you're unhappy, you can change that, Eddie."

"I am unhappy in some ways," he said. "But I don't think I have the courage to make a change, not a real one. It's not just Dorothea. She goes her way and I go mine. Lots of marriages are set up just like that, and I can deal with it. But I've got my mother too. Let's say I head out of here, what happens to her?"

"She seems like a person well able to take care of herself."

"You might be surprised, especially now with everyone pointing fingers at her."

"Sean and I are going to meet with her and go through that. Obviously, whatever she said to Lulu worked. If Lulu believes she had nothing to do with Junior's death, other people will start to believe it too."

"It's not just Junior's death, it's my father. It's no secret that they had a rocky marriage at times, so some people suspect she killed him. I'm not sure that's something she can survive."

"Before we meet with Remmy, you might want to see if she'll tell you what was in her closet that was stolen."

He looked puzzled. "I thought it was just her ring and cash and stuff."

"No, there was something else. Something she wanted back so badly that she offered Junior a lot of money for its return."

Eddie gripped the wheel tighter. "What the hell could it be?"

"I'm hoping you can find out. If she'll tell anyone, I'm assuming she'll tell you."

"I'll try, Michelle, I'll give it my best shot."

He drove her home and walked her up to the door.

"When you come over to speak to Mom, drop by my place afterward, and I'll show you and Sean some of my paintings."

Michelle's face lit up. "I'd like that, Eddie, I'd like that a lot. Well, thanks for a wonderful evening. I haven't had this much fun in a long time."

He took a deep bow, and when he stood again, he handed her his plumed hat. "For you, milady." He added, "Hell, I haven't had this much fun in the last twenty years."

They stood there awkwardly, not looking at each other,

for a long moment, and then Eddie put out his hand, which she immediately shook. "Well, good night," he said.

"Good night, Eddie."

As he drove off with the horse trailer behind his truck, Michelle stood there fingering his cavalry hat and staring after him.

Michelle had very infrequently allowed herself to think about a long-term relationship with a man. First had come the goal of being an Olympian, then a street cop, and then over the next decade she'd pounded her way through the intricacies and hardships of being a Secret Service agent. Those had been *her* expectations, *her* career goals, and she'd met each head-on and conquered them. Now at thirty-two, having settled down in a small town and started a new career, thoughts had begun to creep in about the possibilities of something else besides work, besides clawing her way to the pinnacle of a new career. She'd never really envisioned herself as a mother—though she had no reason to believe she couldn't be a good one—but she could see herself as someone's wife.

She stared at the swirl of dust lingering behind Eddie's departed truck.

And once again she heard Sean's warning ringing in her ears. Eddie *was* married, if unhappily. And so for her that was the end of it.

She went inside and spent the next hour kicking the crap out of her heavy bag.

CHAPTER

54

WHILE MICHELLE WAS AT the reenactment, King received a phone call from Sylvia Diaz at his houseboat.

"We missed you at the funeral and the reception," he said.

"Well, I didn't know the Battles, and I obviously wasn't invited to the reception. And crashing an event like that didn't seem to be a stellar idea."

"You missed some interesting developments." He explained about Remmy and Lulu Oxley but didn't mention seeing Sally Wainwright at Junior's grave. The fewer people who knew about that right now, the better, he thought.

"I need to talk to you. Are you free for dinner tonight?" she asked.

"You sound stressed. Anything wrong?"

"Sean, I think something is very wrong."

That evening King drove to a restaurant on the outskirts of Charlottesville. Sylvia hadn't wanted to meet in Wrightsburg. Her cryptic response to his question had left him full of curiosity. When they were seated at a private table in the back, he didn't waste any time. "Okay, what's going on?"

Sylvia launched into her discovery of Kyle's theft of the prescription drugs and seeing the mysterious woman at the Aphrodisiac.

King sat back, puzzled. "You didn't recognize her voice?"

"No, it was muffled by the door. Kyle obviously didn't know who she was either. And she was armed, so I didn't want to push my luck in finding out."

"No, you did the right thing. A thousand dollars a pop; that should narrow the list down."

"Obviously a wealthy woman or one with access to money."

"I thought it was only the dancers who stayed in those rooms."

"Well, I can't be sure that it *wasn't* one of the dancers," replied Sylvia. "From what I heard she performed some sort of striptease for him, although he became furious when it didn't end in sexual intercourse. I remember him clearly yelling at her for 'shaking her naked ass' right in front of him and then not letting him 'do her,' something vulgar like that. I certainly never saw that side of him at work, thank God."

"What sort of drugs are we talking?"

"Painkillers mostly, but potent ones. Some that if you circumvent the time-release component, or take too many, can give you a very dramatic shock, sometimes life-threatening."

"And you saw her leave?"

"I think it was her, but I couldn't be a hundred percent

sure. If it was, she drove off in a convertible Mercedes-Benz—you know, one of the older styles, like an antique. I couldn't get the license plate, and I couldn't make out the color for sure, but it was dark, maybe a green or dark blue. So if that was her, I guess she wasn't one of the dancers. If so, she would have just stayed at the club."

"We should still be able to trace the car."

"What should I do about Kyle?"

"Seems like it's a police matter. You have the proof and you were a witness."

"Do you think I should confront him with it?"

"No! There's no telling what he might do. I'll speak with Todd tomorrow and see what he thinks. But you better start thinking about finding a new assistant."

She slowly nodded. "I guess I should have seen this coming. Kyle was always cutting things close. I caught him on the computer in the admin office the other day, and he gave me a B.S. story about buying supplies. He was probably fudging the pharmacy inventory while I was standing right there."

"He's obviously good at lying, and while he seems like the nonviolent type, those are just the ones you have to be careful about. I'll handle it first thing in the morning."

She smiled at him. "It's nice to be taken care of for a change."

He returned the smile and looked around. "They have an excellent wine cellar here. Mind if I order something extraordinary?"

"Like I said, it's nice to be taken care of."

"If memory serves me correctly, they have a 1982 Château Ducru-Beaucaillou."

"Ducru-Beaucaillou? My French is a little rusty."

"It means 'beautiful pebble,'" he said, staring at her eyes. "Seems appropriate."

The next two hours went very quickly, and the conversation moved away from Kyle to more personal issues.

"George and I used to come here every year for our anniversary," said Sylvia as she stared out the window at the full moon hovering over them.

"Nice place to celebrate," commented King. "I actually brought Michelle here when we started our agency."

"I was laid up in the hospital so drugged up I didn't even know he'd been killed until a couple of days later."

"What were you in the hospital for?"

"Ruptured diverticulum of the colon. George performed the surgery on me. It became a little more involved once he got in there, and I had a reaction to the anesthesia and my blood pressure bottomed out. Not really a dinner topic, sorry."

"Must be stressful for a doctor to perform surgery on his wife."

"That sort of surgery was his specialty. I think he instinctively knew it might be a little more complicated than the tests showed, and he was right. George was far and away the best surgeon in the area; nationally ranked, in fact. I was in the best possible hands." She suddenly dabbed at her eyes with a napkin.

King reached over and took her hand. "I know that was all very painful for you, Sylvia. I'm really sorry you had to go through that."

She took a deep breath and wiped her eyes. "You'd think I'd get over it at some point. I keep telling myself it's part of life. In fact, whenever I autopsy a murder victim, I try to tell myself that. Death, sometimes violent, unfair death, is part of life. Without that outlook I don't think I could do my job."

He raised his glass to her. "A job you do extraordinarily well."

"Thank you, it's nice to be appreciated."

She looked at him shyly.

"What?" he said.

"I was just wondering why we stopped seeing each other."

"I was starting to wonder the same thing."

She lightly touched his hand. "Maybe we should work on that."

"Maybe we should," said King.

CHAPTER

55

KYLE WAS FURIOUS. HE'D arrived at the motel room right on time, knocked, and no one had answered. He waited outside for another thirty minutes to see if she showed. She didn't. Then he decided to try knocking again. Maybe she'd fallen asleep. Maybe she was drugged out. He tried the knob. It was locked! He looked around. There were only two other cars parked in the lot, and they were far away from this section of the motel. As he was getting into his Jeep, a car pulled into the parking lot. Kyle watched as a large flabby man and a petite woman in a tiny skirt and wobbling unsteadily on four-inch heels got out and went into one of the rooms without looking at him. Kyle shook his head. Well, at least one guy was getting some tonight. He drove off.

All the way back to his apartment he thought of various ways to track down the woman and cruelly punish her for this latest sleight. Most of all he was upset about missing the five-thousand-dollar payday.

He pulled into his parking lot, slammed the door on his Jeep and hurried up the steps. It was after one o'clock in the morning, and he had nothing to show for the lost sleep. But he'd get even. He had what she wanted, more drugs. He would turn the tables on her. He'd go to the Aphrodisiac. If she worked there, he'd find out who she was. And if not, he'd go to the room, confront her, feign retreat and then wait for her to leave the club. He'd follow her home and find out her identity. With that information in hand he'd put the squeeze on her. If she could afford a thousand bucks for fifty dollars' worth of drugs, she could afford to pay a little quiet money.

By the time he opened the door to his apartment, he had most of the plan worked out. He'd commence execution of it tomorrow.

He went to his bedroom and turned on the light. Only it didn't come on. Damn bulb again. Then he noticed the movement by the bed. It was her! Here at his apartment. She was lying on his bed, only a sheet over her. Even in the darkness he could make out the scarf and the glasses she always wore.

"What the hell are you doing here? I waited at the motel for almost an hour." It didn't occur to him to ask how she knew where he lived.

In answer she sat up, let the sheet fall slightly off her shoulders, which were bare. This got his blood going and all his anger quickly dissipated. Then she seductively pulled the sheet far up her thighs, which were also bare. Kyle felt himself growing aroused as she motioned for him to join her on the bed.

"No guns this time, okay?" he managed to stammer.

She nodded her head and then pointed to the bureau

against the wall. Kyle went over and saw the money spread out there.

When he looked back at her, she'd risen and was standing in front of him, the sheet barely covering her. She motioned with a flick of her hand for him to go over to the bed.

He did so smiling. She circled behind him. He turned to face her, his back to the bed.

The sheet dropped.

Her hand came up and Kyle froze. It looked like a gun that she was holding. When she fired, he put up his hands, as though to ward off the bullet.

The air-propelled twin darts attached by fifteen feet of wire to the Taser gun shot out and pierced his thin shirt. With one terrible jolt fifty thousand volts hit him dead in the chest, easily enough to drop a three-hundred-pound NFL lineman much less a scrawny morgue tech. The surge instantly overrode his central nervous system, and he fell backward onto the bed, where he curled into a fetal position as his muscles contracted.

Even though he'd be incapacitated for some time, the woman rushed forward to the bed and pulled the darts free. She put the Taser gun into her bag, which was lying on the floor, and slipped on a pair of gloves. She next pulled out a syringe.

Kyle looked on fearfully as she turned over his paralyzed arm, pulled up his sleeve, put a rubber tourniquet around his forearm to pop up his veins, found a good one and plunged the syringe contents into it. She quickly undid the strap and placed it and the syringe on the nightstand next to the bed.

As Kyle lay twitching on the bed, she stared down at

him. What she'd shot into him was already taking effect. He was starting to convulse more, but it wasn't enough. She took the pillow, held it over his face and pressed down. Two minutes later it was over. She removed the pillow and looked down at him again. She felt for a pulse and found none. Kyle was dead.

Despite appearing to be naked, she was actually wearing panties and a bra. She pulled a sweat suit from her bag, donned it quickly, grabbed the money, searched Kyle's pockets and found the note she'd written to him. She stuffed the note and the bedsheet she'd wrapped around her into the bag. She made sure she'd left nothing behind other than the syringe and rubber tourniquet and left the building.

As she sped away from the dead man's apartment, she took comfort in the fact that she now had one less problem to deal with.

CHAPTER

56

KING AND MICHELLE drove over to see Remmy the next morning.

King filled in Michelle on his conversation with Sylvia. "I spoke with Todd earlier this morning. He's going to pick Kyle up today."

"Any idea who the mystery woman is?"

"I guess the easiest thing to do is go to the club and ask. If she's a regular there, or works there, someone has to know about it."

In turn, Michelle filled in King on the reenactment. "It was amazing, hundreds of people with so much going on all the time. I mean, it was utter chaos, like watching a real battle. Eddie thinks they may show some of the film they took on the local PBS station," she said.

"I've actually been to a couple of those. A woman I used to date when I was in the Service had a brother who was big into them. Had a whole museum of memorabilia and stuff from the Civil War. Muskets, uniforms, swords, even an amputation kit."

"Eddie did a great job. The man has amazing skills and yet his self-esteem is rock-bottom."

"Well, his father's a hard act to follow."

"Yeah, but it's not like he hasn't accomplished anything in his life. And as physical as he is, you should have seen him when he was talking about his twin brother. In fact in some ways he may very well be the most exceptional Battle of them all."

King stared at her with a questioning expression. "And you said he drove you home? Just the two of you?"

"Will you stop with the insinuations? Nothing happened, and nothing is going to happen, between us."

"That's good to hear because the last thing we need is Dorothea or, God forbid, Remmy Battle gunning for us," King shot back.

Eddie met them at the front door of the mansion.

"I've spent the last hour trying to get her to tell me what was in that secret drawer, and getting absolutely nowhere," he reported.

"Well, if she won't tell you, I don't think we're going to crack her," said King.

"Maybe I softened her up some. She's on the rear terrace and expecting you. The coffee's hot; Mason just brought it out along with some ham biscuits."

Eddie walked out to the terrace with them. Remmy closed what looked like a diary that she was writing in. It was an old-fashioned kind with a clasp and lock across it. Remmy placed the journal inside the pocket of her jacket.

As King was greeting Remmy, Eddie motioned Michelle toward him and whispered, "When you're done here, come on by my studio; it's right behind the carriage house. I've got something to show you."

He walked off, and Michelle turned to see Remmy's keen gaze on her.

"I understand you watched Eddie playing soldier," she said slowly.

Michelle joined them at the table. King poured out coffees.

"He's certainly good at it," remarked Michelle. "I had no idea it was so involved."

"Eddie got into it because his father was interested in it. I don't think he really cares for it all that much."

"Well, he certainly looked like he loved it to me."

"Well, looks certainly can be deceiving, can't they?"

The two women gazed at each other for an uncomfortably long time.

King finally broke in. "You're a miracle worker, Remmy."

"Meaning what exactly?"

"Meaning the conversion of Lulu from enemy to friend."

Remmy waved her hand dismissively. "I was wrong and I acknowledged it. Don't make it out to be some grand gesture of benevolence."

"So what made you conclude you were wrong?" asked Michelle as she reached for a biscuit and coffee.

Remmy raised her cup and took a drink before answering. "I made Junior an offer he couldn't refuse. But he did refuse it. And then he got murdered. Doesn't take a rocket scientist to figure there's a lot more to it than I thought."

"But Junior might still have been involved. He might have been killed because of it, in fact," said King.

Remmy settled her stern gaze on him. "Didn't you try your best to convince me he was innocent? Or am I thinking of another Sean King?"

"Just playing devil's advocate."

"I forgot, you're a lawyer. Reminds me why I can't stand the breed."

"I'm glad I took down my shingle, then. I wouldn't want you for an enemy."

"No, you wouldn't," she said bluntly.

"I understand you're quite anxious to get back some property other than your jewelry and cash."

"Eddie's already been here trying, Sean," Remmy said. "And if I won't tell him, I sure as hell am not telling you."

"Is it that bad?" asked King in a very serious tone. "So bad you'd risk more people being murdered?"

"I have my reasons."

"I hope they're damn good ones, but I think you're not only being selfish but shortsighted."

"I'm unaccustomed to being spoken to that way," she snapped.

"I tend to lose my manners during a murder investigation. I trust I have my priorities right," he replied firmly.

"What was in my closet can have nothing to do with anybody getting killed."

"Your husband and Junior may have been killed by the same person. If so, the only connection I see between them is the burglary."

"It can't be, it can't," said Remmy stubbornly.

"And you won't let us be the judge of that?"

"No, I won't," she said steadfastly.

"All right, let's get back to why we're here. Eddie says that people are talking about you maybe having Bobby and Junior killed. He says it's ruining your life."

"Eddie talks too much. I thought I taught him that reserve and stoicism are two of the greatest attributes a person can have."

"But not greater than love," said Michelle. "And he does love you."

"I know that!" snapped Remmy.

"If he's worried about you, there must be a reason," Michelle persisted.

"Eddie worries too much about the wrong things."

"Remmy, we can't help you if you won't confide in us," said King.

"I never said I needed your help."

"Okay, fine. By the way, where were you when Junior was killed?"

"No one has yet told me exactly when he was killed."

After King told her the time parameters, she thought for a bit. "I was here actually, in my room reading."

"Anybody here to verify that?"

"I can."

Mason was standing in the doorway. "I was in the house until ten o'clock that night. Mrs. Battle never came out of her room during that time."

King looked at him for a long moment. "Thanks, Mason." He looked back at Remmy as Mason walked off. "It's nice to have such good, loyal help, isn't it? Last question: why was your wedding ring in the drawer and not on your finger?"

Remmy didn't answer right away. King stared at her, waiting for a response. Finally, she said, "A ring is a symbol of love and commitment."

"Yes," said King expectantly.

"You said that was your last question. I'm sure you can find your way out."

Outside, Michelle said, "Sean, you know it wasn't Remmy who killed Junior."

"That's right. I saw Mason coming out onto the patio. I wanted him to tell us where *he* was at that time."

"That was pretty clever."

"Even cleverer because he said Remmy never came out of her room."

"Meaning what?"

"Meaning that Mason doesn't have an alibi for the time Junior was killed."

"You really think he's a possible suspect?"

"Of course he is, Michelle. He's older but still big and strong enough to have taken on Junior. And you noticed that the killer never spoke to us. He only used his laser aimer to convey his instructions."

"Because if he'd spoken, we would have recognized his voice?"

"Exactly. And he lied about the reason Remmy wasn't wearing her ring."

"Speaking of which, the stoic Mrs. Battle was pretty candid with her answer. No love, no commitment, no ring. Yet she stayed married to the man."

"Lots of marriages work that way, unfortunately. Well, at least she's free of him now."

They reached King's car.

"I'm going to walk over to Eddie's studio," said Michelle.

"I'm going to find Sally and see if she'll be a little more cooperative than her employer. I'll join you at Eddie's after I'm done."

"What do you think Sally will tell you?"

"I'm tired of getting stonewalled on this case," he said, biting out the words. "So she better have a *damn* good explanation of why she was praying in front of Junior's grave."

"Sean King, did you know you're very sexy when you get mad?"

"So they tell me," King said as he marched off to corral the young horsewoman.

CHAPTER

57

KING SAW A HORSE AND rider coming toward him. However, it was Savannah, not Sally, astride a large gelding with two white-mottled forelegs.

She pulled up next to him and dismounted. She wore jeans, riding boots and a corduroy jacket.

"Beautiful day for a ride," he said.

"I can saddle you a mount."

"I haven't ridden in a while."

"Come on, it's like riding a bike."

He motioned to his jacket and dress slacks. "I'm not really dressed for it. How about a rain check?"

"Okay, sure," she said, obviously doubtful he'd ever cash in.

"I'm not just saying that, Savannah. I mean it."

"Okay. Are you here to see my mother?"

"Already did. Unfortunately, it was a short interview."

Savannah couldn't suppress a smile. "And you're surprised?"

"No, I guess I'm an optimist." He looked around. "Have you seen Sally?"

"She's in the stables over there," Savannah said, pointing over King's left shoulder. "Why?"

"Just wondering."

She looked at him suspiciously but then shrugged. "Thanks for spending some time with me after the funeral."

"It was my pleasure. I know how tough things have been for you."

"I think they're going to get tougher. That FBI agent was here again."

"Chip Bailey? What did he want?"

"He wanted to know where I was when Daddy was killed."

"That's a pretty standard question. And what did you tell him?"

"That I was at home in my room. No one saw me, at least that I know of. I guess I fell asleep, because I didn't hear my mother come in. I didn't even find out Daddy had died until the following morning."

"I'm surprised she didn't come and get you when she got the call."

"My bedroom's on the second floor, all the way at the other end of the house from hers. And I've, well, I've been going out nights and not getting back until late. She might have thought I was out and didn't bother to check."

"I see. You don't want to burn the midnight oil too much; it's bad for your complexion."

"I figure I might as well do it while I have the energy. I have a lot of years to be dull and boring."

"I don't think anyone would ever describe you in those terms. Made any decisions for the future?"

"I got a job offer from a big petrochemical company to be a field engineer. The assignment is overseas. I'm thinking about it."

"Well, you'd be, without a doubt, the prettiest field engineer anyone's ever seen."

"You keep talking that way, I might start to think you have intentions."

"I don't think I could keep up with you."

"You might surprise yourself, Mr. King."

As Savannah rode off, King's gaze followed her. He'd forgotten her particular talent: chemical engineering. And she, like many others in this bizarre case, had no alibi for the time her father was killed. And yet that was only one death and one killer. What was the other murderer doing right now? Seeking to add to his list of victims?

He found Sally in the stables mucking the stalls.

She leaned on her shovel and wiped the sweat off her brow.

"I see Savannah's back to riding," said King.

She looked at her shovel. "Never seen her doing this part of the job, though."

King decided to get right down to it. "I saw you at the funeral."

"Mr. Battle had a lot of friends. There sure were tons of people there."

"No, I meant Junior Deaver's funeral."

Sally froze. "Junior Deaver?" she said cautiously.

"Unless you have an identical twin, you were praying over his grave."

Sally started mucking again while King studied her.

"You can tell me or the FBI, it's up to you."

"I don't know what you're talking about, Sean. Why would I be praying over Junior's grave? Like I told you, I hardly knew the man."

"That's what I came here to ask you, because you obviously *did* know him."

"Well, you're wrong."

"Are you sure you want to do it this way?"

"I've got a lot of work to get done today."

"Fine, it's your call. Do you know a good lawyer?"

Sally stopped shoveling and looked at him fearfully. "What would I need with a lawyer? I haven't done anything wrong."

King took the shovel from her and set it aside. Then he drew very close, backing Sally up to one of the horse stall gates. "Let me make this as clear as I can. If you knowingly have material information about either Junior Deaver's murder or the burglary and you fail to come forward to the authorities, that's a crime punishable by imprisonment. And if you're charged with that crime, you're going to need a lawyer. If you don't have one, I can recommend several good ones."

Sally looked like she was a second away from bursting into tears.

"I don't know anything, Sean, I don't!" she wailed.

"Then you have absolutely nothing to worry about. But if you're lying to me, you could go to prison." He handed her back the shovel. "And while they don't have horses there, they do have lots of shit. Of the human variety," he added.

He pulled out one of his business cards and stuck it in the sweatband of her hat. "So when you think it through and realize I'm right, call me. I can help."

As he walked off, Sally took out the card and looked at it, an expression of helplessness on her features.

CHAPTER

58

EDDIE'S STUDIO WAS IN A two-story converted barn in the rear of the carriage house property. Michelle walked in the side door and called out, "Eddie?"

The place had been substantially remodeled inside. There were windows running along the second story and a skylight to give necessary illumination to the artist; worktables, easels and buckets of paintbrushes and other tools were neatly arranged. Large and small canvases in various stages of completion hung on the walls. The smells of oils and turpentine were heavy in the air. Stairs went up to a second-floor landing, where there appeared to be a small windowless room with a door.

"Eddie?" she called out again as she examined some of the works on the wall. The portraits and landscapes were done with meticulous attention to detail. There was one almost finished scene of a Civil War battle that, to Michelle's admittedly inexperienced eye, should have been hanging in a museum.

On another wall were a number of objects neatly hung

and labeled. They appeared to be assorted memorabilia from Eddie's reenactment hobby.

She turned when she heard feet clattering down the stairs. Eddie had on an artist's smock, the front of which was smeared with blue paint, and his hair was charmingly disheveled. Under his arm he was carrying what looked to be a small canvas. It was covered with a cloth.

"Hey, I was just finishing something up," he said.

Michelle pointed to the paintings. "I'm no expert, but I never expected to see this level of work."

He waved off her comment, but his smile betrayed how much it had pleased him. "Technically, I'm right up there, I think. But the really great artists have something— I don't think anyone can really quantify it—that I don't. But that's okay. I'm happy with what I do have, and so are my clients." He took the piece he was carrying and set it up on an empty easel but did not uncover it.

"So, any luck with Mom?"

"When your mother doesn't want to do something, you might as well try moving a mountain. But we'll keep trying. What is it?"

Eddie had turned to her with a broad smile. "Okay, close your eyes."

"What?"

"Just close your eyes."

Michelle hesitated and then did as he asked.

"Okay, now open them."

When she did, she was staring at herself, at least a version of herself on the canvas, wearing the ball gown from the reenactment. Michelle approached the canvas and studied it closely before turning to Eddie in amazement.

"That's why I wanted the Polaroid of you," he explained.

"It's beautiful. How did you do it so fast?"

"Worked on it all night. With the proper motivation a person can accomplish anything. But it doesn't do you justice, Michelle, it really doesn't." He wrapped it up with brown paper and masking tape. "You can take it with you."

"But why did you paint me?"

"You spent all day watching me play soldier, it was the least I could do."

"I enjoyed watching; it wasn't a burden."

"I still appreciate it."

She touched the wrapped painting. "And I appreciate this."

She gave him a hug and was surprised at how tightly he squeezed her; how strong he was. And she squeezed back. For one long moment their bodies were compressed together. He smelled of paint and sweat and something else, something intensely male. Her hands lightly traced the hard muscles of his back and shoulders. She didn't want to let go, but she finally drew back from him, her gaze downcast.

He cupped his hand under her chin and raised it. "Look, I know this is probably getting a little awkward for you. I'm not throwing myself at you. You're not going to wake up tomorrow and find a new car in your driveway. But—"

"Eddie—," she began, but he held up his hand.

"But it's just nice to have a friend is what I'm saying."

"I'd think you'd have lots of those, both men and women."

"I'm more of a loner really. I paint and I fight in pretend battles."

"And you do them both extremely well," she said.

"Yes, you do," said another voice.

They looked over as King came walking in.

"Hey, Eddie," he said.

The men shook hands while Michelle looked on self-consciously.

King glanced around at the art on the walls. "You've really got a tremendous eye."

"You sure my mother didn't pay you to say that?"

King looked at the wall of Civil War memorabilia. "An interesting collection."

"One of my few hobbies." He grinned at Michelle. "You know, Sean, we need to get you into reenactments. I can see you up on a sturdy steed charging right into the teeth of a Union battery, sleeping with the mosquitoes and eating hardtack until your arteries pop."

King glanced at Michelle and smiled. "The day you see that is the day the sky falls and kills us all," he said, paraphrasing Michelle's response to Lulu's pole-dancing offer.

Eddie was about to say something when King's cell phone rang. He answered it, listened and then clicked off, his features very troubled.

"That was Sylvia. Kyle Montgomery's been found dead."

"What!" exclaimed Michelle.

"Who's Kyle Montgomery?" asked Eddie, bewildered.

"Sylvia Diaz's assistant," answered Michelle. "Was he murdered?"

"Sylvia's not sure. She said it looks right now like a

drug overdose, but she's not convinced. She wants us to meet her at Kyle's apartment. Todd's there too."

The two hustled out. Michelle called back over her shoulder, "Eddie, I'll give you a call. Thanks."

As they exited the building, Eddie looked at the wrapped portrait. "But you forgot your paint—" They were already out of earshot. He shrugged in disappointment and carried the painting upstairs.

CHAPTER

59

THE FORENSICS TEAM HAD finished by the time they reached Kyle's apartment. He was still on the bed, his lifeless eyes fixed on the ceiling of the small, dank apartment.

Sylvia was looking down at him when King touched her on the shoulder. She turned, and there were tears in her eyes. She dabbed at them with her hand and straightened up, assuming a more professional appearance.

"It's okay, Sylvia," said King. "You two weren't best friends but I know it still hurts."

She blew her nose into a tissue and nodded at the techs standing by. "You can take him."

They placed Kyle in a body bag and carried it out.

Todd Williams came over to join them.

Michelle said, "So it *was* a drug overdose? We're not looking at another serial killing?"

The chief shook his head. "No watch and no dog collar thing going on."

King was staring at Sylvia. "But on the phone you said you weren't sure it was a drug overdose."

"Certainly, we found indications that it was," she said slowly.

Williams added, "A syringe, rubber tourniquet and a needle mark on his forearm."

Sylvia said, "We need to run tests on any residue in the syringe to see what it was. That'll take a few days. And I'll run toxicology on the body fluids, but we won't know the results of those for at least two weeks."

"You can't tell from the autopsy what was shot into him?" asked Williams.

"Yes and no. If it was heroin, for example, which is a respiratory depressant, there might be some slight heaviness or congestion in the lungs and a foamy mucus in the airway, but it would be far from conclusive. The fact is, if he died of an overdose, the autopsy alone won't reveal what it was for certain. We have to rely on the toxicology results for that. If it was cocaine, the tox report will pick that up. If it was heroin, 6-monoacetylmorphine, a metabolite of heroin, will be found in the body. That's pretty conclusive proof of a heroin overdose."

"Maybe it was a drug from your office."

"Possible, but if the screens find 6-monoacetylmorphine in Kyle's blood or urine and don't find the presence of aspirin or Tylenol, that will be proof enough that it's not a prescription opiate narcotic in his system."

"Tylenol or aspirin?" asked Williams.

"Yes, because prescription opiates are frequently combined with those medications. That's not the case with heroin or cocaine or other street drugs."

"Who found him?" asked Michelle.

"I did," said Williams. "After you called me this morning, I decided to handle it myself. I came here with a deputy. We knocked. There was no answer. His Jeep was parked in front, so we figured he was here. We called his apartment and his cell phone, but there was no answer. We didn't have a warrant to go in, but it was suspicious enough that I went to the super's office and got them to open it. That's when we found him."

"The core body temp and degree of rigor mortis suggest he's been dead less than twelve hours," opined Sylvia.

King checked his watch. "So sometime after midnight or so?"

"Yes."

"And no one saw anyone enter or leave the apartment?" asked King.

"We're still checking on that," said Williams.

"Okay, we need to find this mystery woman at the Aphrodisiac pronto," said King.

"I'm heading over there today," said Williams.

"We'd like to go with you, Todd," said King. "Can you hold off for a couple of hours and meet us there? We'll call you."

"I guess that won't hurt."

"When are you going to do the post, Sylvia?" asked Michelle.

"Right away. I've canceled my patients for the day."

"Now that Kyle is dead, can't you get someone to help you?" said King. "They can send someone from Richmond or Roanoke."

"But on such short notice it won't be right away," said Sylvia.

"But if he did die of an overdose, it won't matter. You

said you won't have confirmation for a couple of weeks," said Williams.

"But there might be other evidence that's slowly disappearing as we speak," said Sylvia sharply. "The body speaks to us after death, Todd, but the longer you wait, the softer the voice becomes."

"Well, I'll help you," said Williams. "I need to attend the post anyway." He added, "It's becoming damn routine."

As they were all walking out, King stopped Sylvia. "Are you okay?"

She looked at him with a sickened expression. "I think it's possible Kyle committed suicide."

"Suicide! Why?"

"He may have suspected I was on to his drug dealing."

"But killing himself, that's a little drastic. And the guy struck me as spineless. And there was no suicide note either."

"Cowards kill themselves, Sean. They're afraid to face the consequences of their actions."

"And, what, you're blaming yourself?"

"If it was suicide, I can think of no other reason than my suspicions."

"That's not fair to you, Sylvia. You didn't ask the guy to steal drugs."

"No, but—"

"Before you beat yourself up over this, why don't you do the post? As good as you are, you can't predict what happened until you do that."

"But even the post won't tell me if the overdose was accidental or intentional."

"The bottom line is, it was Kyle's choice. You had no

control over it. And life is full of enough legitimate guilt without us adding the guilt of others to our burden."

Sylvia managed a weak smile. "You're a very wise man."

"I've had lots of practice. Primarily dealing with my own stupid mistakes."

"I'll call you when I'm done with the post."

"I sincerely hope this is the last one you'll have to do for a long time."

As he started to turn away, she said, "Last night was the most fun I've had in years."

"I can say the same."

As King and Michelle drove off, Michelle looked over at him. "Am I wrong, or have you and Sylvia rekindled your romance?" He shot her a glance but said nothing. "Come on, Sean, don't feed me that line about my being your partner and not your shrink."

"Why not? It's still a valid point."

She slumped back in her seat with a defeated expression. "Okay. Fine."

"What do you care anyway?"

"I care because we're right in the middle of a very complicated murder investigation, and we don't need the best detective on the case and the *brilliant* medical examiner being distracted by a romance."

"If I didn't know better, I'd say you were jealous."

"Oh, please!"

"I said if I didn't know better. And don't worry, right now everything else takes a backseat to this case." He paused and added, "I saw you and Eddie hugging."

She looked at him angrily. "You were spying on us!"

"No, I peeked in the window as I was going to the door to see if you were in there. I didn't know you two were trying to crawl inside each other's bodies."

"That's so unfair, Sean. I was just thanking him for a painting he did of me."

"Oh, he painted a portrait of you? That should make his intentions quite clear."

"He's unhappy."

"And it's not your job to fix that unhappiness," he retorted. "So just let it go, Michelle. The last thing you need right now is for your judgment to be clouded."

Michelle looked ready to argue but remained silent.

King continued, "He's an attractive, fun and nice guy who's had more than his share of tragedy, and to top it off he's caught in a miserable marriage. You wouldn't be the first woman in history to want to help a man like that."

"You sound like you've experienced stuff like that."

"The world is full of *stuff* like that. And none of us are immune to it."

"Okay, okay, I get the message. So where to now?"

"We're going to see Roger Canney. It seems he came into a substantial sum of money right around the time of his wife's death. Its origins are unclear."

"That's interesting."

"You haven't heard the most interesting part. The late Mrs. Canney had a job."

"Really? Where?" Michelle asked.

"Battle Enterprises. Care to guess which executive she was servicing?"

"Bobby Battle!"

"You win the prize."

CHAPTER

60

NO ONE ANSWERED THEIR knock at the Canney residence.

"That's funny," said King. "I called ahead. He said he'd be home."

"At least the housekeeper should be here."

Michelle went over and peeked inside the garage window. "Well, there are two cars in there, a big Beemer and a Range Rover. Unless he pays his housekeeper extremely well, I don't think they belong to her."

King put a hand on the front door, and it swung open. Michelle saw this and immediately took out her gun and rejoined King.

"I swear to God," she whispered, "if he's in there dead with a dog collar around his neck and wearing a watch pointing to the number six, I'm going to scream for an entire week."

They made their way quietly inside. The front room was empty. They cleared each subsequent room before moving on to the next.

Michelle heard the noise first, a grunting sound, appearing to come from the back of the house. They hustled there and looked around. They saw no one, but the sound repeated itself, followed this time by a clanking noise of metal on metal.

Michelle motioned to a door at the end of the hall. King nodded, moved forward and slowly pushed it open with his foot while Michelle covered him. King peered inside, tensed and then relaxed. He opened the door and motioned for Michelle to join him.

Canney was seated with his back to them, earphones on and doing leg presses in his nicely equipped home gym. King pounded on the door, and Canney snapped around and ripped off his headphones.

"What the hell are you doing here?" he demanded.

"I called this morning. You said one o'clock was fine. It's one o'clock. Nobody answered the door and it happened to be open."

Canney stood and put his CD player down and toweled off. "I'm sorry. My housekeeper has the day off, and I must have lost track of time."

"Happens to the best of us," said King. "We can wait if you want to clean up."

"No, I think we can just get down to it. I can't imagine this will take long. Let's sit outside. I made some lemonade."

They went into the large backyard, which had a lap pool, spa and a small cabana-style building as well as intricately planned landscaping.

"Beautiful," commented Michelle.

"Yes, I love it back here."

"It all looks fairly recent," said King. "And you

haven't lived in this house that long, have you? What, three years or so?"

Canney stared pointedly at him as he drank his lemonade. "How did you know?"

"Public records are just that, public. You're retired now. From accounting?"

"Twenty years seemed long enough to worry about other people's money."

"Well, now you have plenty of your own to worry about. I guess accounting pays better than I thought."

"I've made some good investments over the years."

"And your late wife worked too, at Battle Enterprises. She was executive secretary to Bobby Battle, wasn't she? In fact, she was working there when she died in that car accident?"

"Yes. It's not exactly a secret."

"I didn't see you at Battle's funeral."

"That's because I didn't go."

"You hadn't kept in touch with the family?"

"Just because my wife worked there doesn't mean we were friends with them."

"I found a picture of your wife while I was doing my background research. She was a very beautiful woman; had even won some local beauty pageants."

"Megan was extraordinarily attractive, yes. Does this line of conversation have some point?"

"The point being that I had to hunt up pictures of your wife because there are none of her in your home. Nor are there any of your son."

"You mean, not out in the public areas."

"No. When no one answered the door and we found it

open, we thought there was something amiss, so we went room to room, including your bedroom; there are no photos at all of your family."

Canney stood, enraged. "How dare you!"

King remained impassive. "Let me be blunt with you, Rog: you came into your money roughly three years ago, soon after your wife died, in fact. That's when you bought this place. Before then you were an ordinary bean-counter making an ordinary income and doing okay because your wife was working too. Those sorts of people don't suddenly retire *after* they lose their spouse's income, and buy a million-dollar property."

"She had life insurance."

"Fifty thousand dollars. I checked that too."

"What exactly are you implying?"

"I'm not interested in implications. I'd much prefer the truth."

"This interview is over. I believe you know the way out, since you've already searched my house."

King and Michelle rose. "Okay, we can do it the hard way."

"And you can do it with Giles Kinney, my lawyer. He'll tear you apart."

King smiled. "Giles doesn't scare me. I kick his butt on the golf course at least once a week."

CHAPTER

61

KING AND MICHELLE MET
Todd Williams and two of his deputies at the Aphrodisiac
and were soon in Lulu's office questioning her about the
occupant of the room and Kyle's visits there. At first she
denied knowing anything about it but finally admitted
that she'd recently seen Kyle at the club.

"But I don't know who the lady is," she said. "She
doesn't work here. I know that for a fact."

"What, you're in the charity business now, letting
rooms out for free to rich drug users?" said Williams
sarcastically.

"I didn't know anything like that was going on. She
paid for the room, in cash. I just thought she needed a
place to stay."

"Was she here every night?"

"I didn't keep track really. Unless you're going into
one of the performance areas to see the girls or the bars,
you don't have to show ID. We have restaurants and
lounges here too, and a business center. Anyone can come

in and go to one of those places. We are open to the public," she added hotly.

King shook his head. "Come on, Lulu, are you saying that when the woman first came here, you never spoke to her? How the hell did you know what she even wanted?"

"She left cash and a note that said she wanted that room and that room only."

"And you did what? You just gave it to her without question?"

"It's just a room, Sean! And cash is cash. It's not like she was running some criminal business in there. She only came at night. During the day we had the room cleaned, like all the others. There was never anything there. I know it sounds a little weird, and I admit I was curious. In fact, when she first started coming, I kept an eye peeled. There was never any loud noise or stuff like that. Except for this Kyle person, no one ever visited her."

"Did you see her come and go?"

"Sometimes. But she always wore a scarf, long coat and glasses."

"And that didn't make you suspicious? Didn't you ever try to find out who she was? Wait and watch her leave, trace her somehow?"

"Of course I was suspicious, but I'm not one to pry into other people's business either. Live and let live is my motto. If she wanted a private room and didn't want anyone to know who she was, at least she was willing to pay well for the privilege. And so there you are. I'm not into scaring off customers," she added defiantly.

"Well, Kyle Montgomery is dead, possibly murdered, so that puts a different spin on things," said Williams.

Lulu looked at him nervously. "I don't know anything about that. He sure wasn't killed here, so I don't see what this place has to do with it."

"Well, let me enlighten you, then," said the police chief. "We have a witness who says a very heated altercation took place here between Kyle and this woman. We know he was bringing her prescription drugs that he'd stolen from the doctor's office where he worked."

"I don't know anything about that."

Williams continued. "So they had an argument recently, and last night, Kyle dies."

"Well, I didn't kill him, and I don't know who the lady is."

"Did she come here last night?"

"Not that I know of. At least I didn't see her."

"When was the last time you did see her?"

Lulu thought. "I can't be sure. I've had other things on my mind, including a husband to bury," she said, bristling.

"We're going to need to question anyone here who might have seen her."

"Some of those people aren't due into work until later."

"Then right now I want to see the room, and I want to question whoever *is* here who might have seen her."

Lulu looked at him nervously. "Right now?"

"Is there a problem with that?"

"No, it's just that some of the night-shift dancers are still sleeping."

"Sleeping. It's two-thirty in the afternoon!"

"They dance until dawn!"

"All right, let's start with the nondancers, but in the meantime you get those gals up and ready to talk to us. You understand, Lulu?"

"I understand," she said quickly.

As they were leaving, Michelle glanced back and saw Lulu's hand disappear inside a drawer of her desk, just as it had the other time she and King were here.

Once they were outside, Michelle said, "Todd, why don't you collect the people and start the questioning? Sean and I'll poke around a bit."

"Good idea. We'll compare notes later."

"What's up?" said King after the police chief and his men had left them.

"Come on, quick."

Michelle led him outside and to the back of the building where she spotted a staircase leading from the second floor. They stayed concealed behind a Dumpster and waited. Within a minute or so their patience was rewarded. A number of men, some carrying coats over their arms, others with their shirts unbuttoned and untucked and hair sticking up, emerged from a second-floor door and made their way down the outside stairs, climbed into cars parked there and sped off.

King and Michelle looked at each other.

"Appears the Aphrodisiac is living up to its name. Nice catch, Michelle," said King.

"And prostitution is one way to enhance the old revenue stream," added Michelle. "So what do we do about it?"

"I think another talk with Lulu is in order."

"Husband dead and three kids. I know it's a crime,

Sean, but I'm not real excited about helping to send her to prison."

"Perhaps we can show her the error of her ways."

When Lulu returned to her office later, King was sitting behind her desk and Michelle was standing beside him.

"What are you doing in here?" Lulu barked.

In answer King reached inside the drawer and pressed the buzzer they'd found there earlier.

"I hope this second warning doesn't confuse the girls, but at least all the johns have already left the joint."

Lulu's mouth dropped open but she quickly recovered. "What's that supposed to mean?"

"Sit down, Lulu," King said very firmly. "We're here to help you. But if you try to bullshit us even a little bit, we'll just tell Todd to come in here and take over. And then it'll be out of our hands."

Lulu stared fiercely at them but finally sat down, her hands fidgeting in her lap.

"If you want to light up, feel free; we might be here awhile."

Lulu did so, sucking in the smoke and then purging it out her nostrils.

King sat back in his chair. "Okay, explain the setup."

"It's not what you think," Lulu said.

"You're far too smart to do it the old-fashioned way, so I'm sure you have something very creative. I'm anxious to hear what it is."

Lulu looked nervously at them. "I've worked hard for years to build up this place. Long hours, ignoring my kids at times, and Junior too. I've got ulcers and a two-pack-a-day habit. Sure, I'm the minority owner but I really run the place. My partners spend most of their time in Florida. But they're always on me to keep pushing up the profits so they can buy bigger boats and better-looking wives. More, more, more—that's all I hear."

"So you came up with ways to do that with the dancers?"

"My partners suggested it actually. I didn't want to do it but they insisted. Said they'd find another manager who would, and get rid of me. But any girl who didn't want to do it didn't—no questions asked. I wouldn't back down on that." She hesitated and then said, "If I tell you . . ."

"Lulu, like Sean said, we're here to help you," said Michelle.

She suddenly yelled out, "Why? Why do you care?"

King answered, "Because we think you're basically a good person and a mother with three children who need you. You've been under tremendous pressure and you just lost your husband. What you tell us goes no further, you have our word."

Lulu took a deep breath and began. "No money exchanges hands between any of the girls and any of the men. We . . . well, we formed a club of sorts. The members pay an initiation fee to the club to join and then a monthly amount based on . . . well, based on usage. We book it as business networking."

"Well, that's certainly an original way to network. Go on," said King.

"It's a fairly large sum, so the clientele is limited and of a certain level."

"Translation: wealthy guys looking for some action in bed," commented King.

"Anyway, with their membership they have access to

the girls by appointment only. The members are given special words to tell the girls so they know it's okay. They all use protection and there's no dangerous stuff allowed. Anybody gets rough with one of the girls gets kicked out for good. But we've never had any problems. The dancers who participate get extra pay."

"Pretty creative, but it's still illegal, Lulu. This could shut the club down and put you right in prison."

Lulu lit another cigarette and looked like she might be sick. "I know," she said in a trembling voice. "God, I knew this whole thing was stupid."

"And the buzzer in your office is connected to the rooms, to alert the girls and their clients if there's a problem, and they clear out through the rear exit."

"Yes," Lulu said miserably. "And I have people keeping an eye on the entrance to the hallway from time to time."

"So how did Kyle get through, then?"

"The lady left a note and a picture of Kyle telling me he was okay." She put her cigarette out. "I can tell you this much. There was someone who followed Kyle in the night I saw him. One of my lookouts told me about it later."

"That was Sylvia Diaz, the doctor Kyle works for."

"Name sounds familiar."

"She's the local medical examiner. And before you changed doctors, you two shared the same gynecologists."

"I haven't changed my ob-gyn."

"Okay, the point is, she was the witness who saw Kyle here and heard the argument between him and the woman." He paused and said, "You're going to have to put an end to it, Lulu. No more, starting today, or else it all comes tumbling down."

"I'll have to refund the men their money. That's a lot of cash."

"No, you won't. They knowingly participated in an illegal scheme. Tell them they had a close call today and that's it. Tell them if you pay the money back, it can be traced to them if there's a later investigation. I'm certain they'll pass on the money to avoid the risk." He stared at her pointedly. "This is your only way out, Lulu."

She finally nodded in understanding. "I'll call them all today."

"And talk to your partners in Florida. Make it clear to them that the long arm of Virginia law reaches that far south. If they don't want to lose the boats and the babes, they better get off your back and stick to pole dancing and beer, which I'm sure pays a pretty penny."

King rose and motioned for Michelle to join him in leaving. "And with Remmy helping to take care of the kids financially and finishing up your house, you might want to spend less time here and more time at home. It's just a suggestion."

As they were heading out, Lulu called to them. "Look, I owe you a big debt. All I can say is thank you."

King turned back. "I figured you were about due a break. Good luck." He and Michelle started to leave again but paused when Lulu called to them again.

"I do know what kind of car the woman drives. I saw it one time."

"We know too. An older-model Mercedes convertible."

"It was more than that. It was a true classic, a 1959 300 SL Roadster."

"How do you know that?" asked Michelle.

"One of my partners is a car buff. He's got a fleet of fancy ones he keeps down in Naples. He taught me a lot. The one the lady drives is a beauty. It's worth a small fortune."

King muttered something under his breath. "Lulu, consider your debt paid in full. Come on, Michelle." He grabbed her arm and pushed her out the door.

"What's the rush?" asked Michelle.

"I think I know where to find that car."

CHAPTER

62

KING PARKED HIS LEXUS on a side road and got out.

"We'll have to walk from here. I don't want anyone to see us if we can help it."

"Where are we going?"

"Be patient. You'll see soon enough."

They climbed over a rear gate and made their way down a gravel road. Through a break in a long row of one of the twelve-foot hedges planted on either side, Michelle caught a glimpse of the house in the distance and commented, "We're at the Battles'." As King moved away from the direction of the house, she said, "Sean, the house is that way."

"That's not where I'm heading."

"Where, then?"

King pointed up ahead. "To the car barn."

They reached the large structure without being seen. King was able to jimmy open a side door, and they went inside. He made his way along each of the cars on the first floor, looking under their protective cloth covers. Finished with the first floor, they headed up the stairs to the second.

There were a number of covered cars up there, and King started checking each. Arriving at the third vehicle, he lifted off the cover completely and let it drop to the floor. He looked at the vehicle's model name.

"A 300 SL." He knelt down and inspected the tires, running his hand along the tread. He held up one finger for Michelle to see.

"Mud," she said. "But how could someone take this car and no one know about it?"

"Easy. This building isn't used anymore, Sally told us. And it's not visible from the house. And that gravel road we came up leads right to the side road. If she's only driving late at night, chances are good no one would see her."

"*Her.* So I guess it's pretty clear who our sexy stripper/ drug user is."

King straightened up. "Yes, it is. And I guess we better go and talk to her."

"This isn't going to be pretty."

"Trust me: not knowing the truth is even uglier."

They headed in the direction of the mansion. Before they got there, however, King veered off, passed by the stables and went through the gate connecting the carriage house and the Battle mansion properties.

"Sean, where are you going? Savannah'll be at Casa Battle."

King ignored her and kept marching along. She hurried after him. He saw the car parked out front, raced up the steps and pounded on the carriage house's front door. They soon heard footsteps coming and the door opened.

"What do you want?" she asked.

"Can we come in, Dorothea?" asked King. He placed one foot inside the doorway in case he didn't get the answer he wanted.

"Why?" she demanded.

"Kyle Montgomery's dead."

One of Dorothea's hands flew to her chest, and she stepped back as though staggered by a physical blow. "I . . . I don't know who that is."

"We know everything, Dorothea. We traced the car."

"What car?"

"The 300 SL in the car barn you used to drive to the Aphrodisiac."

She stared defiantly at them. "You're wrong."

"We're wasting time," King said impatiently. "You were seen leaving the club, Dorothea. We have a witness who recently saw you get in the car and drive off around five in the morning."

Dorothea's defiant look started to fade.

"This same person heard you and Kyle arguing. You pulled a gun on him. You threatened him—"

"I didn't threaten that little . . ." Dorothea stopped and looked like she might faint.

King said quietly, "I thought you'd want to talk to us first, before the police. But if not, we can go ahead and call them now."

"Oh, my God," she said. Within seconds her hardened exterior simply crumbled and tears slid down her cheeks. King pushed open the door and they went in.

CHAPTER

63

"I DIDN'T KILL HIM, SEAN. I didn't."

"But you were buying drugs from him?"

They were sitting in the living room. King and Michelle were in wing chairs. Dorothea was on the small sofa across from them, clutching the arm of the furniture as though if she let go, she'd topple to the floor.

"I've been under tremendous pressure lately," she began slowly. "I've had some . . . financial reverses."

"Spending a thousand dollars a night on drugs isn't exactly the way to stop financial problems."

She looked at him, stunned. "Did you talk to that little shrimp!"

"Careful, one shouldn't speak ill of the dead. Tell me about that night."

"How much do you know?"

"Enough that if you start lying, I'll know, and that won't make me happy."

"I don't know what came over me, I really don't. I

could tell Kyle wanted to sleep with me. Not that it wasn't obvious. Men are so transparent."

"But you didn't want to sleep with *him*?"

"Of course not. But I'd had a lot to drink. And I'd made up my mind that that night was the last time. Like you said, drugs weren't going to solve my problems. And it wasn't just the money problems. It was the family . . . Marrying into the Battle clan carries with it a lot of pressure and stress."

"I can see having Remmy as a mother-in-law wouldn't exactly be a walk in the park," commented Michelle dryly.

"It was a complete and total nightmare. Everything I did, wore, ate, drank or said was scrutinized. And they weren't tactful about criticism. Bobby was far worse than Remmy. He was such a tyrant. And his mood swings were terrifying. Smiling and happy one minute, screaming and bullying the next. Anyone could be a target, even Remmy. I've started seeing a therapist, trying to tackle my issues in a more constructive way."

"That's good," said King. "But you were telling us about Kyle."

"Yes. Well, when Kyle came with the drugs, I was a little looped and decided to screw with him. So I, well, I . . ." She stopped, her face flushing. "It was idiotic. I know that."

"We know about the striptease. You don't have to elaborate. But you pulled a gun on him."

"He was about to attack me! I had to protect myself."

"And you demanded the money back."

"I'd paid him enough. He was stealing the drugs. His profit margin was a hundred percent. I was just trying to make the transaction a little fairer from my end."

"So you got the money back?"

"Yes. I pretended I was going to shoot him, and he ran out. That's the last time I saw him, I swear."

"How did you end up approaching him in the first place?"

"I knew he worked at Sylvia's office, although we never had any direct contact. I'd gone there for a back injury. The painkillers she prescribed became sort of a necessity, but after my treatment was completed, Sylvia wouldn't write any more prescriptions. But by then I was hooked. I knew Sylvia kept the drugs I wanted at her office. I could tell Kyle was a marginal person: ready, willing and able to do anything for money. And I knew prescription drugs from a medical office were far safer than anything you could buy on the street. Besides, I had no wish to get hooked up with an actual drug dealer. I picked the Aphrodisiac as the rendezvous spot because I'd had lunches and meetings there and knew they had rooms and wouldn't ask any questions."

"And you don't think he knew who you were? He'd obviously seen you at Sylvia's office."

"I always wore glasses and a scarf, kept the lights low and spoke very little. And if he had recognized me, I'm sure he would've tried to blackmail me."

King was looking at her closely when she said this. She caught his look and paled.

"I know this seems really bad, Sean."

"Dorothea, it is really bad. Does Eddie know about any of this?"

"No! Please, you can't tell him. We don't have the

world's greatest marriage, but I still care for him and this will kill him."

"I can't promise you anything, Dorothea. Now, I want to know where you were last night."

"I was here."

"Eddie can corroborate that?" asked Michelle. "He came back early from the reenactment."

"How did you know that?" asked Dorothea.

Michelle looked uncomfortable. "I drove up with Chip Bailey to Middleton to see the battle. Chip had to leave early and Eddie drove me back. He said he wasn't going to stay for the second day of the reenactment."

Dorothea stared at her suspiciously and then said, "Well, he wasn't in the house last night. He was probably in his studio. He sleeps there sometimes."

Michelle started to say something but then stopped.

King said, "So you don't have an alibi. By the way, I called the Jefferson Hotel in Richmond. You never checked in on the night Bobby was killed, like you said you did. The FBI will also have discovered that fact. Were you at the Aphrodisiac that night?"

"Yes. Kyle brought me the drugs around ten o'clock."

"Ironic."

"What is?"

"He was your alibi for your father-in-law's murder, but now he's dead. So unless someone else at the club saw you, there goes your alibi for that murder too."

Dorothea put her head in her hands and started sobbing. Finally, Michelle rose, went into the kitchen and came back with a wet cloth for her.

"Just take it easy, Dorothea," said King. "Kyle's death

hasn't been ruled a murder yet. It might just be a drug overdose. Or even a suicide."

"I can't imagine that man taking his own life. The little I saw of him he was far too interested in furthering his own interests." Dorothea wiped her face with the cloth and then stared across at King. "So where do we go from here?"

"We can't keep your actions secret."

Dorothea's lips started to tremble. "I guess I couldn't expect you would."

"The extent of what has to be revealed is still to be determined, however."

"I didn't kill Kyle Montgomery or my father-in-law!"

"Speaking of the latter, why did you go to the hospital that day?"

"Does it really matter now?"

"It could."

She drew a long breath. "Bobby promised me money, a larger part of his estate. His will needed to be changed to do that. He said he'd do it, but had never given me proof he had."

"So you went there to see if he'd verify he'd done it?"

"I heard he was awake and talking. I didn't know if I'd have another chance. My financial problems would be solved if Bobby had changed his will like he said he would."

"No, you mean they'd be solved when he *died* and you actually got the money," corrected Michelle.

"Yes," Dorothea said quietly as she looked down. "Anyway, when I got there he wasn't coherent, and was back on the ventilator."

"Did Eddie know about this change-in-the-will prospect?"

"No. Eddie thinks we're fine financially. Eddie doesn't worry about anything."

"I think you're wrong there," said Michelle.

"Why would Bobby change his will to favor you and Eddie over Remmy? From what I've heard he'd already provided for you both."

Dorothea smiled tightly. "Can one ever have enough money? I know I can't. And Bobby had so *damn* much of it."

He eyed her steadily. "Bobby was a tough negotiator. So what was the quid pro quo, Dorothea?"

"I'd rather not say," she finally replied. "It's not something I'm exactly proud of."

"Actually, I think I can guess. The little striptease you did for Kyle probably paled in comparison. By the way, why did you drive one of Bobby's classic cars to the Aphrodisiac?"

She looked at him with a triumphant smile. "I figured he owed me at least that. And he never drove them anymore."

"Do you know why?"

"He got tired of them, I guess. The great Bobby Battle was renowned for that. Getting tired of things and then forgetting about them." She stifled a sob.

King stood and looked down at her with little sympathy. "If Kyle's death is ruled a murder, the police will want to question you."

"I suppose it doesn't matter now. It can't get any worse."

"Oh, no, Dorothea, it can get a lot worse."

As they left the house, Michelle said, "How did you

know it was her? I had Savannah pegged as our druggie-stripper."

"No, she couldn't be."

"Why not? You remember the way she flaunted herself at the pool that day."

"Exactly. That was the answer. Sylvia said that when she was at the Aphrodisiac, she overheard Kyle say that the woman was *flaunting* her naked butt."

"Yes, so?"

"Well, Savannah has her name tattooed on *her* butt. Other things being equal, I doubt she'd show it off to Kyle if she wanted to remain incognito. There's only one Savannah in Wrightsburg with a derriere like that."

CHAPTER

64

LATER THAT DAY THEY received word from Sylvia that she'd completed the autopsy of Kyle Montgomery. They arranged to meet at King's office. When she showed up, Todd Williams was with her. A minute later Chip Bailey pulled into the parking lot.

"I called him," explained Williams. "I figured we needed to keep him in the loop, even though Kyle's killing isn't connected to the serial murders."

"Are you sure it's not?" replied King.

Williams looked at him sharply. "Are you *trying* to drive me nuts?"

As they settled themselves in the conference room, Sylvia opened her folder.

"As I said, we won't know the exact cause of death until we get the toxicology screens back," she began. "However, there were some unusual findings on the external exam that lead me to believe his death was suspicious."

"As in suicide by overdose?" asked King.

"No, as in homicide." She paused and then began speaking quickly but firmly. "Kyle was not a known drug user. We found no other drugs or drug paraphernalia in his apartment, and there were no other needle marks on any part of his body."

"But you did find a used syringe with something in it and a needle mark in the arm," commented Bailey.

"The something in the syringe has been confirmed as heroin. Okay, let's say Kyle wanted to kill himself. Heroin is a street drug, so you can never be certain of the dose you're actually injecting. And you also have to wonder where he obtained it. I obviously don't have any in my pharmacy."

Williams said, "But he'd know more than a layperson. And the sad truth is, there are sources of illegal drugs everywhere."

"But if you're going to kill yourself, you're looking to get it right the first time. Bottom line: heroin isn't a good choice for suicide. But more importantly, I found two small superficial puncture wounds in the center of Kyle's chest. I hadn't noticed them at the crime scene because of the poor lighting."

"What sort of punctures?" said Bailey.

"Like tiny needles set barely an inch apart. It's some sort of patterned injury."

"Like from a syringe?" asked Michelle.

"No. And you wouldn't use a syringe on your chest. Arms and legs are by far the best locations for injection purposes."

"Well, what do you think it is, then?" asked King.

"I've seen a case like this before in Richmond, after a

riot. A man went into cardiac arrest and died after police incapacitated him with a Taser gun. A Taser would leave twin marks like I saw on Kyle where the electrified darts impacted the body."

Bailey said, "So somebody shoots him with the Taser and then injects him with an overdose. That's why there was no sign of a struggle."

"I can't be absolutely certain about the Taser, but there's more. I also found small petechiae and hemorrhages in his eyes and mouth."

"That's a sign of asphyxia, of being smothered," said Michelle.

"Exactly. The hemorrhages occur as one struggles for air. Now, there was no evidence of strangulation at autopsy, so I'm thinking he might have been suffocated with an object that would leave no such traces, like a pillow. And heroin is a respiratory depressant; his breathing would already have been very shallow, and that would have aided the person trying to kill him by suffocation."

"So if he was murdered and the person tried to make it look like a suicide, who has the motive to kill him?" asked Bailey.

"Well, the woman he was selling drugs to at the Aphrodisiac for one," said Williams. Bailey looked at him questioningly, and the police chief filled in his colleague.

Bailey said, "So she gets the money back, why kill him?"

"What if Kyle learned who she was and was trying to blackmail her?" suggested Sylvia. "That would be a prime motive for murder: fear of exposure."

"So we need to find this woman, and fast," said Williams.

Michelle and King exchanged glances.

"We know who she is," he said.

They all looked at him in surprise.

"Well, who the hell is she?" asked Williams.

"Dorothea Battle. And she's got no alibi for the time Kyle was killed."

"Dorothea Battle?" The police chief rose from his chair. "Why the hell didn't you tell me this right away, Sean?"

"We just found out ourselves. She admitted it to us."

Williams pulled out his cell phone. "Well, we'll pick her up pronto, then."

"She's at her house."

"You mean you hope she is. If she's flown the coop, I'm holding you responsible."

"I don't think she killed Kyle, Todd."

Williams ignored this and spoke into his phone, ordering the arrest of Dorothea Battle. When that was done, he looked at the private investigator. "And what do you base that conclusion on?"

"Gut instinct."

"Thanks, I'll keep that in mind."

"If Dorothea did kill this guy, we might have three killers out there. The serial killer, the person who killed Bobby Battle and now whoever killed Montgomery," said Bailey.

"Or Dorothea could have killed Bobby," said Williams. He looked at King. "Did she say anything about why she went to see Battle?"

"Dorothea was hoping Bobby had changed his will to give her more money. She said she went to the hospital to make sure he'd done so. As it turned out, he hadn't.

Remmy got the money. So his death didn't benefit Dorothea at all."

Michelle spoke up. "She said he was incoherent. But what if when she visited him, he told her that he hadn't changed his will and in anger she poisoned him?"

King said, "I don't think Battle was capable of answering any questions. He was on the ventilator which makes speech pretty much impossible."

Bailey glanced at King. "How's your theory looking regarding the victims being connected somehow?"

King shrugged. "Still working the angle."

After the others had left, King picked up the phone and made a call. But he put the phone down a few moments later.

"Who were you trying to get in touch with?" asked Michelle.

"Harry Carrick. There was no answer. I'll try again later. Once Dorothea is picked up, the shit will really hit the fan. Harry's friends with Remmy, so I'd like to give him some advance warning. He may want to go by and see her. And Dorothea's going to need a lawyer."

"I wonder if I should find Eddie and tell him."

"Better he hears from someone else. Bailey will probably want to do the honors."

"How come you didn't tell Bailey about Canney's connection to Battle?"

"I don't know if there is a real connection yet. I'd like to be sure."

"But you have your suspicions?"

"Yes, I do. Strong ones."

"Care to share them?"

"My hunch is that Steve Canney was Bobby Battle's child by Mrs. Canney. And that Roger Canney made the old man pay after his wife died. That would explain his sudden wealth and the fact that he has no pictures of his adulterous spouse and the son who wasn't his."

"I'm surprised he waited until she died in the car accident before he started blackmailing Battle," she said.

King stared at his partner. "Car accident?" he said slowly.

"Yes, she was drinking and crashed her car. Don't you remember?"

"I remember very well, thank you."

She noted the faraway look in her partner's eyes. "You're on to something. Care to share?"

He glanced at her. "What if Canney's wife didn't die in a car accident?"

"But she did. They found her in her car at the bottom of a ravine. I told you I checked with Todd on that."

"Right. She died in a car crash. But that doesn't necessarily make it an accident, does it?"

CHAPTER

65

KING EVENTUALLY GOT IN touch with Harry and told him what had happened.

"I'll head straight to the Battles'," he said. "Why don't you and Michelle meet me there?"

It was dinnertime when they all collected at the mansion.

Remmy met the three at the door. "Mason is out right now," she explained.

"You've heard?" asked King.

"Yes. I hardly think she'll pull herself out of this one."

King looked at the older woman with surprise. "Remmy, I know the two of you aren't the best of friends, but she's still married to your son."

"Which is the only reason I have any concern at all."

"Where's Eddie?"

"In town talking with the lawyers. Dorothea hasn't been formally charged yet?"

"They don't even have a firm cause of death yet," Michelle put in. "Until that happens, they can't charge her."

"You don't think she killed the man, do you?" Harry asked Remmy.

She placed her gaze squarely on him. "No, but I didn't think she was buying stolen drugs either."

"There's quite a bit of difference between that and murdering someone," rejoined Harry.

She motioned them in. "Why don't we continue this *fascinating* discussion over dinner?"

Savannah joined them in the dining room. She was dressed in a long skirt, white blouse, dark blue sweater, stockings and low-heeled pumps. Her hair was nicely styled, and she had a modest amount of makeup on.

It took King a moment to realize what he was seeing. Then it struck him: daughter was dressed just like mother. He looked over at Michelle. From her startled expression it was clear she was thinking the very same thing.

Harry sat next to Savannah and struck up a conversation with her while King and Michelle focused on Remmy.

"Dorothea got virtually nothing by Bobby's death," said King. "So there was no motive there."

"Motives needn't be simply financial," replied Remmy as she buttered her roll.

Like your motive for killing your husband? thought King.

"You have something in mind?" asked Michelle.

"No, I'm just stating what I thought was an obvious fact."

"You had no idea Dorothea was taking one of Bobby's cars and renting a place at the Aphrodisiac? Or that she had a drug problem?"

Remmy shook her head. "But then, I'm not my daughter-in-law's keeper, am I?"

"I knew she had a drug problem." All eyes turned to Savannah.

"Did she mention it to you?" asked King.

"No, but I saw her once, I guess she was coming back from that place. It was early in the morning, and I'd gotten up to go for a walk. She was coming up from the direction of the car barn. She was a mess. I was surprised she could even drive home."

"You didn't just assume she was drunk?" asked Michelle.

"After four years of college I know the difference between drunk and high."

"I'm so glad our money bought you such an invaluable education," snapped Remmy.

"Did you confront her about it, Savannah?" asked King.

"No, it was none of my business."

"But didn't you tell anyone, like Eddie?"

"Again, it was none of my business. Dorothea and I aren't close, in case you hadn't noticed."

After dinner Remmy excused herself, saying she had some letters to write, and Savannah was left to say formal good-byes. However, King had to use the bathroom and asked Harry and Michelle to hold up for a minute. As they waited for him to come back, Harry led Savannah over to a corner and started speaking to her in a confidential tone. When King returned, they said their good nights and left.

Harry said, "I didn't mean to ignore you, Michelle, but

I'm worried about Savannah and wanted to speak with her privately."

"Did you notice she's dressing like her mother now?" King said.

"That was one indication something was amiss," said Harry diplomatically. "Remmy is a very intimidating woman, and I guess not even an independent soul like Savannah is immune from her force of will."

"And Remmy writes lots of letters, keeps a journal and presumably gets a lot of letters from friends," commented King.

Harry looked at him quizzically. "I suppose she does. As do I. Is that important?"

"While I was using the bathroom, I happened to pass by the study. Remmy was in there writing out some letters like she said she was going to."

"So?" asked Michelle.

"The one thing that's been bothering me is that we still don't know what was taken from her and Bobby's closets. What if it were letters, or a diary, something like that?"

Harry said, "That would make sense. Women like Remmy often desire a secure place for their confidential letters."

"Letters that could be incriminating somehow," said King. "Not necessarily in a criminal sense, but in a personal one. At least it's something to keep in mind."

They left the house. Michelle had driven over separately. She said good-bye to Harry and King and drove off. Harry climbed into his convertible and waved as he pulled out.

King was getting into his car when he saw the note on his front seat.

It was short and to the point. "I want to talk. I'll meet you at your place at ten tonight." It was signed "Sally."

King looked around but saw no one. He checked his watch. It was nine o'clock. He debated whether to call Michelle and tell her to meet him at his houseboat. Then he thought better of it. That might scare Sally away. He drove off. In one hour part of this mystery might be cleared up, or at least be less muddled. Right now he'd take that.

CHAPTER

66

AN HOUR LATER KING met Sally at the end of his driveway, led her past all the construction on his new home and down the steps to his houseboat.

The young woman was obviously very nervous. To put her at ease, King said, "It's the right thing to do, Sally. It really is. And once you get it off your chest, you'll feel better."

They sat at his small kitchen table as the lake water slowly lapped at the boat's hull. He'd fixed her a cup of hot tea and was now staring at the woman expectantly.

"Junior," he finally said. "You came to tell me about Junior?"

Sally let out a huge breath and plunged in. "I was with him when the burglary happened."

King was startled. "You helped him break in?"

"No! Not at the Battle house. At Junior's house, the new one he's building."

"So he didn't commit the burglary?"

"He couldn't have. We were there from eight at night

until almost four in the morning. And it's a good hour's drive from the Battles'."

"Why were you with Junior at his new house?"

Sally took a drink of the tea and sat back, her face flushed, her cheeks stamped with fresh tears. "Oh, God, I can't believe I'm telling you this."

"Sally? Why were you with him?" King asked pointedly.

"We'd gotten to know each other when he worked at the Battles'. We . . . we were both lonely, I guess."

"You were having an affair with Junior?"

"It's not like that, not at all!" she answered hotly.

"Then tell me what it *was* like," said King calmly.

"We were just friends. At first. I mean, well." She put down the teacup and leaned forward. "He'd told me he was going to be working at the house all night. His wife had the night off and was with the kids. I went there, seduced him, and we had sex. There. That's it. I told you."

"*You* seduced *him*?"

She looked offended. "I'm not always dressed in jeans and covered with horseshit, Sean. I clean up pretty damn well. He was surprised when I showed up there, of course. But I made it clear to him what I was after."

"But I thought Junior really loved Lulu."

"He did, but he's a man after all and I was wearing next to nothing and my offer was pretty tough to refuse. I just wanted sex, no questions and no commitments. And from what he told me, Lulu hadn't been paying him much attention for quite a while. Worked long hours at that club."

"So you found Junior ready, willing and able?"

"Let's put it this way: he wouldn't have been physically capable of committing that burglary. Hell, *I* could barely walk when it was over."

King put up a hand. "Okay, okay, I don't need any more details."

Sally rubbed her eyes. "The thing is, I really liked him. I know he was big and tough-looking, but he was really a sweet guy underneath."

"Why didn't you come forward when Junior was arrested for the burglary?"

"He wouldn't let me! He said he'd rather go to jail than let Lulu find out."

"Okay, I guess I can see that. What else?"

"That's it. I snuck away from the Battle funeral to say my good-byes over Junior's grave. I didn't think anyone had seen me." She looked down at the table. "Will all this have to come out?"

"Maybe not, now that Junior's dead and Remmy is convinced of his innocence. And I guess there's no reason to ruin Lulu's memory of her husband."

"He did love her, Sean; I was just a onetime fling, that's all." She added in a very small voice, "I guess that's all I ever am."

After Sally had left, King thought about calling Michelle but decided to let it wait until morning. It had been a long day. He went to bed.

＊　　＊　　＊

Outside the houseboat the man had watched Sally
leave. He had used the listening device he'd planted to
hear the entire conversation between the two. He
looked up at the houseboat as the last light was
extinguished there. He'd wait until Sean King was fully
asleep, and then he was going to pay him one final visit.

CHAPTER

67

MICHELLE HAD DRIVEN home, done some kickboxing on the heavy bag hanging in her basement, put away some laundry and actually cleaned her kitchen. After that she showered and was thinking about going to bed but had grown very restless. Her mind kept returning to the murders. Was there something they were overlooking? King had suggested that Mrs. Canney hadn't died in a car accident, that she had been murdered. If so, by whom?

Her head buzzing, she decided to go for a drive; that always helped her think more clearly. Her route took her past her and King's office. She parked and went inside, figuring she'd go over her voluminous notes on the investigation she kept in her desk to see if anything clicked.

As she passed through the small office foyer, she saw some telephone messages on the part-time receptionist's desk. There was one for King from a Billy Edwards. The name sounded familiar, but she couldn't quite place it. The area code was from the Los Angeles area. It was still early enough there, she decided. One thing that annoyed her about working with King was that he kept things incredibly close to the vest, even at the expense of his partner. This might be a chance for her to get the jump on him. She called Edwards. On the third ring the phone was picked up.

"Billy Edwards?"

"That's right. Who's this?"

"Michelle Maxwell. I'm partners with Sean King in Wrightsburg, Virginia. I believe he called you?"

"That's right. I was just getting back to him."

"He's out right now and asked me to return the call."

"Fine with me. So what do you want to know about the time I worked at the Battles'?"

Now the name clicked. Billy Edwards was the mechanic for Bobby Battle's classic car collection. He'd been let go the day after Bobby and Remmy's argument, the one Sally Wainwright had overheard.

"That's right," Michelle said quickly. "We understand you were let go very abruptly."

Edwards laughed. "Try thrown out on my ass with no warning."

"By Bobby Battle?"

"The one and only. I heard on the news that he died. Is that right?"

"Yes. Did he give any reason for letting you go?"

"Nope. But he didn't have to. It didn't have anything to do with my work, I know that. Now, I admit I was pissed with how it was handled, but the man treated me good. Paid me a nice severance and wrote a damn fine reference that helped me get another job pretty quick out in Ohio working for another rich guy with a car collection bigger than Battle's."

"Good for you. Now, we understand that the night before you were let go he and Mrs. Battle had an argument in the car barn."

"Remmy Battle, now, there's a real piece of work. Let me tell you, those two were equally matched, like Godzilla butting heads with King Kong."

"Agreed. But did you know anything about an argument?"

"No. How'd you find out about it?"

"I'm afraid I can't tell you that, it's confidential."

"Uh-huh. I bet you it was Sally Wainwright, wasn't it?"

"Why do you say that?"

"Because she liked going down there and hanging out by herself. Of course she'd go down there with me sometimes too," he added with a chuckle. "Oh, yeah, we had some good times together, me and Sally."

"So you two were . . . seeing each other."

"No. It was just messing around. She was wild, let me tell you. If Battle had known what we'd done inside some of his vehicles . . ."

"Really?"

"Hell, yes. But I wasn't the only one."

"Who else?"

"Is Mason still working there?"

"Yes."

"Well, there you go."

Michelle couldn't hide her astonishment. "Mason was sleeping with Sally?"

"At least that's what she said." He added, "I never personally saw them doing it. But she's a pretty girl. I probably shouldn't be saying this to a woman, but you all live in the same house together, you know, things happen. You see her running around in something skimpy or coming out of the bathroom in a little towel, hey, we're only human. I'm not apologizing for it."

"I get the picture. Anyone else?"

"Probably, but I don't have names for you."

"Sally said that Bobby had just pulled in driving the Rolls-Royce when he and Remmy got into their argument."

"The Rolls? It was a beauty. Only something like five in the whole world. Did he end up getting rid of it?"

"Apparently, he did so the very next day."

"I thought he would."

Michelle stiffened. "Why do you say that?"

"The morning I got canned I went to get my tools and stuff from the car barn. I always had a thing for that Rolls. That was one sweet machine. Anyway, this was the last time I was going to see it. Not like I'd be buying one of my own." Edwards laughed.

Michelle, however, was as taut as a strung bow. "So what did you do?"

"I wanted to take one last look at it. Pulled the cover off and sat in it, pretending it was mine."

"Right, right," said Michelle impatiently. "But why did you think Battle was going to get rid of the car?"

"Because when I was covering it back up, I noticed that the left front fender was dented and one of the headlights had been cracked. It had to have happened the night before because I'd just checked the car that afternoon and it was fine. It wasn't all that much damage really, but a car like that you're talking thousands of dollars in repairs. And you can't get parts for a vehicle like that anymore. It was a real shame. I guess Battle hit something and was pissed off. The guy hated anything to be out of sync. He used to come down to the barn and ream me if he found oil on the floor or a license plate hung crooked. It probably made him sick to see the damage on that Rolls. If he couldn't fix it just right, he'd get rid of it. Just the way the man was."

"Did you ever tell anyone the Rolls-Royce had been damaged?"

"No. It was his car; he could do what he wanted with it."

"Do you remember the exact date it was damaged?"

"Well, it must've happened the night before I got fired. Like I said, I'd checked it that afternoon and there was no damage."

"I understand that. But what date was that?"

Edwards was silent for a bit. "It was over three years ago, I know that. In the fall or thereabouts. I did some work for a company down in North Carolina until the job in Ohio came through. Maybe September. No, I think it was October or maybe November. At least I think," he said with less confidence.

"You can't be any more specific?"

"Look, I have a hard time remembering where I was last week, much less three years ago. I've moved around quite a bit since then."

"Could you look up your payment stubs from when you worked at the Battles'? Or from the jobs in North Carolina or Ohio? That would narrow it down."

"Lady, I live in a one-bedroom apartment in West Hollywood. I don't have room to keep stuff like that. I barely have space for clothes."

"Well, if you remember, will you please call me back?"

"Sure, if it's important."

"It's very important."

Michelle put down the phone and sat at her desk. Over three years ago in the fall. Yet if it *had* been the fall, it would be about three and a half years ago, since it was springtime right now. She sat bolt upright. *Wait a minute,* she said to herself. *Sally Wainwright would probably remember the exact date.* She checked her watch. It was too late to call her. They could do it in the morning. Right now, though, she wanted to get ahold of King and tell him what she'd learned.

She called his cell phone but there was no answer. She left a message. He didn't have a hard-line number at his houseboat. He was probably asleep. She stared at her phone, mulling over what to do. Part of her said to call it a night and go home, yet as she looked down at her phone, she started to get a very strange feeling. Sean was a light sleeper. Why hadn't he answered? His caller ID would have shown it was her. Unless he couldn't answer the phone! She grabbed her keys and raced to her truck.

CHAPTER

68

SEAN KING MOVED around uncomfortably in his bed. As the boat rocked, a small moan escaped from his lips as a fire raged in his brain. He didn't awaken, though. It was no nightmare that was assaulting him. His body was being drained of the ability to absorb oxygen. He was being slowly and quietly put to death.

Headlights cut through the darkness as Michelle pulled up in the Whale and climbed out. She made her way quickly down the stairway to the houseboat.

"Sean?" Michelle called out as she banged on the houseboat door. "Sean?" She looked around. His car was parked up there. He had to be here. "Sean?"

She tried the door latch. It was locked. She went around the walkway and peered in one of the side windows. She could see nothing. She pounded on the window of what she knew was the bedroom he slept in.

"Sean?" She thought she heard a sound. She listened more intently. It was a moan.

She raced back to the front door and put her shoulder against it, but it didn't budge. She stepped back and then sprang forward with a powerful, thudding side kick and broke open the door where the lock met the doorjamb. She raced inside, her pistol out. She felt an immediate heaviness in her lungs, which increased her level of panic. There was a humming coming from somewhere, and even as she raced forward through the houseboat's darkened interior, she felt cold tendrils of something clutching at her. She stumbled over things before hitting the light switch, and the darkened room became bright.

"Sean? Sean?" she screamed.

She reached him, tried to awaken him, but he wouldn't come around. She dragged him out of his bed, through the cabin, out of the houseboat and into the open air, even as her own breath became more and more labored. He lay motionless on the deck, his face a very frightening cherry red. *Carbon monoxide poisoning.* She bent over him, pulled her hair out of her face and began mouth-to-mouth.

"Breathe, Sean, breathe, damn it. Breathe!"

She kept pumping air into him, giving him every ounce of hers she could until she started feeling sick and dizzy. And still she persisted.

"Breathe. Come on, Sean, please, please! Breathe for me, Sean, breathe for me, baby, please. Sean, don't do this to me. Don't you do this to me. Come on, you bastard, just breathe!"

She checked his pulse and then lifted up his T-shirt and

listened to the beats of his heart. They were barely there. She pushed more air into his lungs and then took precious seconds to call 911. She kept going. She was ready to begin CPR if he went into cardiac arrest. But his heart was still beating, she could hear it. If only his lungs would start doing their damn job. She kept pushing air into him until Michelle thought she would pass out herself. *He looks dead. He's gone. I've failed.*

"Please, Sean, please, don't do this. Don't give up. I'm here, I'm here, Sean. Come on, you can do it. You can do it." She followed one enormous breath after another, willing each one down his throat with all possible speed, to impact with his lungs, expand them, scream at his brain, telling it the fight wasn't over.

You can do this, Sean. It's not your time, damn it, it's not your time. Don't leave me, Sean King. Don't you do it.

She swore and puffed. Puffed and swore, screaming encouragement, trying to reach him wherever he might be, life, death or in between.

Stay with me, Sean. Stay with me. It's not your time. It's not. Trust me.

And finally, it started to turn. His chest began to rise and fall with greater force and regularity; the bright red discoloration of his face began to lighten. She ran and got some water from the houseboat and spread it over his face. Where was the ambulance? They should have been here by now. He was doing better, but his condition could change any second. And if he'd been severely oxygen-deprived for a long time, might there be brain damage? She pushed this troubling thought from her mind and kept tending to him.

As Michelle poured the last of the water over King's face and stood to get more, she glanced down and froze. The laser dot was right between her breasts, dead on her heart.

She didn't hesitate, mainly because she was sick of playing catch-up to a killer always one step ahead of them. And she was furious for missing him the last time, when Junior had died. With dizzying quickness she leaped to one side and in the same motion pulled and fired her pistol. She emptied her entire mag, spreading the shots over a wide enough area to find—she hoped to God—this person who'd taken so much from so many.

She rolled, came up into a squat behind the houseboat's solid rail, dropped the spent mag and slammed in a fresh one. She chambered a round with a quick pull of the slide and peered over the boat's gunwale. Then she heard it, feet running away. She was about to go after her would-be assassin when King moaned very loudly. She was by his side in an instant, all thoughts of the fleeing killer gone. King was trying to sit up, his breath coming in large bursts. An instant later he was violently sick to his stomach. Michelle dipped a cloth in the lake and wiped his face clean and then held him as tightly as she could.

"Sit back, Sean, sit back, it's okay. I'm here. Just lie back. I've got you." She tried to fight back the tears, now tears of happiness. She finally decided to just let them pour down her cheeks. She felt like shrieking for joy as she hugged the man to her chest.

"What happened?" he said weakly. "What the hell happened?"

"Save your breath; the ambulance is on its way."

He focused on her as she cradled his head in her lap. "Are you okay?"

It was only then that Michelle realized she'd been shot. It wasn't the pain, at least not initially; it was the blood flowing down her arm. She felt the hole in her shirtsleeve where the slug had gone through. Just a graze, she thought. No bullet in there, at least she didn't think so. She ripped off the bottom part of her sleeve and fashioned a bandage to stop the blood loss.

"Michelle, are *you* okay?" King said again, more urgently, though his eyes had closed.

"Never better," she lied.

"SOMEBODY BLOCKED UP the vents on your heating system, Sean," Todd Williams told King and Michelle at the hospital later. He was there along with two of his deputies and Sylvia. "All the fumes came back into the cabin. You're lucky Michelle got there when she did."

"I almost didn't," she said, rubbing her injured arm, which was now in a sling.

King scowled at her from the bed. "You said you were okay. I don't believe getting shot qualifies as being okay," he grumbled.

"It was just a nick."

"Not quite, Michelle," said Sylvia. "It's on the inside of your arm. Another inch and it could have hit your torso and the damage would have been far worse."

Michelle shrugged off this dire pronouncement and said, "Anyone find the bullet or the shooter?"

"No on both counts," said Williams. "The slug's probably in the lake. The shooter, who the hell knows?"

"Well, one good thing came of it," said King. They all

looked at him. "If the killer wanted to get rid of me, we must be getting closer."

"Well, we're not going to catch him while I'm sitting here," said Williams.

After he had departed, Sylvia said to King, "You can't go back to your houseboat. You can stay at my place; I've got plenty of room."

Michelle stood and said firmly, "He's bunking at my house. I'll be able to keep an eye on him there."

King looked awkwardly at the two women. "She's right, Sylvia. You've got a lot going on. You can't exactly sit around and babysit me, although I feel fine."

Michelle shook her head. "You heard what the doctor said, Sean. You have to take it easy for a few days."

"That's right," said Sylvia. "They've pumped you full of oxygen, and you might feel fine now, but your body's undergone a shock, and if you overdo it, you'll end up right back here." She looked at Michelle. "Well, you take care of yourself too."

"I'll be fine, thanks."

Sylvia gave King a hug, whispered something in his ear and then left.

"What'd she say?" asked Michelle.

"Don't I have any secrets?"

"Not from me. I just saved your life. Not the first time either."

King sighed. "Okay. She said not to scare her like that again."

"That was it?"

"I'm sorry if you're disappointed. What, did you expect her to profess her eternal love? A couple needs to work up to that. At least three meals, a movie and some heavy petting, or so I've heard."

"Smart-ass. Shows you're getting better."

"Can we get out of here now?"

"They want to keep you for observation for a while longer."

"Damn it, all I need is some fresh air, and you can't get any of that in a hospital."

"Okay, I'll see what I can do. We can run by your place so you can pick up your things."

"Can you drive with that arm?"

"Drive *and* shoot. The way things are going we'll probably need both."

As they pulled out of the parking lot an hour later in Michelle's truck, King said grumpily, "Well, at least this time they didn't blow up my house."

"I admire a man who can find the silver lining in all situations."

"Now I face only one more challenge."

Michelle looked at him with a confused expression. "What's that?"

"Surviving at your house."

It was barely light outside when Sally Wainwright rose from her bed to start her work. Horses needed to be fed, ridden and groomed. Stalls needed to be mucked and bridles and saddle cinches mended, plus a host of other chores that would make the hours race by. Always the first one up, and usually the first in bed, she was moving more slowly this morning after her late night. She was scared of what might happen after her conversation with Sean King. Yet like he'd said, it was the right thing to do. At least now everyone would know Junior had been innocent.

She dressed and headed out into the crisp morning air, her quick strides carrying her rapidly to the stables. She approached the stall of the first horse, one she was dutifully trying to break in. She wondered how much longer she'd be working here. Only Savannah and Eddie rode, and with Savannah possibly leaving, would there be any need for horses and stables? Maybe it was time to move on anyway. Too much tragedy, too much death. She started shivering just thinking about it.

The serrated knife sliced cleanly through Sally's neck, severing the carotid arteries and jugular veins, cutting so deeply, in fact, that it carved into her cervical spine on its jagged crescent path from her left to her right ear. She sputtered, tried to speak, felt the blood rushing down the front of her shirt, emptying far faster than it was possible for her body to replenish. She dropped first to her knees and then onto her face. Sally Wainwright's stunned brain realized she'd been murdered an instant before she died.

Her killer used the rake to push Sally over on her back. She stared up but couldn't see the person now, of course. The rake came down directly on her face, breaking her nose. Another blow caved in one of her cheeks; a third blow shattered her left eye socket. By the time the blows stopped raining down, Sally's mother would not have recognized her own daughter.

The rake and knife were dropped beside the body as the killer continued to hover. The face held an expression

of fury, of hatred for the fallen woman. A moment later
Sally was alone in her death, the straw all around soaked
through with her blood. The only sound was that of the
horse as it jostled the stable door, waiting impatiently for
its morning ride; a ride that wouldn't be coming.

CHAPTER

70

KING SETTLED HIMSELF IN the bed in the tiny guest room of Michelle's small cottage. As the sky lightened, he could hear Michelle in the kitchen clanking dishes and utensils, and he shuddered to think what inedible concoction she was making for him this time. She was forever trying to get him to drink power shakes and eat energy bars with low carbs, no carbs, or just the "right" carbs, promising him his body would feel the miraculous change overnight.

"I'm not really hungry," he called out weakly. "Just fix yourself something, maybe some cardboard with a little tofu."

The pots continued to clank and water ran and he distinctly heard the crack of eggs and then a blender starting up.

"Oh, God," he groaned, and lay back against the pillows. *Raw eggs in a blender with who knows what.* He decided to start thinking about the case, to take his mind off the impending gustatory nightmare.

Seven deaths starting with Rhonda Tyler and ending, at

least so far, with Kyle Montgomery. Five of the deaths he believed were by the same killer. Bobby Battle and Kyle were not, he thought. Whether they'd been killed by the same person, he didn't know. And now his life had been almost taken, and Michelle's as well. There seemed to be an abundance of potential suspects and a dearth of clues. At every stage the killer or killers seemed to be one step ahead. They'd gone to see Junior, but the killer had gotten there first. Sylvia had told him about Kyle and the thefts and the lady at the Aphrodisiac. By the time they'd started investigating that, Kyle too was dead. Sally had come to tell him about her sexual encounter with Junior, and an attempt had been made on his life shortly thereafter.

He sat upright in bed.

Sally!

"Michelle," he called out. The clattering was still going on. She obviously couldn't hear him. He got up and staggered into the kitchen. His balance was still off. She was at the sink cutting up an onion and putting it into the blender, where a yellowish-green ooze currently resided.

She turned and saw him. "What are you doing up?" she said in a scolding tone.

"We have to check on Sally."

"Sally? Why?"

"She came to see me last night with some important information. Right after she left, I went to sleep. That's when my heater was messed with." He told Michelle about Sally's being with Junior on the night of the burglary.

"Well, that qualifies as a stunning development. And you're afraid the person who tried to kill us might have seen Sally there too?"

"Nothing would surprise me with this guy. He always seems to know everything in advance."

Michelle wiped off her hands, picked up her cell phone and called Todd Williams. She relayed a message to the chief and clicked off. "He's heading over there with some of his men right now."

"Maybe we should go there too."

"The only place you're going is back to bed."

"Look at you: you've been shot, and you're still assaulting eggs and knifing onions."

"Just go get in bed. I'm sure Sally's okay. Todd promised to call."

King reluctantly did so. He supposed the odds were very long against anything having happened to Sally so quickly.

Savannah was beating on the door of the carriage house so hard her hands were starting to bruise. Dorothea finally answered the door in her robe. Savannah nearly fell inside.

Dorothea saw the terrified look on the woman's face and said, "My God, Savannah, what is it?"

She pointed in the direction of the nearby stables. "I found . . . I found Sally. In the stables. She's dead. Her head crushed. Oh, my God, she's dead!" she shrieked.

Dorothea looked frantically around as though the killer might be hiding in her foyer. She raced up the stairs to the bedroom, where Eddie lay sleeping.

"Eddie! Savannah found Sally dead in the stables. Eddie!"

He lay motionless in the bed. She drew closer. "Eddie!"

She grabbed his shoulders and shook him violently. "Eddie, wake up."

All she got in return was a small groan. She checked his pulse. It was very faint, as was his breathing, terrifyingly so. She grabbed a glass of water off the nightstand and threw it in his face. This did nothing. She lifted his right eyelid. The pupil was a pinprick. The drug-savvy Dorothea knew what that meant. She picked up the phone and called 911, then she ran back down the stairs where Savannah was squatting right by the door, sobbing. She was dressed in her riding clothes, Dorothea noted, and her boots had left mud all over the foyer.

Todd Williams rose from beside the body and nodded. Sylvia came forward to examine Sally while the forensics team searched for clues. Chip Bailey stood next to the stable's double door and watched the proceedings as Williams joined him.

"How's Eddie?" asked Bailey.

"He's still unconscious. I don't know if he's been poisoned or what. I don't know what the hell is going on anymore. I mean, who would want to kill Sally and Eddie?"

"I didn't think the girl had anything to do with any of this."

Sylvia rose from the body after a few minutes and joined the two lawmen.

"Her throat was cut from ear to ear almost. The blood loss was horrific. Death would have been in a minute or so. And then her face was smashed to a pulp."

"So you're sure her throat was cut first?" asked Bailey.

"Yes. She was dead when the blows hit her."

"Time of death?"

"No more than four hours or so. I did a rectal temp, and the minimal degree of rigor mortis substantiates that."

Williams checked his watch. "So about five-thirty this morning."

"Looks to be. There's no sign of rape or sexual assault. Whoever killed her struck from behind and is right-handed. The throat slash was executed left to right."

"And Savannah found her?" said Bailey.

"She was going riding and came upon the body," said Williams. "At least that's what I think she said. She was crying so hard I really couldn't be sure."

"And she went to the carriage house to get help?" said Bailey.

"It's situated closer to the stables than the mansion or the house where Sally stayed," pointed out Williams.

"And Dorothea answered the door, tried to rouse Eddie and then called for help."

"Right."

Bailey mulled this over. "So Dorothea and Eddie were in bed together. Dorothea was okay, but Eddie had been given some poison or other."

"I haven't taken a complete statement from Dorothea yet," said Williams.

"I think you'd better."

"No, what *I* think I'd better do is call Sean and Michelle," said Williams. "They phoned about Sally this morning, before we got the call from Dorothea. They obviously know some things we don't."

CHAPTER

71

AS KING WAS WAITING FOR the call from Williams, Michelle came in carrying a tray balanced in her one good arm.

He frowned at her. "I should be waiting on you."

"Here, this'll be good for you." She arranged the tray and pointed out its contents. "My famous mega-power shake, dry cereal with sliced banana and as a little treat, low-carb bread with avocado spread."

"What's in the power shake? No, never mind, I don't want to know." He took a tiny sip of the shake and quickly put it down. "I think it needs to breathe a bit."

"It's not wine, Sean."

"No, it's certainly not," he said firmly. He wiped his mouth with a napkin. "I never got around to asking why you were coming to my house so late last night."

"Oh, damn, I forgot all about it. Billy Edwards, Battle's ex-mechanic, called from L.A."

King sat straight up. "What did he say?"

Michelle filled him in about the damage to the Rolls.

Before she'd even finished, King was out of the bed and grabbing his clothes.

"What are you doing?" she asked in amazement.

"We've got someone to see, and fast."

"Who?"

"Roger Canney."

They arrived at Canney's house only to find no one home. They peered in the darkened windows and tried all the doors, but they were locked. King noted the morning's newspaper on the front steps. They were standing in the driveway when a man came by walking two large basset hounds—or rather, they were walking him.

"He's not home," called out the man, who was wearing a Maryland Terrapins basketball cap. "Saw him leave, oh, about two hours ago when I was doing my jog."

King looked at his watch. "Pretty early."

"He had some bags with him he loaded in the car. Guess he's going on a trip."

"Which car? Beemer or Range Rover?" asked Michelle.

"Range Rover."

"Did he say where he was going?"

"Nope. Blew out of here so fast he almost ran me over."

They thanked the man, climbed in Michelle's truck and drove off.

"I'm going to call Todd and tell him to put out an APB on Canney," said King.

"Sean, what's going on?"

"Think about how Mrs. Canney died."

"She was drunk and died in a car accident. But you suggested she might have been murdered."

"Right. Murdered and knocked back into that ravine when her car was hit by a very heavy Rolls-Royce driven by Bobby Battle. Both events occurred about three and a half years ago."

"You're saying Bobby Battle killed Mrs. Canney. Why?"

"What if it wasn't Roger Canney who first initiated a blackmail scheme against Battle? Maybe it was Mrs. Canney who threatened to reveal Battle as her son's father, and Battle didn't respond the way she'd intended or he got tired of paying. Then Roger Canney blackmails Battle over his wife's death."

"But how would Roger Canney have known Battle was involved in his wife's death?"

"Canney might have known about his wife's plan to blackmail Battle. Or it's still very possible he came up with the scheme and his wife helped him put the screws to Battle. Then his wife is conveniently killed? He's a smart guy. Even if he didn't have actual proof of the murder, he'd put two and two together."

"So he confronts Battle, tells him he knows he killed his wife *and* fathered Steve, and he wants money to keep it quiet."

King nodded. "In seeking to avoid blackmail over an illegitimate child by killing Mrs. Canney, Battle ironically might have set himself up to be blackmailed for murder."

"But wouldn't Battle have realized that Canney had to

reveal his complicity in the blackmail scheme if he went to the police claiming Battle murdered his wife? I mean, he'd have to give them some plausible motive."

"He could simply use the fact of the illegitimate son. He could've claimed ignorance of any blackmail scheme or the source of any monies, blaming that on his dead wife."

"Nice guy."

"Yeah."

"Looks like we spooked him into running."

"Let's hope he hasn't run too far. We need him to fill in a lot of holes."

Just as King was about to call Williams, the police chief called him. King told him what Sally had disclosed to him the night before, as well as his suspicions of Roger Canney and the man's flight. Williams arranged for the APB and then asked them to meet him at the Battles'. He refused to say why or answer their questions about Sally.

King slumped back in his seat with a hopeless expression. *She's dead.*

CHAPTER

72

WHEN THEY ARRIVED AT the Battles', Williams and Chip Bailey led King and Michelle to the stables. On the way Williams broke the news about Sally and what had happened to Eddie. King turned pale and put a hand against a section of fencing. Michelle wedged her good arm up under his.

"Just take it easy. We don't need you going down too."

"The knife used to kill Sally was taken right off the Peg-Board inside the stables and was dropped at the crime scene," Bailey told them. "Same thing with the rake. Sylvia just left, but she said death would have been pretty fast."

"Can we see the body?" asked King.

"It's not pretty, Sean. If I were you, I wouldn't," replied Williams.

"I need to," said King firmly.

Williams reluctantly led them inside and over to Sally's corpse.

"My God," said Michelle.

"It was like the killer was furious at her about something," said Williams. "Just kept on beating her in the head." He looked at King. "Maybe Sally knew more than she was telling."

"Maybe," said King slowly as he pulled his gaze away. He stood solemnly outside the stables and watched as Sally's body was carried out in a black pouch.

As the doors on the ambulance clunked shut, he turned to Williams. "This was my fault. I forced her to tell me the truth and never even thought she might be in danger because of it."

"You were fighting for your life, Sean," countered Williams. "You didn't really have an opportunity to think about anything else."

"How's Eddie doing?" asked Michelle.

Bailey answered, "I just called the hospital. They said he's still unconscious but out of danger."

"Do they know what it was yet?"

"No. I was going to drop by the hospital later, if you want to come along. Right now I intend to talk to Dorothea again. And after that, Savannah, although I hear she's a wreck."

As they walked along, Williams turned to King. "If this thing pans out on Canney, I'm going to owe you one. I never would have picked up on that."

"That's just one piece of the puzzle, Todd," replied King.

Dorothea met them at her house. She looked pale and drawn. While Williams, King and Michelle offered words of commiseration, Chip Bailey volunteered no such niceties. He looked at her with a mixture of anger and determination. They stepped around the muddied sections of the entryway and went to the living room.

"What time did you and Eddie go to bed?" asked Williams.

"About half past midnight. He'd been out in his studio working. But we didn't go to sleep then. Not until about an hour later." She smiled in an embarrassed fashion. "I didn't think that possibly being implicated in a murder could do so much for one's sex life. But Eddie's been wonderful throughout this ordeal."

"A good man is hard to find in times of trouble," said Michelle tightly.

"I'm starting to realize that," she answered with surprising sincerity.

Bailey broke in. "He was drugged, Dorothea. I've talked to the doctors at the hospital, and they said he's under the influence of some powerful narcotic."

She suddenly looked frightened. "That's what I can't understand. I . . . I have to tell you that when Savannah started banging on our door, I woke up in a total fog. I still don't feel quite all together."

Bailey looked at her suspiciously and said, "You didn't mention anything like that when we came by this morning."

Dorothea spoke quickly. "Everything was happening so fast. Savannah was a mess, Sally was dead and I couldn't wake Eddie. God, it was all like a nightmare."

"What time did Savannah come to your door?" asked Bailey.

"A little past eight. I remember looking at the clock in the foyer."

"What did Eddie have to eat or drink last night?"

"We had dinner, nothing unusual. Some wine after dinner, and then he went to his studio to paint and I did some paperwork in my home office."

"Can we see the leftovers from the meal and the bottle of wine?" asked Bailey.

"There weren't any leftovers. I think the bottle of wine is around here somewhere."

"I'd appreciate if you could show me where it is before I leave," said Bailey.

Her features became defiant. "What exactly are you trying to prove?"

He eyed her coolly. "Somehow Eddie was slipped something last night that knocked him out so completely he's still not fully recovered. It had to be administered somehow."

"Well, I have no idea how it was done," she said hotly.

"That's okay, it's my job to figure that out," said Bailey. "The drugs you bought from Kyle: do you have any of them here?"

"I . . . I'm not sure. I can look."

"No. I tell you what I'm going to do: I'm going to have your home searched. Do you have a problem with that?"

Dorothea rose on unsteady legs. "I think I should speak to my attorney first."

Bailey stood too. "Fine, you do that. Meantime I'll get a search warrant issued. I'm posting one of my agents outside the house just in case something important decides to walk out. And we can check drains, and you're on septic here, so any evidence that happens to get flushed we can find."

"Your insinuations are ridiculous," she cried. "I didn't kill Sally or drug my husband."

"Too bad for you we don't have a final cause of death on Kyle Montgomery. If we did, you might be in jail right now. That would've been a nice alibi for you."

Bailey walked out while Dorothea looked at King pitifully. "Sean, what is going on?" He dashed forward and caught her before she hit the floor. He eased her onto the couch.

He turned to Michelle. "Get me some water."

Michelle rushed off and King looked back at Dorothea. She gripped his arm.

"God, I feel so bad. My head is splitting and my stomach's doing flip-flops."

"I'm going to have Mason come and look after you."

She clenched his arm even more tightly. "I didn't do anything, Sean. You have to believe that."

Michelle came back in with the water, and Dorothea drank it down.

"You do believe me, don't you?" she said pleadingly.

"Let me put it this way: I believe you as much as I believe anyone right now."

As King, Michelle and Williams left, they spotted Bailey talking to one of his men and pointing at the house. They walked over to him.

"You sure didn't cut Dorothea any slack, Chip," said Williams.

"I wasn't aware she deserved any," shot back the FBI agent.

"It's been a pretty traumatic morning for her, actually the last few days."

"If all of it's her own doing, why should I feel sorry for the woman?"

"You think she drugged her husband, then slipped out and killed Sally?" asked King.

"I think it's entirely possible she drugged Eddie and that someone else killed Sally while Eddie was unconscious. The stables are close enough to the carriage house that if there was a fight or Sally was able to scream, Eddie might have heard and come to her rescue. With him drugged that couldn't happen."

"And whom do you think Dorothea was partnered with in all this?"

"If I knew that, we could probably all go home."

"And the motive for killing Sally?"

"She knew more than she told anyone, including you. She said she was Junior's alibi. Well, we only have her word for that, because she only came forward after Junior was dead. He can't corroborate it. Now, suppose she *wasn't* with him the night of the burglary? Suppose she was helping someone break in the mansion or doing it herself?"

"If so, why would she come forward with the story about being with Junior?" asked Williams.

King answered, "Because that gives *her* an alibi for the burglary."

"Exactly," said Bailey, glaring triumphantly at Williams.

"That's actually not a bad theory, Chip," said King.

"Thanks. I have my moments." He climbed in his car and drove off.

CHAPTER

73

EDDIE FINALLY STARTED
to come to around three o'clock that afternoon.

Williams, Bailey, King and Michelle had gathered in his hospital room. He looked up at them from his bed, all pale, twitchy and disheveled. Remmy sat next to her son, holding his hand in a firm grip and rubbing his forehead with a wet cloth. "God, Eddie, don't you scare me like that again."

"It wasn't exactly my idea," he said in a very tired voice.

"What do you remember about last night?" asked King.

"Dorothea and I had dinner, where we talked about, you know, recent events. I'd been at the lawyer's for a while before that."

"Why didn't she go with you to see the attorney?" asked Michelle sharply.

"I wanted her to but she didn't want to go. As crazy as it sounds, I think she believes if she ignores all of this, it'll go away. Anyway, after dinner I went to my studio, to clear my head of all this stuff." He glanced sideways at Michelle before continuing. "Around midnight or so I came in and went upstairs to bed. Dorothea was still awake. She was actually *very* awake, if you know what I mean," he added, obviously embarrassed.

Remmy snorted. "Unbelievable to me under the circumstances, but I gave up trying to understand your wife years ago."

"It was as much me as her, okay?" he said harshly to his mother. His gaze, however, remained on Michelle. "I guess it was sort of a circle-the-wagon mentality. But I admit the timing was strange."

"What happened after that?" prompted King.

"I went to sleep. I mean, I guess I really went to sleep. The next thing I know I wake up and I'm in the hospital. What the hell was it?"

"The docs said morphine sulfate, also known as MS Contin," answered Williams. "Guaranteed to knock you out for eight, nine hours or longer."

"But why?" asked Eddie. "What was accomplished by that?"

King looked at Williams. "You haven't told him?"

"Told me what?" demanded Eddie.

Williams looked down at him. "Sally Wainwright was murdered around five-thirty this morning."

Eddie sat up so fast he almost pulled out his IV line. "What!" he yelled. "Sally?"

"Eddie!" cried out his mother as she pushed him back down. "You're going to hurt yourself."

Eddie suddenly got a wild look and shot up again. "My God! Dorothea! Is she okay?"

"She's fine," said Williams quickly. "Absolutely fine."

"For now," muttered Bailey.

Eddie sank back down but clutched his mother's arm. "Somebody killed Sally in her sleep?"

King said, "No, she was killed in the stable."

"But why Sally?" Eddie demanded.

Williams looked at King, who said, "She'd come forward with important information that ruled out Junior's having committed the burglary at your mother's home."

Now Remmy looked surprised. "I'd already figured he hadn't done it, but how could Sally possibly have proof of that?"

"She did, and we're going to leave it at that for now," said Williams.

"Did what she tell you implicate someone else?" asked Eddie.

"No," admitted King.

"Then why kill her?"

"I don't have the answer to that. I don't have the answer to a lot of things."

Bailey spoke up. "But what we do know, Eddie, is that you were drugged last night, and while you were out, someone killed Sally. Someone who knew her routine and that she'd be in the stables at that hour of the morning."

Everyone remained silent for an uncomfortably long moment until Eddie exclaimed, "Are you suggesting that my wife—"

Bailey broke in. "I'm not suggesting anything. I'm just stating a plain fact. But Dorothea *has* come under suspicion."

Eddie shook his head. "She's a respected business-woman."

"With a drug problem, and possibly a murder suspect," pointed out Remmy in a sharp tone.

"Shut up, Mother!" yelled Eddie.

This caught all of them off guard. Remmy slowly let go of her son's hand.

Eddie pointed his finger accusingly at Bailey. "If you think for one minute that Dorothea drugged me and then killed Sally, you're wasting everyone's time while the real killer is getting away."

"It's our duty to investigate all possible leads," said Bailey calmly.

"Including ludicrous ones?"

"You better get some rest, Eddie," said King gently. "You've had a hard night."

"Fine, I'd really like to be alone right now anyway."

Eddie looked away from them all, his forearm over his face.

Remmy rose and headed to the door. "I'll come and check on you later, son."

"Whatever," he answered curtly.

Remmy went to the door, then turned to Williams. "You know, it seems to me that we're no further along than we were on day one. A lot of people killed and no progress." She shot Bailey a vicious look. "And that includes the illustrious FBI. Makes me wonder what the hell I pay taxes for." She left the room.

The men followed her out.

Michelle paused at the door and glanced back at Eddie. He still lay there, his face covered. She quietly left.

CHAPTER

74

TWO DAYS PASSED WITH NO sign of Roger Canney despite Chip Bailey and Chief Williams having put in place an area lockdown.

"It's like he popped into a damn hole somewhere," complained the frustrated FBI agent at one meeting of the investigative team.

With eight murders in total now and the attempted killings of King and Michelle, Wrightsburg was over-flowing with law enforcement folks fighting over turf, evidence and the proper way to satiate the horde of media that had invaded the town. Hardly a citizen had not been interviewed by a reporter from some organization. One could not watch the national news or read the *Washington Post, New York Times,* or *USA Today* without seeing a story about the Wrightsburg slayings. Pundit after pundit proposed one solution after another, most having nothing to do with the actual facts of the case. People were putting their homes on the market at an alarming clip, business was down across the board; it didn't seem too far-fetched to think the town might cease to exist if the killer or killers weren't soon found. Business and political leaders were, not surprisingly, calling for Chief Williams's head, along with his top—if recently appointed—deputies, King and Maxwell. Bailey too was feeling the heat from his superiors, but he went about his business, methodically running down any lead that looked promising, though most petered out.

Eddie was released from the hospital about the time Sylvia completed the autopsy on Sally; not that the cause of her death had ever been in doubt. No new leads had materialized, but at least no one else had died either.

In the midst of all this chaos and scrutiny, when it seemed like the entire town would implode any second, Sean King pulled out two bottles from his portable wine cooler and went to dinner with Michelle at Harry Carrick's home.

As she exited her cottage and climbed into the Lexus convertible, King's eyes had widened at the sight of her. "You look beautiful, Michelle," he said, scrutinizing the clingy dress that stopped about midthigh and showed off a healthy dose of her Olympian legs. She also sported a stylish blue wrap around her shoulders; she was no longer wearing the sling. She wore makeup, and it appeared she'd even washed her hair, and hardly any of it was dangling in her face. It was a stunning contrast to her usual jeans, windbreakers, sneakers and running suits and flyaway tresses.

For his part King was dressed in a suit and tie and even had a handkerchief in his coat's breast pocket.

"I wanted to make a nice impression on *Harry*," she

said hastily. "But my, I didn't expect such accolades from you."

"I'm not sure I know what you're talking about."

"I found the breakfast and lunch I made you in the trash can again. If you don't like my cooking, just say so. It's not like it would hurt my feelings."

In his best Bogart imitation King said, "Aw, angel, you shouldn't waste time in the kitchen. Not your style, angel."

She smiled and said, "Thank God for small favors."

"But with that said, the tuna dish you made the other night was really good."

"High praise coming from you."

"I tell you what: the next meal we'll make together. I've got a few tricks I can show you."

"Okay, that's a deal."

"How's the arm?"

"Like I said, just a scratch."

As they drove with the top down along the winding country roads on a warm, fine evening covered by a vast sky of stars, Michelle glanced at him admiringly and observed, "You look pretty spiffy yourself."

"Like Eddie Battle, I can clean up well on occasion." He smiled to show he was joking.

"Are we the only guests?"

"Yes, since I was the one who suggested we get together."

"You? Why?"

"It's time we sat down and talked this case through, and I do my best thinking over a good bottle of wine or two."

"Are you sure you just didn't want to escape another meal at my house?"

"Thought never occurred to me."

Harry's house was large and old and its interior beautifully decorated.

He met them at the door and led them into the library, where, despite the warmth of the evening, a cozy fire was burning. The old lawyer was wearing a snappy three-piece suit with stylishly muted checks. A carnation was pinned to his jacket lapel. He poured them drinks, and they sat on a soft, cracked leather sofa in front of the fire. The couch looked as though it had carried the posteriors of at least five generations.

He raised his glass. "A toast to my two good friends." They drank to that, and then Harry added after eyeing Michelle, "And really, I believe another toast is in order." He lifted his glass once more. "To one of the most lovely women I've ever encountered. Michelle, you look extraordinarily beautiful tonight."

Michelle smiled and glanced at King. "Now, if I could only cook."

King started to say something but seemed to think better of it and hastily took a sip of his cocktail.

"What an incredibly interesting place," said Michelle as she looked around at the built-in, worm-eaten wooden shelves stuffed with what looked to be ancient tomes.

Harry's gaze followed hers around the library. "Of course it's haunted, as it should be for a place that saw the light of the eighteenth century."

"Haunted?" said Michelle.

"Oh, yes. I've seen numerous apparitions over the years. Several I consider to be regulars. Since my return here, I've felt a real duty to get to know them, considering I'll be joining them in the not-all-too-distant future."

"You've got a long time left, Harry," commented King.

"What would we do without you?" said Michelle, tapping her whiskey glass against Harry's tumbler of bourbon.

"Even before the other branch of the Lee family was building its fortress at Stratford Hall, my line was laying the brick and mortar for this." Harry checked his pocket watch. "Calpurnia serves promptly at seven-thirty. That gives us a little time to talk before the meal, although I'm sure I can guess our dinner topic."

"Calpurnia?" asked Michelle.

"Calpurnia is my cook and housekeeper; a delightful lady who's been with me for years. I discovered her when I was serving on the supreme court in Richmond, and she graciously agreed to return with me here. I'd be utterly lost without Calpurnia."

He took a sip of his bourbon, set down his glass and put his hands together, his features now very serious.

"We must solve this thing, and soon, you know. It's not like people are going to stop being killed simply because we wish it."

"I know," said King. He stood and faced them, his back to the fire. "I've been giving this a lot of thought, having had not much else to do while recovering from that deep draft I took of carbon monoxide. Now, there've been eight deaths thus far." He held up the fingers on one of his hands. "But I want to talk about only five, at least at first. And I want to begin with Rhonda Tyler."

"The dancer," said Harry.

"The prostitute."

"You're sure?" said Michelle.

"I checked with Lulu. Tyler was one of the ones who opted for the 'extra pay' structure."

"What's that?" asked Harry curiously.

"A little sideline of the Aphrodisiac; it's since been shut down," said King vaguely.

Harry nodded in a knowing way. "I always suspected that was happening. I mean, you can't let men watch naked girls, ply them with alcohol and not expect some to want more than to merely play voyeur."

"Exactly. So Rhonda was a prostitute. Was that why she was killed?"

Michelle ventured an answer. "Well, prostitutes are probably the number one victim pool of serial killers."

"Right again. So are we simply dealing with an 'ordinary' serial killer who opted to start with this 'classic' victim pool, or is there something else going on?"

"What do you mean, Sean?" asked Harry.

"I mean, was Tyler a symbol or was her death more personal?"

"How can we answer that with the little we know?" said Michelle.

"Let me answer a question with a question. Could Bobby Battle have enjoyed the services of Rhonda Tyler? She was at the Aphrodisiac before Bobby had his stroke. He was known to frequent the place, although Lulu was pretty vague on the last time she'd seen him there."

"I hadn't considered that angle," said Harry quietly. "But let's say he did sleep with her. Why would that make her a target for our killer along with at least four other people who seem to have no connection?"

"What if some of the other victims did have connections to Battle?"

"Such as?"

Michelle answered, "Sean thinks Steve Canney was Bobby's illegitimate son. His mother had worked for Battle and probably gotten pregnant by him, and we think Roger Canney was blackmailing Bobby. We also think Bobby may have been involved in Mrs. Canney's death three and a half years ago, and that's when the blackmail started."

"My God!" exclaimed Harry.

"But, Sean," said Michelle, "I've been thinking about this too. Bobby openly had affairs with women, slept with prostitutes. If what you say is true, why would he care if the truth came out about an illegitimate son? Why would he allow himself to be blackmailed over a sexual encounter?"

"I think I can answer that," said Harry. "Just about the time period you're talking about Bobby was in the middle of selling his company. Many local lawyers I knew were working on the deal on Battle's behalf, so I heard all the war stories about the negotiations. The buyer was a large multinational corporation with a sterling reputation. And Bobby was the very public face of his company."

"So news of an illegitimate son wouldn't have helped the negotiations," said King.

"Precisely. As a matter of fact, the deal did go through

and made Bobby more money than he could possibly have spent in several lifetimes. It was probably a good thing."

"Why do you say that?" asked King.

"Battle had always been eccentric, but for some years he was growing more and more bizarre in his behavior. Violent mood swings, bouts of depression followed by times of unrealistic euphoria. And his mind wasn't what it was. One of the most brilliant engineers and businessmen of his day, he was forgetting names and important items. I really wasn't surprised about the stroke. In fact, I suspected he suffered numerous minor ones previously that had affected his mind. But we're getting far afield from the topic of blackmail." Harry turned to King. "Sorry for the detour."

"No, we need all the information we can get. The timing of the sale of Bobby's company makes me believe it was only Roger Canney who had the blackmail plan. One would think that Mrs. Canney would know who the father of her son was, or at least that Bobby could have been the father. Steven Canney was seventeen when he died. If she'd wanted to come forward and make a claim, she wouldn't have waited all those years. It's not like Bobby wasn't rich seventeen years ago too."

Harry picked up this line of reasoning. "But Roger Canney might have known Steve wasn't his biological son and been waiting for his wife to die before putting the screws to Bobby. Perhaps he waited because his wife wouldn't have gone along. He certainly would have known of the potential sale of the man's company. That was publicly disclosed."

"Or maybe," said Michelle, "Roger Canney didn't want to wait for his wife to die 'naturally,' so he sped up the process by running her off the road, freeing him to begin his blackmail scheme."

"But it was Bobby's car that was damaged right around the time of her death," King said. "So it seems far more likely that Bobby killed her."

"I'm just pointing out that Roger Canney might've had a motive to kill her too," Michelle replied.

King looked at her admiringly. "That's a good point, Michelle. I hadn't really considered that."

"So where does that leave us?" she wanted to know.

The bell for dinner interrupted them.

"I've told Calpurnia that a dinner bell is quite old-fashioned, but she claims my hearing's not what it was, and it's the only way she can get my attention without trudging all over the house to find me. Shall we?"

CHAPTER

75

SEAN HAD UNCORKED both bottles of wine upon his arrival so that they could properly breathe before dinner. At the table he poured out the first one. "This is a La Croix de Peyrolie out of Lussac-St-Emilion."

"And I'm sure it has some wonderfully nifty history," said Michelle as she smelled it.

"It's made by the appropriately named Carole Bouquet, who used to be a famous model and was a James Bond girl in one of the films—*For Your Eyes Only*, I believe. The other bottle is a Ma Vérité de Gérard Depardieu, Haut-Médoc."

"Let me guess, made by the actor of the same name," chanced Harry.

"Yes. These wines are really up and coming, and I only bring them out on special occasions."

"Harry and I feel so honored," said Michelle, smirking.

They toasted and began their meal, which was served by Calpurnia. She was about sixty years of age and over six feet tall, blocky of build and with thick gray hair pulled back in a harsh bun. She looked like every child's worst school-cafeteria-worker nightmare. Yet the food was spectacular.

As Calpurnia left them, Harry said, "Now, Michelle was asking where your speculations about Steven Canney's lineage and Rhonda Tyler's possible liaison with Bobby Battle left us."

"With the fact that two of the victims might be connected to Bobby Battle. Does it stand to reason that more are as well?"

"Janice Pembroke?" said Michelle.

"No. I figure her simply as a person in the wrong place at the wrong time," answered King.

"Diane Hinson? She was a lawyer. Maybe she was working on some corporate deal with Bobby," Michelle suggested.

King shook his head. "Doubtful. She was a trial lawyer, mostly criminal work. I made a lot of inquiries and could find no one who could place them together at any time. Let's leave Hinson for the moment and move on. Next up is Junior Deaver. He had a clear connection to the Battles."

"Right. He worked for them and was also accused of stealing from them," said Michelle.

"But the burglary occurred *after* Bobby had his stroke," said Harry.

"I never thought that Bobby was killing anyone," said King, "perhaps other than Mrs. Canney. But we have three people with possible connections to Bobby Battle. Each was killed using the M.O. of an infamous serial killer, a watch was placed on the wrists and a letter was subsequently received."

Michelle looked unconvinced. "Granted, Pembroke might have been killed merely because she was with Canney, yet Hinson was killed in the manner of the Night Stalker. But you say she has no connection to Battle."

"Her watch was set to one minute past four," said King. He paused and said, "And remember, Pembroke's watch was set to one minute past two. The others were right on the hour."

"So Hinson's and Pembroke's were one tick off," said Michelle slowly.

"Exactly." King looked at her puzzled. "One tick off? There's something familiar about that phrase, but I can't think of what it is."

"So the killer is intentionally telling us, via the watches, that some victims are, what, slightly off?"

"I think he's telling us that Tyler, Canney and Junior were killed intentionally because of their connection to Bobby. Pembroke and Hinson were not specifically targeted, because they had no such connection."

"All right, let's assume Pembroke was killed because she was with Canney. Why was Hinson murdered?" asked Michelle.

"So we'd run down numerous paths trying to have it all make sense but it never would. For our killer's purposes having Pembroke die at the same time as Canney was simply gravy. It muddied the waters even more. If Canney had been alone, I bet we'd have had another murder like Hinson's to cover up the connection to Bobby. And it also explains why the killer used the word 'kid' instead of 'kids' in his letter following the teenagers' deaths. Only one kid was his target: Steve Canney."

"But, Sean, if the killer really wanted to throw us off, why set some of the watches so they were one tick off? If he'd kept them all on the hour, chances are you'd never have stumbled on this line of reasoning."

"For some reason I think this guy is trying to play fair by giving us a legitimate clue."

"Or he's just screwing with us," said Michelle.

"Possible, but I don't think so."

Michelle still looked skeptical. "All right, let's assume all that's true. Now we have Bobby Battle as a possible common denominator. But you don't think he was killed by the same person. Isn't his being linked to yet another killer too huge of a coincidence? And then we have Kyle and Sally. How do those deaths fit in?"

"Despite what Sylvia found, Kyle may have been a suicide. And Sally may have been killed because she didn't come forward about the alibi for Junior."

"I'm not following, Sean," said Harry.

"If Junior was killed only because he stole from the Battles, then once the killer found out he really hadn't committed the burglary, that meant Junior was killed for no reason. The killer revenged himself and in his sick mind perhaps thought he was avenging Junior as well by killing Sally. He might have foregone his trademark watch and infamous serial killer indicia in her case because he was too incensed or didn't consider her to be important enough. And he didn't have much time to plan it. Sally only told me the truth barely seven hours before she was killed."

"Well," said Michelle, "her face being crushed by

repeated blows after she was dead maybe fits with the theory of revenge. Someone in a rage."

"Right. A man capable of ferocious attack and—" King froze. "Seven hours."

"What is it, Sean?" asked Harry.

"I'm not sure," he said at last. "What I just said about seven hours, it struck me somehow, but not the way I thought it would." He thought for a moment and then shook his head. "Sorry, probably a slightly premature senior moment."

"What about Chip Bailey's theory that Sally lied about being with Junior and committed or helped commit the burglary?" asked Michelle.

Harry's eyebrows went up. "That's an intriguing conjecture."

"Yes, it is," said King slowly. "And not one we can entirely discount right now, although my instincts tell me he's wrong."

They continued with their meal and also finished off the second bottle of wine. Afterward in the library they sipped coffee that Harry poured for them. He offered them an after-dinner cognac, but they both declined.

"I have to drive home," said King. "The wine was plenty."

"And I have to look after him while he drives us home," added Michelle, smiling.

The room had grown chilly, and Michelle stood in front of the fire warming her long legs. "Dresses can be very drafty," she said self-consciously.

Harry turned to King. "What's your opinion of Dorothea?"

"Well, the source of the drug Eddie was given wasn't the wine, nor did they find any of the drugs Dorothea had purchased from Kyle," said King. "However, I checked with Sylvia. The morphine sulfate Eddie was given was a drug she kept in her pharmacy and may have been one of the drugs Kyle brought to Dorothea at the Aphrodisiac. And Dorothea has no alibi for the time Kyle was killed. She said she was at home, but Eddie didn't see her."

"Actually, he was out in his studio all night painting a picture of me," said Michelle in an embarrassed tone.

King eyed her closely but said nothing.

Harry looked at her curiously for a moment and then said, "So she was buying the drugs, and she's a possible suspect in both Battle's and Kyle Montgomery's deaths. She was also the person who had the best opportunity to drug Eddie, and lived very near where Sally was killed. All circumstantial obviously, but still compelling."

"And she's been depressed due to the financial setbacks and family issues she told us about," said Michelle. "A troubled woman all around."

King replied, "I don't disagree with you, but I'm having a hard time finding her motive. She said Bobby had promised to change his will to benefit her, but he didn't. So there goes her motive to kill him."

"Unless she found out he hadn't and was so furious she murdered him," said Michelle.

Harry rose and stood next to Michelle in front of the fire. "At over seventy, one's whole body becomes drafty regardless of the amount of clothing or the relative heat of the room," he explained.

Returning to the discussion, he said, "There might be a

third possibility. We've been focused on what was taken from Remmy's closet, but what was stolen from Bobby's closet?"

They both stared at him but said nothing.

Harry continued. "The will that left everything to Remmy is the one that's being used by the lawyers. It was drawn up many years ago."

"How do you know that?" asked Michelle.

"The lawyer who drafted it was a former clerk of mine, currently a partner at a firm in Charlottesville. They had the original, and that's the will that's being probated."

"Did anyone look for another, more recent will?" asked King.

"That's the point. I don't think so. But what if a later will was the thing stolen from Bobby's closet during the burglary?"

King said, "But if it was in Bobby's secret compartment, which Remmy told us she was unaware of, she wouldn't have had the opportunity to destroy it."

"I'm not saying it was Remmy. Bobby had a stroke, he was delirious, talking gibberish at the hospital, so I heard," said Harry.

"And maybe he mentioned another will," said King, snapping his fingers.

"So anyone who heard him could have committed the burglary," said Harry.

"If Dorothea had it, though, she would have made it public, wouldn't she?"

"But there'd be the little matter of where it came from," said Harry. "I don't think she would want to confess to burglary."

King looked puzzled. "But, Harry, we're overlooking something. Bobby's death was well publicized. Whoever drew up the new will would have come forward."

"Maybe he didn't use a law firm to draft it."

"If he did it himself, he'd still need witnesses."

"Not if it were a holographic will, entirely in his hand-writing."

"So if there is such a will, who has it, and why aren't they making it public?"

"A question to which I would dearly love the answer," remarked Harry as he finished off his snifter of cognac.

CHAPTER

76

KING AND MICHELLE SAID good night to Harry and drove off. The weather was still nice enough to keep the top down. However, Michelle tugged her wrap more tightly around her shoulders.

"I can put up the top if you want," said King, noting her movement.

"No, the breeze feels wonderful and the air smells so good."

"Spring in rural Virginia, can't beat it."

"I feel like we made some progress tonight."

"At least we took the time to talk out different angles. That's always helpful."

She glanced at him with a suspicious look. "As usual you're saying less than you know."

He pretended to be offended by her remark; however, his smile betrayed this effort. "I'm not conceding I *know* anything. But I do suspect some things that I might not have mentioned."

"Such as, *partner*?"

"Such as I've spent a wonderful evening over two fabulous bottles of wine with an attractive young woman, and all I've talked about is murder and mayhem."

"You're stalling. And mentioning the wine before mentioning me says a lot."

"Well, I've known those bottles of wine longer than I've known you."

"Thanks a lot, but you're still stalling."

The SUV hit them from behind so hard that if they hadn't been wearing their seat belts, they both would have gone headfirst through the windshield.

"What the hell!" yelled out King as he looked in his rearview mirror. "Where did they come from?" The words were barely out of his mouth before they were rammed again. King fought the wheel, trying to keep the two-door Lexus coupe on the windy road.

Michelle kicked off her heels and pushed her bare feet against the floorboard to steady herself. Reaching into her bag, she slid out her gun, chambered a round and punched off the safety pretty much all in one smooth motion.

"Can you see the driver?" asked King.

"Not with the damn headlights shining in my face. But it has to be the killer."

King pulled out his cell phone. "This time we're going to nail the bastard."

"Look out, here he comes again," yelled Michelle.

The next impact by the far heavier vehicle almost lifted the rear of the Lexus off the road. King's cell phone was knocked out of his hand, banged against the windshield and then went rocketing backward. It clanged off the hood of the SUV, hit the street and broke apart.

King tangled with the wheel again and managed to regain control as the two vehicles uncoupled. King's car was outweighed by at least a ton. Still the Lexus coupe was far more nimble than the beast attacking them, and it had three hundred horses under the hood. Calling on all of them when they hit a straightaway, King punched the gas and the Lexus leaped forward, leaving the other vehicle far behind.

Michelle undid her safety belt.

"What the hell are you doing?" cried King.

"You can't outrun him on these windy roads, and I can't get a decent shot off with my belt on. Just keep ahead of him."

"Wait a minute, call 911 first."

"I can't. I didn't bring my cell phone. My purse was too small for it *and* my gun."

King looked at her incredulously. "You didn't bring your phone but you brought your gun?"

"I think I have my priorities right," she said sharply. "What can I do with a phone: call him to death?"

She turned around in her seat, leaned over it and placed her elbow on the headrest of the rear seat. "Keep ahead of him," she repeated.

"Well, damn it, you keep from getting killed," he shot back.

The truck came powering up again for another collision of metal on metal, but before it could make contact, King shot across to the other side of the road, whipped back and rat-tat-tatted on the gravel shoulder before regaining the hard surface. He downshifted and nailed the hairpin turn at fifty, tires screaming. He suddenly felt the right wheels losing touch with the asphalt, and he lurched his two hundred pounds to that side, grabbing hold of Michelle's right hip and pushing her sideways against the passenger door.

"I'm not being fresh. I just need the ballast. Stay there for a sec."

He dropped his speed a couple of mphs and exhaled a sigh of relief as the rubber attached itself once more to terra firma.

They hit another straightaway that King knew would run for a quarter of a mile before a series of serpentine curves would confront them. He smashed down on the gas so hard he was sure his loafers would be hitting the pavement in another quarter inch. As he ripped right through triple digits on the speedometer, the trees flashed by at such dizzying speed he would've started puking had he bothered to look.

Behind him the driver of the truck wound it up to well over a hundred on the quarter-mile stretch, keeping well within striking distance. King hit 130 and looked for another gear to grab, but the Lexus didn't have any more to give. All he could think about was, *How many air bags does the damn car have?* He hoped it was at least a dozen; it looked like they would need every one because the series of curves was flying at them. If he slowed down, they were dead; if he kept this speed, they'd be equally dead.

Michelle eyed the headlights bearing down on them and then slid her gaze up to the driver's silhouette. She inched forward, finally resting her right elbow on the top part of the car's trunk, and took aim with both hands on her pistol.

They hit the curvy area, and King braked hard to sixty

when the signs said twenty, but the traffic engineers had undoubtedly not taken into account murderous SUVs in their calculations of highway safety. This allowed the truck to make up significant ground. "He's coming up," warned King. "I can't go any faster without us flipping."

"Just hold it steady. If he doesn't back off, I'm going to take out his front tire."

Their pursuer came within fifty feet and then twenty. He had to see that she had him dead in her sights, Michelle thought, and yet he wasn't giving an inch of ground. Then the SUV took an incredible leap forward as the driver gunned it.

King had seen this and mimicked the man's efforts. The Lexus shot forward, the truck right on their ass. King arched his body and stamped both feet on the gas as though that would give them the turbocharge they so desperately needed.

What he hadn't counted on was a family of deer choosing that moment to amble across the road.

"Look out!" screamed King. He whipped the wheel to the left and then to the right. They went off the road and pinballed alongside a stretch of guardrail as the Bambis scattered. King felt the guardrail imprint its signature on his once beautiful convertible rivet by screeching rivet. He regained the road and looked back. The driver of the truck had smashed on his brakes to avoid the deer, but the SUV had never left the road, and it was barreling down on them once more.

King didn't have time to get back up to cruising speed, and anyway, the engine's peculiar whine made him wonder if the guardrail had done more than simply cosmetic

damage. What was certain was that the speedometer had
dropped to under ninety and was staying there.

"Brace yourself," cried out Michelle. "Here comes the
son of a bitch." She fired her gun twice right as the truck
ate into the rear of the Lexus, ripping a hole in the car and
taking what little was left of the molded bumper and
flinging it into the woods. Michelle was thrust forward
from the collision toward the rear of the car. As King saw
her legs flying past him, he reached out with his free hand
and clamped down on her ankle, looping his arm around
her limb and holding on for dear life. They hit another
straightaway, and he somehow coaxed more speed from
the car, leaving the truck behind again.

"Shit!" yelled Michelle.

"Are you hurt?"

"No, I got off a couple shots, but I lost my gun. Damn
it, I've had that SIG for five years."

"Will you forget the gun; this guy's trying to kill us."

"Well, if I had my gun, I could kill him before he kills
us. I don't know if I hit anything. He slammed into us
right as I fired." She yelled out, "Wait a minute!"

"What?"

"There it is. My gun landed on the lip of the rear
spoiler. It's wedged there."

"No way—don't you even think about it, lady."

"Just hold on to my leg. I can almost reach it."

"Damn it, Michelle, you're going to give me a heart attack, and I'm about to have one as it is."

So focused was King on her that he didn't see the SUV
speed up and come alongside until the last instant.

"Hold on," he screamed as he instantly downshifted,

leaping over gears in a way that probably voided every manufacturer's warranty Lexus offered. He could almost hear the car screaming at him to *Just stop it!* and he expected to see his transmission vomited all over the road. He plunged to twenty clicks on the speedometer, both feet on the brakes now, then came to a thudding stop, wheels smoking, as the g's raced down his torso and washed off his toes. Michelle had a death grip around the rear headrest, her bare feet braced against the back of his seat.

King's body was misfiring in so many ways he figured cardiac arrest was the least he could expect. He slammed the car into reverse, jammed down on the accelerator, firewalled what was left of his engine, and rocketed backward.

The SUV had stopped so hard that its tires seemed ablaze, such was the volume of smoke pouring from them. The driver cut a swift 180 and was coming at them full tilt, the SUV's grille resembling bared teeth looking to devour them. It was gaining with every revolution of the wheel.

Michelle stopped inching toward her gun and eyed her partner, who was looking backward as he drove. "You can't drive faster backward than he can forward, Sean."

"Thanks for telling me." His knuckles were turning purple from his grip on the wheel. "Hold on to everything you can. On the count of five I'm cutting a J."

"You must be nuts."

"Yes, I must be."

By cutting a J he meant that from a fast reverse driving position he was going to whip the car into a 180-degree turn, probably on two wheels, slam it into drive, fire the turbos and rocket off in the opposite direction. All that in one neat motion, preferably without killing them both.

Sweat broke over King's brow as he prayed that all his Secret Service training would come back to him so many years later. He clamped on the door with his free hand for leverage, braced his left foot against the floorboard as a fulcrum point, gauged the exact right moment and whipped the wheel hard, letting go of it completely and then clamping down on it. It worked to perfection. He leapfrogged over the first two forward gears, gunned it and shot ahead. However, five seconds later the SUV was chasing them and gaining.

Smoke was now coming out of the Lexus's hood, and every single gauge King was staring at was foretelling their doom. Their speed dropped to sixty, then fifty. It was over.

"Sean, here he comes!" screamed Michelle.

"There's not a damn thing I can do about it," he shouted back, hopelessness evolving to rage in the course of a single breath.

The SUV roared past, pulled back and took its two and one half tons and broadsided them. King kept one hand on the wheel and clamped the other on Michelle's ankle as she struggled to get the gun. His fingers dug in so tightly on her skin that he knew he was drawing blood. His arm and shoulder were being torqued almost beyond limit.

"Are you okay?" he called out, gritting his teeth against the pain as he could feel her full weight pulling against his tendons.

"I am now, I've got the gun."

"Well, good, because the bastard's coming again. Hold on!"

He looked over to see the black SUV swerve toward him about the same time he felt Michelle's limb twist around in his hand.

"What are you do—" He didn't have time to finish his sentence. The SUV clipped the rear end of the Lexus, and the car did what King had feared all along. It started to fishtail, and then it went into a 360, totally out of control.

"Hold on!" he called out hoarsely as seemingly every ounce of belly bile started to march upward to incinerate his throat. As a Secret Service agent King had trained relentlessly to master the maneuvers of vehicles in the most hazardous conditions imaginable. Warmed up by the J-turn, he just let instinct take over. Instead of fighting the movements of the car, he went with them, turning the wheel toward the spin instead of against it and beating back the natural impulse to crush his brakes. The thing he was most fearful of was the car rolling. If it did, Michelle was dead and he probably would be too or at best a quad. King didn't know how many revolutions the car took, but the low-built, bottom-heavy 3,800-pound Lexus held the road despite jettisoning a good deal of its tire rubber and a bunch of its metal guts.

The car finally came to a stop facing in the direction of where they'd been heading; the black SUV was just up ahead and moving away from them fast, apparently having decided to give up the fight. Michelle's gun fired, and the rear tires of the SUV disintegrated as the ordnance ripped into them. The vehicle started to whip around, went into a 360 and then did what the Lexus had steadfastly refused to: it rolled. Three shuddering flips, and it came to rest on its shattered roof along the right shoulder of the road far ahead of them, a trail of metal, glass and rubber left in its turbulent wake.

King sped forward, as much as he could in his wrecked car, while Michelle slid down in the seat next to him.

"Sean?"

"What?"

"You can let go of my leg."

"What? Oh, right." He released his death grip.

"I know; I was scared too." She gave his hand a comforting squeeze as they looked at each other and drew long, thankful breaths.

"That was some damn fine driving, Agent King," she said gratefully.

"And I sincerely hope it's the last time I ever have to do it."

They pulled next to the wreck and got out. They advanced toward the car; Michelle had her pistol ready. King managed to wrench the driver's door open.

The man lunged toward them.

Michelle was ready to fire, but then her finger relaxed against the trigger.

The driver was upside down and bound by his seat belt. When King had opened the car door, he had plunged through the opening.

The head was so bloody and mangled King didn't bother checking for a pulse.

"Who is it?" she asked.

"I can't tell; it's so damn dark out here. Wait a minute."

He ran over and pulled the Lexus up so that its headlights were pointed right at the dead man.

They looked at the body now outlined in bright light.

It was Roger Canney.

CHAPTER

77

AT TEN O'CLOCK IN THE morning the Deavers' double-wide trailer was empty. The kids were back in school, and Lulu was at work. Priscilla Oxley had driven off to a mom-and-pop store for cigarettes and some more tonic to wash down her cherished vodka. Meanwhile a truck was parked behind a stand of trees that bordered the paved road leading to the gravel one the trailer was situated on. The man inside the truck had watched as Priscilla sped by in her LTD, a cigarette in one hand and a cell phone in the other as she steered with her dimpled knees.

The man immediately got out and made his way through the woods until he was on the edge of the clearing by the trailer. Luther, the old dog, moseyed out from the rear shed, cocked its head in the man's direction as it caught his smell, gave a tired bark and then retreated back to the shed. A minute later the man was inside the trailer after picking the simple front-door lock and made his way swiftly to the small bedroom-office that was located at one end.

Junior Deaver had never been much of a businessman and was a worse recordkeeper, but fortunately, his wife was very strong in both those areas. Junior's construction company files were organized and easily accessible. Keeping one ear attuned for anyone coming, the man went through the files, which were conveniently arranged in chronological order. When he finished, he noted that he'd compiled a fairly lengthy list. One of these people had to be it.

He folded the list and put it away in his pocket and replaced all the files to their proper place. Then he left the way he'd come. As he returned to his truck, Priscilla Oxley drove past on her way back to the trailer with her tobacco and tonic. A lucky woman, he thought. Five minutes earlier and she would have been dead.

He drove off, his precious list in his pocket. He thought about the burglary that had been unjustly blamed on Junior Deaver. He tried to recall every detail he'd heard of the crime. There was something there he was definitely missing. In the same vein he went over and over again the circumstances of Bobby's death. Who was unaccounted for who might want the bastard dead? There were several possible suspects but no one he truly believed could have killed the old man. It would have taken nerve and knowledge, attributes he possessed in abundance and that he respected in others. He hoped for the day to be able to tell the impostor of his admiration, right before he slit his throat.

Perhaps he should have made Sally talk before he killed her. Yet what could she really have known? She was with Junior, she'd said. They'd had sex. She was a stupid woman who preferred spending her days with four-legged beasts and her nights with two-legged ones. She deserved the quick death she'd gotten. *What's one less Sally Wainwright on the planet anyway?* he asked himself.

He'd killed six people so far, one of them in error, a mistake he'd made retribution for at least in his way. It wasn't like he could pull out the rosary for this; no confessional could possibly contain his sins. He'd missed eliminating King and Maxwell, which frustrated him greatly. They were no doubt right now spinning new theories about what was really going on, and one day they might just alight on the right one. As complicated as it all seemed, the pair might figure it all out and ruin everything. It would be risky, but he was going to have to try again to kill them, in a way that wouldn't fail. It would take time to come up with such a scenario, and in the meantime he'd pay close attention to the intelligence he received from his bugs and try to stay a step ahead. It would be tight, but if he kept his head and stuck to his plan, it would turn out all right.

He was confident he was going to win. He had the most powerful advantage of all: he wasn't afraid to die for ultimate victory. He doubted his opponents felt the same.

Yet now he had another component of his plan to put into place.

A successful exit.

78

"YOU CAN'T BELIEVE Roger Canney's the one," said King heatedly.

They were at police headquarters, around a long conference table. Williams and Bailey stared back at him doubtfully. Michelle doodled on a pad in front of her while simultaneously watching her partner closely.

"He tried to kill both of you," pointed out Bailey.

King said, "Because we pretty much accused Canney of blackmailing Bobby Battle. The fact he tried to kill us pretty conclusively proves we were right. And if Canney did kill his wife, he'd probably be terrified we'd uncover that too. He goes on the run, we think. But he's really still in the area and tries to kill us. That doesn't mean he committed all those other murders."

Bailey shook his head. "He'd have to know or at least believe you'd shared your suspicions with us. And his method of trying to kill you was pretty stupid. Someone could have driven by and seen it all. And he used his own vehicle to try and kill you."

"I didn't say he was a smart criminal. Frankly, I think

he became unhinged. He'd been living on easy street for years thinking he's safe. And then his son's murdered and we stumble upon the blackmail. Maybe he just snapped. And if you do paternity testing on both the Canneys and Bobby, I'll think you'll find out who Steve Canney's real father was," added King.

"Okay, then, maybe Canney killed his son and his girl-friend and Bobby Battle, and then killed the prostitute and Diane Hinson to muddy the waters."

"And Junior Deaver?" pointed out King. "How does he fit into it?"

"Canney could have hired him to burglarize the Battles' house," said Bailey.

"For what reason?" shot back King.

"Well, if Battle and Mrs. Canney *were* having an affair, maybe Battle had something belonging to his lover that Roger Canney wanted back. Or Canney was afraid Battle had something incriminating on him. But then Junior also steals items from Remmy too, and Canney's ticked about that or is afraid Junior will give him away. So he kills him. By going after you two he showed he didn't mind murdering someone who got in his way."

"And Sally's death?" asked Michelle. "How does that figure in?"

"From what you've told us she was—and not to speak ill of the dead—a gal who'd jump into bed with anything wearing pants. Maybe Junior told her about Canney, and Canney found out and had to kill her too," said Bailey, who smiled broadly, obviously pleased with himself.

King sat back, shaking his head.

"It does sort of make sense, Sean," conceded Williams.

"It's wrong, Todd," said King very firmly. "All wrong."

"So give me an alternative theory that fits the facts," challenged Bailey.

"Right now I can't, but I'm telling you that if you stop looking for the real killer—or more likely, killers—other people could die."

"We're not going to stop, Sean," said Williams, "but if no more people are killed, it's pretty good evidence Canney is the one."

"You don't believe that, Todd, no matter how much you want to." King rose. "Come on, Michelle, I need some air."

Outside the police station, King leaned against Michelle's truck, shoved his hands in his pockets and scattered a bunch of gravel with an angry thrust of his foot.

"You know, either Chip Bailey is the biggest idiot I've ever met or . . ."

"Or maybe he's right, and you can't bring yourself to admit it," finished Michelle.

"Oh, you think so? Damn, my own partner conspiring against me," he said with a resigned grin. "Maybe I am wrong."

Michelle shrugged. "I think pinning the whole thing on Canney is way too much of a stretch, but like Bailey said, we don't have much of an alternative theory."

"There are things we know, things that are dangling right in front of our faces that we're not even seeing. If I could just grab them and hang on, I know it would lead us where we need to go. But it's driving me crazy that I can't see them."

"I think I know a remedy."

He looked at her dubiously. "I'm not running in a marathon or going bungee jumping in order to get my brain firing better."

"What I'm thinking requires no physical exertion at all."

"An absolutely stunning concept, coming from you."

Michelle stared at the beautiful blue sky. "I say it's boating time. Nothing like a spin on the water to get the mental juices flowing again, especially on a day like this."

"We don't have time—" King stopped and his expression turned softer. "Okay, after nearly being killed twice, maybe a little break wouldn't be so bad."

"I knew you'd see my logic. Sea-Doos or jet boat?"

"Jet boat. I'm getting tired of you always wanting to race on the Sea-Doos."

"That's just because I always beat you."

CHAPTER

79

KING WAS AT THE WHEEL, and Michelle sat next to him in the twenty-foot Bombardier jet boat as they cruised along at thirty knots over the lake's calm surface. The summer season was still a ways off, so they had the water pretty much to themselves.

"How much of Cardinal Lake have you seen?" asked King.

"A lot. I don't let the grass grow under my feet."

King went on in a pedantic tone. "You know, this lake was formed by damming up two rivers and letting the water back up over ten years. The end result was a very deep thirty-mile-long lake with excellent fishing, water sports and about two hundred coves and inlets."

"Wow, you sound just like the real estate agent who sold me my place. Do you also refinance mortgages?"

They headed toward the hydroelectric dam, which was really two dams, an upper and a lower one. Then they hit the main channel and turned west. Where the two rivers came together, King headed north until they came to a smaller channel that doglegged north and then east. They kept this heading, passing the even-numbered red channel markers that ran upriver, until he pulled back on the throttle and steered straight into a small uninhabited cove. A few minutes later they'd anchored down in about twenty feet of clear water, and King pulled out a basket of food and a cooler with sodas and water he'd put together.

"I'm going to swim before we eat," said Michelle.

"How's your arm?"

"Will you stop with the arm? It was only a nick to begin with."

"Why do I think if you took a thirty-thirty round through your chest, you'd only ask for a Band-Aid, and a small one at that?"

She stripped down to her one-piece swimsuit and dove in.

"God, the water's great," she said after coming back up.

King eyed his instrument panel. "Water temp's seventy-five, still a little cool for me. I'm an eighty-one, eighty-two kind of guy."

"You mean you're a wimp."

"That's another way of putting it, yes."

After they'd had their lunch, King pulled up the anchor and they started off again. Michelle pointed to a long, wide point up ahead. It was quite a sight: a six-slip boat dock with a gazebo, bar, dining area and equipment sheds and about six thousand square feet of decking, all encased in cedar siding and shake roofing. It just begged for an *Architectural Digest* spread.

"That's pretty impressive. Who owns it?"

"What, you lose your sense of direction on the water? That's Casa Battle."

"What! I didn't even know they were on the lake."

"You don't put up a mansion in Wrightsburg without lakefront access. They have the whole point plus about twenty more acres. Their dock is a ways from the main house. In fact, you can't even see the mansion from the lake. I think they designed it that way so there wouldn't be gawkers coming by on boats all the time. They use golf carts to come and go."

"What a life." She squinted against the intense sunlight. "Who's that out there on the sailboat?"

King grabbed his binoculars and zeroed in on the skipper of the other boat. "Savannah." He pondered for a moment, then fingered the throttle forward and steered toward the sailboat.

"What are you doing?"

"Going fishing."

They drew close to the sailboat that was little more than a Sunfish. Savannah had one hand on the tiller and the other on a can of Coke. She waved when she saw who it was.

"Great minds think alike," called out King.

Savannah had a long tank shirt on over her two-piece bathing suit. Her hair was wet and pulled back in a ponytail, and her shoulders and face had already started to redden from the sun.

"The water's amazing," she said.

"Sean won't go in until it hits bathwater status," said Michelle.

"Don't know what you're missing, Mr. King," said Savannah.

"Well, I could be tempted if you two were to join me."

They each took a minute to drop their anchors, and

then first Savannah and then Michelle dove in. When they came up, King was still sitting on his boat's swim platform, his feet dangling in the water.

"What are you doing, Sean?" said Michelle.

"I said I could be *tempted,* not that I'd actually do it."

Michelle and Savannah looked at each other, a silent communication passing between the two women. They both went under the water. When they came back up next to where King sat, each had one of his feet in her hands.

"Oh, no, you—," began King. Whatever else he was about to say was lost as he was pulled into the lake and immediately went under. He came up spitting water and cursing loudly.

"These aren't swim trunks!" he shouted.

"They are now," replied Savannah smugly.

After a half hour in the water they navigated their boats to the dock and sat in the gazebo drinking beers that Savannah fetched from the bar fridge.

Michelle looked around at the mountain and water vistas. "Quite a view."

"This is really my favorite part of the whole place," said Savannah.

King eyed the Battles' collection of boats. "I've been out on the big Sea Ray cruiser, but I don't remember that Formula 353 FasTech. It's a beauty."

"Daddy had just bought it last winter. The marina folks came and prepped it for summer. We haven't even put any hours on the engine yet. Eddie's the real boater in the family. I just like to ride on them and catch some sun and drink beer. Eddie said he'd take it out soon and break it in. I understand it's really fast, got some monster engines."

King said, "I'll say, twin five-hundred-horsepower Merc EFIs; a top speed north of seventy and a cruising speed at right about double nickels. Tell Eddie I'd be glad to help him break it in."

"My, my," Savannah said in an exaggerated southern accent, "and here I was having such a dee-lightful time on my little old no-horsepower sailboat."

"It's clearly a guy thing, Savannah," commented Michelle, shooting her partner an amused glance. "I didn't know you were so into racing boats."

"It's easy to be when you can't afford them."

There was a bit of silence, and King slowly put down his beer and looked at the youngest Battle with a serious expression.

"You didn't come here just to admire me in my bikini and lust over our boats, did you?" she asked, returning his gaze with a hopeful look that held out the possibility that that indeed was all he was interested in.

"We do have some questions to ask you."

Savannah immediately looked away and her expression became pained. "Sally?"

"Among other things."

"That's one reason I came down here to go sailing, to get away from it." She shook her head. "I'll never get that out of my head. Never. It was so awful, Sean, so awful."

He put his hand over hers and squeezed for a moment before letting go. "But it only gets worse if we don't catch the person who did it."

"I told Todd and Agent Bailey everything I know. I didn't even know Sally was in the stables until . . ."

"And then you ran to your brother's home?" said

Michelle. Savannah nodded. "Dorothea answered the door. How did she seem?"

"I don't really remember. I was hysterical. I remember her going to get Eddie, but then she couldn't wake him. Then all hell broke loose. I just stood over by the door the whole time. I was afraid to move. When they came and got Eddie, I ran back to my room and pulled the covers over my head." She put her drink down and went over and sat on the dock, her feet in the water.

King stared at her curiously. What the hell was gnawing at his brain, begging him to decipher it? He finally shook his head in frustration. It just wasn't coming.

"Is your mother home?" he asked.

"No, she went out. Something to do with the lawyers and probate."

"Would you mind if we took another look at the closets in your parents' bedrooms?"

She swiveled around on her bottom to look at him. "I thought you already did that."

"Never hurts to check a second time. It might help."

They climbed in the golf cart Savannah had ridden down in and headed up to the house. Savannah led them in through the rear entrance and up the stairs to the third level.

"I keep telling Mama that if she's going to stay here, she needs to have an elevator put in."

"Climbing stairs is good exercise," said Michelle.

"Don't listen to her," said King. "Get the elevator."

Savannah opened the door to her mother's bedroom and stopped dead. "Oh," she exclaimed. "What are you doing in here?"

King moved past her and looked at Mason suspiciously.

The butler gazed back at them unperturbed. "Just tidying up your mother's room, Savannah. The maids rarely do a good enough job." Now he looked at King and Michelle with equal suspicion. "Can I help you with something?"

"Um," began Savannah, her upper teeth biting into her lower lip.

"You're dripping on the rug," Mason pointed out.

"We were swimming in the lake," explained Michelle.

"Nice day for it." He continued to stare at them questioningly.

"We're here to take another look at Remmy's closet, Mason," said King. "As part of the investigation."

"But I thought because Mr. Deaver is dead that there's no longer an investigation to pursue."

"You'd think so, wouldn't you, but that's not actually the case," said King politely.

Mason turned to Savannah. "Have you checked with your mother about this?"

King answered, "She took us through it once before, Mason. I can't imagine she'd have a problem with a second time."

"I always like to make sure of these things, Sean."

"You see, because we know Junior didn't do it and Remmy is now friends with his widow, it's up to us to find out who did take those things. It's in Remmy's interest of course to see that happens. But if you want to call her and bother her while she's with the probate lawyers, that's fine. We'll just wait right here."

King could see Mason working through all this in his head. Finally, he shrugged. "I can't see that it will hurt anything. Just try and keep things neat. Mrs. Battle is very particular."

"Yes, she is," said King.

Mason left, and they went immediately into Remmy's closet and accessed the hidden drawer, examining it minutely but finding nothing.

"Maybe you'll have better luck in Daddy's room," said Savannah.

As they were leaving the closet, King stopped to look at some photos on the shelf across from Remmy's bed. Savannah stood next to him.

"That's me when I was twelve, fat and ugly. God, I can still feel those braces on my teeth."

King held up another photo, an old one, with two babies in it.

Savannah pointed as she spoke. "That's Eddie and Bobby Jr. I never knew him, of course; he died before I was born. No, I'm sorry, that's Eddie on the left and Bobby Jr. on the right." She still looked unsure. "Well, that's embarrassing, not knowing your own flesh and blood."

"Well, they were twins," said King, putting the photo back.

They moved to Bobby's bedroom but had no success there either, at least not at first. But as King went over the drawer inch by inch, he stiffened. "Can you get me a flashlight?" he asked Savannah.

"Mama keeps one in her nightstand in case the power goes out." Savannah ran and got it.

King shone it in the drawer. "Look at this." They all peered in.

"It looks like letters," observed Michelle.

"That's definitely a *k*, and either a *c* or an *o*."

Michelle looked more closely. "Then there's some space, and that's a *p* followed by what looks to be either an *a* or an *o*."

King straightened up, looking thoughtful. "It appears something was lying in this drawer, and those letters somehow stained the wood, imprinting it."

"It might have gotten wet," suggested Savannah.

King leaned in and took a long whiff of the drawer. He looked at Savannah. "Did Bobby drink in his room?"

"Daddy drink? He has a whole bar in that piece of furniture that looks like a credenza across from his bed. Why?"

"Because it smells like Scotch in the drawer."

"That might account for the moisture," said Michelle, who took a whiff. "He was looking at whatever it was, spilled his drink in the drawer, and the letters got transferred from the paper to the bottom of the drawer."

King went into the bedroom and came back with a pen and paper he'd taken from Battle's desk. He wrote the words down with the approximate spaces in between.

Kc_____ pa, Ko_____ pa, Ko_____ po

"Kc-pa, Ko-pa, or Ko-po," he said slowly. "Ring any bells?" Savannah shook her head.

"Obviously, there are letters we're missing. If we were

playing *Wheel of Fortune,* here's where I'd ask for a couple of vowels," said Michelle. "What do you think, Sean?"

He took a moment before answering. "Somehow this may be the whole key right here, if I can just think of what it means."

Michelle had a sudden inspiration. While Savannah was scrutinizing the letters King had written down, Michelle whispered in her partner's ear, "Maybe it's from Battle's holographic will that Harry thought might exist?"

None of them heard the bedroom door close quietly behind the person who'd been listening in. Nor did they hear the sound of soft footfalls moving down the hall to the stairway.

80

SEAN KING SAT STRAIGHT up in bed like someone had frisked him with a cattle prod.

Seven hours! My God, seven hours! But not really seven hours, more likely longer than that. The seven-hour reference had made him think about Sally's death. She had died barely seven hours after telling him about Junior. That was one major point. However, the seven-hour time difference had just now made him recognize a startling fact, so startling that with that one revelation everything else started tumbling into place.

He fumbled around and found his watch on the night-stand. It was one o'clock in the morning. He staggered out of his bed, tripped over something Michelle had carelessly left on the guest room floor and fell down grabbing at his big toe. He felt around and found the object. It was a twenty-pound dumbbell.

"For Chrissakes," he yelled at no one in particular. He got up, rubbing his foot, and limped down the hallway to her bedroom. He was about to burst in when he thought better of it. Surprising Michelle Maxwell like that could earn him a one-way ticket to the morgue.

He rapped on the door. "Are you decent?"

A sleepy voice filtered through the one-inch wood of the door. "What?"

"If you still keep that fifty-caliber machine gun under your pillow, don't pull it. I come in peace."

He went inside and flicked on the light. She was sitting up in bed, rubbing at her eyes.

"I like your choice in lingerie," he said, eyeing her baggy gray sweat suit emblazoned with the acronym WIFLE, which stood for Women in Federal Law Enforcement. "You wear that on your honeymoon, and your hubby will never let you out of bed."

She looked at him irritably. "Is that why you woke me up, to critique my pajamas?"

He sat next to her. "No, I have something I need you to do while I'm gone."

"Gone? Gone where?"

"I've got some things to look into."

"I'll go with you."

"No, I need you here. I want you to keep an eye on the Battles."

"The Battles. Which ones?"

"All of them."

"How exactly can I do that?"

"I'll call Remmy and say that you need to ask some more questions. She'll bring everyone together at her house, and that'll make it easier for you."

"What exactly am I supposed to ask them?"

"You'll think of plenty of things, don't worry."

She crossed her arms and looked at him stubbornly. "What the hell is going on?"

"I'm not sure yet, but I really need you to do this."

"You're keeping things from me again. You know I hate that."

"I don't know anything definite yet. But you'll be the first to know. I swear."

"Will you at least tell me what the things are you're going to check into?"

"All right. I'm going to have a friend of mine look at Bobby's autopsy results."

"Why?"

"Next," he said, ignoring her question, "I'm going over to UVA Hospital and do a little research into certain narcotics. Then I'm going to do a little antiquing."

She raised her eyebrows. "Antiquing?"

"After that I'm going to visit Bobby Battle's family physician. I have some questions to ask that might clear up a lot. Last but not least I'm heading to D.C. to purchase a certain device that might assist us greatly. "

"And that's all you're going to tell me?"

"Yes."

"Gee, thanks for all your trust in me."

He rose. "Listen to me, Michelle. If I told you exactly what I'm thinking and I turn out to be completely wrong, it might make you trust the wrong person. Until I know if I'm right or not, keep one thing in mind: until we catch this person, no one is your friend. And I mean no one."

She stared back at him. "Are you trying to scare me?"

"No, I'm trying to keep both of us alive. We've already taken two shots. I don't want the third to be the charm."

CHAPTER

81

WHILE KING WAS HAVING his late night epiphany and conference with Michelle, a man with murder on his mind had entered the residence of Jean and Harold Robinson. Wearing a black hood, he'd opened the basement-door lock and slipped inside. It was easy when one had a key, and he did, having used the impressions he'd taken at the shopping mall to create one. Before entering the house he'd cut off the phone lines. Inside, he moved quickly up the stairs, the layout of the home well known to him. There were four occupants, and he knew where each was located, having scouted out the residence several times. For good measure he'd also studied a schematic of the house that was conveniently displayed on the builder's Web site.

As he'd deduced in the shopping mall where he'd first spotted the soccer mom Jean Robinson, the family had a security system but didn't use it. The three children—the infant he had waved to in the van and two older boys—were asleep on the upstairs level. The wife and husband had a master suite on the main level, only the husband wasn't home, which was why he was here tonight.

The heat came on with a shudder, flooding the house with gas-heated air. Under the cover of the sound he flashed down the hall to the master bedroom. He listened at the door for one-two-three beats. All he heard were the soft snores of Mrs. Robinson, waiting for him without even knowing she was. He opened the door and closed it softly behind him. His eyes had long since adjusted to the dark. Jean Robinson was a small lump on the left side of the California King bed. She wore a white sheer nightie. He'd been peering in her window when she was changing into it. She had a bad habit of not closing the blinds all the way and leaving the light on when she undressed. Because the window faced the backyard, she probably assumed it was private. She'd assumed incorrectly, of course, as most people did about having any privacy at all. There was always someone watching. Always.

She'd gotten back in shape quickly after her third child. Her tummy was flat once more, her breasts still large from nursing the infant, her legs slender, her butt fleshy but in a very attractive way. Her husband no doubt loved her, and they had a healthy sex life together. Yet what did that really matter to him? He wasn't here to rape the woman, only to kill her.

The gag was stuffed in her mouth in an instant, cutting off any sound she might have made. After a second of confusion as to what was happening to her, every muscle in her body tensed. He pushed against her from behind, crushing her to the bed. Yet she was stronger than he would have thought; she fought back. Her hand reached back, gripped the hood and pulled it off.

He panicked and slammed her head against the hard wood of the headboard, once, twice, a third time, until he felt her go limp. Once more into the solid oak, and he thought he heard her skull fracture, if one could hear such a thing. While one forearm levered into the back of her neck, his free hand frantically sought out his hood. He found it gripped in her fist. Yanking it free, he pulled it back on. Putting his arm under her small waist, he lifted her completely off the bed and slammed her headfirst against the wood one final time.

He flipped her over and looked at her eyes. They were open, staring, lifeless; the blood from her crushed head ran down, staining her exposed breasts. He pulled the nightie all the way off and flung it across the room. He lifted her naked body up and set it on the floor. He took the steak knife he'd pilfered from the Robinsons' kitchen and proceeded to mark her skin in very intricate ways. The police should have no trouble getting this one, he thought as he worked away. He took the risk of switching on a small light on the nightstand and used the knife blade to dig under her fingernails, extracting pieces of his hood from them. These he put in his pocket.

He took her watch from the nightstand, set it to six, pulled out the stem and wrapped the band around her wrist.

Finished, he felt for her pulse, just to be sure. It had gone for good. Jean Robinson had ceased to be. Next stop for the woman, the licensed butcher, Dr. Diaz. Harold Robinson was now a widower with three young boys to care for. And the world would go on, which proved his point entirely that none of it really mattered. *We're all replaceable.*

He grabbed the nightie, which might have traces of him on it, and stuffed it into his pocket. He didn't have the luxury of vacuuming up after himself, because of the home's other occupants; indeed, he was fortunate that the sounds of their mother's being beaten to death hadn't roused the two older boys.

He turned back once more to look at his work. Yes, it was all nicely set up—first-rate, in fact.

Here's to you, Mrs. Robinson.

He went to the kitchen, found her purse, took out her cell phone, hit the directory, obtained the number he wanted and called the good husband, who was on the road, not too far from here. He said four simple words. "Your wife is dead." He then hung up and turned off the phone. He reached up on top of the kitchen cabinet and retrieved the bug he'd planted there in an earlier burglary. He'd no longer need it.

Now he had one more task to perform, and then it would be over, at least for tonight. He started to the back stairs leading to the basement.

"Mom?"

He froze there in the hallway as the light in the upper hall came on. Footsteps approached; they were short, halting strides; bare feet sliding along wood flooring.

"Mom?"

The little boy appeared at the top of the stairs and looked down. In one hand he clutched a stuffed dog that he was dragging along. He was clad in white underpants and a Spider-Man T-shirt. He rubbed sleepy eyes with a small, dimpled fist.

"Mommy?" he said again. Still looking down, he finally saw the shadow of black hood at the bottom of the stairs.

"Daddy?"

The killer stood there and stared back up at the child. His gloved hand slipped to his pocket, fingered a knife. It would be over in an instant. A deuce instead of only one dead, what did it matter? *Mother and son, what the hell does it matter?* He tensed to do this very thing. Yet he made not a move. He simply stared at the small frame outlined in the weak light; the potential eyewitness.

"Daddy?" he said again, now his voice rising with fear when no answer came.

He snapped back just in time. "It's Daddy, son, go back to sleep."

"I thought you had to go, Daddy."

"I forgot something, Tommy, that's all. Go back to sleep before you wake up your brothers. You know once your little brother starts to cry, it's all over. And give Bucky a kiss for me," he added, referring to the stuffed bear. While he couldn't exactly imitate the father's voice, knowing the son's name, that he had brothers and other intimate details would certainly put the little boy at ease.

He'd researched the Robinsons thoroughly. He knew everything from their nicknames to their Social Security numbers to their favorite restaurant to the various sports the two older boys, Tommy and Jeff, played: Tommy baseball and Jeff soccer. He knew that Harold Robinson had left the house at a little before midnight on his way to Washington,

D.C. . . . that their mother loved them very much . . . that tonight he'd taken that person away from them forever. He'd done so solely because she'd had the great misfortune to pass by his radar while shopping for milk and eggs. It could have been anyone's mother. Anyone's. But it just happened to be Tommy's. And twelve-year-old Jeff's. And little one-year-old Andy's, who'd had the colic his first six months of life. It was amazing the intimate details people shared if one just listened. Yet no one did listen anymore, except perhaps priests. And killers like him.

He let go of the knife in his pocket. Tommy would have the chance to grow up. One Robinson was enough for tonight.

"Go back to bed, son," he said again more firmly.

"Okay, Daddy. I love you." The little boy turned and headed back down the hall.

Black hood stood there for far too long, staring up at the empty space where sleepy Tommy had been, where he'd said, I love you, Daddy. He should be making his escape; finishing up his last task. *I love you, Daddy.*

He suddenly felt ashamed to even be in the same house with the child who'd said that to him, however mistakenly. He cursed himself. *Go, go now. The husband is probably right now phoning the police. Go, you idiot!*

Down in the unfinished basement he shone his light on the capped piping that marked a future toilet area. He unscrewed the cap, took out the large Baggie of items, stuffed it in the pipe and screwed the cap back on just so. In planting evidence one could neither be too obvious nor too obtuse. His fence-straddling would have to be perfect.

He slipped outside, crossed the backyard and made his

way to his blue VW parked several blocks off. He took off his hood as he drove away. Then he did something he'd never done before. He drove directly to the home where he'd just committed perhaps his most heinous crime of all. The murdered mother was in her bedroom. Tommy was in his—the third dormer window from his left. The kids got up at seven to be ready for school. If their mother wasn't up by then, they'd go and get her. He checked his watch; it was one o'clock now. Tommy perhaps had six more hours of normalcy. "Enjoy them, Tommy," he mumbled to the dark window. *"Enjoy them . . . And I'm sorry."*

He drove off, licking at the salt of the tears sliding down his cheeks.

CHAPTER

82

KING HAD ALREADY LEFT in a rental car by the time Todd Williams called Michelle with the news of Jean Robinson's death. When she arrived at the stricken home, it was surrounded with police and emergency vehicles. Neighbors stared terrified from windows and porches. There was not a child to be seen anywhere. The three Robinson children had gone to a nearby relative's home with their father.

Michelle found Williams, Sylvia and Bailey in the master bedroom; all three were staring down at the former lady of the house.

Michelle recoiled slightly as she saw what had been done to the woman.

Sylvia looked over at her, and nodded in understanding. "Stigmata."

Jean Robinson's palms and feet had been mutilated as though to resemble the markings of Jesus on the cross. And her body had been laid out too, like the son of God on that piece of chiseled wood.

Bailey said wearily, "Bobby Joe Lucas. He did the

exact same thing to fourteen women in Kansas and Missouri in the early 1970s, after raping them."

"I'm pretty certain no rape occurred here," said Sylvia.

"I wasn't suggesting that. Lucas died of a heart attack in prison in 1987. And her nightgown is missing according to the husband. That would fit our killer's M.O."

"Where's Sean?" asked Williams.

"Out getting some questions answered."

Bailey looked at her suspiciously. "Where?"

"Don't really know."

"I didn't think Batman went anywhere without Robin," said the FBI agent sarcastically.

Before Michelle could fire back a response, Williams said, "Well, can't you call him? He'll want to know about this."

"His cell phone was broken during the chase with Roger Canney. He hasn't replaced it yet."

"I'm sure he'll hear about this soon enough," said Sylvia. "Bad news always travels faster than good."

"Where's the husband?"

Williams answered, "With the kids. He was on the road when it happened. He's a salesman with a high-tech outfit. He said he got a call from his wife's cell phone a little before one o'clock this morning. The voice said his wife was dead. He tried calling her cell phone back but there was no answer. Then he tried calling the house but the line wasn't working. We later found the wires had been cut. So he called 911."

"When did Robinson arrive here?"

"About an hour after my men. He was on his way to Washington for a sales conference."

"He likes to travel pretty late at night."

"He said he wanted to put his kids to bed and spend time with his wife before he left," answered Bailey.

"Any reason to suspect him?" asked Michelle.

"Other than that there was no forced entry, none that we can see," replied Williams.

"And no one saw anything?" she asked.

"There were only the three kids here. The infant of course can't help us. The oldest boy—"

A female deputy rushed into the room. "Chief, I just finished interviewing Tommy, the middle child. He said his father was in the house last night when he woke up. He doesn't know what time it was. He said his father told him he forgot something, to go back to bed."

At this instant another deputy burst in. "We found something in the plumb pipe in the basement."

They placed the Baggie taken from the plumb pipe on the dining room table and observed its contents through the clear material.

"St. Christopher's medal, belly ring, gold anklet, belt buckle and an amethyst ring," inventoried Williams.

"All the things taken from each of the first five victims," said Bailey.

Williams immediately turned to one of his deputies. "I want Harold Robinson taken into custody right now."

CHAPTER

83

KING'S FIRST STOP HAD been a physician friend of his in Lynchburg who was also a well-respected pathologist. They'd gone over Battle's autopsy results very carefully. A more detailed report had been prepared by Sylvia, which included the toxicology results and microscopic examination of Battle's brain tissue.

"From the gross finding of the unusual wrinkling on the thoracic aorta and the microscopic lesions on the brain, I certainly can't discount it, Sean," said his learned friend. "Those certainly are telltale signs of the disease."

"One more question," said King. "Can it affect the fetus?"

"Do you mean can it cross the placenta? Absolutely."

King's next stop was UVA Hospital, where he met with a professor in the pharmacology department. This was really what had started it all going in his mind.

He quickly received confirmation of his suspicions.

The professor informed him that "a person who abuses strong narcotics builds up a tolerance to them. Over time the desired effect is diminished, and higher doses of the drugs are required to achieve the desired result."

King had thanked him and went back to his car. *Well, I certainly know someone who's been taking strong narcotics: Dorothea.*

His next target was an antique shop in Charlottesville's downtown mall area that he'd been to several times. With the shop owner's help he found the object he was looking for.

"It's a cipher disk," explained the owner. He pointed to the round piece of metal that had an outer ring of letters and an inner one. "You can decode encrypted messages that way. You move the rings to line up the two sets of letters: *a* for *e*, *s* for *w* and so on."

"And if you're off by one letter or one *tick*, the whole meaning of the message changes? One tick off?"

"That's a good way to phrase it. One tick off and the whole thing changes."

"You just don't know how unbelievably satisfying that is." King purchased the cipher disk and left, the curious owner staring after him.

A little later he was speaking with Bobby Battle's private physician, a prominent doctor in the area and a man he knew well.

He discussed the results of the autopsy with the gentleman, who looked at the report very carefully and then took off his wire-rim glasses and said cautiously, "I've only been his doctor the last twenty years, you know."

"But you've noted changes?"

"In his personality, yes, I suppose. But he was getting

on in years. Half my patients have personality changes when they get to that age."

"But in Bobby's case did you suspect that was the cause?"

"Not necessarily. Usually, it's a case of mild dementia or the beginnings of Alzheimer's. Obviously, I didn't have the benefit of a postmortem exam."

"Did you run any tests while he was seeing you?"

"The symptoms weren't extreme, and you know what he was like. If he didn't want any tests run, none would be. However, these autopsy results could indicate he'd reached an advanced stage. I emphasize the word *could*."

"Did you ever talk to Remmy about it?"

"It wasn't my place and I had no hard proof. I suspected she knew that something was amiss," he hastily added.

"Yet they had Savannah."

"Typically, penicillin has been very effective against the disease. And the fact is, Savannah is hale and hearty."

"If Bobby had it, how long could it have been in his body?"

"Decades. It's chronic. It can have a long evolution in the body if left untreated."

"So he might have contracted it after he had Savannah?"

"Or he could have had it before. In the late stage it's not sexually transmittable, so even if he had it when Savannah was conceived, there would have been no danger for the fetus."

"Yet Remmy could have contracted it."

"I don't know her doctor, but if she had, I'd imagine she would have sought treatment."

King spoke with the doctor for several more minutes, then thanked the man and left.

He had one more stop to make. He phoned ahead to make sure the shop was open. Two hours later he was pulling into a parking garage in downtown D.C. Minutes after that he was walking into a very special retail store, where he spoke for some time with one of the employees there.

"It'll do the job?" King asked the employee, holding up the piece of equipment the man had given him in response to his request.

"Without a doubt."

King drove back to his houseboat, a big smile on his face. As he'd learned over the years, information was *king*.

He'd just walked into his houseboat when he heard footsteps outside. He looked out the window and saw Michelle hustling toward the dock.

He stepped outside as she ran up to him.

"I've been looking everywhere for you," she said.

"What's up?"

"They think they found the killer."

King looked at her in bewilderment. "What? Who?"

"Come on, there's a lot you need to be filled in on."

They ran for her truck.

CHAPTER

84

"AND THE LITTLE BOY'S *certain* it was his father?" asked King for the third time.

They were at police headquarters going over the events at the Robinson house the night before.

"That's what he said," answered Williams. "I don't know why he'd lie about it."

"But he told you he was at the top of the stairs looking down into the dark."

"His father spoke to him. Knew his name, his brother's name, and that there was a baby upstairs and even the name of Tommy's stuffed animal. Who else could it be?" King didn't respond; he sat back and fiddled with a pen he was holding.

Williams continued. "And we found all the items taken from each of the five murder victims in the man's house."

"Any prints on them?" asked King sharply.

"None. But that hardly surprises me. We haven't found fingerprints at any of the other crime scenes either."

"Pretty convenient, leaving all the evidence at his house."

"No, we were damn lucky to stumble on it. My deputy only noticed it because the cap was screwed on crooked while the other pipe caps were on straight. He was down there looking for ways the guy got in and spotted it."

"What's Robinson's story?"

"He left the house at midnight and was almost halfway to D.C. when he got the phone call."

"He didn't stop anywhere?"

"No. His wife's cell phone did ring on his at that time. We checked. But he could have been standing right in his house and done that with both phones."

"Yet he showed up over an hour after you got to the house?" said King stubbornly.

"So he drove around all that time giving himself an alibi. And he really didn't seem all that choked up that his wife was dead. He took the kids and went to a relative's house."

"And his motivation for killing all those people?"

"He's a serial killer disguised as a dad in the burbs. It wouldn't be the first time. He picked his victims out and did them."

"But what about the connection between Deaver, Canney and Battle?"

"Coincidence, or the connection was wrong."

"And the theory of why he killed his wife?" persisted King.

"Maybe she suspected him," offered Bailey. "And he had to take her out before those suspicions became dangerous, and he tried to tie it to the serial killings. The guy's on the road alone a lot at night, perfect for a serial killer. Right now we're looking into his whereabouts at the time each of the murders took place. It was a risk, killing her in his own home. But he might have felt he had no choice. Had his kid not seen him, we never would have suspected."

"Yep, my gut tells me he's our guy," said Williams.

"Yet his son talks to him and the boy's still alive?" said King.

Bailey answered, "Maybe even an animal like that has his limits. Or maybe he thought his son was half-asleep and wouldn't remember the conversation, or that no one would believe him if the boy did tell someone. You're a lawyer. A defense counsel could have a field day with a kid that young."

King sat back in exasperation while Bailey eyed him closely. "Your partner said you were out doing some investigating of your own. Find anything?"

There was just enough mirth behind the FBI agent's question to make King want to strangle the man. As if sensing this, Michelle, for once, put a calming hand on his shoulder.

"Just be cool," she whispered under her breath.

"Is this where I'm supposed to say, 'Screw you, Michelle'?" he muttered back.

Instead, he stood and said, "Well, if he *is* the guy, I congratulate you. Just keep us informed." He took out his deputy badge. "Do you want this back, *Chief*?"

"No. It's not *officially* over until we get a confession or some more evidence."

"Good, because I like being a deputy right now. In fact, it might come in handy."

He walked out.

"Talk about your sour grapes," said Bailey.

Michelle immediately rose to her partner's defense. "We don't know for sure Robinson is the guy."

"Well, we're fast approaching that point," Bailey replied.

Michelle stood to leave.

"Oh, Michelle," said Bailey, "be sure and keep us informed of any more *progress* you two make. I'm sure it'll prove invaluable to the investigation."

"Chip, that's the smartest thing you've said since I met you."

She followed King outside.

"So what do you think?" she asked.

"I think we'll let them keep Robinson locked up. He'll probably be safer in jail."

"But you don't think he did it?"

"No, I *know* he didn't do it."

"But you know who did?"

"I'm getting there. Did you have a chance to talk to the Battles?"

"Not after all this went down. Do you still want me to?"

King thought for a moment, his hand tapping the roof of her truck as he did so.

"No, we'll just cut to the main course. We're running out of time."

"You think he'll kill again?"

"He's arranged it so the police think the killer's locked up in jail. That's his way out. Even so, odds are Robinson must have an alibi for at least one of the murders. But the longer we wait, the less chance we have of nailing the real murderer."

"If he won't strike again, why keep Robinson in jail?"

"Because if he gets out, I'm convinced he'll be found in some alley with a bullet in his brain and a handy note clutched in his cold, dead hand that reads, 'I did it.'"

"So what do we do now?"

King opened the door of her truck. "Now it's time to take our best shot. And hope to God it's a knockout."

CHAPTER

85

HE WAS HALFWAY through running down the list he'd taken from Junior Deaver's trailer. The others would take time, but he'd bought himself some breathing space. The police had arrested Harold Robinson. He'd actually been fortunate Tommy had woken up and identified his father as being in the house, as the papers had reported. That plus the discovery of the items belonging to the five victims seemed to confirm Robinson as the perpetrator of the killing spree. Which had been his intent all along. Whether it would hold up he didn't know. If Robinson had an alibi for at least one of the killings, it might sink the whole ship, but until that time he had room in which to work. And Robinson's wife, a natural corroborator for her husband's whereabouts, was dead. That would make the police's alibi-checking a little more difficult. There was one more killing to do, but he wasn't concerned about the police connecting it to the previous murders and letting Robinson off the hook. They'd never find the body of his next victim. Indeed, there'd be nothing left to find.

He'd recently gleaned one very intriguing piece of information. When he'd checked the recording from the phone bug planted in King and Maxwell's office, he'd heard the conversation Michelle had with Billy Edwards. Over three and a half years ago the great Bobby Battle and his imperious wife had had an argument in the car barn. And the Rolls-Royce had been damaged. Over three and a half years ago. The day before Edwards had been let go, in fact.

He sat mulling this over. There was something . . . If only he could remember what it was. He finally turned back to his list, which showed the people Junior Deaver had done work for in the recent past. He figured that if someone had set up Junior for the burglary, they'd have to have had access to his trailer and personal items. He further deduced that the person who'd committed the burglary had probably killed Bobby Battle. This act had not only stolen his glory but ruined everything he'd worked for. For that sin only the ultimate punishment would do.

Michelle and King were huddled in their office.

"Okay, Sean, no more glib responses, no more bullshit answers. I'm tired of being kept in the dark. You said we had to give this guy our best punch and hope it's a knockout. I want to know everything you know. And I want to know it right now."

"Michelle—"

"Everything now, Sean, or you can look for another partner!"

King sat back and sighed heavily. "Okay, I know who

killed Bobby Battle. I spoke to a bunch of doctors, did my antique shopping, made some other inquiries and figured out some pieces of the puzzle, and it all holds up."

"Who is it!"

"Let me just say first that you're not going to believe it."

"Fine, I won't believe it."

King fiddled with a paper clip on his desk. "Harry Carrick killed Bobby Battle."

"Are you out of your mind? What possible motivation could Harry—"

King broke in. "The oldest possible one. He's in love with Remmy. Has been for decades."

"But are you saying he burglarized the Battles' house too?"

"Yes. Remember, he's old friends with the Battles. It would be relatively easy for him to get a key to their house and also obtain the pass code to the security system. Then he just busts the window and makes it look like a break-in. Harry said Junior had done work for him. You saw Junior's truck. It was full of tools, clothes. Harry could have taken whatever he needed from there to incriminate Junior. And on top of that he was a prosecutor and circuit judge for years, so he's no neophyte around fingerprints. He could have lifted one of Junior's and planted it at the Battles'."

"But why would he steal from the Battles?"

"I believe Bobby had incriminating evidence of their affair in his closet's secret cache. If so, he'd likely make it look as though Remmy's secret cupboard was the real target while he was really after what was in Bobby's."

"What sort of incriminating evidence would Bobby have had?"

In answer King opened his drawer and pulled out a photo. He turned it around and pointed to the back.

"Kc-pa? Ko-pa? Why don't we try Kodak paper?"

Michelle slowly reached out and took the photo. She ran her fingers over the words "Kodak paper" imprinted across the back. "And it partially leached off onto the drawer." King nodded. "So he had a photo of Remmy and Harry in some compromising position?"

"It must be. That's why Harry brought up his theory of a stolen will from Bobby's closet, to throw us off the track. The way I see it Harry and Remmy must've been in on this together. They had to get the photo back but make it look like a burglary in which Remmy's things were all that were taken. Under that theory, Remmy would have given Harry the key and the pass code. What they probably didn't realize was that the security system has an archives feature. Without Remmy knowing, I checked that log. At one-thirty in the morning when the burglary took place, the security system was turned off by someone inputting the access code. No one had ever checked that before because everyone assumed it was a burglary."

"So they get the photo."

"And then there's only one more thing to do."

"Kill Battle," said Michelle, and her voice broke. "I can't believe this, Sean, I can't. Not Harry."

"Look at it from Harry's point of view. The woman he loved was married to a monster. Remember he was at the hospital the morning Bobby died. He told us the hospital had called him in because he's their general counsel."

"You mean he's not!"

"No, he is, but they didn't call him. He came in on his own. He arranged to meet us as we were leaving. He told us he was an old friend of Bobby's. He asked if we'd seen Remmy. All things to throw off any suspicion we might ever have about him."

"So the night Battle was killed?"

"Remmy left the hospital at ten or so. She signaled to Harry, who was waiting in the parking lot probably dressed in hospital scrubs. He's the hospital's general counsel. He knows its shift change time. He goes in, moves the camera, shoots the stuff in the bag, drops the false clues and leaves."

"But Remmy's being there incriminates her. Why would they have done it that way? Why have Remmy anywhere near there?"

"That's why they planted the evidence that it was the serial killer's doing. I checked: Remmy was already rich, even without Bobby's leaving her property in the will. So there was no motive there. And because Remmy was there, people will actually believe she might have been set up. They might initially suspect her, but over time they'd start to think like you did: if she really did do it, there'd be no way she'd be near that room on the night Battle died."

"And what were she and Harry going to do? Wait a bit and get married?"

"No, I suspect that after a discreet interval Remmy would move away. Then a little while later Harry would do the same. Next stop, maybe a private island in Greece."

Michelle drew a long breath and slowly let it out. "So now what do we do?"

"We're having dinner with Remmy and Harry."

"What! Are you kidding?"

"No, we're having dinner at Harry's home." He sat forward. "Michelle, they made a mistake, a small one, but it was enough. Using a little surveillance device I bought in D.C., I have all the proof I need."

"Does Todd or Bailey know about this?"

"No, just us. I'll never approve of what Harry and Remmy did, but I thought they deserved to have this handled as discreetly and with as much dignity as possible."

"When?" she asked.

"Tomorrow night at seven. Harry's out of town until tomorrow afternoon. It'll just be the four of us there. Once they realize we know the truth and have the evidence, I have no doubt they'll confess and come with us very quietly. Then we'll turn them over to Todd."

"I have a bad feeling about this, Sean. A really bad feeling."

"Do you think I like it? Harry was a Virginia Supreme Court justice; he's been a good friend of mine for years."

"I know, but—"

"However much you like Harry, you have to put that aside. Bobby Battle was an awful person in many ways. I also learned that he probably was suffering from a chronic disease he may have transmitted to Remmy."

"Oh, my God!"

"But regardless," King continued, "he didn't deserve to be murdered." He looked at her and said quietly, "There, I've told you all I know." A pause, then, "Are you with me on this, Michelle?"

"I'm with you," she answered quietly.

CHAPTER

86

KING HAD ASKED HARRY to give Calpurnia the night off so he could make dinner for the four of them.

"You've got quite a kitchen, Harry," said King as he and Michelle put the meal on the table. "I appreciate your letting me come early to get things done."

Harry looked at the elaborately prepared meal. "Really, Sean, I have to think I made out far better than you on the arrangement."

Harry was dressed in one of his finest suits, though it seemed a little snug over his frame. "My weight hasn't changed in forty years, but its location has," he'd explained in a mock depressed tone.

"Yes, indeed," said Remmy, who was also dressed very handsomely. She and Harry sat side by side across from Sean and Michelle in the large dining room.

"I just trust that your drive home will be far less eventful than it was the last time you dined with me."

"Actually, I think this evening may hold its own unique points of interest," said King vaguely as he started serving the food. Michelle meanwhile looked on with a distracted expression.

"Michelle, my dear, what's wrong?" said Harry.

She glanced up at him quickly. "Nothing, just not feeling all that great. Probably just a spring bug."

The meal went uneventfully. They ate dessert and then moved on to the library for coffee. The night had turned chilly and the fire was warming. King went over to an enormous wood-and-stamped-tin room divider that sat diagonally against one corner.

"This is a beautiful piece," he said.

"Eighteenth century," answered Harry. "It was handmade from materials right here on the property."

King stood in front of the fire. He glanced nervously at Michelle and then said, "I'm afraid I've been a little deceitful tonight."

Harry and Remmy stopped chatting and looked up in surprise.

Remmy said, "What?"

"The purpose of this dinner wasn't really social."

Harry set down his coffee and glanced at Remmy and then at Michelle, who kept her head down and her hand buried in the pocket of her jacket. "I don't understand, Sean. Do you mean you want to talk about the case some more?"

"No, I don't really need to talk about the case any more. I think I know all I need to know."

The two continued to glance curiously at him.

Michelle finally blurted out, "Sean, just tell them."

Harry said, "Tell us what?"

The hand in which Remmy was holding her cup and saucer started to shake.

They all turned as the man in the black hood came into the room, his gun out and its red laser aimed dead on Harry's heart.

King immediately stepped between black hood and Harry.

"This stops now," King said quietly. "No more killing."

"Get out of my way or you'll die first!"

Remmy rose. The pistol swiveled in her direction. "Sit down!" said the man sharply.

King took a step forward but stopped when the pistol came in his direction once more. "Michelle," said black hood, "take your gun out and put it on the table. Now! No heroics," he added.

She did so, gripping it by the muzzle.

"You can't kill us all, can you?" said King.

"I'm thinking about it, I really am," shot back the man as he eyed Remmy.

"Well, then I guess it's time to clear up your misperception," said King calmly. "Remmy and Harry had nothing to do with Bobby's death. It was a setup. A setup to bring you in." He paused and added, "I found the bug."

The gunman took a step back, his pistol dropped a notch. "What?"

"The conversation you heard between Michelle and me was staged. Okay!"

He snapped his fingers, and the room instantly filled with heavily armed police and FBI agents. They came out from behind the enormous room divider, the large cabinet in the corner and behind the thick drapes. With a dozen guns to his one, black hood backed up against the wall.

"Drop it," said Todd Williams, his gun leveled right at the circle in crosshairs etched on the black hood.

Michelle had picked up her gun and was aiming at the exact same spot. Black hood seemed to be thinking of whether to go for it. His body seemed to tense.

"Drop it!" roared Williams, who obviously sensed what the man was doing.

"It would really be better if you did," said King in a level voice. "At least that way you may be able to clear up a few remaining pieces. I think you owe us that."

"Oh, you do, do you?" Despite the sarcasm, the man let the pistol fall to the floor. He was immediately tackled by the police and handcuffed.

"The house has been surrounded all day," said King as they pulled the man back up. "We knew exactly where you were at all times. When I went over to admire that piece of furniture, I was actually given the signal you were in the house and I could start my little act." He paused. "We had Harry and Remmy in safe places so you wouldn't get a chance to jump the gun on us. We did it on *our* terms. It was actually refreshing." King walked over to the prisoner. "Do you mind?" He glanced at the prisoner's manacled hands. "Since you're in no position to remove it yourself."

"Doesn't matter now, does it?"

King glanced over at Remmy. "I realize you already know from his voice, Remmy, but, Harry, you better hold her anyway."

Harry placed a protective arm around Remmy's shaking shoulders. She put a hand to her mouth, stifling back a sob.

King lifted off the hood. The man flinched slightly as the fabric slid across his strong features.

"It's all over, Eddie," proclaimed King.

Surrounded by armed men, manacled and caught in the act, Eddie Battle actually had the temerity to smile. "You really think so, Sean?"

"Yes, I do."

"Hell, I'll take that bet, old buddy."

CHAPTER

87

"I STILL DON'T UNDER-stand how you figured it out, Sean," said Williams.

The police chief, Sylvia and Chip Bailey were gathered at King and Maxwell's office.

King bent a paper clip into a triangle before answering. "Seven hours," he said. "Seven hours, that's what got me thinking in Eddie's direction."

"You mentioned that before," said Williams.

"But it wasn't a literal clue. It made me start thinking about the drug that Eddie was given, or rather self-administered."

"Morphine sulfate," said Michelle.

"Right. I spoke with a narcotics expert. He told me that an average dose of the drug will knock you out for *eight* to *nine* hours unless the person it's given to is prone to using heavy-duty narcotics. Then its effects would be diminished. Well, Dorothea was just such a heavy-narcotics user. I believe Eddie slipped her the drug around two o'clock that night after they'd had sex. Yet because she'd built up resistance through her own drug use, the morphine's effects were reduced. In fact, she'd almost *fully* recovered less than six hours later—before eight o'clock, in fact, the time Savannah came and told her about Sally's being killed."

"But she mentioned she was in a fog," said Bailey.

"And she was, but coming out of it. We just thought she was lying, trying to cover up. However, Eddie couldn't give himself the morphine sulfate until after he'd killed Sally, not before, say, six o'clock or so. He started to come out of the effects of it around three in the afternoon, about *nine* hours after he took it, or the normal length of time the drug would render someone unconscious. That could only be possible if he took it *after* Sally was killed. The seven-hour reference that kept bugging me came from Sally's being killed less than seven hours after she told me about Junior. That made me start thinking about how long Eddie was knocked out, and it just didn't add up. Particularly if you believed Dorothea was drugged too, since they recovered at very different times. Even with her built-up tolerance it was far too much of a discrepancy."

Williams slapped his leg. "Damn, I never even thought of that." He pointed a big finger at Bailey. "Neither did you."

King continued. "Conceivably, if the killer wasn't Eddie, he might have drugged Eddie, but he would have done it well in advance of killing Sally so Eddie would've been safely unconscious. He wouldn't have waited until *after* he'd killed Sally. What would have been the point? And typically, a murderer wants to get away, not take time injecting a knockout drug into some-one for no reason."

"That makes sense," admitted Bailey.

"And the seven hours also made me start thinking about something else. If Sally was killed because of what she told me barely seven hours earlier, then my houseboat had to be bugged. How else could Eddie have known about it so quickly? He might have followed Sally to my place and been listening from his car. Anyway, I had to do something about that, so I got this."

He held up the small device. "It's a transmitter detector and frequency grabber with a range of one to three mega-hertz. It also has a sixteen-section bar graph to indicate RF strength so it'll home right in on the location of the bug."

"You found the bug but didn't remove it?" said Bailey.

"No. So long as Eddie thought the intelligence he gath-ered on it was valid, then I could use that to set him up."

"It was brave of Harry and Remmy to play along," said Michelle.

"Neither one of them knew it was Eddie until he spoke. I regret shocking Remmy like that, but I thought burden-ing her with the knowledge of her son's guilt beforehand would have been even worse."

"I was nervous about it," said Williams. "I mean, we had the place surrounded, but still he could have shot somebody."

"I was sure he wouldn't, not when he realized Harry had nothing to do with Bobby's death. Eddie played fair, I'll give him that. He killed, but he did so for specific rea-sons. But, just in case, I had Harry wear the bulletproof vest. It made his suit a little tight, but it was well worth the inconvenience. And of course, having a dozen armed lawmen in the same room didn't hurt." He opened his desk and took out another object.

"What's that?" asked Sylvia, looking at it curiously.

"It's a cipher disk, a way of decoding encrypted messages. This version was used by the Confederate army during the Civil War. Eddie has one in his artist's studio." He moved the disk around. "If you're just one tick off, like one minute on a watch face, the entire meaning of what you're saying changes. One tick, that's all it takes. I'm sure that's where Eddie got the idea for altering the watch times, depending on the victim. It would appeal to both his creative side and his love of Civil War history."

"But what I don't get is, he had alibis," protested Bailey. "We checked. For instance, when Canney, Pembroke and Hinson were killed, he was attending Civil War reenactments."

"Yes. But at night the reenactors sleep in their vehicles or else in their own tents. Eddie could easily slip out and no one would miss him. I clocked it on the map. At each murder he was only at most a two-hour drive away. He easily could be back in time to fight the next day."

Bailey said, "Wait a minute. We found people who'd been at those reenactments. They remembered Eddie's truck being there virtually the whole time. That's documented."

King answered, "I'm sure his truck *was* there. But his truck also has a tow hitch. I checked. At the two reenactments you're talking about, he didn't bring his horse trailer. But he could have towed another *car* close to the reenactment area and hidden it in the woods. Then he uses that vehicle to get to and from the murders, and everyone would believe he'd never left because his truck was still there. In fact, I think we'll find out that he had another car hidden somewhere that he used."

"God," said Sylvia, letting out a long breath. "We've all been so blind."

"Okay, Sean, you've told us how you figured it out, now tell us why. Why did Eddie kill all those people?" asked Williams.

"And in stupid-people language, if you can manage it," said Sylvia with a smile, repeating the phrase King had used at the morgue when she'd been about to explain the cause of Rhonda Tyler's death.

King didn't smile back. "Eddie Battle is a very complex man. And this plan has been forming in his mind for a very long time. I think it all started with the death of his twin brother."

"Bobby Jr., the one who was born severely retarded," said Bailey.

"No, Bobby Jr. wasn't born that way; he was born infected with *syphilis*. The brain damage came later."

"Syphilis?" exclaimed Bailey.

King picked up two pictures from his desk. "When Michelle and I were in Remmy's bedroom, Savannah showed us this picture of the twins when they were infants. She couldn't tell them apart." He picked up the other photo. "This is a picture of Bobby Jr. shortly before he died, which Mason showed us. The change in his features, the manifestations of the hydrocephalus and the problems with his teeth and eyes are very apparent. It was passed through to him by his mother when he was in the womb."

"Hutchinson's teeth, mulberry molars, optic nerve atrophy," said Sylvia as she stared at the young man's photo. "Yet how did Remmy contract syphilis?"

"From her husband. He was contagious either when he impregnated Remmy with the twins or had intercourse with her during the first or second trimester of that pregnancy."

"And syphilis can cross the placenta," said Sylvia in a hushed tone.

"Exactly. Bobby Jr. eventually became brain-damaged and suffered the other effects because it wasn't treated. He later died from cancer, but I'm sure the syphilis had severely weakened his body."

"But why wasn't it treated?" asked Sylvia.

"I've had a very awkward conversation with Remmy about that. She said that when her son started exhibiting strange symptoms, Bobby refused to take the boy to the doctor. He wouldn't even acknowledge he was ill. He probably wouldn't even admit to himself he had syphilis, because apparently he never went for treatment either. Anyway, by the time Remmy sought medical help, it was too late. The disease had done irreversible damage. Remember, this was over thirty years ago, and the level of medical knowledge wasn't nearly as far along as it is today. She's lived with that guilt for years."

"It's hard to believe a woman like Remmy wouldn't have taken her son to a doctor immediately," said Michelle.

"That's exactly what I was thinking," said Sylvia.

"I think there's a lot we don't know about Remmy and her relationship with her husband," said King. "A woman who talks with adoration and pride about her husband but doesn't wear her wedding ring and doesn't care if she gets it back? Those are some deep waters we'll never plumb entirely."

"But they had Savannah years later and she's okay," pointed out Bailey.

"Bobby was no longer contagious by then, and Remmy had received treatment for syphilis years before." King put the photos away and continued. "Now, historically, one major way the disease is spread is through sexual intercourse with prostitutes. As we know, Bobby had the reputation of consorting with such women. He contracted the disease from a prostitute and passed it to Remmy, who unwittingly passed it to Bobby Jr. He and Eddie weren't identical twins, but fraternal, so they didn't share the same amniotic fluid. That's probably why Eddie wasn't infected."

"And Eddie found out about this?" asked Bailey.

"Yes, although how I'm not sure. But I think he's been harboring this knowledge for a long time. A powder keg waiting to blow. I think Eddie too felt enormous guilt. He knew it was only by luck that he escaped that same fate. From all accounts he loved his brother very much."

"So Rhonda Tyler was—," began Williams.

"Eddie's way of symbolically punishing the prostitute who'd infected his father all those years ago and thus doomed his brother. Tyler had the great misfortune to come across Eddie at some point."

"The unusual wrinkling on Bobby's aorta and the brain

lesions," said Sylvia. "All that points to syphilis," she said in a very chagrined tone, putting a hand over her eyes.

"You weren't really looking for it, Sylvia," said King kindly. "And those things could be caused by other diseases as well."

Michelle picked up the explanation. "Steve Canney had to die because his mother had an affair with Bobby that produced Steve. His mother was dead, so Steve had to be sacrificed in her place."

"Eddie is devoted to Remmy," said King. "I'm sure he saw the bastard child as a direct slap against her. Janice Pembroke was simply in the wrong place, wrong time."

"One tick off," said Bailey.

"Right. Same with Diane Hinson. One tick off, to cover his tracks and to further break the connection between the victims."

"And Junior Deaver?"

"Eddie thought he'd stolen from his mother. That was enough. When he found out he'd been wrong, he took it out on Sally. You can see his sense of fair play and justice, however twisted. The mud prints in their foyer should have told me it was him. Savannah said she never moved away from the doorway, but there were muddy prints all over. They were from Eddie's boots, not Savannah's. He was cutting it tight. He had no idea when Dorothea would come out of the drug's effects, and he had to take the morphine too. He probably didn't even notice the mud. As we could tell from the beating he gave Sally, he was slightly crazed."

"Slightly!" exclaimed Williams.

"And then he set up Harold Robinson to take the fall. Why he picked him I don't know."

"Wait a minute. The man the little boy saw was Eddie?" asked Michelle.

"Yes."

"Why didn't Eddie just kill him too?"

"He might have thought if the boy believed it was his dad, it would help to seal Robinson's fate further. That actually happened. Or maybe despite all he's done, he couldn't bring himself to kill a child. As I said, Eddie is a very complex man."

"You mean a monster," said Williams.

"Does Dorothea know?" asked Sylvia.

Bailey nodded. "I told her. Remmy and Savannah joined me in giving her the news. That's one stricken family, let me tell you."

"But why did Eddie impersonate famous serial killers?" asked Williams.

King inclined his head at Bailey. "I think that was directed at you, Chip."

"Me?"

"It would make sense if he wanted to flaunt his superiority. Beat you at your own area of expertise."

"But why? We were friends. I saved his life."

"No, you blew his kidnapping scheme out of the water."

Bailey came right out of his chair. "What?"

"I'm convinced he arranged his own kidnapping. He hired the man you killed. He wanted to punish his father for the death of his brother two years before, and the only way the twenty-year-old college student could think to do that was by smashing him in the wallet to the tune of five million dollars. I'm sure he was the one who was burning the money after you killed his partner. He didn't want his father to get it back. But he ran out of time. He had to tie himself back up and play dumb when you got there. I told you he'd been harboring this hatred for his father a long time."

"Unbelievable," said Bailey as he slowly sat back down. "That's unbelievable," he said again. "And all these years he's pretended everything was great and he was really hating my guts?"

"Eddie is a consummate actor and liar. And let's put it this way: consider yourself very fortunate you weren't found with a watch around your wrist."

"Jesus!" the FBI agent said.

"But, Sean," said Williams, "it's been twenty years between the kidnapping and all these murders. What set Eddie off?"

"I believe it was his father's stroke. Perhaps he felt Bobby would die before he could show him his version of justice. I don't know that for sure, but the timing I think is beyond coincidence."

"So what now?" asked Michelle.

Williams answered, "Eddie's being arraigned tomorrow at the courthouse."

"No doubt his trial will get a change of venue," said King. "If it goes that far."

"What, you mean insanity?" asked Williams. "No way. The bastard knew exactly what he was doing."

"In a way he was exorcising demons that have been with him most of his life," said King. "I'm not excusing anything he did, and if he gets the death penalty, so be it.

But if he hadn't had Bobby Battle as his father, I don't think any of this would have happened."

They all looked at each other in silence.

"And there but for the grace of God go I," said Sylvia in a very low voice.

CHAPTER

88

WHEN EDDIE BATTLE WAS driven over to the courthouse the next morning in a special convoy provided by state police and uniformed FBI agents, the crowd of townspeople and media was so enormous the convoy couldn't get through. Indeed, fueled by the national attention the story had received, seemingly everyone from a five-state area had come to watch. And there was an angry look to the throng.

"Shit," bellowed Chief Williams as he stared out at the crowds from the lead van. "I was afraid of this. We've been getting death threats against Battle ever since the story broke about his capture." He eyed the mobs in their way. "No telling if somebody out there has a gun either." He scrutinized a group of tough-looking men standing beside pickup trucks with building materials in the beds.

"That's probably a bunch of Junior's good old boys, and they don't look like they're here to pat Eddie on the head."

"Isn't there an underground entrance to the courthouse?" said Bailey, who was in the rear seat behind Williams.

"Don't you think if there were I would have already gone there? Maybe we should take him back to the jail and let it settle down."

"Settle down! It's not going to settle down for months. We might as well get it over with now, while we have the manpower with us."

Williams studied the crowd some more, then barked into his walkie-talkie. "Okay, let's move it right down the middle of the street. Take it slow; I don't want any civil lawsuits because we ran over somebody. We'll pull onto the lawn directly by the front steps. You clear and secure that area. I want a ring of body armor there, you under- stand? Then we'll open the doors and hustle him through fast for his arraignment. But before he comes back out, we're going to disperse this damn crowd and get these media trucks out of here, that's for damn sure."

"You're gonna have a big First Amendment problem with that, Todd," said Bailey.

"To hell with the First Amendment! I've got a prisoner to keep alive. Even if it's just so they can execute him."

The area was secured, the van pulled in front and Eddie Battle was whisked into the courthouse as screams and epithets rained down on the men encircling him, along with bottles, cans, rocks and other thrown items but fortunately no bullets.

Battle's court-appointed lawyers met him outside the courtroom. They spoke briefly and went inside, where Eddie pleaded not guilty. His counsel didn't ask for bail to be set, not that such a request would have been seriously considered. His lawyers might have been terrified that a free Eddie would come and visit them in the middle of the night.

"We'll be in touch," said his lead attorney, a tall, portly woman with a bad haircut.

"I'm sure," said Eddie, his strong body nearly bursting out of the too small orange prison jumpsuit. "You think you can get me off with good behavior?"

Eddie and his bodyguards headed back out but were stopped by Williams and Bailey long before they got to the exit doors.

"We're looking at a near riot out there," said Williams. "Before we can get him out, we have to deal with it. I've ordered pepper spray and tear gas if they won't disperse on their own."

Eddie smiled. "Looks like I really lighted up old Wrightsburg's fire, Todd."

"Shut up!" screamed Williams, but that did nothing to wipe the smile off Eddie's face. It just grew bigger.

"Now, you have to protect me, *Todd*. You can't let them kill me or the media will be pissed. You can't deprive them of the show. Think of the ratings. Think of the ad dollars."

"I said shut up!" Williams moved toward him but Bailey got between them.

"That's stupid, Todd, don't even think it."

"Hey, thanks, Chippy. You've always been such a good friend," said Eddie.

Bailey whipped around, and his hand went toward his gun.

Now Williams stepped in. "Okay, Chip, we're not

going to let him do this to us." He bellowed to two of his deputies. "Take him to the holding cage on the second floor. We'll come get him when the crowd's under control."

"Good luck," called out Eddie as the deputies led him away. "Don't let me down now."

CHAPTER

89

ONE OF THE DEPUTIES WAS by the outside door; the other hovered by the window.

"It *looks* like a damn riot there," said the one by the window. He was Eddie's height, well built, with curly hair. "There goes the tear gas."

"Tear gas!" said the other, a short cop with a bulldog chest, wide waist and broad hips that caused all the gear on his belt to stick out sideways. "Wish I were out there shooting some of that stuff at those sumbitches."

"Well, go on, I got things here."

"No can do. The chief said to stay put." He glanced in the direction of the holding cell where Eddie Battle sat silently watching them. "This mutha's killed a bunch of people. Dude's crazy."

"They don't riot for jaywalkers, boys," said Eddie.

They both looked at him. The big cop laughed. "That's a good one. They don't riot for jaywalkers."

The short cop looked at his partner.

"Go on," said the big cop. "This dude's going nowhere."

"Well, look here, if you see the chief coming, radio me. I'll be back in a flash."

"Roger that."

The short cop left, and it was just Eddie and the big cop.

Eddie rose and moved to the door. "You got a cigarette?"

"Right, like I'm falling for that one. My mother didn't raise no idiots. You just stay over there and I'll stay over here."

"Come on, they searched every crevice I have and some I didn't even know I had. I've got nothing to hurt you with. I really need a smoke."

"Uh-huh." The big cop kept looking out the window. He glanced back every now and then to check on Eddie but eventually kept his gaze on the goings-on outside.

Eddie Battle had massive forearms with thick, pronounced veins. One of these veins was bigger and thicker than the others, a fact probably noted by the police who searched him, but not raising any suspicion. It was a vein after all, full of blood. However, to someone as skilled as Eddie Battle, a vein was not always a vein. This vein, in fact, was made of plastic, resin and rubber and was completely hollow. In the course of his reenactment career Eddie had become very adept at makeup, disguises, costuming and creating fake wounds and scars. He sat back down in the shadows for a bit, working on the artificial vein with his fingers. It finally "ruptured," and he slid out the very slender items that had been hidden there. The risk that he might be caught had been very real, and he'd taken some very real measures to deal with that eventuality. No search of his person, however thorough, would have turned up the pick and tension tool hidden in the hollow vein.

He kept his eyes on the big cop still looking out the window. He moved forward quietly, draped his manacled hands through the bars of the cell such that they covered the lock. He inserted the instruments in the lock and slowly worked it. He'd practiced this very maneuver for hours at a time on an old cell-door lock he had salvaged from a prison that had been torn down. Finally, through the tension tool and lockpick he could feel the tumblers start to fall into place. There was a loud noise from outside, and he used that moment to cover the sound of the lock clicking open. He held on to the bars and slipped his instruments between his wrist and manacles.

"Hey, dumb-ass! Hey, I'm talking to you, you big stupid piece of flesh."

The big cop turned and eyed him. "Why don't you just stuff it! I ain't the one going to no electric chair."

"Lethal injection, you moron."

"Right, that's my point, so who's the dumb-ass?"

"From where I'm looking you are." *Come on, big guy, just step this way.*

"Keep right on talking."

"What, sticks and stones'll break your bones, but words will never hurt you? How the hell did somebody like you get to be a cop? But not a real cop, just a country bumpkin." *Come on, you know you want a piece of me. Here, coppie, coppie.*

"Us country bumpkins caught you, now, didn't we?"

"An ex–Secret Service agent did, dumb-shit. Your police chief I could've eaten for breakfast any day of the week." Eddie glanced at the man's hand and saw the wedding band. "After I screwed your little woman, that is. Damn, she was a tasty thing."

"Uh-huh." A bead of sweat broke over the back of the cop's thick neck. His pistol hand clenched and unclenched.

Almost there.

"Are your kids as ugly as you are, or did you and your fat-ass wife adopt so you wouldn't have any little freaks running around?"

The cop whirled around and strode toward the cell, his big low-quarter shoes thumping on the painted concrete floor with each step. "All right, you piece of shit, you're damn lucky you're in there—"

Eddie kicked the door open, and the heavy metal caught the cop flush in the face. He went down hard. Eddie charged out, the chain binding his hands went around the cop's neck and Eddie flexed his powerful arms. In thirty seconds there was no more big cop. Eddie searched the body, got the keys to the manacles and was free. He raced over, locked the door to the hallway, pulled the dead officer into the cell, switched clothes and set him on the bunk propped against the wall.

Eddie put on the cop's sunglasses and broad-brimmed hat, unlocked the door and glanced down the hallway. There were officers stationed along this corridor.

Not a problem, there was always the window. He shut the door, raced over and looked out. Fortunately for him, the police had now herded the crowd to the other side of the building. He glanced down. It wouldn't be easy, but the alternative was far more unpalatable. And he had a job to finish. He opened the window, climbed out, felt for the ledge below with his feet and hit it squarely. He squatted, gripped the slender edge of brick with his strong fingers, eased his body off but held on, swinging. He glanced to the right and left. He swung out, did it again, a little farther this time, and then once more, until his body was almost parallel with the ledge. On the fourth swing he let go, the man on the flying trapeze. He hit the outcropping of roof on the first floor of the building, caught his balance and then lowered himself to the ground.

Instead of running away, he marched to the other side of the building and right into the middle of the crowd, fighting his way through at the same time he pretended to be helping quell the riot. He reached a number of empty squad cars, looking in one after another until he spotted keys in the ignition of a bulky Ford Mercury. He climbed in, backed it out and drove off. The riot was still going on, the network personnel gleefully filming all of it for the national audience. However, they'd just missed the biggest scoop of all: the successful escape of Eddie Lee Battle.

He found a pack of gum in the ashtray, popped a piece of Juicy Fruit in his mouth and turned the police radio on high so he could learn instantly when they discovered he was no longer in custody. He breathed the fresh air and flicked a wave to a kid walking his bike along the side of the road. He slowed the squad car and rolled down the window.

"Hey, you gonna grow up to be a good law-abiding person, son?"

"Yes, sir, mister," called out the little boy. "I wanna be just like you."

He tossed the kid a stick of gum. "No, you don't, son." *You don't want to be like me. I'm terminal; only got a few days to live.*

But he looked on the bright side as he sped up. He was free and he was back in business. And he only had one more to go. One more!

It felt so damn good.

CHAPTER

90

"So who killed Bobby Battle and Kyle Montgomery?" asked Michelle.

They were sitting on King's dock catching some sun after returning from a morning ride on their Sea-Doos.

"Nothing's clicked yet. Maybe I used up all my little gray cells catching Eddie."

"Well, Dorothea had the best motive to kill Kyle."

"And she had the opportunity to kill Bobby as well. And maybe the motivation. If he didn't live up to his part of the bargain and give her a bigger piece of the estate."

Michelle looked troubled. "I know you concocted all that stuff about Remmy and Harry, but you don't really think—"

"Harry has an alibi, an ironclad one. At the time of Battle's death he was giving a speech to the Virginia State Bar in Charlottesville."

Michelle looked relieved. "And Remmy?"

Now King looked troubled. "I don't know, Michelle, I just don't know. She certainly had good reason to want to kill him."

"Or maybe someone who wanted to be the next lord of the manor did it."

He looked at her strangely and was about to respond when his cell phone rang.

He answered, listened, and his face turned ashen. He clicked off.

"This is really, really bad, isn't it?" she said fearfully.

"Eddie's escaped."

All the Battles were given round-the-clock security at their home. Harry Carrick, King and Michelle joined them there, since their lives were conceivably in danger too. A massive three-state manhunt jointly conducted by the FBI and area police was begun, but two days later there was no sign of Eddie.

King and Michelle were in the dining room having coffee with Sylvia, Bailey and Williams and talking about the case.

"Eddie's a very experienced outdoorsman. And he knows this country better than most," pointed out Bailey. "He's hunted over it and explored it for most of his life. He can live on next to nothing for weeks."

"Thanks, Chip, that's very encouraging," Williams said sourly. "We'll find the son of a bitch, but I can't promise to bring him in alive."

"I don't think Eddie will let that happen again," King said.

"Wouldn't he have fled the area as fast as possible?" asked Michelle.

King shook his head. "Too many roadblocks and police at all the bus and train stations and the airport. The police car he stole was found abandoned on a back road. I think he took to the hills."

Williams nodded at this. "His best chance is to lay low around here, change his appearance as much as he can, and when things quiet down a bit, he makes his run."

King didn't look convinced.

Williams noted this and said, "You disagree?"

"I think he's hanging around but not for the purpose you think."

"What, then?"

"Someone killed his father."

"So?"

"So I think Eddie wanted that all to himself. I think Bobby was supposed to be the final victim in all this, if the stroke didn't kill him first." King glanced at Michelle. "He came to see us, claiming his mother was upset about people thinking she had Junior and her husband killed. He knew she hadn't done it. He wanted us to find out who had. And you remember when we were having drinks with him at the Sage Gentleman. He said his father just had to live."

"So he could kill him," said Michelle.

"So what the hell is he going to do, go after the person who killed Bobby?" said Williams. "We don't even know who that is, Sean."

"But if we run that person down, we have a good shot at nailing Eddie."

"I'd appreciate it if you would not plot the capture and execution of my only remaining son in my house."

They all turned to see Remmy standing there. She'd

rarely come into the mansion's public spaces. When she did, she spoke to no one, not even Harry. Her meals were delivered to her bedroom.

King rose from his chair. "I'm sorry, Remmy, we didn't see you standing there."

"Why should I be? This is only my house and my dining room, and those cups you're drinking out of are mine too, in case you'd forgotten."

King glanced at Williams. "I know this arrangement is awkward—"

"To put it mildly," she interrupted.

Williams said, "It's just a lot easier having all of you in the same place, Remmy."

"Oh, I'm glad it's easier for some people; it's certainly not for me."

"We can go to a hotel," suggested Michelle, but Remmy dismissed this remark with a decisive wave of her hand.

"Never let it be said I shirked my civic duty, even if it does mean losing my son." She stalked out of the room.

They all looked at each other nervously.

"This really is an impossible situation for her," said Sylvia.

"Do you think any of us like it?" rebutted Michelle. "Eddie is a mass murderer. She has to learn to accept that."

King took on a thoughtful look as he stirred more sugar into his coffee. "Speaking of which, I hope all of you realize that the case against Eddie isn't ironclad."

"What the hell are you talking about?" protested Williams. "He showed up at Harry's house with a zodiac mask on, ready to kill all of you. And now he's escaped and killed a deputy in the process."

"Right. But not knowing what happened between him and the deputy, there might be a claim for self-defense or manslaughter. The cell door was open, and a defense counsel could make the claim that the deputy was trying to hurry along the process of justice and Eddie just fought back. Now, I'm as certain he's guilty of all those murders as though I'd seen him commit them. But you don't have to convince me, you have to convince a neutral jury, maybe one from another part of the state or even a different state. So where's your direct evidence that he committed the murders?"

Williams was still bristling. "All the stuff you said. His motivation, the cipher disk, drugging Dorothea."

"That's theorizing and speculation, Todd," said King firmly. "We need physical evidence tying him to the crimes; do we have it?"

Sylvia spoke up. "If you'd asked me before the murder of Jean Robinson, I'd probably say no. However, I found a hair follicle with root attached to it on the floor next to her bed. I don't know how it got there, but the color and texture told me it wasn't hers or her husband's. I've sent it for typing along with a sample of Eddie's DNA. If it matches, we have him, at least for that murder."

"And hopefully ballistics will match the slugs shot into our car tires when Junior was killed to the gun taken from Eddie," pointed out Michelle.

"Just let me get hold of him," said Williams. "We'll have a confession in no time."

"*If* we get hold of him," said Michelle.

"He can hide for a while, but we'll eventually catch him," said the police chief confidently.

"The person he's after," said King. "That's the key. We find him, we find Eddie."

"You really think that?" said Bailey.

"No," replied King, "I know it. He's got one more to go. Just one more. And we have to get there before he does."

CHAPTER

91

EDDIE SAT BACK ON THE small cot in his cave. He'd rested, eaten and planned. He had a battery-powered TV/radio/police scanner and had kept abreast of the search developments, which was fairly easy since there were none. However, he was limited in his movements. He could only go out at night, and it was a long hike to the battered old truck he'd hidden away in a patch of woods just for this contingency.

After all these years of bouncing from thing to thing, never really etching an identity anywhere, he'd finally found his niche: fugitive killer. He laughed, rose, stretched, dropped to the ground and did a hundred push-ups and an equal number of sit-ups. He had wedged a steel bar between two jagged outcroppings of rock farther back in the cave. He did twenty-five quick pull-ups and then five with each arm. He dropped to the ground, breathing hard. He wasn't twenty anymore, but for his age he wasn't doing too badly. Big cop would no doubt have attested to that.

He slid the pistol out of its holster and chambered

body-armor-piercing ammo he'd purchased on the black market with as much ease as clicking a mouse key. Hell, you could buy anything on the Net—guns, ammo, women, children, marriage, divorce, happiness, death—if you just knew where to look. But it was only one gun against a thousand, far worse odds than even at the Alamo.

And yet a man with nothing to live for is a powerful man indeed. Perhaps unbeatable. Had he read that somewhere or just made it up? Whatever, it would become his coda from this point forward.

They'd eventually hunt him down and kill him. Of that he was certain. But it didn't matter so long as he got to his father's killer first. That's all that really mattered now. Wow, he'd certainly streamlined his life. He laughed again.

He took the list from his pocket. The names were dwindling, but he wasn't sure he could manage now to get to them all. However, after much thought he might just have come upon a shortcut. He'd try it out tonight. Two more deaths: his father's killer and his own. And then Wrightsburg could get back to normal. His family could move forward with fresh lives, finally free of their monster patriarch.

He lay back down on the cot, listened with one ear to the radio and with the other to any noise coming from outside. The cave's isolated location and well-hidden entrance made it highly unlikely anyone would come near. However, if they had the misfortune to, he'd give them a proper burial. He was not a monster; in his case the apple had fallen far from the tree.

I am not my father's son. And thank you, Jesus, for that. But I'll be seeing you soon, Pop. Maybe the devil will bunk us together. For all time. We'll talk.

He cracked his thick knuckles and dreamed of such an encounter as the afternoon receded into night. The night when he'd be on the move. To his shortcut. To his last target. And then the big curtain would come down on the Eddie Lee Battle Show. There'd be no encore. He was getting tired. *Good-bye, everybody, it was cool while it lasted.*

Just one more to go . . . Or maybe more? Yes, maybe more. What did it matter after all?

CHAPTER

92

THE SMALL BUILDING housing the *Wrightsburg Gazette* was dark and empty at this hour of the night. There was no alarm system and no night watchman either, for what was there to steal from the venerable but money-losing *Gazette* other than paper? Cash was tight at the daily publication, and the owner didn't like to waste it on protecting things he believed didn't need it.

The back door's simple lock turned and then opened, and Eddie moved inside, shutting the door behind him. He shot across to the small room at the back of the printing area. He pushed open the door to this windowless section, shone his light around at the flat file cabinets stacked one on top of the other and started reading the labels on the fronts.

He found the one he wanted, opened it, lifted out the spool of old-fashioned microfiche and went to one of the terminals that lined the outside ring of the room. He sat down, inserted the spool into the reader, clicked on the light behind the screen and turned on the machine. He knew the date he was looking for, and he quickly found the story he wanted. Of course, it all fit now, all the things he'd heard over the last few years, the little clues here and there. Another thought struck him as he remembered something Chip Bailey had once told him. It had happened before, not in this country, but in another.

Yes, now it all makes perfect sense.

He removed the spool and replaced it in the file cabinet. He was about to leave but paused, thinking something over, finally breaking into a smile. *Why not?* He picked up a Sharpie pen from a holder on one of the tables and went over to the wall. He wrote the four letters large on the concrete wall. They couldn't very well miss it, could they? Not that they'd have any clue what it actually meant. He wanted to get there first after all. They could come and pick up the pieces after it was all over.

He admired his handiwork for a moment and then slipped back out. His truck was parked about a mile off, on a dirt road that he very much doubted the police would be covering. He kept to the wood line as he made his way back.

Chip Bailey sat up in bed, confused for a moment, then realized what the noise was. It was his cell phone ringing. He groped around, found the light in his small motel room and clicked on the phone. It was Chief Williams; his message was terse but drove from him thoughts of sleep.

Someone had just broken into the *Wrightsburg Gazette*. The description of the person fit Eddie Battle. They were locking down the entire area. Bailey was dressed in a minute, put on his belt clip and slipped his gun inside. He ran to his car and jumped in.

The knife hit him in the chest with such force that the hilt smacked into Bailey's sternum. The dying FBI agent tried to look around, to see who'd just killed him, but the blade had nearly severed his heart in two. He slumped back against the seat, his head tilted to one side.

Eddie rose up from the backseat and let go of the knife. He'd passed by the motel on his way back to his truck. Seeing Bailey's car in the parking lot, he'd thought it appropriate to pay back his old friend for "saving him" all those years ago. He might not get another chance. He'd dialed Bailey's cell phone, a number well known to him, from a pay phone. He'd imitated Williams just well enough that the groggy FBI agent would not have picked up on the difference.

Well, that inattention to detail had certainly cost him.

Sorry, Chip, you snooze you lose. And you weren't that good of an agent anyway. Pretty damn inept and pompous actually. And you wanted to be my stepfather so badly. Those big bucks are quite the attraction, aren't they, old Chip? Old buddy. Old pal.

Eddie climbed out of the car. He made it to his truck in half an hour, keeping well out of sight of the roads. It was now time to sleep and prepare. And then to act on the information he'd obtained tonight.

His shortcut to determine the identity of the person who'd killed his father had worked to perfection. He just hoped the "execution" on the other end would be as flawless.

*   *   *

"It was *his* knife," Williams told King and Michelle at the Battles' house. "His prints were on it. Eddie's not trying to hide that he did it. Hell, he's probably proud of it."

Chip Bailey's body had been found the following morning by one of his men. The death of the veteran FBI agent had staggered everyone.

"Pretty damn ballsy for Eddie to come out of hiding to take out Chip like that," said King.

"I'm not sure that's the only reason he came out," replied the police chief. "You two better come with me."

He drove them to the *Gazette* building and pointed out the word on the wall that Eddie had written there.

TEAT

King looked at the word and then glanced at Williams. "Teat? What, like a cow's teat? You're sure this was Eddie's doing and not some kid's prank?"

"No, I'm not sure. It looks like just that, in fact. But the *Gazette* isn't that far from the motel where Chip was killed."

King looked around the room. "What would he want from here?"

Michelle pointed to the numerous microfiche files. "Maybe he was looking for something in there."

"That's a lot to look at when you don't know what you're looking for," said King. He turned to Williams with a concerned expression. "You better watch your back, Todd."

"I'm not looking to get a knife in my chest. I've got

twenty-four/seven protection on me. I wish Chip had done the same."

"Maybe he thought it could never happen to him," said Michelle. "Or maybe he was too proud."

"Or maybe he really believed Eddie was his friend," commented Williams.

"Some friend," remarked King. "How's the search coming?"

"Way too many back roads and woods. And apparently, everybody within a four-state area has called in and said they saw Eddie. He's ten feet tall with claws and has body parts dangling out of his blood-encrusted mouth. I swear to holy Jesus I don't know how anybody gets convicted in this country, I really don't."

"It only takes one good lead," Michelle reminded him.

"I might die of old age before that happens," Williams shot back.

Michelle looked at her partner. "What do you think, Sean?"

He shook his head wearily. "I think after all this, Eddie's in the driver's seat and we're back at square one."

CHAPTER

93

KING AND SYLVIA HAD just finished dinner at her home. King had taken leave of the armed camp at Casa Battle. However, there was a deputy at the end of Sylvia's driveway just to make sure their private meal wouldn't be interrupted.

Sylvia played with the bracelet on her left wrist. "Where do you think he is?"

King shrugged. "Either a thousand miles away or ten feet, it's hard to say."

"He crushed Jean Robinson's skull, you know. And the windpipe of that police officer at the courthouse too. And he stabbed Chip Bailey so hard the knife blade hit the man's spinal cord! Not to mention what he did to Sally Wainwright and all those other people *and* almost killing you."

"And yet he didn't kill Tommy Robinson."

"You think that excuses what he's done?" she said sharply.

He looked at her over the rim of his wineglass. "No." He rose and picked up the bottle of wine he'd brought.

"This vintage is best drunk outside." He was tired of talking about Eddie. He was sick of it actually.

They walked down the steps to Sylvia's small dock.

"When did you put up the gazebo?" he asked.

"Last year. I like to sit and just look."

"You've got a nice spot to do it, although you ought to think about putting in a boat slip."

"I get seasick. And I'm not that good a swimmer."

"I'd be proud to teach you."

They sat and drank the wine.

"I'll get you out on my boat. It's actually a very safe lake," King said after a while.

"You're sure about that?"

"Absolutely."

The man alternated between swimming just below the surface for fifty feet and then coming up shallow, only his face out of the water, and taking a breath before heading back under. He came up one last time, treading water and looking around. It was just as he'd thought: they hadn't secured the dock. Why would they think of that? They were only the police.

Eddie swam the short distance to the dock with methodical strokes. In his black wet suit he was pretty much invisible. He reached the swim ladder, eased himself out of the water and then stopped, listening. He made a detailed sweep of the surrounding area before continuing up and onto the dock, then pulling up the watertight pouch that was tied to his foot. He took his gun out of the pouch and checked his watch. He'd have to move fast. It wasn't like he could make a quiet exit, although there were rumbles of thunder in the distance. He'd heard on his radio that a major storm was heading in: high winds, rain and lots of lightning and thunder. He couldn't have asked for a better night. The natural elements were always his friend, it seemed. That was good, because he didn't have any others.

He went to the storage shed, worked the combo on the lock, opened the door and went in. He grabbed the gear he'd need, hit the switch on the electric lift and hurried back out, the lift remote in hand.

The Formula FasTech was lowering into the water. Before he'd been caught, he'd had the foresight to make sure it was completely ready to roll. The dealer who'd sold it to his father had said it was one of the fastest boats—if not *the* fastest—on the lake. Well, depending on how things went, he might just need every knot it could produce.

He climbed into the cockpit. When the boat was fully in the water, he hit the stop button on the lift remote. All became silent again. He wouldn't turn on his running lights until he was well out onto the water, if even then. It was fortunate for him that no one else in his family was really much of a boater. There'd be no one coming down to the dock at this hour of the night. Lucky for them. He was in a killing mood, family or not. He couldn't seem to help himself now.

He waited, waited. There it was, the enormous crack of thunder as the storm began its barrage. He fired the twin Mercs almost simultaneously, and a thousand horsepower instantly lit up under him. He hit the captain's switch, which sent most of the engines' noise under the water. He eased back on the throttle, and the boat edged out of its slip. He turned the bow to the cove's opening, nudged the throttle forward and did about ten knots heading away from the house. He felt the hull trembling a bit under him, as though the Mercs were angry he wasn't pushing them harder, getting up on plane, blasting all comers away. He patted the dash. *That will come later, I promise.*

Once he hit an open channel, he went to half-speed and the FasTech immediately leaped to thirty-five knots, the Mercs still not entirely happy but getting there. He eyed the colorful GPS screen in the center of his dash and made his heading to the southeast at 150 degrees. There were no other boats on the water, and he knew the lake intimately. The channels were well marked with lighted buoys: red buoys blinking even numbers upriver and green buoys blinking odd numbers downriver. Shoals were marked in startling white light. He knew where they all were any-way. The only trouble one could get into was in the coves where low spots weren't always marked and the land jut-ted out randomly. However, his father had purchased a radar add-on for the FasTech, so he wasn't worried about running aground, even in the coves. *Thanks, Dad, I owe you, you son of a bitch.*

He kept his running lights off and upped his speed to fifty knots. He alternated between looking over the bow and glancing at the GPS. The Mercs were now fairly con-tent; at least the hull had stopped trembling. He was up on plane and running smooth, though the storm was really blowing in now. He turned on his VHF radio and listened to the weather report. All small craft were being ordered off the water. People were being told to batten down the hatches. It was going to be a damn fine corker of a storm.

Thank you, Jesus. He'd have the whole show to himself. He changed course when he hit the main channel and pointed his bow to the southwest now, 220 degrees on the compass. It was not all that far by water really. It was far longer by car, which was why he'd taken the boat. And anyway, the cops were watching all the roads. However, there was only one police boat on the water, and it only worked weekends when the lake was most crowded. There'd be no one out here to give him trouble tonight.

He stood at the wheel and let the wind whip across his face and lift his hair. As the breeze kicked up, so did the chop; edges of frothing white outlined the tops of the dark waves now. However, the FasTech ate through the two-footers and kept right on plowing. Eddie looked at the ominous sky. He'd always loved the outdoors. Riding horses, playing soldier, camping under the wide, wide sky, painting breathtaking sunrises, hunting and fishing, coming to understand how one thing worked with another, fed off each other.

It was all coming to an end, though. He understood quite clearly that this would be his last ride. Surprising how fast it had come. He was very strong and healthy, and yet his life expectancy had topped out at age forty. Yet when it was done, he would have accomplished everything he'd set out to do. How many people could claim that? He'd lived his life exactly on his terms, not his father's or his mother's or anyone else's. His alone.

It was a lie he told himself every day.

He opened the cooler and pulled out the single beer

he'd put in there before he'd been arrested. He hadn't known then that he'd need the boat, only that he might.

The beer was warm, of course, all the ice long since melted. But it tasted so good. He held up the metal against his face and rammed the throttle to full forward. The Mercs woke up from their wimpy cruising speed, and the boat screamed to seventy nautical miles per hour and then beyond. The hills that rose up from the man-made lake flew past him; the thousands of trees dotting their skin were silent sentinels to his last hurrah. *The Charge of Eddie Lee Battle and His Trusty Light Brigade.* God, was he in his element.

"Into the breach once more," he screamed to the dark, flashing skies as the rain started to pour. He licked the drops off his face. "A man's greatest virtue is the courage of one against all. When it seems darkest, then there shall be light, if only from the pulse of one beating heart," he proclaimed, quoting the purple prose of some long-dead Civil War–era writer who'd probably never shouldered a musket in his life. As if on cue the sky was suddenly lit by a billion-candlepower stab of lightning and the thunder roared as the storm began to unleash itself.

The scream of the Mercs matched Mother Nature decibel for decibel. The wake behind him was enormous, but the ride was smooth, so damn smooth, high up on plane as he was. Almost three-quarters of the thirty-five-foot boat was out of the water, blowing right through three-footers now. He was a frigging jet. Nobody could catch him.

Nobody!

CHAPTER

94

MICHELLE PACED IN HER room at Casa Battle like a caged beast looking for any possible opening to squeeze through to freedom. King had gone to Sylvia's for dinner. Why that bothered her she wasn't sure. Well, maybe she was sure. She hadn't been invited. And why exactly did that surprise her?

She finally bolted from her room, took the main stairs two at a time and went into the family room. She hadn't seen Remmy all day. Dorothea was probably asleep. She slept a lot. Who could blame her? She was ruined financially, had a drug problem, was still suspected of murdering Kyle Montgomery, and her husband had turned out to be a deranged killer and was on the loose. If it were Michelle, she'd probably sleep for the rest of her life.

She stopped when she saw Savannah coming down the hall. The young woman was no longer dressing like her mother. Perhaps the invincibility of Remmy Battle was wearing thin. She had on low-slung jeans that showed the top edge of her black thong panties, a short off-the-shoulder blouse and no shoes on her feet, the toe-nails painted a candy-apple red.

She looked up in surprise when she saw Michelle there, as though she wasn't even aware the woman had been staying with them all this time.

"How's it going, Savannah?"

Savannah's face clouded over. "Oh, just great. Father dead, sister-in-law a vegetable, mother whacked out, brother a serial killer. How's it going with you?"

"Sorry, poor choice of words."

"Forget it. It's not like you've had it easy either."

"Compared to your family, I think everyone on earth has had it easy." She paused, wondering whether to simply go back to her room and sulk. Rejecting that option, she said, "I was going to make some coffee. You interested?"

Savannah hesitated before answering, "Sure, it's not like I've got any plans."

The two women sat on a couch in the family room with their cups of coffee.

Michelle looked toward the window where the rain was starting to ping against the panes. "Sounds like a storm is really blowing in," she said. "I hope Sean gets back soon."

"He's at Sylvia's?"

"That's right. He just went for dinner."

"Are you two sleeping together?"

Michelle flinched at this blunt question. "Who, me and Sylvia?" she joked.

"You know who I mean."

"No, we're not. Not that it's any of your business."

"If I worked with Sean, I'd sleep with him."

"Good for you. But not really good for a stellar working relationship."

"You like him, don't you?"

"Yes, and I respect him. And I'm glad we're business partners."

"But that's all?"

"Why are you so interested in this?"

"Probably because I don't think I'll ever have anything like that. I mean someone in my life."

"What, are you crazy? You're young, beautiful and rich. You'll have your pick of any man you want. That's just the way the world works."

Savannah stared at her pointedly. "No, I won't."

"Of course you will. Why wouldn't you?"

Savannah started biting her nails.

Michelle reached over and snatched the hand out of Savannah's mouth. "Little kids bite their nails, Savannah. And while we're asking each other blunt questions, why don't you get your name taken off your ass? That might help your marriage prospects, if you're so worried about it."

"That wouldn't help."

Michelle eyed her warily. "Why the poor-little-me routine?"

Savannah suddenly exploded. "Because what if I'm as crazy as the rest of my family? My father was totally screwed up. My brother's a killer. Now I found out my other brother had syphilis. My mother is a freak unto herself. Even my sister-in-law is a total mess. It's a disease. You come into contact with the Battles, you're doomed. So what the hell chance do I have? I've got no chance.

None!" She dropped her cup of coffee on the floor, pulled herself into a ball and started sobbing.

Michelle stared at her for a long moment, wondering if she even wanted to get involved in this. Finally, she reached over and hugged the woman tightly, said soothing words to her without really knowing their source. As the thunder boomed outside, Savannah's sobs started to recede, but the young woman still clung to Michelle as though she were the only friend she'd ever had or ever would have.

All Michelle really wanted to do was get out of this place as fast as she could. She would even tackle the homicidal Eddie head-on, so long as it was away from Casa Battle. And yet she stayed right there and embraced the sobbing woman and whispered comforting things into her ear. Michelle held her like she was her own flesh and blood, silently thanking God she wasn't. For who knew, Savannah could well be right about everything she'd just said. Maybe the Battles were cursed.

CHAPTER

95

"THIS REALLY HAS BEEN a wonderful evening, Sean."

He and Sylvia had returned to the house and were sitting in the small glass-enclosed patio off the kitchen, observing the bad weather coming in.

"I love watching storms on the lake," she said. "It's even prettier in the daytime, when you can see it come right over the mountain's crest."

She turned to see him staring at her. "What?"

"I was just thinking there's something far lovelier than a storm, and it's sitting right next to me."

She smiled. "Is that a leftover pickup line from your college days?"

"Yes, but the big difference is I mean it now."

They moved closer to each other, his arm went around her shoulders and she rested her head against his chest.

"Like I said before, it's nice to be taken care of for a change," she said.

"You two really make a great couple, you really do."

Sylvia screamed and jerked up. King half rose from the

couch before he saw it was pointless with the gun pointed at him. He sat back.

Eddie Battle leaned against the doorway, still in his wet suit, aiming his pistol first at Sean and then at Sylvia. The laser aimer danced across their torsos like a red-hot ember on a puppeteer's string.

"In fact, you're so adorable if I had a camera I'd take a photo."

"What the hell do you want, Eddie?"

"What do I want? What do I want, Sean?"

King moved in front of Sylvia as Eddie stepped into the room.

"That's what I asked."

"You know, I like you. I really do. I'm not pissed that you're the one who ran me down. It was a nice little battle of wits. In fact, I figured it would be you. That's why I tried to take out you and Michelle at your houseboat."

"Why don't you save everybody a lot of trouble and just give yourself up? There's a deputy right outside."

"No, not right outside, Sean," he corrected. "He's at the end of the driveway in his cruiser. I checked. And with the storm howling I could shoot both of you, throw a party, and he'd never even know it."

"Okay, so where does that leave us?"

"That leaves us with both of you coming with me. We're going to take a little spin on the lake."

King edged one hand down and pressed it against the side pocket of his jacket. His new cell phone was in that pocket.

"On the lake? There's a lightning storm!" said Sylvia.

King felt the number pad through his coat. *Keep him occupied, Sylvia.*

As if she could read his thought, she said, "And you can't get away by water."

"I'm not trying to get away. I gave up on that notion a long time ago."

King found the speed dial number he wanted, pressed it, then felt for and pushed the call button. He would have to time this just right.

As soon as he heard the call go through and the voice started to say hello, he shouted, "Damn it, Eddie, this is crazy. What, you're into kidnapping now?"

"Yeah, I was getting tired of just killing. Let's go."

"We're not getting in your boat and that's it."

Eddie lined up his laser aimer on Sylvia's forehead. "Then I'll just shoot her right here. It's up to you. I don't really give a shit."

"Just take me, then," said King.

"That's not part of the plan, old pal. *Both* of you."

"Where're you taking us?"

"And spoil the surprise?" In one terrifying instant the countenance of a man who'd slaughtered nine people confronted them. "Now, Sean. Right now."

For some reason that wasn't even apparent to her, after leaving Savannah Michelle had gone over to Eddie's studio to look around. She didn't believe for a minute that the man was lurking around his home; there were armed police everywhere and Eddie was no fool. But as she went from painting to painting, she couldn't help but wonder how a man who'd killed so many could have done such beautiful work. It didn't seem possible that the same mind and body could house such an artist and such a terrifying killer. She shuddered and hugged herself. To think she'd had feelings for him. What did that say about her judgment? Her perception of other people? How could she trust her instincts ever again? This horrible thought put a burn in her belly. She bent over, suddenly dizzy and nauseous; she wedged her forearms against her thighs as she fought the urge to collapse.

God, how could you have been so damn blind? But then she remembered what was said about some of the most famous killers in history. That they didn't look or act like murderers. They were charming, fun to be around; you felt compelled to like them. That was the most frightening aspect of all. *They were you and they were me.*

She straightened back up when her phone rang. She answered it but no one said anything. And then she heard King's voice screaming something, only one word of which she really caught. But it was enough.

"Eddie!"

Still listening and piecing together what was happening at the other end of the wireless connection, she looked around, spotted a hard-line phone on a table next to one of Eddie's easels and called Todd Williams.

"They're at Sylvia's—at least I think they are."

"Holy shit. But there's a deputy with Sean."

"He may already be dead."

"I'm on my way."

"Me too."

Michelle put the cell phone to her ear as she raced back

to the Battle mansion. She sprinted to her room, grabbed her truck keys and ran back outside. She was about to jump in her truck but then stopped and ran back inside. She hurtled to Savannah's room and threw open the door. Savannah was on her bed. She jumped up when Michelle burst in. Michelle covered the speaker hole of her phone so nothing she said would reach Eddie Battle's ears.

"My God, what is it?" asked Savannah.

"I need your phone."

"What?"

"Give me your damn cell phone!"

Seconds later Michelle was climbing in her truck, her phone still pressed to her ear, straining to hear anything that might help her figure out where Sean was.

Wait a minute. She heard something. What was it?

"Boat!" Sean was asking where Eddie was taking them on the boat. She heard that clearly.

She punched in the numbers on the phone she'd taken from Savannah.

"Todd, they're on a boat on the lake."

"A boat! Where the hell did Eddie get a boat?"

"There's a bunch of them at the dock here. Including a really fast one."

"Shit!"

"Todd, do you have a boat?" she asked frantically.

"No. I mean the Game and Inland Fisheries people have one, but I'm not sure where it is right now."

"Well, that's just great!" Michelle thought quickly. *Idiot.* Of course.

"How fast can you get here?"

"What, uh, ten minutes," answered Williams.

"Make it five and meet me at the Battles' dock. It's a hike, but there's a golf cart you can take. The path is lighted, and there are signs pointing the way."

"But what about you?"

"What about me what!" she cried out.

"Don't you need the cart?"

"It'll just slow me down. Now listen really carefully, on your way here you need to get on the horn to the Game people, find that boat and get some armed men out onto the water. Make sure you lock down all roads that have lake access. And call the FBI and the state police and get a chopper up here with a big searchlight pronto. Tell them to roll out SWAT or Hostage Rescue. We're going to need some snipers."

"That'll all take time, Michelle."

"Which we have none of, so just do it!"

"It's a big lake. Over five hundred miles of shoreline. Lots of places to hide."

"Thanks for the pep talk. Just get your ass here."

She clicked off, jumped out of her truck, ran around behind the house and raced at the top of her speed down to the dock along the lighted path. She kept listening on her phone for helpful sounds, but all she could hear was a roar. If they were in the boat, the engines would drown everything else out.

She reached the dock, hit a switch, and the entire area blazed with light. At that instant an enormous streak of horizontal lightning shot across the sky followed by a snap of thunder so loud she put her hands to her ears.

Her gaze immediately caught the empty slip. "Shit, he's in the FasTech."

She got back on the phone. "Todd, he's in a Formula FasTech. A thirty-five-footer, white with a red—"

"I know that make of boat. You got any idea of the engines that thing's got?"

"Yeah, twin Mercs, five hundred horses each with kick-ass Bravo screws. If you're not here in three minutes, I leave without you." She clicked off.

"Okay, what do we got?" she asked herself as she ran from slip to slip. Sea-Doos were nimble and fast but they had no running lights, and she couldn't exactly see big Todd being able to either hang on to her while she drove or else maneuver one by himself. Plus, after the lopsided road duel with Roger Canney, if it came down to a battle of the boats, she wanted a little more beef on her side.

She stopped at the big Sea Ray performance cruiser berthed in one slip. It clearly couldn't match the FasTech in speed, but it was a big boat with big engines—that's all she needed. She shot the lock off the storage shed, went in, found the keys for the Sea Ray and the remote for the lift the Sea Ray was on and got the boat ready.

Todd Williams came flying up in the golf cart minutes later. He grabbed a life jacket and climbed on board.

"I got hold of everybody. The Game folks are putting their boat in at Haley Point Bridge, that's fifteen miles upriver. Both the FBI and the state police are sending choppers and snipers just as fast as they can. I got roadblocks setting up at all lake access roads."

"Good. Now take this and listen carefully. Sean may give us some clues as to where they are." Williams took the phone and held it to his ear.

Michelle hit reverse throttle, and they sped backward out

of the slip so fast Williams fell against the gunwale and almost pitched over the side.

Righting himself, he said, "Shit, Michelle, do you know how to drive this thing? It's not a damn rowboat."

"I'm a fast learner. Sylvia's house—tell me approximately how far it is from here and the compass heading."

Todd gave her his best estimate, and she swiftly calculated time, distance and route. Actually, while at the Secret Service she'd become quite an accomplished sailor, piloting everything from cigarette boats while guarding former presidents with a love for bone-jarring speed on the water to docile paddleboats with said former presidents' grandchildren as her very precious passengers.

"Okay, hold on."

She pointed the bow out to the open channel and slammed the throttle all the way forward. The big Sea Ray groaned a bit at first, like it was waking up. But then its props cut hard into the water, spitting it in all directions. Its bow rose up in the air like a cagey bronco ready to relieve its rider of his perch, and the boat took an enormous leap forward. They were fully on plane within seconds, and the boat blasted right through forty knots as Michelle headed directly into the jaws of the approaching storm on a twenty-thousand-acre lake without having any idea where she was supposed to be going.

CHAPTER

96

"COME ON, WHERE ARE you taking us, Eddie?" King called out over the sounds of the twin Mercs mixed with the thunderstorm.

He was bound hand and foot with fishing line and was lying on his side on the deck next to the captain's chair. Sylvia sat in the stern seat, similarly bound, as Eddie drove standing up, the wind whipping his thick hair around.

"What do you care? It's not like there's a return ticket from this trip."

"So why kill us? You filled out your scorecard. You got everybody you were after."

"Not everybody, old buddy. By the way, I won the bet."

"What bet?"

"When you caught me, you said it was over, I said it wasn't."

"Congratulations."

Eddie changed course to the east, cutting across a big wave that jolted the FasTech hard. King hit his head on the molded fiberglass behind him.

"If you don't slow it down, you'll kill us long before you get to where you're going."

In response Eddie eased the throttle forward even more.

"Eddie, please," wailed Sylvia from the back.

"Shut up!"

"Eddie—," she began again.

Eddie turned and fired a bullet within an inch of Sylvia's left ear. She screamed and threw herself on the deck.

With an enormous crack a thin bolt of lightning hit a tree on a small island as they flashed by. The oak exploded, sending charred wood sailing into the water. The accompanying clap of thunder was far louder even than the Mercs.

King inched himself forward. Tied up like this, he had no chance against someone as physically strong as Battle. Even in a fair fight he probably couldn't hold his own. He glanced back at Sylvia. She still lay on the deck. He could hear her sobs over all the other sounds. He struggled to sit up, finally making it. He slid his back against the side of the boat and managed to finally hoist himself into a seat next to Eddie.

Eddie looked over at him and smiled. "You like the view from there?"

King gazed around. He knew the lake well, although as every experienced sailor knew, things looked very different in the pitch-dark. Yet at that moment they passed a landmark that he recognized, a five-story condo building built on a clay point that jutted out into one of the lake's main channels. He shouted, "Looks like we're heading east, to the dam." He prayed his cell phone connection was still open. If it wasn't and Michelle tried to call him back, he couldn't hit the answer button, and the ringing sound would give it away in any event.

"East to the dam?" he said again, even more loudly.

"You know your lake," said Eddie, who took another swig of his warm beer, seeming to savor every drop.

"I know why you killed all those people, Eddie."

"No, you don't."

"I figured it out. Tyler, Canney, Junior, Sally. And Hinson and Pembroke to throw us off. One tick off, right? One tick."

"You don't know shit."

"Your father was a horrible man, Eddie. I know he drove you to this. You killed because of him, what he did to your mother, your brother."

Eddie pointed his pistol at King's head. "I said you don't know shit about why I did it."

King bit his lip, trying to keep his nerves in check, not exactly an easy thing to do right now. "Okay, suppose you tell me?"

"What does it matter, Sean? I'm a psycho, okay? If they don't burn me in the chair, they should just lock me up and throw away the key. Let somebody slit my belly while I'm asleep in my cell. Then everybody can just take a nice long breath. No more Eddie. It's cool, no more Eddie, and the world just keeps right on trucking." He eyed King and smiled. "Hey, at least when *you* die, there'll be plenty of people to mourn you. I don't have anybody."

"Dorothea?"

"Yeah, right."

"Remmy will."

"You think so?"

"You don't?"

Eddie shook his head. "Let's just not go there."

"Tell me about Steve Canney."

"What's to tell?"

"You're an honorable man, Eddie. You should've lived a hundred and fifty years ago. So grant a condemned man his last request. Talk to me."

Eddie finally smiled. "What the hell? Okay, here it is. I'd just gotten back from college. My parents were on the outs again. Savannah was about two years old, and Dad was already tired of her. I knew the bastard was screwing around again. I followed him and saw him with the Canney woman. When she had her son, I broke into the hospital, checked the blood-type records. Roger Canney wasn't the father. I knew who was."

"Was Savannah Bobby and Remmy's child?"

"Oh, yeah. I think Dad believed Mom was really going to divorce him this time. So she suddenly ended up very pregnant. Whether the sex was consensual or not, you'd have to ask her."

"Why the hell didn't they just divorce?"

"Bobby Battle's wife leaving him? No way that control freak would ever let that happen. That would've been a sign of failure. The great Bobby Battle never failed. Never!"

"Remmy could have divorced him if she'd wanted to."

"I guess she didn't want to."

King debated whether to ask the next question, deciding this might be the only chance he got. He was also thinking that the longer he kept Eddie talking, the longer he and Sylvia would stay alive. And who knew, he might just be able to persuade him to let them both live. "Why didn't you kill the boy, Eddie? Tommy Robinson?"

"Figured he'd set up his old man, make my life easier."

"Come on, you couldn't be sure of that."

"So there was no reason to kill him. So what? You think that makes me a Boy Scout because I managed not to kill one stinking kid? You saw what I did to Sally. What the hell did she ever do to me, huh? I smashed her face down to the bone." He looked down and eased back on the throttle.

The storm was growing fiercer by the minute, and even the FasTech was having difficulty cutting through the now massive wakes. Formula built some of the best boats in the world, and King prayed the fiberglass of this boat could withstand the beating it was taking. Yet they were only one lightning strike from being incinerated when the fuel tank ignited.

"And Junior?"

"That one I felt really shitty about. That stupid Sally. Why didn't she come forward? Hell, I liked Junior."

"He wouldn't let her tell the truth. He didn't want to hurt his wife."

"See, there you go. Always better to tell the truth. They'd both be alive if they'd just done that." Eddie sucked the last drop of beer out of the can and tossed it overboard. He rocked his head back and forth, loosening the thick muscles in his neck. "You've killed people before, Sean."

"Only when they were trying to kill me."

"I know that, I wasn't lumping us together. What did it feel like, right before you saw them die and you knew you'd done it?"

King at first thought Eddie was making light of this, but when he caught the man's gaze locked on the darkness ahead of them, he understand exactly what Eddie was really asking.

"It felt like a piece of me died with them."

"I guess that's where you and I are different."

"You mean you enjoyed it?"

"No, I mean I was already dead when I started killing." He flexed his arms and shook his head clear. "I wasn't always this way. I never hurt anyone or anything. I wasn't one of those people who started out torturing animals and worked my way up to humans. The kind of crap Chip Bailey went on and on about."

"I never thought you were a run-of-the-mill serial killer."

"Is that right?" Eddie smiled. "I wanted to play in the NFL. I was good enough, a damn good college player. Could've made it in the pros. Well, maybe I could, maybe I couldn't. Strong as an ox, good wheels, and I hated to lose—man, I hated that. But it didn't happen, just wasn't in the cards. You know, you're right. I was born too late. The 1800s would've suited me a lot better. I'm freaking lost in this century."

"When did you find out the truth about your brother?"

Eddie eased his gaze over to King and then checked the rear, where Sylvia had once more perched on the edge of the stern seat. Looking back at King, he said slowly, "Why are you asking that?"

"I think that's where all this started, that's why."

"Oh, what, my big excuse?"

"Most men in your position would be begging for justification, a legal defense, something to explain it."

"I guess I'm not most men, then."

"Syphilis. When did you know that's what it was?"

Eddie pulled back on the throttle some more, and the FasTech slowed to thirty knots. Still fast, but at least the boat's props weren't coming out of the water every furlong.

"When I was nineteen," Eddie said slowly, still looking out over the bow into the distance as though he were attempting a dead-reckoning calculation. "They didn't know I found out. They were just feeding me lies about why my brother was dead. But I learned the truth—oh, yeah, I did. They weren't going to slip that shit by me. No way."

"So shortly before the kidnapping scheme."

Eddie smiled. "I can't believe I was able to keep that secret all these years. I guess Chip was really surprised."

"To put it mildly." King glanced at Sylvia, but she was simply looking out over the dark waters, flinching at every burst of lightning and clap of thunder. King could feel his dinner coming back up on him, the seas were so rough. He fought through this urge to retch and said, "Did you ever confront your father about it?"

"What was to confront? He was the indomitable Bobby Battle. Bastard could do no wrong. He never admitted what he did to his own son. He rubbed his crotch against every hooker around, brought the shit home, killed Bobby and didn't even give a crap. That sure as hell didn't surprise me. He didn't give a shit that he'd murdered his own flesh and blood. Damn brain dissolving, eyes falling out, teeth rotting. His last years he was in agony all the time, I mean all the time. It was like someone had taken this beautiful painting and wiped turpentine all over it. I knew Bobby was still in there, but I couldn't see him anymore." Eddie blinked rapidly. "Every day, man, I just watched him waste away. When he started getting really ill, I said, take him to the doctor. Damn it, help Bobby, help him. Please! And they never would. I was just a kid, they said. I didn't understand, they said. I understood, man. I sure as hell did, just too late for Bobby."

"I've heard your brother was a really wonderful person, even with all the pain and hardship he suffered."

Eddie's features brightened. "You should've seen him, Sean. The sweetest guy. He was everything I wasn't. Before his brain started going, he was smart, man, I mean really smart. He taught me shit, helped me, took care of me. He was my big brother. There wasn't anything we wouldn't do for each other. The times we had together." King watched as salty tears started to slide down Eddie's cheeks to mix with the rain. "And then he just started getting sicker and sicker. Mom finally took him to a specialist; she never told me what the person said, but Bobby just kept getting worse. He died four days after our eighteenth birthday. Dad was gone on some business thing. Mom wouldn't come in the room. I held my brother, held him until he passed, and then I just kept right on holding him till they made me let go." He paused and added, "Bobby was the only real friend I ever had. He's the only person I know who ever really loved me."

"You said your father's reaction didn't surprise you. Did something else?" King asked curiously.

"You really want to know what surprised me? You really want to know?"

To King, Battle seemed like a little boy desperately eager to share a long-held secret.

"Yes, I really do."

"That my mother, my steel-backboned dear mama, didn't raise one finger to save her own son. Her own damn son. Now, explain that one to me, will you?"

"I can't, Eddie. I don't know why."

Eddie took a deep, replenishing breath. "Join the club." He throttled back even more. "Okay, we're here." As the boat slowed, King looked around to see if he could tell where they were. It was very dark and his bearings were off-kilter, but something looked very familiar about their location.

Eddie pulled a knife out of his watertight pouch and pointed it at King, who flinched back in panic.

"Eddie, you don't want to do this. We can get you help."

"I'm beyond help, Sean, but thanks for the offer."

Sylvia cried out from the back. "Please, Eddie, don't do it."

Eddie stared at her, suddenly grinned and motioned her toward him. When she didn't budge, he pulled his gun. "Next one goes right into your brain, Doc. Get your ass up here."

She hobbled forward trembling with fear. He sliced

through the fishing line binding her and pushed her down the stairs and into the forward cabin and shut the door behind her. He then slipped the knife blade under the line binding King's feet and cut through it cleanly.

"Move to the back of the boat, Sean." He shoved his pistol into the man's back for emphasis.

"What are you doing, Eddie?"

"Just coming full circle, man, full circle. Now step up on the gunwale and turn around."

"Are you going to shoot me here or while I'm in the water?"

In answer Eddie took his knife and sliced cleanly through the bindings around King's wrists, freeing him. King looked at him warily.

"I'm not getting this, Eddie."

"No, you're *not* getting it, at least from me." With a sudden thrust Eddie hit King hard in the chest with one of his massive forearms. King shot backward out over the water and went under headfirst.

Eddie raced back to the cockpit, slammed the throttle forward, and the FasTech shot off before King even had a chance to break the surface.

When he did come up, he saw the FasTech circle around and head back toward him.

King turned and started swimming away. Why hadn't the bastard shot him and left it at that? Why run him over with the boat? As the FasTech bore down on him, King could almost feel the massive props eating into his flesh, turning the lake water red with his blood.

At the last instant the boat veered away and passed

him. Eddie called out, "Thanks for asking about my brother, Sean. It just saved your life. Have a good one."

The boat roared away, quickly turning into a speck before completely disappearing into the darkness.

King screamed, "Sylvia! Sylvia!" but it was useless. He turned, looked around, and it finally struck him why his surroundings looked so familiar. The dock he was now staring at was *his* dock. They were in his cove! And there sat his jet boat in its slip.

And yet the FasTech was already out of sight. How could he possibly find them in time?

And then it hit him, what Eddie had said. *Full circle. He's coming full circle.*

King swam toward the dock with all his might.

CHAPTER

97

MICHELLE WAS FLYING through the darkness on the Sea Ray heading toward Sylvia's home when Williams came up beside her.

"The connection was lost on your phone," he said glumly.

"It's probably the storm."

"Yeah, probably," he said.

She looked to the sky. "I don't see a chopper."

"Damn, Michelle, in this weather? What'd you expect? You can't risk a bunch of people's lives like that."

"Why the hell not? I spent nine years of my life doing that at the Secret Service!"

"Come on, we're doing all we can—"

"What's that?" she said suddenly.

"What's what?"

"It's the phone!" she screamed. "My phone, where is it?"

"Back on the seat."

"Take the wheel."

She snatched up the phone and hit the answer button. Her heart leaped when she heard his voice.

"Michelle, could you hear anything on the phone?"

"Yes, Todd and I are in a boat heading to Sylvia's right now. We called out everybody."

"Listen, Eddie's still got Sylvia. He's headed to the cove below where the first body was found. Do you know where that is?"

"Yes."

"I'm heading there in my boat right now."

Michelle raced to the cockpit with the phone pressed to her ear, grabbed the wheel and plowed the Sea Ray into a thunderous turn, pitching its deck almost perpendicular with the water. Williams fell down again.

"I'm on my way. Ten minutes. We'll send everybody there. Oh, and Sean?"

"Yeah?"

"Thanks for being alive."

Eddie aimed the bow right at the ring of red clay that stuck out from the cove he was in, cut power and ran the FasTech right up onto it. He started to open the door to the cabin.

"Okay, Doc, let's go."

The stream of fire extinguisher fluid hit him flush in the face. He staggered back and was hit on the head with the canister. Blinded, he grabbed at his face and dropped to his knees. But he sensed Sylvia racing past him, and reached out and tripped her with one of his big arms.

"Get away from me, you bastard, get away from me," she screamed.

Eddie wiped his face off with his hand, his eyes stinging like crazy. He grabbed her by the scruff of her shirt, lifted her completely up in the air and threw her onto the hard clay shore, where she landed with a thud and lay still.

He opened a storage bin and lifted out the short-handled ax, jumped off the bow, and his feet hit dirt. He waded out into the water and dipped his head below the surface to clean off the crap she had shot him with. He stood, gazed out at the lake and the lightning crackling in the distance, took a deep breath, turned and walked over to her.

"Get up."

Sylvia said nothing.

"I said get up." He emphasized this point with a foot in her ribs.

"I think my arm's broken," she whimpered.

"Which one?"

"My left."

He reached down, grabbed her left arm and pulled her up as she shrieked in pain.

"Damn it, you're killing me, you bastard!"

"That's right. I am." He dragged her along into the woods.

King's boat flew through the water. He glanced behind him and saw the wink of lights about five hundred yards behind. He clicked on his phone, which had somehow survived its dunking in the water.

"Is that you behind me?" he asked.

Michelle answered, "And coming up fast."

King slowed the boat as he maneuvered into the narrow inlet. As soon as he saw the beached FasTech, he cut his running lights.

"Okay," he said into the phone, "looks like they're out of the boat."

Michelle's cruiser appeared at the mouth of the inlet. She powered down, cut her lights and coasted into shallow water next to the jet boat.

"Are you armed?" she called across.

He held up his pistol. "I stopped at my houseboat before I headed back out."

Michelle and Todd grabbed flashlights out of the Sea Ray's cabin, and the three climbed off their boats and waded to shore, their pistols aimed at the FasTech just in case Eddie was lying in wait.

Covering each other, they quickly made a search of the boat and found nothing except a used fire extinguisher.

They headed to shore and then into the woods.

"We'll spread out," said King, "but keep visual contact. No lights yet. He could pick us off easy that way."

A bolt of lightning hit on the hill opposite them with such force that the ground seemed to shake.

"If the damn lightning doesn't get us first," muttered Williams.

They threaded their way up to the crest of the hill and peered over.

"Two hundred yards and to the right is where the first body was found, if I'm not mistaken," whispered King.

"About that," said Michelle.

"We'll take it slow and easy," said Williams. "This guy's nuts but cagey as hell. I'm not looking to end up like Chip—"

Sylvia's scream hit them all right in the gut.

King tore down the hill, Michelle right on his heels, with Williams rumbling along in the rear.

98

"PLEASE, GOD, DON'T DO it." Sylvia was on her knees, head flush against the top of a rotted stump, with Eddie's knee in the middle of her back holding her in this position.

"Please," she continued to wail. "Please."

"Shut up!"

"Why are you doing this? Why?"

He stuffed his pistol in the gear belt he'd put on in the boat and pulled out a black hood from the inside of his wet suit. He donned the hood, adjusting the eye holes so he could see. It wasn't the circle-with-crosshairs one the police had confiscated, but it would do just fine for this impromptu execution.

He swung up the ax in one strong hand.

"Any last words?"

Sylvia was nearly unconscious with pain and fear. She started to mutter something.

Eddie laughed. "Are you praying? Shit! Fine, you had your chance."

He raised the ax over his head. Yet before he could bring it down on her neck, the handle of the ax exploded.

"Helluva shot, Maxwell," muttered Williams as they hurtled forward.

If they thought Eddie was simply going to surrender, they quickly saw that wasn't the case.

He jumped sideways, far enough to reach a steep incline, and he rolled and slid down to the bottom. He was up in an instant and sprinted off.

King ran up to Sylvia and cradled her.

"It's okay, Sylvia," gently whispered King. "You're okay."

There was a flash of motion.

"Michelle!" screamed out King. "Don't!"

She cleared the crest, rolled down and hit the bottom. Up just as fast as Eddie, she sprinted after him.

"Damn it," screamed King. He handed Sylvia over to Williams and raced after his partner.

As King ran along, he could only tell where he was heading when the pitch-blackness was lit by lightning. Or when he heard the crash of footsteps up ahead.

"Why the hell are you doing this?" he called out to Michelle even though he knew she couldn't hear him.

After spending the last hour with Eddie Battle he had no desire to ever go near the man again unless he was behind bars with twelve guards surrounding him. And maybe even then he'd take a pass.

He stopped suddenly because the sounds up ahead had ceased.

"Michelle?" he hissed. "Michelle?" He gripped his pistol and swung it in arcs, periodically looking over his shoulder in case Eddie had circled around to rear-flank him.

Up ahead Michelle was staring at a clump of brush with great intensity. She glanced down every so often to see if the tiny red light was dancing across her body. She eased her pistol's muzzle through a small gap in the wild holly bush she was hidden behind and parted its branches slightly. There was slight movement to her right, but it turned out to be a squirrel.

She heard a noise behind her and whipped around.

"Michelle?"

It was King, about twenty feet away. He'd taken a different path and was separated from her by a wall of bramble.

"Stay back," she said between clenched teeth. "He's stopped right up ahead."

She turned and waited. One lightning flash; that was all she needed. She edged around the bush, backtracked a bit and then slowly made her way down and around with the goal of coming up behind Eddie.

The flash of lightning. She heard the noise to her right. She pivoted and fired in the same instant. There was an explosion in front of her as a spark of red-hot light erupted for an instant and then vanished.

She couldn't know it, but Eddie had at the same time been circling around her and had fired at the exact same instant as she. Beating odds of probably a billion to one, the two bullets had collided, causing the explosive spark she'd seen.

Eddie hit her low and hard, driving the breath right out of her before drilling her into the dirt almost face-first. It was a textbook tackle. Mud, leaves and twigs were pushed so far into her mouth she could barely breathe. Michelle twisted her body around and tried to kick at him, but he was on top of her pinning her down. He was unbelievably strong; she couldn't come close to breaking his iron grip with her fingers; it was like a child trying to escape from her daddy. She tried to get up, but she didn't have nearly the strength to do it with his 220-plus pounds clenched around her.

Damn it. She spit shit out of her mouth. If she could just push him away, she could deliver stunning blows with her feet that might give her a chance. But he was simply too strong. She felt the hand go around her throat while he kept the other one locked on her arms. She thrashed wildly around trying to throw him off, but she had no leverage. She tried to call out but couldn't. She started to lose focus. Her brain felt heavy, her limbs started to twitch.

Is this it? Is it?

And then everything relaxed. The weight was lifted. She was free, and Michelle knew she'd just died at the hands of Eddie Lee Battle. She turned to see his face peering down at her, smiling at what he'd just done.

Only he wasn't looking at her. She sat up, scooted away from him and only then saw what he was staring at.

King was standing there. Both hands were around his pistol grips, the weapon pointed directly at Eddie, who was backing away a little. King's clothes were torn to shreds and his face and hands bloodied from where he'd fought through the bramble to reach them.

"I wouldn't have killed her, Sean."

King was trembling with rage. "Yeah, right, you bastard."

Eddie continued to back away, his hands up.

"Another step, and you get it between the eyes, Eddie."

Eddie stopped, but he started to lower his hands.

"Keep 'em up," barked King.

Michelle rose and looked around for her pistol.

"Hey, Sean, just go ahead and shoot," said Eddie wearily. "Save the state a lot of money housing me on death row."

"We're not doing it that way."

"Just do it, Sean. I'm beat, man. I got nothing left."

"You'll make it. Have no fear."

"You think so?"

"In fact, I'll bet you—"

"The hell you say, you're on—"

Eddie leaped, his hand sliding to his back; he pulled the pistol.

Michelle screamed.

The shot was fired.

King walked over and looked down at Battle lying there. He kicked the pistol away with his foot, stared at the blood pouring down from Eddie's shoulder where the bullet had impacted before exiting out the man's back.

"I won the bet this time, Eddie."

Eddie smiled weakly up at him. "Just one tick off, man. One tick off."

CHAPTER

99

EDDIE BATTLE PLEADED guilty to every murder he'd committed. In return for fully cooperating with the authorities and answering all their questions, and because there was some doubt as to his mental stability, his attorneys were able to broker a deal that would send him to prison without the possibility of ever being free again. There was immediate reaction from all corners. Pro-death-penalty activists marched in the streets of Wrightsburg. There were calls for impeachment of the governor, the prosecutors and the judge assigned to the case. The Battle family—at least what remained of them—was ankle-deep in death threats. It was predicted that whatever maximum security prison he was sent to, Battle would be dead within a month.

King hadn't followed much of this. After shooting Eddie he'd helped carry him and Sylvia down to the boats where they'd been taken to the hospital. Both had fully recovered, though King doubted Sylvia would ever be the same after her terrifying experience.

Hell, I might never be the same, thought King.

He'd taken long rides on his boat, driving across in the daylight what he'd covered that awful night. He and Michelle had talked about it some but had mostly avoided the subject. They were drained enough. However, she'd been effusive in her thanks for saving her.

She kept shaking her head at the memory of it. "I've never felt so helpless like that before, Sean. I've never encountered a man that strong before. It was like he was possessed by something not of this world."

"I think he was," replied King.

All of which brought King to where he was right now, sitting at his desk and wondering what Eddie had meant by his last words while lying bleeding on that hill.

"Just one tick off, man." The five words beat into his head, and he couldn't get rid of them. He finally rose from his desk and drove over to the Battles'. Remmy was home, Mason told him.

There were several pieces of luggage stacked in the foyer.

"Someone going on a trip?" asked King.

"Savannah's taken a job overseas. She's leaving today."

Lucky her, thought King as Mason led him down the hallway.

Remmy seemed a very pale version of her former self. She was sipping from her cup of coffee. King felt certain it was actually nine-tenths Mr. Beam.

"I hear Savannah's moving out," he said after Mason had left them.

"Yes, but she said she might come back for Christmas," the mother said hopefully.

Or not, thought King.

"Is Dorothea out of rehab?"

"Yes. She's back next door. I'm going to help her with her money problems."

"That's good to know. No reason not to spread the wealth. And she is family. The police no longer suspect her in Kyle's death?"

"I don't think they do. I doubt they'll ever solve that."

"You never know."

Neither said a word about Eddie. What was there to say anyway?

King was anxious to leave, so he decided to just get to it. "Remmy, I came here to ask you one question. It's about a former employee of yours, Billy Edwards?"

She looked at him sharply. "The mechanic?"

"That's right."

"What's the question?"

"I need the exact date when he left."

"The payroll records will show that."

"I was hoping you'd say that." He looked at her expectantly.

"Do you want them now?"

"Right now."

When she returned with them, King had turned to leave but then something made him stop.

He stared down at the meticulously groomed and attired Remington Battle sitting there in a beautiful old chair, the epitome of the aristocratic southern grande dame.

She glanced up. "Is there something else?" she asked him coldly.

"Was it worth it?"

"Was what worth it?"

"Being Bobby Battle's wife. Was it worth losing both your sons?"

"How dare you!" she said sharply. "Do you realize the hell I've been through?"

"Yeah, it's really been a piece of cake for me too. Why don't you try answering my question?"

"Why should I?" she retorted.

"Call it a gracious act by a refined and dignified lady."

"Your sarcasm is absolutely lost on me."

"Then let me lay it straight out for you. Bobby Jr. was your child. How could you just let him die?"

"It wasn't like that!" she said, her voice rising. "You think it was an either/or choice? You think I didn't love my son?"

"Words are easy, it's the actions that are hard, Remmy. Like standing up to your husband. Like telling him you didn't give a shit where he got the disease but that *your* son was getting treatment for it. It's not like it's that hard to diagnose, even back then. You put the kid on penicillin and chances are extremely good you'd have *both* your sons in your life right now. Did you ever think about it in those terms?"

Remmy started to say something and then stopped. She set her cup of coffee down and folded her hands in her lap.

"Maybe I wasn't as strong back then as I am now." King saw the glimmer of tears in her eyes. "But I finally did make the right decision. I took Bobby Jr. to all sorts of specialists."

"But it was too late."

"Yes," Remmy said quietly. "And then the cancer came. And he just couldn't fight it off." She brushed at her tears, reached for her coffee but then stopped and looked up at him.

"Everyone has to make choices in life, Sean," she said.

"And lots of people make the wrong choices."

Remmy seemed about to make some biting comment, but King stopped her cold when he took a photo off the shelf and held it up. It was of Eddie and Bobby Jr. as children. She suddenly put a hand to her mouth as though to stifle a sob. She looked at him, the tears sliding down her cheeks now. "Bobby was a very different man when we first married. Maybe that's the one I was clinging to, hoping he'd come back."

King put the photo back. "I think any man who lets his own son die without lifting a hand to save him isn't a man worth waiting for."

He walked out and never looked back.

As King came outside, he saw a driver was loading Savannah's bags into a black sedan. Savannah climbed out of the car and approached King.

She said, "I wanted to see you before I left. I heard some of what you said to my mother. I wasn't eavesdropping. I was just passing by."

"Frankly, I don't know whether to pity or loathe her."

She stared at the house. "She always wanted to be the matriarch of this great southern family. You know, sort of a dynasty."

"She didn't quite make it," commented King.

Savannah stared at him. "That's the thing . . . I think

she made herself believe that she *had* made it. She hated my father in private and yet idolized him in public. She loved her sons and yet sacrificed them to preserve her marriage. It makes no sense. All I know is I'm getting the hell away. I'll spend the next ten years trying to figure it out. But I'm going to do it from a distance."

They hugged, and King held the car door for her.

"Best of luck, Savannah."

"Oh, Sean, please tell Michelle thanks for everything she did."

"I will."

"And tell her I took her advice on my tattoo."

King looked at her quizzically but said nothing. He waved as the car sped off.

King drove to the *Wrightsburg Gazette* and unwittingly sat at the same microfiche machine that Eddie had when he broke in that night.

King raced through the spool of back issues until he found the date he was looking for, the day Edwards had been let go. He didn't find what he was searching for. Then it occurred to him that it might have happened too late to make the next day's edition. He forwarded to the day after that. He didn't have to read far. It was front-page news. He read the story carefully, sat back and then finally laid his head down on the desk as his mind began to creep into areas that were truly unthinkable.

When he rose back up, he noted the wall Eddie had written on. It had been cleaned off, but there were still traces of the word he'd written there.

TEAT

A few days before, he'd played with various combinations of the word: *tent, test, text.* Nothing seemed to work. Yet he didn't believe Eddie would have written that word if it wasn't important.

King pulled the cipher disk out of his pocket and played with it. He had taken to carrying it around for some reason. Long ago it was discovered that frequency analysis could break an encryption of fair length. The method was straightforward. Some letters of the alphabet occur far more frequently than others. And the letter that occurs far more often than all others is the letter *e.* This discovery had put the code-breakers on top for quite some time until the encryption folks once more got the upper hand centuries later.

King spun the outer ring of the cipher disk around until the letter *e* was lined up with the letter *a.* One tick off. He looked at the wall and in his mind's eye changed one letter, *e* for an *a.* Now it read:

TEET

That made no sense either. What was a teet? As a long shot he left and went back to his office, went to a search engine on the Internet and typed in the word *teet,* and for the hell of it, the word *crime.* He didn't expect to find anything. However, a long list came up. Probably all garbage, he thought. And yet when he looked at the very first listing, he suddenly sat up.

"Oh, my God," he said. He read all that was there and sat back. He felt his forehead: it was damp with sweat, his whole body was. "Oh, my God," he said again.

He stood slowly. He was glad Michelle was out. He couldn't have faced her. Not right now.

King had some things to track down, just to make sure. And then he was going to have to just face it. He knew it would be one of the hardest things he'd ever had to do.

CHAPTER

100

TWO DAYS LATER KING pulled up into the parking lot and got out of his car. He went inside the office building, asked for Sylvia and was directed back to her office.

She was at her desk in her medical office, her left arm in a sling. She looked up and smiled, then came around and gave him a hug.

"Do you feel halfway human yet?" she asked.

"I'm getting there," he said quietly. "How's the arm?"

"Almost as good as new."

He sat down across from her while she perched on the edge of her desk.

"I haven't seen much of you lately."

"I've been kind of busy," he answered.

"I've got tickets to a play in D.C. for next Saturday. Would it be too forward to ask if you'd like to join me? Separate hotel rooms, of course. You'll be perfectly safe."

King glanced over at the coatrack. The woman's coat,

sweater and shoes were neatly arranged either on or next to the rack.

"Is something wrong, Sean?"

He looked back at her. "Sylvia, why do you think Eddie came after us?"

Her demeanor instantly changed. "He's crazy. We helped bring him down. Or at least you did. He hated you for it."

"But he let me go. And he kept *you*. He had you bent over a tree stump, about to cut your head off. Like an executioner."

Her face twisted angrily. "Sean, the man had killed nine people already, most at random."

He took a piece of paper out of his pocket and handed it to her. She sat back behind her desk and slowly read it.

She looked up. "It's the newspaper article about my husband's death."

"He was the victim of a hit-and-run driver, case was never solved."

"I'm well aware of that," she said coldly, sliding the paper back across. "So?"

"So the same night George Diaz was killed Bobby Battle's Rolls-Royce was damaged. The next day the Rolls was gone, and so was the mechanic who looked after Bobby's collection."

"Are you saying this mechanic person killed my husband?"

"No, I'm saying Bobby Battle did."

She looked at him, stunned. "Why in the hell would he do that?"

"Because he was avenging you. He was avenging the woman he loved."

Sylvia rose, her fingers digging into her desktop. "What the hell are you trying to do here?"

Now King's demeanor changed. He sat forward. "Sit down, Sylvia, I have a lot more to say."

"I—"

"Sit!"

She slowly sank back into her chair, without ever taking her gaze off him.

"You told me once that you'd seen Lulu Oxley at the gynecologist you both used. You intimated she'd changed docs. But she didn't change docs. You did."

"So is that a crime?"

"I'm getting to that. I got the name of your new ob-gyn from your old doctor, and then I went to see your new gynecologist. She was way up in D.C. Why so far away, Sylvia?"

"That s none of your damn business."

"When you had your surgery three and a half years ago, your husband performed it. He was the best, you said. Only he had another agenda when he opened you up. I've discovered after talking to a surgeon friend of mine that the procedure to correct a ruptured diverticulum is one of the very few that would allow the surgeon to do something 'extra' in the pelvic region that most likely wouldn't be noticed by anyone assisting him."

"Would you *please* get to the point!" she exclaimed.

"I know, Sylvia."

"You know what?" she said fiercely.

"That a tubal ligation was performed on you without your knowledge that rendered you infertile."

There was a long silence. "You don't know what you're talking—"

King interrupted. "George Diaz corrected your diverticulitis and operated on your colon all right, but at the same time he also stapled your fallopian tubes shut. And he did it on purpose. You couldn't go to your old ob-gyn with those staples in you: how could you explain them? So you went to a new one, probably with dummy records, and she removed them. I went to see her with a bogus story about my 'wife' and her fallopian tube problem. I said you'd recommended her because you said she'd done such a wonderful job on you. Because of confidentiality restrictions she couldn't tell me much, but it was just enough to confirm my suspicions. And the damage was permanent, wasn't it? You'd never have children."

"You bastard, how dare you—"

King interrupted her again. "Your husband found out you and Bobby were lovers. You fell for the old man just like hundreds before you. And George took his revenge for your infidelity. And then you took yours." He picked up the photo of George Diaz off her desk and laid it face-down. "You don't have to keep up the facade of the poor, pining widow for me."

"I was lying flat on my back in the hospital when George was killed!"

"That's right. But I'm betting your husband told you what he did. He'd want you to know how he'd avenged himself for your betrayal. And you called Bobby and told him all about it. And he took his Rolls-Royce, went over to your house, saw Diaz out walking, and that was that. At first I thought Bobby had run Roger Canney's wife off the road and killed her, because her death also occurred around the time George was killed. But hers was a simple car accident. Your husband's death was murder."

"It's all conjecture. And even if it happened as you say, I did nothing wrong. Nothing."

"The wrong comes later. Because you killed Bobby by injecting a lethal dose of potassium chloride into his nutrition bag."

"Get out of my office."

"I'll go when I've had my say," he shot back.

"First you say I'm the man's lover, and then you say I'm his murderer. What possible motivation would I have for killing him?"

"You were afraid of being exposed," King said simply. "On the very day he was killed we saw you at Diane Hinson's home. Michelle told you Bobby was conscious, but that he was just rambling, calling out people's names, saying stuff, totally incoherent. You were terrified he'd say your name, talk about your relationship. Then everything might come out. Maybe he'd already thrown you aside by then. So maybe you owed him nothing. I don't know that for sure, but I do know that you went and killed him. For a doctor it would be easy. You knew the hospital routine. You put the poison in the bag and not the tube, and you left the feather and watch because you wanted the murder attributed to the other killer. You were very quick to support my theory of a family member having killed Bobby. But you made a mistake. You didn't take anything from his hospital room. Those thefts from the other victims, the St.

Christopher's medal and the like, weren't revealed to the public or to you. So you didn't know to copy that detail."

Sylvia shook her head. "You're crazy. You're as crazy as Eddie, you know that? And to think I was looking forward to rekindling what we had."

"Right, me too. Guess I'm really lucky."

Her face twisted hideously. "All right, you've had your say, now get out. And if you repeat one word of it, I'll sue you for slander."

"I'm not finished yet, Sylvia."

"Oh, there's more insane talk to come?"

"A lot more. You were also the one who burglarized the Battles' home."

"You just don't stop, do you?"

"Bobby had probably given you the access code and a key. Junior had done work for you, you told us that. You got the stuff to frame him easily enough, and who better to forge a print than a medical examiner? I'm not sure how you did that, but I know with a very experienced person that it's possible."

"Why would I burglarize their home? What would I want with Remmy's wedding ring?"

"You didn't care about the ring! There was something else you were after. Battle was in a coma in the hospital. You weren't sure if Remmy knew about Bobby's secret cache. You weren't even sure what you wanted was in there, but you had to look. In Bobby's closet you knew where the secret drawer was, but you didn't know how to open it and had to break in. Someone would obviously see that, so you broke into Remmy's closet to make it look like a burglary and framed Junior for it. You'd probably heard from Bobby that Remmy had a secret cupboard in her closet, but he didn't know its exact location. That's why you had to bust everything up, looking for it."

"And what exactly was I supposed to have stolen?"

"A picture of you and Bobby together. Some of the lettering from the back of the Kodak paper had stained the drawer. He might have told you he kept it there. Either way, you had to get it back. Because if he died and the photo was discovered, people might start putting the pieces together about your husband's death. And even if you weren't to blame for that, no one would believe you. And maybe it seemed pretty ironic your ending up with Remmy's wedding ring. Did you ever wear it in the privacy of your home?"

"Okay, that's it! Get out! Now!"

King didn't budge. "And did you really have to kill Kyle? What, was he trying to blackmail you?"

"I didn't kill him. He was stealing from me!"

King glanced over at the coatrack. "You were doing Hinson's post the night Battle was killed. You said Kyle came to the morgue that night, but you didn't mention that you'd seen or spoken to him, only that he'd accessed the door, and that was recorded on the security log."

"I never saw him. I was in the back working on Hinson."

"Not around ten o'clock you weren't. And that's probably what Kyle saw, or, more to the point, *didn't* see." He pointed at the neatly arranged things by the coatrack. "Your jacket, shoes and such you *always* place there when you're here working. And it's also pretty strange to perform an autopsy at night and without assistance or a witness, as you did with Hinson. You gave Todd such a hard time about him ducking the other autopsies, but you didn't want him at Hinson's, because you had someplace else to be. Namely, killing Bobby during the nurse changeover. You feigned illness when Todd called you later that night about Battle's death because you had to complete Hinson's post, or else you couldn't bring yourself to see Battle's body so soon after you'd killed him."

"That's crazy. And I wanted to perform the autopsy as quickly as possible. The body will only give clues for a certain period of—"

"Save the lecture for somebody who cares," said King. "I'm betting Kyle put all this together and tried to blackmail you. So you came to me with the perfectly true fact that he was stealing drugs and selling them, and I told you I'd have Todd see Kyle the next day. Only by then you'd killed him. Maybe you went right after we finished dinner. And during the post you conveniently found enough evidence to make it look like murder. And of course there was Dorothea ready to take the blame, which I'm certain was your intent. In fact, I bet you recognized her at the Aphrodisiac and knew she was Kyle's drug client."

He looked over at her. She was simply staring blankly at him now. "But was it all worth it for a monster like Battle? Was it, Sylvia? You were just one in a hundred. He didn't love you. He didn't love anyone."

She picked up the phone. "Unless you leave right now I'm calling the police."

King rose. "Oh, just so you know, Eddie put me onto this. He knew you'd killed his father; that's why he was going to kill you."

"So now you're listening to convicted murderers?"

"Ever heard of a guy named Teet Haerm?"

"No."

"He lived in Sweden. Maybe still does. He was accused of killing some people back in the eighties. He was arrested and convicted, but it was later overturned and he was set free."

"And what exactly does that have to do with me?" she said icily.

"Teet Haerm was the *medical examiner* for the city of Stockholm. It's said that he even performed the autopsies on some of his victims. Probably the only time that had ever happened. At least until now. Eddie left a clue behind, only he misspelled it on purpose. He wanted to get to you first after all." He paused and added, "I don't know if Teet was guilty or not, but I know you are."

"And you can't prove one word of anything you've said."

"You're right, I can't," conceded King. "At least not right now. But let me tell you something, lady, I'm not going to stop trying. In the meantime I hope your guilt will ruin your life."

King walked out the door, shutting it firmly behind him.

CHAPTER

101

KING AND MICHELLE
boarded the small plane and flew down to South Carolina.
From there they drove an hour to the maximum security
prison Eddie Battle had been transferred to and where he
would spend the rest of his life. Michelle chose to wait
outside while King went in.

Eddie was brought in wearing shackles and surrounded by four beefy guards who never took their eyes
off him. Eddie's hair was shaved to the scalp, and there
were scars and wounds on his face and forearms which
King knew had been inflicted since he'd been incarcer-
ated. He wondered how many others were hidden under
the jumpsuit. He sat down across from Eddie. They were
separated by inch-thick Plexiglas. King had already been
instructed on all the visitor's rules, chief of which was to
make no sudden moves and never ever try to have any
physical contact with the prisoner.

King knew he'd have no trouble following those
procedures.

"I'd ask you how it's going, but I can see."

Eddie shrugged. "It's not that bad. Pretty basic stuff. Kill or be killed and I'm still here." He eyed King with a curious look. "Didn't expect to be seeing you again."

"I had a few questions to ask you. And then I had something to tell you. What do you want first?"

"Give me the questions. The boys in here don't have many. Spend most of my time in the library. Lifting weights, playing ball, getting some of the boys organized into a team. They won't let me paint, though. Guess they're afraid I'll drown somebody in a bucket. Shoot."

"First question: Did your father's stroke start everything in motion?"

Eddie nodded. "I'd been thinking about it for a while. Wasn't sure if I'd have the balls to actually do it. When the old man went down, it just snapped in my head. Now or never."

"Second question: Why kill Steve Canney? I thought you did it for your mother, but now I know that wasn't the case."

Eddie shifted in his seat, the shackles rattling. One of the guards looked over. Eddie smiled and waved before looking back at King. "My parents let my brother die, and my old man goes off and has another son with some slut. Well, I didn't want or need another brother. This Canney kid grew up healthy and strong. That should've been Bobby, you hear me? It should've been Bobby." His voice rose higher, and now all four guards looked over. King didn't know if he was more frightened of Eddie or them.

"Third question: What made you kill Junior? At first I thought it was because you believed he'd stolen from your mother. Now I know you wouldn't have cared about that. So why?"

"There was a drawing of my brother that got busted up during the burglary."

"Your mother showed me it."

"It was a drawing of Bobby before he got really sick." Eddie paused and put his shackled hands on the wood in front of him. "I was the one who drew it. I loved that picture. And I wanted it in Mom's room so she'd always know what she did. When I saw it smashed up, I knew I'd kill whoever had done it. I thought Junior had broken it. That was his death sentence."

King suppressed a shudder at Eddie's reasoning for murder and said, "In case you're interested, this has all really hit Remmy hard, though she tries not to show it."

"She's just lucky I didn't have the guts to kill *her*."

"Did you come up with the plan to impersonate famous serial killers because of Chip Bailey?"

Eddie grinned. "Old Chippy. Bragged all the time about how much smarter he was than everyone else, how much he knew about serial killers, their M.O. He claimed he could run down the smartest of them. Well, I took him up on that challenge. I think the results speak for themselves."

"If your father hadn't been murdered, what would you have done?"

"Killed him. But before I did I was going to tell him about all the people I'd killed and why. I wanted him to know what he'd done. For once in his life I wanted him to take responsibility."

"Last question. Why'd you take something from each of your victims?"

"So I could plant them at Harold Robinson's, to put the blame on him." He paused, his brow wrinkled, and he finally said in a low voice, "I guess I'm just like my old man."

King understood that this was by far the harshest sentence Eddie could have been given, and it was a self-imposed one. That was why he had asked the question.

"So what'd you come here to tell me?"

King sunk his voice low. "That you were right about Sylvia. I confronted her with it all, but I can't prove any of it, though I'll keep trying."

"Did you figure out my 'Teet' clue?"

"Yeah."

"Found out about him when I went down to the FBI at Quantico with Chip once."

"Sylvia's moved away from Wrightsburg, probably set up a new life under another name."

"Lucky her."

"I haven't told anyone else about it, not even Michelle."

"I guess it doesn't matter."

"It *does* matter, Eddie, there's just nothing I can do about it right now. I have no proof. She covered her tracks really well, but I'll keep trying." King rose. "I won't be back to see you."

"I know." As Eddie started to rise, he called out, "Hey, Sean, can you tell Michelle I wouldn't have really hurt her that night? And tell her I enjoyed our dance together."

The last image King had of the man was him shuffling

off surrounded by the guards. And then Eddie Battle was gone. King hoped forever.

As he was leaving the prison, King was stopped and given a package at the visitor's center. He was only told that it had been mailed here and they were to hold it for him. It was actually addressed to Michelle. He got back in the car.

"What's that?" she asked.

"It's for you. We'll stop for lunch at that diner we passed earlier, and you can open it."

It was truly a greasy spoon full of truckers, but the food was good and the coffee hot. They found a spot near the back and ate their lunch.

"Don't you want to know how he is?" asked King.

"No. Why, did he ask about me?"

King hesitated and said, "No, he never mentioned you."

Michelle swallowed her bite and chased it with some coffee.

"One thing still has me puzzled," she said.

"Really, only one thing?" King attempted a smile.

"What was in her closet safe that Remmy wanted back so badly?"

"I think they were letters from a certain gentleman acquaintance of hers."

"So she *was* having an affair?"

"No, this was a case of unrequited love. The gentleman in question would have it no other way with a married woman. But she wanted his letters back."

"I wonder who it could have—" She stopped, eyes huge. "Not—"

"Yes," said King quickly. "Yes. But it was a long

time ago, and he did nothing to be ashamed of. He simply cared for a woman who turned out not to have deserved it."

"God, that's so sad."

He helped her rip open the package. They both sat staring at the object.

It was the painting of Michelle in the ball gown that Eddie had done.

King looked at her and then at the painting but said nothing. They paid their bill and left. Before they got in the car, Michelle threw the painting in the diner's Dumpster.

"Ready to go home?" King asked as she climbed in the driver's seat.

"Oh, yeah."

Michelle punched the gas, and they drove off in a swirl of dust.

ACKNOWLEDGMENTS

To Michelle, it's hard to believe, novel number ten and counting. I wouldn't have wanted to share the ride with anyone else.

To Rick Horgan, for helping me see the forest *and* the trees when I really need to.

To Maureen, Jamie and Larry, for all you do, and for being such terrific friends.

To Tina Andreadis, for being a dear friend and a major reason why the public knows who I am.

To the rest of the Warner Books crew for all your hard work and support. I know the books don't sell themselves.

To Aaron Priest, for always being there for me.

To Lucy Childs and Lisa Erbach Vance, for all that you do.

To Maria Rejt, for your thoughtful editorial comments.

To Dr. Monica Smiddy, for all your forensics wizardry. You'd make a great teacher.

To Dr. Marcella Fierro, for patiently answering all of my questions and giving me a behind-the-scenes look at the medical examiner's office in Richmond.

To Dr. Catherine Broome, for making this author seem far more knowledgeable about medical matters than I actually am.

To Bob Schule, my resident wine expert, stellar proofreader and great friend.

To Dr. Alli Guleria and her husband, Dr. Anshu Guleria, for helping me on medical matters, for allowing me to borrow your really cool cars for the story and for being such wonderful friends. Consultants are great, aren't they?

To Jennifer Steinberg, for all your excellent research. I haven't stumped you yet, but I'll keep trying.

To Lynette and Deborah, for all you do every day to keep me straight. I know it's not an easy task.